SALAR JANG'S PASSION

Musharraf Farooqi

SUMMERSDALE

Summersdale Publishers Ltd
46 West Street
Chichester
West Sussex
PO19 1RP
UK

www.summersdale.com

Printed and bound in Great Britain.

ISBN: 184024 224 8

This edition published 2002
First published 2001 by HarperCollins Publishers, India

Cover design by Blue Lemon Design Consultancy
www.bluelemondesign.co.uk

Author's Note

For information on the habits of the termites and for the passages quoted in Dr Adbari's article, *Termites: A Study in Social Behaviour* by P. E. Howse (1970, Hutchinson University Library, London), and *A Natural History of Termites* by Frances L. Behnke (1977, Charles Scribner's Sons, New York), have been used as sources.

The passage quoted in Dr Adbari's article is taken from E. P. Evans' book, *The Criminal Prosecution and Capital Punishment of Animals: The Lost History of Europe's Animal Trials* (1987, Faber and Faber Limited, London)

About the Author

Musharraf Farooqi was born in 1968 in Hyderabad, Pakistan. He worked as a journalist in Karachi and started the literary magazine *Cipher*. He moved to Toronto in 1994. He has translated the poetry of modern Urdu poet, Afzal Ahmed Syed, and is currently working on the English translation of the Urdu classic, *Dastan-e Amir Hamza*. This is his first novel.

For Michelle

Dramatis Personae

Main Characters

Salar Jang: An eccentric, rich old man in his seventies, shopping around for a bride.

Mirzban Yunani: An absent-minded genius researching the evolution of eternity.

Bano Tamanna: The industrious wife of Mirzban Yunani. Daughter of Salar Jang.

Muneemji: Salar Jang's factotum, Bano Tamanna's guardian.

Mushtri Khanam: An attractive but crabby spinster. Younger sister of Mirzban Yunani.

Ladlay Qalabaz: Mushtri Khanam's lover.

Others

Basmati: Mirzban Yunani's temperamental neighbour.

Begum Basmati: Basmati's wife. Friend of Bano Tamanna.

Bhai Qamoosi: An individualistic man and a confirmed bachelor.

Bilotti: A geriatric vegetable vendor of Topee Mohalla.

Chhalawa: Waiter at the Chhalawa Hotel.

Imam Jubba: Priest of the Topee Mohalla mosque.

Kaskas brothers: Wrestlers.

Kotwal: A notorious tomcat.

Lumboo: The neighbourhood sweeper.

Lumboo's Lashkar: The eleven children of Lumboo.

Madaar Sahib: An advertiser in the matrimonial columns.

Master Puchranga: A cinema billboard painter. Friend of Mirza Poya.

Mirza Poya: A cinema fan. Friend of Ladlay Qalabaz and Master Puchranga.

Parwana: Bano Tamanna's lawyer.

Qudratullah: A widower. Manager of Desh Bank. In love with Mushtri Khanam.

Tabaq Sahib: Mirzban Yunani's neighbour.

Unnab: A cock-fighter who lives in Topee Mohalla.

Glossary

Acchha! – Really! OK!

Alhamd'o'lillah – Praise the God!

Allah'o'Akbar – God is Great!

Aqiqa – The feast given at the ceremony of shaving an infant's head on the sixth day after its birth.

Ashura – The tenth day of the Islamic month of Moharram on which Husein, Prophet Muhammad's grandson, was killed. According to folk belief, Doomsday would fall on Ashura.

Ayatul-Kursi – A prayer to safeguard from calamities.

Bara'at – A bridegroom's entourage.

Bhang – A beverage made by crushing hemp leaves.

Bibi – A form of address used for respectable women.

Biryani – A rice and meat dish.

Bismillah – I begin in the name of God!

Bohni – Day's first sale.

Chaddar – A coverlet.

Chamkeela – Something which shines. (The pangolin was given this name because of his shining silvery scales.)

Chandni – A white sheet spread on the floor for seating.

Chappal – Sandals.

Chhalawa – A cherubic ghoul.

Chowkidar – A watchman.

Degchi – A cooking pot.

Desi Kushti – A form of Greek wrestling.

Dholki – A small drum which is drummed with fingers.

Divan – A collection of verses/poetry.

Duldul – A ceremonial horse paraded in the Islamic month of Moharram in the memory of the horse ridden by Husein, Prophet Muhammad's grandson, who died along with his accomplices in the battle of Kerbala.

Fay – The twenty-sixth letter of the Urdu alphabet.

Ghagra – A long skirt with many gathers worn by women in Rajasthan.

Gharara – A divided flared long skirt with many gathers.

Ghungroo – An ankle strap studded with small bells.

Goonda – Ruffian.

Hafiz – Someone who has memorised the entire Qur'an.

Haleem – A thick, spicy broth made with ground lentils and shredded beef.

Insha'allah – God willing!

Isme-Azam – According to Islamic belief, the supreme word which can unravel the secrets of the universe and deliver one from all adversities.

Janab – The equivalent of Sir, as used in addressing someone formally.

Kalma – The basic tenet of Islamic faith.

Karahi – A round, deep-frying bowl.

Kathputli – A wooden puppet common to the South Asian region. It originated in the Rajasthan desert.

Kewra – Oris water. A leaf whose essence is used to flavour food dishes.

Khilaat – A piece of brocaded cloth awarded as a favour in the Indian courts.

Kiryana Merchant – Grocer.

Kotwal – Superintendent of Police.

Kutcha Qila – Makeshift fort.

Lashkar – An army.

Manjha – A skein coated to give it a sharp edge, used in kite-fighting.

Masha'allah! – Praise of God!

Maulvi – A person who leads prayers in a mosque.

Minbar – The pedestal in a mosque from where the priest reads out sermons.

Mohalla – A neighbourhood.

Moondha – A chair woven with reeds and jute-string.

Naan – Flat, leavened bread baked in a clay oven.

Naskh – A kind of font commonly used for Arabic texts; less commonly used for Persian and Urdu texts.

Nastaleeq – A kind of font commonly used for Persian and Urdu texts.

Nauz'obillah – God forbid!

Navafil – Plural of *nuffil*. Votive prayers.

Nazrana – Alms.

Newar – Cotton belt used to weave beds.

Nikah – The Muslim wedding contract.

Nikah Nama – The Muslim wedding contract document.

Palla – A fish found in Indus River.

Papad – A crisp spicy wafer made from rice or lentil flour.

Patay Khan – The protagonist in all *kathputli* shows who takes on different personages.

Patka – A bridegroom's headgear.

Pehlwan – A wrestler.

Pir – A saint.

Pukka Qila – Impregnable fort.

Putli – See *Kathputli*

Qalandar – A person who is supposedly invested with spiritual powers. Qalandars might indulge in *bhang* addiction.

Qasr-e Yunani – The Palace of the Yunanis.

Qawwal – A singer specialising in the *qawwali* form of singing popular in South Asia.

Qila – Fort.

Rusgullay – A sweetmeat made with dried curdled milk.

Seth – Proprietor.

Shabe-Bara'at – The fourteenth night in the Islamic month of Shab'an on which the tree of life sheds leaves written with names of those who are to die the following year.

Shahi Tukra – A dessert made with bread, evaporated milk and caramel.

Shah Tazia – The biggest *tazia* in a group. See *Tazia*.

Shehr – City.

Sherwani – A long formal coat for men.

Soyem – The third day of death.

Surah-e Noor – A Quranic verse believed to ward off harmful creatures.

Tamasha – A show.

Tazia – Replica of Imam Husein's tomb paraded during Moharram on a float.

Tonga – A cart provided with seats, driven by a horse.

Tonga-wala – A tonga-cart driver.

Tota – Snippet of a pornographic film inserted at random between another screening. This illegal practice is common in some cinema houses because of the strict censorship policy.

Umrah – A visit to Mekkah and Medinah to perform the rituals of Hajj. While Hajj is performed at a particular time of the year, Umrah could be performed any time.

Valima – Marriage-feast given by the bridegroom.

SALAR JANG'S PASSION

The termites appeared soon after the rains. The walls of Purana Shehr houses were plastered with mud and straw to keep them cool in summer. During the prolonged rains, the old roofs developed cracks and water seeped into the walls. The smell of wet mud and straw tempted the termites from the bowels of the earth, and since those rains the walls of Purana Shehr became their permanent domicile. But in the beginning, nobody noticed the persistence of fine, sawdust-like particles under wooden doors and beams, since the sweeperess swept them away early in the morning. And no one took an interest in the sporadic appearance of dark, symmetrically-winged insects resembling flying ants, except for Mirzban Yunani, who, remembering the proverb relating to the numbered days of a winged ant, was greatly scandalised to see a pair coupling in mid-flight.

Topee Mohalla was the sad realisation of a government plan to build residences for non-gazetted officers on the outskirts of Purana Shehr, and indebted to the ingenuity of the contractor who was awarded the tender for the scheme, it had turned out more like an abstract metaphysical idea than an architectural concept. The buildings closed on each other from all sides and while in winter the close passageways afforded some sense of warmth, in summer they allowed no circulation, and this ganglion of mostly blind alleys remained dank and humid for the greater part of the year.

The masons had planned these dwellings as they built – adding a small room or a scullery when there was some extra mortar and bricks left at the end of the day, and making a door or improvising a window when they were short of material. And since the contract for wooden fixtures was awarded to another contractor, there was all the more reason. When the latter arrived on the scene, it was too late for protest, and he realised that re-negotiating the conditions of the tender would mean a review and the almost inevitable awarding of the contract to somebody else. However, not to be outdone by the mason, the carpenter, too, found the cheapest wood from an auction and without treating the rafters of the beams and the frames of the windows by dipping them in neem water, to proof them against woodworms and termites, he had them fixed in their positions, made a reasonable profit, and declared his job done. A month after that the Yunanis moved into the new quarters, along with some other families. Bano Tamanna, exultant over the possession of these new lodgings, had the words 'Qasr-e Yunani' engraved in marble on the front wall.

While building the Qasr-e Yunani, the masons apparently had had alternate days of surplus and low supplies. As a result there was a profusion of inlets and portals and an equally munificent growth of shelves, counters and mantles throughout the house. Bano Tamanna's room had as many as three doors and five windows. Mirzban Yunani's room, which was adjacent, had an array of shelves protruding out of the walls and encroaching upon the living space, with vaults and mantles covering almost every wall.

That monsoon all elements of nature seemed involved in a conspiracy to smother human life. In the mist which had enveloped the city, the smell of wood soaking in the wood-stalls, and wet earth lingered. Humidity, at an unprecedented one hundred per cent, had broken all known records. Sweat-soaked clothes clung like second skins and had to be changed at least twice a day. Those who wore glasses wiped their lenses continuously to clean them, and others kept scrubbing their dripping faces with towels and handkerchiefs. In the winding alleys the rainwater had still not dried under the layers of leaves which the autumn winds had blown over there, and they became the hospice of insect life.

Towards the end of summer the rain crows appeared in the night skies and the monsoon rains triggered terrestrial and aerial insect attacks. The children's ears needed protection from the centipedes that crawled out from under the money-plant pots with their subterranean neighbours. An array of small and large grasshoppers lined every surface, and both excited and frightened the Yunanis' granddaughters who were visiting. Mushtri Khanam got rid of the earthworms which had wriggled out from the mud-creases between brick-paved floors by sprinkling salt on them, which dehydrated them and also purged the foul odour which they emanated when dead.

When the rain stopped, the night air laden with insect smells, picked up the chorus of the cicadas and the toads from the wet ground. This nocturnal orchestra slowly faded out as the moon moved westwards.

In Qasr-e Yunani the smell of food and accumulating laundry had been growing for days. Near Mirzban's bedroom wall one could distinguish the fading aroma of the peas-pulao, cooked almost a week ago, and the strong base smell of the detergent in the steaming bucket where Bano Tamanna had left the soaking laundry; and as one moved away from the wall and closer to the kitchen, one passed through corridors demarcated by the distinct scent of pakoras, shami kebabs and fish cutlets. These abated close to the latrine, where a new set of odours took over.

Mirzban was in the courtyard going over the list of weekend chores when he heard the knocking on the door. Finding Bano Tamanna busy in the kitchen and knowing well that although his sister, Mushtri Khanam, was awake, she would not get out of her bed until lunch was served, he got up to see to the door. He was a diminutive man who had been a public school teacher, and satisfied the limited expectations of that office for the last several years. The job was eminently suitable to his disposition and left him enough time to indulge in his unbridled and ceaseless abstractions.

When he heard Mirzban's door latch open, the municipality clerk was already knocking at Basmati's house across the alley. After Mirzban had confirmed the address, the clerk removed the pen stuck behind his ear, scratched something into the well-thumbed sheets of paper in his hand, and then addressing Mirzban in the gruff voice of the government functionary who had been delayed in the performance of his public office, asked him to cover the food, gather the children and pets into the courtyard, and tell the women to take purdah while the house was being fumigated. The operation would take ten minutes, he informed Mirzban. Then reminding him to be alert for the fumigator's knock, he went across to where the notary, Ladlay Qalabaz, was leaning out from the door. He rented the upper story from the Basmatis and had come down to open the door since they were out.

A few weeks after the rains had stopped and the water had seeped into the ground leaving pools of muck everywhere, the municipality fumigators went all around town annihilating the insects and the swarms of mosquitoes which had bred in the city dumps, and now threatened an outbreak of malarial fever. The fumigation was an impressive city-wide operation in which almost every employee of the municipality participated. Even the dog-catchers of the municipality assisted in the formidable task of spraying Purana Shehr.

After the monsoons Bano Tamanna always greeted the fumigators' arrival with enthusiasm. That was the time when her granddaughters would come to visit, and she took every precaution to save them from being bitten by the armies of insects.

With the torrents of rain, black ants came pouring out, and their multitudes carpeted the whole house, from the front door to the storeroom. Sweeping them away with the broom was quite a task. They soon reclaimed lost ground in greater numbers, and often scaled the straws of the broom and nipped the hand. During those rains, it seemed the earth exhaled some nefarious vapour, as these insects came out intoxicated with a unique viciousness. Resting the foot for more than a moment in their mad and arbitrary itineraries was a provocation which they countered by sinking their incisors into the membrane between the toes, and even when they were killed, often remained clinging to the flesh. Wherever one stepped, ants flattened under chappals with small squishing sounds, and a fringe of their carcasses lined the sides of the courtyard walls when the rain water receded.

In the evening, buzzing swarms of mosquitoes hovered in the skies, and every time the veranda doors were opened, a few sneaked in. The rest found their way through the slits and crevices in the door, unless blocked out with old clothes. The children had the kind of blood mosquitoes were drawn to. So before starting her preparations for dinner, Bano Tamanna smeared the flat lid of the *degchi* with hair-oil, and swooped and swatted for a good half hour until the lid turned black with mosquitoes stuck to the oily surface.

Mirzban went to look for Bano Tamanna in the kitchen where she was grating mince to give her the news of the fumigator's arrival. Then he went inside to inform Mushtri Khanam, while Bano Tamanna herded the rabbits and drove them out in the open from their home between the corridors of piled books, and from under a sofa laden with numerous volumes of outdated encyclopaedias and other miscellaneous paper which Mirzban kept picking up from junk-shops.

Eventually, the masked fumigator arrived, trudging heavily, with the DDT cylinder strapped on his back. After spraying the inside of the house, he sealed it by spraying the cracks in the outer walls, where the insects had found tentative shelter, and left the alley carpeted with dead lizards, ants, cockroaches, centipedes, beetles and toads. After the fumigator's visit, the butterflies were not seen around for a long time, the twitter of the song birds diminished, and afternoons were notably robbed of the hum of the bumble bees.

During the fumigation Mirzban kept a close watch on the rabbits and twice he was obliged to lift them by their ears and throw them back behind the pile of kitchen utensils where they had been temporarily confined. With her dupatta tied around her face to keep her from inhaling the fumes, Mushtri Khanam hovered around the tin chest which contained her modest dowry of domestic comforts: tea cosies, steam iron, prayer mat, pillow cases, and other miscellaneous things. All this was collected by Mushtri Khanam herself, one item at a time, over several years. Although the chest was locked, Mushtri still kept an eye on the fumigators, and studied their movements closely to nip any potential act of thievery in the bud.

The mould of Mushtri Khanam's manifestation attracted dried-up widowers, confirmed bachelors and henpecked husbands alike. She could have been classified as attractive if she had ever cared to smile. But years of stern guard over her virtue, with an eye to invest it in some long-term profitable plan, had robbed her aspect of any soft contours. Although in her early middle-age now, she had so masterfully retained herself in youthful quarters, chiefly on the merit of her vanity box and her tightly trussed up coiffure – which greatly rid her face of wrinkles by its strong pull – that it was equally difficult to approximate the number of years she was removed from either maidenhood or spinsterhood.

Mushtri Khanam's recent posting to Desh Bank's Topee Mohalla branch caused much commotion among its phylum of clerks who had become unaccustomed to a womanly form in their midst, since the demise of the old accounts clerk a few years ago. Punctuated by vulgar slang and many such vernacular amusements, their office hours were dedicated to the hopeless, and therefore indispensable and ceaseless, perusal of ledger books, account histories and credit vouchers, when they were plunged into a wholesale awakening with Mushtri Khanam's advent; like the stir caused among certain marshland insects by a sudden welcome drizzle, which otherwise lie dehydrated in the days of drought, buried in dry sand.

It would be a grave injustice to say that Mushtri Khanam's eyes, like the watchful eyes of an astute spider, were unmindful of the agitation her presence had occasioned in the bank. Or that they had failed to notice the transformation of grey heads into dark heads since her arrival. Or that her olfactory senses were proof to the oppressive whiff of pomade cream, for which her colleagues' scalps had recently developed a voracious appetite. Nor were her ears deaf to the Pathan gunman's comments, who confidentially leaned over the clerks' desks, and in an audible whisper complimented them on their renewed youth. This seemingly innocent caper of the Pathan gunman was masterfully executed, and not only embarrassed both Mushtri Khanam and the clerks, but also seemed to suggest to everyone that it was high time the jovial gunman was acknowledged as a referee in the case.

But from the point of view of the bank clerks, any meaningful commerce was difficult, if not impossible, without beholding the object of their tender passions from a point of vantage. The tallest among the dandy bank clerks was the average-height cashier, and he found Mushtri Khanam, with her eyes some thirty degrees above his plane of perception, to be devoid of any sensible message for his perusal. The cashier would not have so summarily given up Mushtri Khanam's pursuit, had he known that the five feet and two inches of Mushtri Khanam's natural height were supplemented by another five inches of heel, cleverly camouflaged under the folds of her sari. Wearing the five-inch heel, perhaps, was a defensive ploy employed by Mushtri Khanam to keep the office world under intimidation. And moreover, this was not exactly the herd of swine before which a matron of Mushtri Khanam's calibre was about to cast her pearls.

So Mushtri kept a low profile, and played the old, back-breaking solitaire of the office spinsters, at which she was now becoming an old hand.

The spinster's solitaire consisted of the following moves. The spinster would station herself in a corner of the office and actively resist all attempts at being approached for courtship. For in her world courtship does not find favour and is not promoted. Any tenders submitted to her overt or covert notice should come marked *Matrimony* in block letters. Only then would they be considered at the bidding. That, however, made the majority of the office's male population ineligible for they were already married, and put a great pressure on the average unmarried clerk since it was understood that once married, the woman would have to resign from work, leaving only the husband's salary for household finances. Such a hardship was also unacceptable to the spinster since she was used to a financial independence that allowed her to spend money in her own capricious ways. In short, such were the obstacles, erected high and low by circumstances on the way to an office spinster's heart, and unless it was to melt by itself, its conquest was well nigh impossible. In the beginning, however, the general office public being unaware of the decorum of Mushtri's world, made several abortive attempts to probe the strength of her defence and the extent of her fortifications, and as was only natural, in those endeavours they were rudely enlightened.

Gradually, as she settled into her role, Mushtri brought her frigid and discomfiting stare into play, which caused anyone caught in the act of contemplating her form, to be wretchedly employed for the rest of the day, in the examination of the mottled waste basket even after she had trained her gaze away. Slowly Mushtri's watch over the clerks grew so acute, that her presence in their midst became like the deployment of a sentry in the cell of the condemned. The clerks were even robbed of any freedom to do justice to their natural feelings among themselves. The sudden raptures and transports of joy into which the whole bank had been thrown upon the sight of Mushtri Khanam's femininity gradually subsided, and gave way to a definitive dread and avoidance of her person. That suited Mushtri very well and she soon firmly established herself in her new workplace. The grey heads made a gradual comeback; the sales of pomade cream suffered. The drought that had succeeded the false drizzle became complete, and all the marshland insects were lulled back to an arid and extensive subterranean sleep. Despondency returned among clerical ranks, and all past joy was forever purged from the bank's recollection. Even the patriarchal gunman, greatly impressed by this turn of events, and caught by the prevailing dread of Mushtri Khanam, felt obliged to make her tea during the break before he took a cup to the manager, Qudratullah the widower.

How the termites survived the fumigation and the DDT vapour is understandable, for it could not possibly have reached the insides of the wall where their armies spawned. During swarming season the termite workers perforated the nests with exits for the exodus of the insects. Born in the labyrinths of darkness the winged royalty emerged from their nests groping for light. And when their nuptial flight had claimed another darkness for their nest they unburdened themselves of the wings. And for a few days after the swarms had left the nests, the ground remained strewn with their wings, until the wind blew them away.

The day the first swarm materialised, and unbeknown to him, a pair fell into Mushtri's bowl of gravy. Mirzban was uncomfortably watching her interrogate his wife. With her eyes fixed on her brother, Mushtri Khanam was quizzing

Bano Tamanna about the length of time Bano's father, Salar Jang, intended to stay. He was arriving the next day by train. Bano Tamanna had cleared the table and gone inside to prepare her room for his stay and shift the beds into the veranda for herself and her granddaughters. The duration of Salar's visits were indefinite. They could terminate in a week or extend to a few months. Whenever Salar or anyone from Bano Tamanna's family came to stay, Mushtri Khanam became sullen and fidgety, and irritated everyone with her sharp retorts to the simplest queries. Salar had mentioned a stay of a couple of weeks or at most a month. He was planning to buy a house in Purana Shehr as his own house upcountry was bought by the government since it was in the way of a new roadway being built and his tenants were giving him trouble with another building he owned. Bano Tamanna's was not a definite answer, and therefore not satisfactory for Mushtri. Mirzban listened to Bano Tamanna's confused and evasive reply to his sister with growing embarrassment but due to Mushtri's austere gaze on himself, he could find neither courage to change the subject nor the presence of mind to stop her from eating the bread dipped in gravy on top of which the insects were stranded.

Although Salar's proud countenance and deep-set eyes did not reveal it, the paralysis of the left side of his face, rheumatism, and unsuccessful lawsuits had devastated his health and family possessions. In his seventies now, his movements had been greatly restricted because of rheumatism and his body had shrunk around his long, aristocratic bones, except for the cartilaginous ears which proudly stuck out of the patriarch's cranium and reminded the world of the lost glory of his illustrious health and magnificent fortune.

In the days of his youth when he broke headstrong horses, and even much later, Salar's was an imposing presence, with his six foot-three height and three-hundred pounds of muscle and bone. One of the finest riders in the princely state of Gulmoha, his days were spent looking after the family orchards and indulging in equestrian sports, in which he participated with the British cavalry officers. His stable which sported Arabs and Thoroughbreds, the latter gifts from the British Indian Cavalry, was the pride of Gulmoha. When he was not in the saddle, Salar could be seen surveying his estate riding in a phaeton. His hookah was specially fired for these trips – the clay bowl filled with fermented, perfumed tobacco and the base with rosewater. The silver-tipped tube of the hookah clenched in his fist, he went on his rounds blowing clouds of redolent tobacco smoke.

When his first child was born after two years of Salar's marriage, he had already given up hope of ever becoming a father from his then wife. Bano Tamanna's mother completed the thousand *navafil* in prayer after she recovered from childbirth. All the farm-hands got a month's rations, a hundred yards of cloth and one gold coin each, during the celebrations that followed. The horses and the pigeons too, were rewarded for their prayers for Salar's progeny. The stallions had to bear the weight of new Morocco leather saddles and the pigeons gold rings in their feet. But all these festivities were short-lived. The second child, a boy, was stillborn. Two more children, both boys, died in infancy. Salar became bitter and lost interest in his household. He moved his bed to the men's quarters and immersed himself in farm administration. Heartbroken, his wife took to her bed. Salar started avoiding her, suspecting that she had some malignant disease. He was correct in his assumption but his disregard for her condition only made it worse. Bano Tamanna's mother died of consumption the following year.

Relieved of all household responsibilities, Salar applied himself to his boyhood passions of poetry and pigeon-breeding. In those days he had a thousand and one pigeons which lived under the able guardianship of Muneemji, a skeletal being who had been Salar's adjutant for over fifty years. Muneemji had groomed Salar's horses as a boy. As a young man, he administered Salar's orchards and kept a record of the produce. He was up before the sun, checking the horses, kicking the servants awake and feeding pigeons. He went to bed last, after inspecting the wings of the prize pigeons, checking the water in their cages and shouting at the servants for their general clumsiness, one last time before he went to bed. Bano Tamanna was brought up jointly by Muneemji and Salar's younger sister who died a year before Partition.

Partition brought many changes. Salar was not sure if he could migrate with his horses and pigeons as the long train journey was extremely perilous. So he had to part with his aviary. Most of the birds had to be presented to his arch rivals, who knew their caprices and could afford their care. A few horses were stolen one night, the rest were distributed among the area's nobility.

His circumstances significantly reduced, Salar no longer travelled with a battery of servants, although once in the new country he soon reclaimed a small estate for the one he had left behind, and instituted a new aviary of pigeons, albeit on a smaller scale. Muneemji who was now in his seventies himself, and walked with a stoop and carried a cane for balance, still did most of Salar's work, and having nobody to shout at, grumbled to himself. The loss of past grandeur was not something Salar quite overcame or even understood. He tried to compensate for that loss of status by a spate of marriages.

He was in his fifties then. Partition had left behind many widows and even in his depleted status Salar was considered a good match. But none of these marriages lasted more than a few months. He soon got disenchanted with these woeful matrons, one of whom he buried with her *nikah nama*, and the rest he exonerated from his duty without any preface. They occasionally wrote to him, cursing him for their ill treatment and offering to come back if he mended his ways. One of them even claimed to have had a baby by him. But that was all in the past as far as Salar was concerned, and he never wrote back or entertained any of those plaints.

Mirzban arrived at the railway station in a tonga to receive his father-in-law and his retinue of pigeons. The loudspeakers were blaring the destination of the approaching train, the platform's number where it would pull in, and the hours by which another train was late. Vendors waited with pots full of boiled eggs and kettles of tea fitted on braziers to ambush the transit passengers. The railway tracks were splattered with the faeces of hundreds of commuters who had relieved themselves through the train's open-ended toilets. The whole railway system was subservient to the random will of the engine-drivers who plied the trains at their pleasure and it was safer to attend to the call of nature on the train itself, rather than use the platform washroom. Therefore, these markings increased whenever a train stopped at the station, and swarms of flies which covered them rose in the air every time someone spat on the tracks. On the same shit-splashed tracks a group of children had put coins to be flattened beneath the wheels of the heavy railway engine, and some were trading these elliptical shapes for marbles or humming-tops.

The arrival of the train was no less an event than the Day of Reckoning. A great commotion broke out on the platform and inside the train itself the moment it pulled in. Mirzban saw Muneemji's shiny bald head sticking out of a bogey. He had not seen Mirzban and even before the train pulled up, he was beckoning the coolies to help out with the luggage. The sleepy passengers pushed each other to get down and the coolies snatched their luggage from their hands even as they struggled out of the bogies. The vendors pushed aside those coming out while trying to reach potential customers inside. Scuffles broke out and the coolies, their shiny brass licence plates tied on their arms, each balancing anywhere from three to four suitcases on their turbaned heads, rushed to the tonga-walas for whom they worked on commission. Children were sometimes separated from their parents in the bustle.

Salar always tried to defray the expense of his visit by bringing crates of mangoes, seasonal fruit, or poultry. Sometimes he even passed amounts to Bano Tamanna for the household expenses which she accepted without Mirzban's knowledge after mildly reproving her father for his extravagance. When the first surge of commotion had subsided, together with Muneemji and two coolies, Mirzban helped out with a hamper containing cherries and fifty-odd crates of birds. These were priceless, pedigree pigeons and went wherever Salar went. Everything was loaded onto five tongas after some haggling for fare, in which the coolies mediated. Jolting and creaking the procession started, with Mirzban in the last tonga. Stray dogs followed them, and to be heard amidst their barking Salar had to raise his voice. And every time Salar attempted to be heard, he immediately broke into fits of coughing, and the dogs barked all the more. The crates of pigeons arrived safely and by the time they reached home, one by one the dogs had also scattered.

Unsuspecting that he was being watched, Muneemji moved slowly in the Sessions Court premises among the corridors of chameleon-infested neem trees, bogus lawyers, and seedy typists, where the drone of metal keys on countless old typewriters, and the cling-clang of convicts walking about in chains and leg-irons made an ungodly music, hourly punctuated by the strike of the clock tower. Whenever a convict in handcuffs and leg-irons went by, mothers covered their children's eyes with their hands and asked them to atone for sins they might be likely to commit in the future.

The complex of three adjoining houses upcountry which Salar had received in reparation after Partition, was in a state of turmoil. His tenants had refused to pay a five per cent increase in rent, proposed for the first time in thirteen years. When Muneemji had failed in his negotiations, Salar, in order to teach his tenants a lesson, decided to file a lawsuit against them in Purana Shehr, so that they would be obliged to travel some eight hundred miles by train from upcountry for every hearing. The main reason for choosing Purana Shehr was his daughter's house, which was commodious enough if not very comfortable, and where he could entrench himself while the preliminaries of the case were being settled. With that view Muneemji had come to the Sessions Court to hire a lawyer for Salar.

In one corner of the court premises, an array of four-wheelers lay abandoned. The original owners of these trucks and wagons, confiscated by the police at some time, had long ago abandoned their claims on their property. The reasons were as many as there were vehicles. The regular transportation of cauldrons of complimentary biryani and korma from the hotel kitchens to the police stations took its toll on the remaining roadworthy vehicles. The vehicles failed to attract any bids in the police auction, and, ultimately, they were sent back to the court premises to rust. At that point some enterprising people came up with the proposal that if they be allowed to use the wagons during the day, they would not grudge a nominal rent. It was money coming in, and the Superintendent of Police, to whom this proposal was forwarded, could find no fault with the idea. So a whole battalion of typists, and a few not so well-to-do lawyers, moved into the vehicles, set up their respective trades, and hung out their boards.

Ladlay Qalabaz, Notary Public & Oath Commissioner,

conducted his practice from one such wagon. A short, dark-complexioned, bespectacled man with a bushy moustache and a smug expression, Ladlay was parked in a four-wheeler from which the seats had been removed to make room for a small table, and the dashboard served the dual purpose of filing cabinet and shelf. With his head thrust out from his office Ladlay was evaluating the crowd in the courtyard with a scavenging eye when Muneemji walked into view. He had seen Muneemji come and go from Qasr-e Yunani and knew his name from the sweeper. Therefore his expression immediately changed from hawkish to benign before their eyes could meet. 'Please! Be seated,' Ladlay beckoned Muneemji to step inside the office where a small pedestal fan was provided. A wooden bench was lying outside but the invitation to step inside the vehicle's inner sanctum showed more respect and greater privilege. As Muneemji was stepping inside, somebody with a hurried look also dropped by, and Ladlay engaged him as well.

Once inside the rusting wagon Muneemji looked around. An extension wire ran from vehicle to vehicle, supplying power to these offices, which was obtained free by a metal hook from a nearby electricity pole.

Someone was toasting papads on an electric heater in a nearby van, and from time to time the papad aroma wafted into the air and tingled Muneemji's nose. As Muneemji turned his head to locate the origin of that appetising smell he saw a curious little man carrying a teapot, stealthily turn a corner then look back, and apparently satisfied that no one was following him, bring Ladlay the tea on tiptoes. His manner was most intriguing.

This was Chhalawa of the Chhalawa Hotel, a meek, wiry character, who commuted barefoot to and from the hotel kitchen, some hundred times a day, carrying tea, arrowroot biscuits and shortbread to all corners of Purana Shehr. Myths describe Chhalawa as a cherubic ghoul who, crawling on all fours could travel hundreds of miles in the flash of an eye. Many chhalawas saw action while in service with Solomon's army. The Chhalawa of the hotel, neither cherubic nor given to quadrupedal motion, derived his nickname from rumours of having been seen at many different places at the same time. It was said that there was no public or private spot in Purana Shehr where Chhalawa had not set foot and that there was no path, no matter how circuitous and buried deep into the nether quarters of the city, which his feet had not trodden. Chhalawa went about the city on his mud-caked feet with his head hung low, coins jingling in his grimy money-jacket, carrying a kettle and cups for the established clients of the Chhalawa Hotel who had, over the years, developed a taste, and an immunity, to the potion sold by that enterprise in the name of tea. Chhalawa was easily frightened by the sight of a policeman, and his shifty gait was specially adopted to keep out of sight of the constabulary.

As Chhalawa came near, he looked closely at Muneemji bending a little over his tray to get a clearer view of the van's inside and greeted Muneemji gaily with a wink and a nod. He put the tray on the van's floor. Ladlay did not look up from the typewriter and seemed engrossed in his typing.

'Ladlay Sahib! My money! It is one month now!' Chhalawa bleated. Ladlay started and the dance of his fat, hairy fingers on the typewriter was interrupted. He looked out of the van to see if someone was calling him from outside. Muneemji had seen Ladlay look from the corner of his eye as Chhalawa put down the tray on the floor earlier but he silently watched the act Ladlay was putting up. After some effort Ladlay eventually found Chhalawa standing right behind him. 'Aha! Brother Chhalawa! I was just going to call for some tea for my guest here. Good thing you came around. Leave the tea on the floor.'

'Ladlay Sahib! I was asking for my money; I have to close my monthly account at the hotel. You have to clear your dues today.' Chhalawa was already moving towards the tray lying on the floor. It appeared to Muneemji that he was going to pick it up but he faltered for a moment, and Ladlay took advantage of his slight indecision to secure it before Chhalawa's hands could reach it.

'I am not running away anywhere, brother Chhalawa!' Ladlay said jocularly, 'I am still alive and my life is the proof that you shall not be deprived of my company any time soon. Come, now! Come along! You can pick up your money when you come back for the cups and kettle,' he said, raising his voice. At this a sudden expression of panic appeared on brother Chhalawa's face and he ambled away in his strange manner, silently pleading with him with his anxious eyes not to compromise his presence. However, he kept looking over his shoulder every few steps and moving his finger in an admonishing manner as a reminder to the notary of his return. Ladlay graciously smiled in reply, waving his hand as if to offer his commiserations in advance to Chhalawa for a visit which was destined to failure in the realisation of its end. Then shaking his head with the air of a man to whom the ephemeral nature of the world had become fully manifest, he turned towards Muneemji and asked him to describe his business as he began pouring the tea. Muneemji briefly described the facts of the matter to the notary who sat listening with a most solemn expression on his face and kept nodding from time to time to express his utmost endorsement and approval of Salar's intended course of action.

'I must congratulate your Sahib on this remarkable idea,' Ladlay said after listening to Muneemji describe Salar's plan, and taking out a big white handkerchief to wipe his neck and brow, and the carriage of his typewriter where particles of dust had settled. 'I would be very honoured to be of any assistance to a patrician like Salar Sahib. You may not have recognised me, but I live right opposite Mirzban Sahib's house. He is a first-rate person and his family is very devout.'

'Really now ... you must come from the nobility yourself to speak well of another!' Hearing Ladlay praise Mirzban and his family by which he meant Bano Tamanna, Muneemji overlooked his small cunning game with Chhalawa and immediately put him on an equal footing with Mirzban's family. 'You must come and see Salar Sahib either today or tomorrow,' he told Ladlay. 'Wah! Wah! What could be better than having your neighbour for your advocate? Right on the spot when you need him. Night and day!' Muneemji continued, happily.

'Don't be deceived by appearances, Muneemji!' Ladlay observed. 'Times are bad. These days you cannot trust your own flesh and blood. My present circumstances make it sound ridiculous and I am not given to bragging anyway but ...' Muneemji helplessly tried to protest that Ladlay not explain his origins as they were obviously noble, but the notary continued, '... I too came from a good family. You think I do not realise what worthy people like Salar Sahib have to put up with? I see hundreds of cases everyday. It is the nature of my work and I will tell you something else. If you ask me, I see the indications of Doomsday become more and more clear everyday. A father can no longer trust his son; amongst themselves brothers thirst after each other's blood. People may say that we lawyers are worse than the thieves and murderers we represent. But I ask you this, where does all that filth come from?' Ladlay paused and looked askance at Muneemji who once again had been distracted by the tempting smell of the papads. But when Ladlay did not take up his monologue after the short pause, and the notary's silence became uncomfortable, Muneemji forced a general comment. 'Of course. No, I fully agree with you. Yours is a thankless but vital office.'

Visibly animated, Ladlay continued. 'I agree that a lawyer's is dirty work. But then who will plead for justice?'

'Who else! Of course!' Muneemji tried not to make his reply sound indifferent and as he looked up he saw Ladlay quickly look away.

Mushtri had finished adjusting the gramophone needle on her favourite record, and after tucking hair-pins in her coiffure she had picked up the newspaper when Ladlay was showed in by Muneemji. Mushtri was at first puzzled. She had seen Ladlay coming and going out of the house across the alley where he had recently rented a room. She knew he was a lawyer of sorts and sometimes from her window she saw him smoking a cigarette in the balcony. At times she had been conscious of his eyes looking at her but she did not give it much thought and as a rule never acknowledged his greetings when she ran into him going to work. So she made a face and muttering something disagreeable, laid herself in the easy-chair to listen to a song. It was an old romantic number, and one of those genderless film songs which can be sung by both the hero and the heroine.

It was still afternoon but the sky was once more overcast and Mushtri had turned on the ceiling lamp. The light attracted the moths who thronged close to the bulb. They collided with everything and the floor was soon covered with their transparent wings, which the red ants began laboriously removing to their nests. Divested of their wings, shiny moths, like emaciated caterpillars, crept around. Some were crushed on the armrest under Mushtri's elbows and on the floor under her feet.

Outdoors, bats were hovering around, preying on the mosquitoes and miscellaneous moths and beetles. Mushtri heard Bano Tamanna instructing her granddaughters to go outdoors with their ears covered, so that a bat does not clutch on to them, and saw her opening the scullery door and putting the tongs over the lighted stove. There were no known cases of bats hanging by children's ears, but everyone knew the cure – just in case – which was to apply red-hot fire irons to the bat which ostensibly made it relinquish its hold. Mushtri Khanam kept a pair in the scullery for Lumboo the sweeper to carry half-dead rats out to the neighbourhood dump which were found bleeding under the newar beds in the morning after a close brush with the cats in the night.

Suddenly the room was filled with a foul oily fetor. As she slapped her arm to get rid of the creeping moths Mushtri had squashed one of the tiny flying beetles which emitted a noxious smell when crushed. Mushtri had turned to the film supplement when her attention was attracted by the rustle of a lizard which suddenly darted from behind the lamp shade to catch a moth, and disappeared into its hideout with its prey. She looked up eagerly to see what the lizard would do next.

It reappeared shortly. But this time instead of bolting at them it altogether ignored the moths, some of which even hit it before falling to the ground, and looked right across Mushtri's line of vision. Mushtri followed its gaze and to her surprise found a butterfly fluttering in the veranda. The manner in which the butterfly had materialised was totally unexpected since they were not usually seen when it was about to rain. Perhaps a draught of wind which had begun to blow outside and promised a gale with its sandy smell had forced her inside the open lattices. The lizard turned to watch as the butterfly rose and made an ellipse round the bulb. It flew to the other corner of the room and turned back. The lizard, which had lurched forward in her direction, stopped in its tracks. As it dived close to where Mushtri was seated, it seemed that the butterfly was seeking the bulb's light, falling on the floor from an angle, but all of a sudden it rose again, and before it could hit the ceiling, the lizard which had run some distance along the ceiling in anticipation of the insect's trajectory, caught it with a small lurch.

Her neck stiff with alertness, Mushtri sat up and watched the lizard with the butterfly in its mouth with a peculiar, almost dreamy fascination. The lizard shook its head sideways to shove the butterfly down its gullet. The slow movement of the insect's wings stopped, and it disappeared with a few successive jerks of the lizard's head.

A faint crease of a smile appeared on Mushtri's face before she slipped into her torpid reading again. It was this smile which Ladlay noticed as he came out of Salar's room and stepped out of the veranda into the gale. The moths were slowly diminishing in number. After resting a while the lizard had come out to forage again.

For some months now, Desh Bank's manager, Qudratullah the widower, had been enduring a daily affliction, dating from Mushtri Khanam's transfer to his branch. Being of a retiring disposition, and averse to any public audit of conduct, Qudratullah had furtively watched the ebb and flow of the tide which had washed Mushtri Khanam's form to his shores. Behind the glass screen where he sipped his tea, and scrutinised the ambience with his inflamed eyes, lay a silently suffering soul – quite forgotten but full of promise.

In the course of his career, the principal idea which had guided Qudratullah's sense of what was expected of him in a situation, was retreat. Retreat in the face of conflict, retreat in the event of disagreement, retreat in circumstances where he was forced to take a conscientious or even conscious stand: in short, retreat from pressures of all kinds. That might not have won him many battles in the field, but it came quite handy in the bank system and he promptly rose from an accountant to a full-fledged branch manager. One of his efforts after being promoted to manager was to have himself transferred to a bank where his history as an accountant was not known. In his own bank the stigma of once being a servile accountant among other lowly accountants was hard to wash, and subsequently robbed him of the charm of wielding power over the covey of his colleagues who knew him from his humbler days. Upon the retirement of Desh Bank's Topee Mohalla branch manager, he arrived there with a deeply entrenched antipathy for clerks. Qudratullah therefore regarded Mushtri Khanam's routing of the clerks' corps with that degree of approbation which almost made her conquest a shared glory.

Her strength of character complemented Qudratullah's complaisance. Together they would rule over the bank, until their retirement, while their clerical staff would be raised under her severe discipline. That was the reach of Qudratullah's fancy at that early stage. But like any responsible head of a commonwealth, Qudratullah needed to take the precaution of engaging Mushtri Khanam's association in this long-term venture from a position of advantage. So he decided to go about it in the cloak of a patron, bestowing his bounty as a favour and an aid to boost the newcomer's enthusiasm in her work. It was necessary to dispel any suspicions of amorous proceedings, both of the clerks' and Mushtri Khanam's, thereby giving the popular tongue no chance to lash him with its venomous thongs, and the public eye no glimpse of his real designs. To complete these necessary calculations took Qudratullah some time, since planning a strategy was not something which came easily to him, but in due course everything was ready. But how this office association was to be cultivated further, Qudratullah did not provision for, since it rested entirely on Mushtri Khanam's response.

Qudratullah had made a list of accounts to be entrusted to Mushtri Khanam over a period of time, and being of a nature which needed constant monitoring, they were calculated to bring him into close and extensive congress with his subject, and in proximity of his object. Mushtri Khanam's towering figure was neutralised by Qudratullah's hierarchy, and as to her glaring eyes, in the manager's chamber they did not glare with half the intensity. Probably it was on account of the office not being well lit, as the only window was kept shut or probably on account of Qudratullah's eyes. He wore tinted eyeglasses indoors since his eyes became sore during the summers, and remained thus plagued until the end of the monsoons. Because his room was a little dark, and since the bulb of the small lamp shed its light on the table and his visitors from over his shoulders, in the initial phases of his plan Qudratullah had a good chance of surveying Mushtri Khanam over the brim of his teacup, although the rising steam occasionally fogged his vision. Every time Mushtri walked into his room, Qudratullah could hear her sari rippling against her flesh with the click-clock of her heels on the tiled floor, which made his own flesh creep with excitement and sent shivers down his spine. And after she was gone, Qudratullah's feet beat a tattoo on the floor as he smelled the strong oil-based perfume of her hands on the mildewy official documents. These meetings naturally extended, and gradually made Qudratullah more wretched and miserable than he had ever been.

The vanity of the clerks blocked their suspicions of Qudratullah's designs, as they did not expect old Qudratullah to fly in the face of their defeat, and to soar where they had singed their wings. So they welcomed the few hours of respite every afternoon when Mushtri Khanam was in the manager's office poring over files and ledgers, and during that interval they became very snappy. Indeed they saw in Mushtri Khanam's labouring over those dead credit accounts, and in her being dictated letters to, and in all such secretarial duties which befell her instead of one of them, her condign punishment.

It did not take Mushtri Khanam long to discern in

Qudratullah's assignments his focal end. On identical pretexts she had been subjected to odious labour under different bosses in different offices and had become frustrated with the routine. It was unfair, Mushtri Khanam thought, that she must work twice as hard for someone to get close to her. However, his being a widower without an issue had removed many difficulties in Qudratullah's case, which other professional married men had posed in the past, and therefore Mushtri Khanam persevered. But this time she had decided on a sterner course of action, knowing full well how vulnerable Qudratullah was despite his dark glasses and his attempt at maintaining an official tone.

People had begun to notice termite tunnels on the walls of their houses and minor damage to books and documents. The tunnels were brushed with brooms, and after they had been exposed and left in the sun for a while the books and papers were put back in the swept shelves. The humid weather persisted and something like a mist hung over the city. It was more noticeable in the mornings and it subsided a little only on days when the sun came out for a few hours. But the weather was mostly overcast and the sun shone only now and then.

Then it was observed that the termites had also damaged the frames of the doors and windows in storerooms and drawing-rooms which were mostly kept shut. This time more serious notice was taken of the damage. The carpenter was called to a few houses. With his adze he scraped the damaged portions, soaked the wood in kerosene oil and patched up the damaged portions by hammering new strips of wood. The repaired areas were planed, filled up with putty, and painted. The carpenter also said that the next time they installed any fixture, he would advise them to use teak wood, which although a little expensive was naturally termite proof. In a few houses people took exception to this counsel. The carpenter bought his own wood and since teak wood was expensive, it was alleged that he suggested using it so that he could make more money. The people called the carpenter all sorts of names and talked about how mercenary the artisans of the day had become.

Soon it was discovered that Topee Mohalla alone was not singled out by the termites. Termite attacks were reported all over Purana Shehr. In some places the problem was quite severe and people had suffered heavy damages.

In due course many theories were put forward to explain and justify the origin of the termites. Most of these originated from the Chhalawa Hotel.

The Chhalawa Hotel, being right across from the Sessions Court building, was usually inundated with lawyers during the day. A break of two hours in the afternoon, between the end of the first court session and the start of the second, invariably found them positioned on the well-engraved and inscribed wooden benches of the Chhalawa Hotel. All the cunning strategies for the defence as well as for the prosecution were crafted under its thatched roof. Their black suits and grimy elasticated bow-ties had become suffused with the potent reek of rat piss which presided over the hotel, and only struck the new visitors to that establishment, since the olfactory devices of its old patrons had become immune to the odour long ago. The lawyers were easily distinguishable in the streets by that smell, and, as a natural consequence, this smell came to be associated with veteran Purana Shehr lawyers more than it did with its author.

While the Chhalawa Hotel catered mostly to lawyers and their clients in the day, in the evenings it became the hub of neighbourhood men who gathered there to discuss their miscellaneous affairs. That evening too, the neighbours were gathered there. In the kitchen the proprietor's cat snoozed over the crate of eggs, and every time the cook had an order to make an omelette, he had to lift one of her limbs to dig under her for an egg, while the cat remained fast asleep. Basmati Sahib had not arrived yet and Tabaq Sahib was busily spreading a dollop of butter on his toast with his forefinger, while Bhai Qamoosi stared at the walls of the Chhalawa Hotel mindlessly. They were decorated with posters of celestial quadrupeds, seemingly graminivorous, but of a nondescript zoology, flying all over God's cosmos without any tangible destiny. Their burdens were saintly men of advanced age in princely garbs, whose right hands, wielding scimitars, were raised over their heads in menacing gestures. These posters, the originals of which were produced by the same illustrator employed by the spiritual quarterlies to embellish their title pages – for the style was unmistakable – had hung in the Chhalawa Hotel since time immemorial. In the line of their hazardous duty they had acquired a rich deposit of the flies' scat, their corners had become dog-eared and the food vapour which constantly hung about the place had significantly diminished their glazed aspect.

'Here he is!' Tabaq Sahib shouted. Bhai Qamoosi looked away from the posters and saw Basmati enter the hotel, wiping his brow with a handkerchief. Basmati took the seat next to him, across from Tabaq Sahib, who sucked his greasy finger, wiped it on his hair, and took a bite from his toast.

'Did you hear at all what Bhai Qamoosi had to say?' Tabaq Sahib sat up as he asked Basmati, pulling up one leg and tucking it under his other thigh to become comfortable.

Basmati's head was turned as he signalled the counter-boy to send over a cup of tea. 'What does Bhai Qamoosi say *now*?' he asked.

As someone who looked for external causes, Tabaq Sahib subscribed to the school of belief which put the genesis of the termites in the miasma which had enveloped the city. The termites had rained down, he maintained, and seeped into the earth with the rainwater. Furthermore, he considered the termite outbreak the earthly forfeit for the worldly

iniquities of the people of Purana Shehr, which was welcome
in the sense that it should, undoubtedly, give them immunity
from any retributive justice in the hereafter. Bhai Qamoosi
disagreed with this line of thinking. He considered it
unenlightened to look for hidden meanings behind simple
facts, and was telling Tabaq Sahib the same on their way to
Chhalawa Hotel. Now Tabaq Sahib brought it up again to
solicit Basmati's help against Bhai Qamoosi.

Basmati sat listening to Bhai Qamoosi's ideas with a
patronising fortitude. Although he differed in his theory of
the termites from Tabaq Sahib, they still shared common
ground in attributing their origin to a divine source. Basmati's
explanation was that the tremors which had shaken the city a
few months ago had moved the layers of earth, and the
termites consigned to Hell, which, as everyone knew flamed
at the centre of the earth, had escaped from their prison.
That the termites had come from God to do His will, was
his thesis too.

After Bhai Qamoosi had finished speaking Basmati began
in a grave voice, 'I do not know how you get these ideas in
your head, Bhai Qamoosi! May God in his plentiful clemency
forgive you for these heresies!' Here Tabaq Sahib nodded
his head. 'But let me tell you something,' Basmati continued
in a changed tone of voice, 'just today I promised to sacrifice
a white billy-goat as expiation for my sins after what my
wife saw the other day!'

'What, Basmati? What did your wife see? Let us know
too!' Tabaq Sahib become animated by Basmati's mysterious
tone. Bhai Qamoosi also leaned forward interestedly and
looked at Basmati to continue. But Basmati took advantage
of the waiter putting his cup of tea on the table to prolong
his silence a bit longer.

'Now will you stop this nonsense and tell us, or what?'
Tabaq Sahib asked anxiously as Basmati proceeded to blow
over his cup and take a sip.

'If you remember,' Basmati began in a barely audible whisper, forcing both Tabaq Sahib and Bhai Qamoosi to lean towards him, 'the sky cleared for a few minutes yesterday, late in the afternoon?'

'Yes! Yes!' Tabaq confirmed eagerly, picking up his cup of tea and bringing it to his lips, 'What of that?'

'Well, my wife was putting the clothes out to dry on the line around sunset when she happened to look up at the sky ...'

'What did she see there?' Tabaq Sahib's voice was choked with fright.

Basmati glanced around to see if anyone was listening. Then he looked at Bhai Qamoosi and Tabaq Sahib and signalling them with a nod to bring their heads closer, said in an even softer whisper, 'The western sky was red!'

'You don't say so!' Tabaq Sahib's hand holding the cup had frozen and his eyes were bulging out. Basmati continued, 'And in the red sky, a fluttering black flag!'

'No!' said Tabaq Sahib as he moved away in alarm and almost crashed his cup into the saucer.

'Yes!' said Basmati triumphantly, and looked at Bhai Qamoosi to come up with an explanation for this historic augur symbolic for the visitation of tempests, which his wife had been a witness to. But Bhai Qamoosi avoided getting into arguments with Basmati, knowing his galvanic temperament, and therefore he silently kept wiping his shirt on which some tea from Tabaq Sahib's cup had splashed.

'Allah!' Tabaq Sahib muttered with a flushed face, his nostrils flaring. The radio in Chhalawa Hotel was broadcasting a *qawwali*.

The lawsuit had been worded by Ladlay and approved by Salar, and a date had been granted for the hearing. A plan of action was agreed upon and Ladlay retired promising to call again within a couple of days after completing the necessary paperwork and making a steel trap of a case against the tenants. With his circumlocutive flattery Ladlay had made his way into Salar's heart. Lawyers were a necessary evil in Salar's life as the means to achieve certain ends. He had been through more lawyers than most men during his numerous lawsuits and was extremely weary of their tricks. The ideas he entertained about them were already hardened. Therefore, at first he received Ladlay with his customary circumspection. However, the notary from the very beginning showed extreme humility, understanding, and deference to Salar's wishes of retribution, and offered several wily devices to make each one of Salar's tenants not only remember his grandmother, but also the taste of his mother's milk on the day she ended her confinement. Like the arch fox who offered the alibi of a bad cold to the lion when he asked him how his den smelt, Ladlay quickly learned to anticipate Salar's moods and to stick to the legal aspect and refrain from making value judgements about his client's wild propositions. He was often present at the private conferences between Salar and Muneemji, and was gradually, and not unwillingly, employed into other interesting occupations by his patron.

In a duffel-bag which always accompanied him, along with his tobacco pouch, shaving kit, a shoe-horn and miscellaneous such effects, Salar carried two notebooks which contained the sum total of his poetry. Tucked inside one of the notebooks was a commendatory note by a reputed poet of Salar's time, meant to be printed on the dust jacket of his collection, in the event of its publication. This book's publication along with the erection of his tombstone were Salar Jang's two major worldly concerns. This last fixation was paradoxical because nothing weighed heavier on Salar's mind or frightened him more, than the idea of his death. But he had already composed a couplet in the third person, which admonished Salar for his misdeeds in the world, and in the same breath, negotiated and secured his redemption from Providence. This was probably done with a view to exorcise any thoughts of death. But now that it was done, he wanted to see it engraved in marble for his tombstone. Salar had reminded Mirzban several times to look into it, but his absent-mindedness always came between Mirzban and his pledges. Salar now mentioned his wishes to Ladlay and he readily agreed to find both the publisher and the engraver.

Within a couple of days Ladlay offered to introduce Salar to the man who had engraved his father's tombstone. But there was a small complication. This engraver only worked in the Nastaleeq font, and in the course of his poetic career Salar had become wary of Nastaleeq because it was the preferred font of the katibs. Technically the katib was a calligrapher whom the poets employed to embellish their manuscripts. But the katibs, not happy with their job description, did more than just blindly copy the couplets. Oftentimes they added words to a couplet to balance the metre and sometimes even changed a whole line, thereby greatly improving the verse. The poets never appreciated this editorial input, rendered free of any charge. But the katibs held their ground. Salar being a poet had had his fill of them and the Nastaleeq font. His demise, he was determined, would not be recorded in the katib's preferred font. So the search had to begin anew for an engraver who did work in the Naskh, the alternate font of the conservative literary establishment. Several weeks passed. Then Ladlay brought the sad intelligence that the only engraver in Pukka Qila who did work in Naskh had died some years ago and ironically, filled a grave where a tombstone commemorated his life in Nastaleeq.

The Kaskas Brothers were the last exponents of the *desi kushti* style of wrestling. Like Salar their circumstances too, had been abridged compared to the glorious past, when the *pehlwans* fought at the head of the armies, and directed troops from their howdahs atop royal elephants. It was an outdated and outmoded form of wrestling in which the body weight of the *pehlwan*, rather than any wrestling skills, decided the victor. One of their ancestors had defeated some famous Russian wrestler ages ago, and that was the single laurel on whose strength their family still got a yearly grant and food subsidies from the government. It consisted of one lamb per head, ten kilos of milk, two kilos of dried fruit, ten pounds of pure ghee, and two kilos of mutton soup per day. The water component of milk was vomited out after it had curdled in their stomachs. That was their daily diet, and after five hundred push-ups and one thousand sit-ups in the afternoon, they drained a bowl of warm milk mixed with poppy seeds, and peacefully slept for the rest of the day.

Salar had a keen interest in this antiquated sport. Besides, the Kaskas Brothers also shared his interest in pigeon breeding. When he heard that the *pehlwans* were in Purana Shehr to inaugurate a clay-ring, he invited them over to see his collection.

When the five tongas carrying one *pehlwan* each rolled into Topee Mohalla, the whole neighbourhood turned out to see them. Women's heads peeped from behind doors; children clapped and in their juvenile enthusiasm, shouted abuse from a distance, as the *pehlwans* stepped down from their tongas. Each of them weighed close to five-hundred pounds and had enormous swinging bellies which gave them a swaggering motion. They were perspiring profusely under their colourful turbans. Clad in muslin kurtas which were sticking to their skins and silk dhotis they looked not quite unlike a pack of pedigree bovines turned out for the annual cattle show.

Muneemji was at the door to receive them. They had two hours before their train left the station, so they refused to have anything except some sherbet. After that they headed straight for the roof. Salar ignored Bano Tamanna's agitation and her whispered entreaties to take them one at a time to the roof for fear that it may cave-in under their combined weight. While the wooden staircase and the roof creaked, Bano Tamanna stood at the foot of the staircase with her granddaughters reciting *Ayatul-Kursi*, to thwart the imminent roof collapse.

Climbing the narrow and winding staircase presented a problem for the *pehlwans*. On each step they had to stop, pull the other foot up, bounce their bellies and with the momentum be carried to the next step. From the roof, the five *pehlwans* climbing up looked like one giant caterpillar winding its course up the helical-staircase. The shed on the roof where the pigeons were billeted was carpeted with newspapers to keep the birds' refuse containing undigested seeds from damaging the surface. If allowed to sink roots in the mud plaster they spread fast. At night Muneemji slept on a charpai near the shed to keep a check on marauding felines, and Salar sat down there, exhausted after climbing the staircase, while Muneemji handed out the prize pigeons to him, and Salar passed them on to the guests. Breathing heavily, as they were completely out of breath themselves after climbing twenty-odd stairs, the *pehlwans* held the pigeons in their hands with infantile delight. They spread out the pigeons' wings and blew warm air under them. Their tired eyes gleamed with pleasure and they giggled like young girls as they passed the pigeons around and baby-talked them. They congratulated Salar on his wonderful collection and offered to buy it off him for any price he had to offer. Salar showing no interest in any such commerce, they nodded their heads in understanding, shook hands all around, rolled down the stairs, had some more sherbet, chatted with Salar and Muneemji in the drawing room, and then mounting their conveyances from wooden stools which the drivers had put out for them, they, and a horde of neighbourhood urchins following them barefoot, disappeared in the tongas' dust, as Bano Tamanna heaved a sigh of relief.

It was over sherbet that the conversation had drifted towards Noor-e Firdousi, the Nightingale of the Battlefield. The *pehlwans* had performed *Umrah* and upon return their group photo with Noor-e Firdousi had recently been printed in daily *Qandeel*.

The favours of Noor-e Firdousi were courted by the country's top brass. The mistress of choice of the pudgy generals, the magic of her lyrics never failed to enliven the spirits of their vanquished army, whose humiliation had more than once been mollified by the strain of her vocal chords, singing the praise of victory-in-defeat. A pointless war had delivered Noor-e Firdousi from ignominious obscurity into the hands of renown. When the war erupted, Noor-e Firdousi was a radio vocalist and had recently recorded the national anthem whose memory was fresh in people's ears. The station manager's efforts to forward one of his *qawwal* lovers were repudiated by the head office during their search for a singer with a voice full of patriotism and pathos. They decided in Firdousi's favour who was invited to record the songs. In the middle of the war, a dam developed a breach, inundating hundreds of thousands of acres of agricultural land and farmers' settlements on both sides of the border, making it necessary for the forces to be called back to help in flood-relief work. Both armies in dire straits, a five-year peace treaty was signed and prisoners of war were exchanged, bringing an uneventful war to its merited end. In this national farce, Noor-e Firdousi, then twenty, emerged as the sole winner in a war which had produced no heroes. In a military ceremony she was decorated with the title of 'The Nightingale of the Battlefield,' and garlanded by the president.

Moving from radio to the cinema became natural for Firdousi, whose appearance on the big screen was an event unsurpassed in the country's cinematic history. She outdid herself in her seductive artfulness. The hero tried to commit suicide immediately after the filming of the last scene. Unconfirmed rumours attributed his rash act to unrequited love. Unheard-of scenes were witnessed in the cinema houses around the country. Several couples became estranged as the husbands felt cheated by their wives' simple ways and plain looks, after their exposure to the Nightingale's cloying audience. After such a momentous start, Firdousi's way to fame and fortune was guaranteed, and soon she was all over, and remained there for what seemed an eternity.

In her fifties and fitted with gold incisors, the voluptuous Nightingale still competed with advantage over much younger and comelier girls in the contraband trade of seduction. She had been tempting public restraint for over two decades now, rolled in Banarasi saris and a double brassiere lined with silk, with her ample rolls of fat hanging in pendulous love-handles. Although short and portly, she dominated the screen with her triple chins, a pair of small mistrustful eyes, and her rippling curls styled into dos of bouffant proportions.

The couch acrobatics of Noor-e Firdousi were legendary. Numerous first-hand accounts attested to the carnal dexterity of the madam in her advanced age. Several interesting jokes, unspeakable, yet somehow in wide circulation, did daily rounds with equal viciousness among the two circles of the under-privileged bureaucracy and the have-not proletariat. Many clever contortions and cunning treats, which Noor-e Firdousi had demonstrated to the delight of her martial patrons, over thirty-five years of active service, were remembered with relish. One manoeuvre in particular – whereby the Nightingale, balancing her lover over her copious legs, suspended him in mid-air at a certain climactic juncture – was always the subject of much citation.

Intrigued, and anxious to verify the stories of Firdousi's many talents, the *pehlwans* had sought audience with Firdousi, and sheepishly narrated the story of their success to Muneemji and Salar Jang that eventful afternoon.

The eldest brother in the group of *pehlwans* looked uncomfortably at his brothers and produced a reluctant mumble as if debating the wisdom of committing himself. The brothers looked the other way. One of them scratched his armpit, the other shook his leg. But none of this suggested objection. Perhaps the brothers too wished to refresh their memory. Their bellies acting like bolsters and their arms folded in front of them, they were leaning forward in their *moondhas*, displaying a wealth of gold rings and bracelets.

'*Janab!*' he started, touching the lobes of his ears, a comprehensive gesture which suggests the multifarious emotions of repentance, awe and rapture variously, but for the present presented the latter two, 'Neither us, nor our fathers or grandfathers have seen a woman quite like her.' Here he crossed his arms, repeated the gesture, and looked at his brothers to solicit their approval. Except for the one looking at the ceiling thoughtfully and who continued to giggle to himself, the others shook their heads in mute approval of their brother's comments without raising their eyes from the ground.

'Even her secretary, what's his name …?' he asked.

'Lamroo!' the chuckling one interjected and snorted again.

'Yes, Lamroo! Lamroo too is a most unbelievable man. He insisted that we take off our turbans and hang them on the same stand where a brigadier's or colonel's cap was hanging. He was quite casual with them. As a result the folds of my turban came loose, but he did not give us time.

'Lamroo let me in while the brigadier was still putting on his pants, and when he saw me he uttered the pained shriek of a bitch on whose tail somebody has stepped. He shouted at Lamroo to keep the eunuchs out of the quarters while he was inside. When I heard that I decided to twist the neck of that son of a bitch then and there, but Lamroo fell at my feet and clung to my legs. He is a good man. And then Madame Firdousi beseeched me in God's name. That bastard also took fright when he realised whom he had abused and sobered up.

'For this very reason we do not touch the heathen bottle. A man loses all sense. Our fathers and grandfathers died reminding us never to touch the bottle. They were very pious people, *Janab*! Let there be no mistake about it. They knew what was right and what was wrong. We try not to blemish their name. That's the best we can do if we need forgiveness from God,' the *pehlwan* said, and became silent.

Muneemji looked at Salar from the corner of his eyes and discovering that the *pehlwan*'s silence had made him restless, interposed after a while.

'So, Firdousi received you after that brigadier had left?'

'And why wouldn't she receive us, Muneemji Sahib? We are not thieves. We went there as her honoured guests. But one thing I must tell you. Firdousi knows how a guest is shown respect. And this is the woman who, when the president got emotional and started crying, kicked him in the belly saying she was not his mother. She did not care about the presidential bodyguards listening in the parlour. Now this is what I call a woman! Lamroo told us this, it's not as if we are making it up.'

Here the *pehlwan* paused and entreated his brothers with his gaze to make some supportive gesture or sound. Muneemji crossed his legs on the *moondha*. But the *pehlwans* were unaffected. Perhaps they were soporific from the pleasant coolness in the room. Salar was visibly restive, and Muneemji felt that he should break the deadlock.

'So, then ...!' Muneemji said and cleared his throat.

'What to tell, *Janab*! What a woman! By God! Hardly had I mounted her than she moved under me. It felt like the earth had moved. You experience the same dizzying feeling when there is a tremor. Your head reels. I took fright. One must fear God's disasters. We are *pehlwans*, but where is the guarantee for life even for a djinn in an earthquake. I tried to dismount and groped for my dhoti. But my arms had gone to sleep, she was clutching them so tight. Now we do not spend sixteen hours everyday in the clay-ring getting sodomised. You won't believe me, but my hands could only grasp air. Even before I knew it, I was in the air. God is my witness. She had carried me on her legs. I felt ashamed. I also felt fear that now she might throw me over. You can expect anything from a woman who could lift you on her legs. In my heart I invoked the Almighty and summoned His help. I said to myself, 'This woman has lifted me and will try to abase me. This is her game. If I take fright now I won't be able to show face even to myself, let alone anybody else.' So, in the name of the Almighty, I thrust myself at her, while still suspended in such humiliation. At the same time, I managed to get hold of her wrists and twisted them. Now I am a good six-and-a-half maunds, and it was her turn to take fright. A horse is after all a horse, a buffalo but a buffalo! She cried, her legs slipped under me, I fell right between her thighs and was all over her in a minute. She laughed. I also laughed even though I still felt a little afraid. Between her laughter she told me that nobody had tried that on her yet. Afterwards she did not try any more of her tricks. But by God, she is a lioness.'

Salar gasped. Muneemji looked at him, but the *pehlwan* continued. 'By God! She is a woman one would be proud to have stock with, if only she were not a whore! Let me tell you this! Only a boy born from a good coupling makes a good *pehlwan*. Our matches were made very carefully. Our wives are themselves the daughters of the djinns. As long as the Kaskas family is alive, *desi kushti* will never be forgotten in the world. The president also patronises us. The whole country has given us honour. We will never let you down. Free-style is nothing. It's all cat shit – good for neither plastering nor finishing.' The *pehlwan* terminated his monologue on a high note and after panting heavily for a few minutes became drowsy like his brothers. However, Salar was far from being inert. Even Muneemji became a little apprehensive when he saw Salar's face looking taut and flushed.

Salar had remained quiet during the whole discourse. He had sat scratching and scraping his chin and scalp, signs of deep thought and the stress of his mental absorption, respectively. Not even in the evening when he was alone with Muneemji, and asked him to look under his pillow for the stationery, did he mention a word about Firdousi to him. Muneemji was a malicious gossip and a walking repository of family scandals which he narrated with contemptuous relish whenever Salar gave him the nod, and therefore he found Salar's silence unusual. Salar only discussed the plans for the next day with him and the time they had to show up at a certain house in Pukka Qila.

One did not hear many sounds in Purana Shehr. It moved quietly with measured steps, without running into momentous events. At around nine o'clock in the evening the whole city wore a deserted look, and the silence was only broken by the solitary night-watchman who circumscribed the city on a bicycle, blowing his whistle. Sometimes the emaciated lion in the zoo avenged himself on the city, for the stolen meat from his rations, spoiling the nightly peace by roaring as loud and as long as he could.

Mirzban could hear the roars in his sleep. But when he woke up with a dry sensation in his throat which was almost choking, and the noise broke upon him with its full throaty resplendence, he realised it was Salar's loud snores from the other room, which sometimes even woke up the old man himself with a start.

The glass of water on his table was all but empty. Still

thirsty after draining it, he crept to the courtyard half-asleep, where a pitcher of water was left overnight to cool in the night air. The pleasant night breeze caressed Mirzban's face, as he carefully replaced the lid. He looked up. The morning star was glowing brightly in the eastern skies, and the moon was hanging low. An empty bed was lying close to him, and Mirzban lay down to enjoy the night. Folding his arms behind his head for a pillow, he surveyed the sky dotted with stars. The sky was the shawl of God, and stars were the small holes through which His light shone, he remembered his mother telling him as a child. In the eye of his mind Mirzban tried to grasp the world as it would look from the heavens looking down, and he saw the sky so tightly wrapped around the ball of life, and the image became so vivid, that he almost felt his own body being squeezed by the weight of the firmament.

The Eternal God behind the perfect sphere who had neither beginning nor end! Looking heavenwards the thought occurred to Mirzban, stirring up his fancy and sending sleep farther from his eyes. The wind opened the bedroom door and Salar's snores flowed into the courtyard. A rain-bird flew by screeching. Agitated by these intrusions in his peaceful reverie, Mirzban stirred uncomfortably in bed, in an effort to concentrate his excited fancy. He raised his head a little by straining his neck to see how the sky lay and marvelled at the sheer expanse of the heavens.

The concept of eternity always fascinated Mirzban with its promise of infinite idleness. But it was not some vulgar employment of this perpetual convenience which attracted him. What enticed Mirzban was the regal and eternal leisure to reflect and contemplate on life inherent in the idea. Nothing became an omnipotent being more than eternal life, he thought.

From there, Mirzban's thoughts turned to the genesis of that virtue shortly. Eternity must have come into being with

God, he postulated. It was the environment for God's element. Without eternity, God would be base like all other life: will not, indeed, *exist!* The germ of Eternity was Time. So Time must have existed before all. It occurred to Mirzban that it sounded blasphemous. But before the frenzy of his thoughts could overcome this compunction, he espied a bird in the sky where there was none before. Mirzban's first thought was that it was the same rain-crow which had disturbed him earlier. It had suddenly risen into the skies and was restlessly flapping its wings. Then almost as suddenly it became still, and plummeted. There was time enough for Mirzban to realise its trajectory, but not to clear out. It brushed the back of his head even as he was darting out of the bed. For a moment, until his vision cleared after the impact had subsided, Mirzban found himself groping about in darkness and felt a burning sensation where the bird had hit him. The bird was now quiet and motionless. Gathering it carefully and turning it over in his hands, Mirzban became by degrees convinced that it was a chappal, not a bird, whose gyrations he had mistaken for the flapping of a bird's wings. He was still wondering about the cause for this calamity which had struck him unsolicited, when he was distracted by hair-raising cries of 'Thief! Thief!' which suddenly rent the peaceful air, and were so dreadful that it seemed the felon was now inculpating himself further with homicide.

With the shoe still in his hand, Mirzban stood motionless listening in the courtyard. Soon other voices joined the solitary cry. Doors were being unlatched, and presently the alleys of Topee Mohalla rang up with the sound of running feet and desperate inquiries about the crime and its precursor. Without any forewarning Muneemji sprang up in his bed on the roof, like a corpse rising in its coffin, and in his cracked voice was shouting something unintelligible. However, the initial chorus soon subsided and gave way to loud inquiring voices. A knot of people was hotly discussing something in the alley. Mirzban, brought back to life by this turbulence, peeped out of the house and discovering nothing hostile in the air, joined the group. From a distance the lamp of the chowkidar's cycle was coming towards them.

It seemed that Basmati Sahib, unable to fall asleep in his bedroom due to the humidity, had come out in the courtyard, where he saw a shadow on the wall. Basmati's own vivid visions of burglars hiding behind walls and in porches had become twice as redoubtable in the wake of his recently coming into a ten thousand rupee prize-bond, and it had become a first principle with him to exorcise shadows with the handiest footwear. After his first impulse was satisfied, he had raised the alarm. They were his cries which Mirzban had heard, although in the dim light of the alley lamp Basmati looked quite unruffled, and no signs of physical violence, which might have justified his gruesome screeches, were anywhere visible on his person.

At that point Mirzban became aware that he was still holding in his hand the Peshawari chappal which had hit him. At that instant Basmati, standing in the alley with only one slipper on and talking hotly to a sleepy Ladlay, also happened to look at him, and recognising his property, immediately laid violent hands upon Mirzban's collar. There was no knowing what harm the impulsive Basmati would have done, if Ladlay and others had not interceded, or if Mirzban was slow to clarify his position. Although it was not in Basmati's nature to be so easily pacified, once the facts were known, he was not allowed to prevail by other neighbours. Wrenching the slipper from Mirzban's hand, and casting him a look of unmitigated suspicion, Basmati turned his back on him and retired to his home in the retinue of Tabaq Sahib and a few other sympathisers, who had tagged along, guided by the temptation to gossip over steaming cups of tea, and anticipating an early breakfast at Basmati's expense.

Other people were also returning to their houses, cursing

Basmati under their breath for creating such pandemonium at that ungodly hour on a week night. Muneemji was stooping dangerously forward from Mirzban's roof, discoursing with the chowkidar and Ladlay. Nobody had found any trace of the thief. It was probable that Basmati Sahib had been taken in by the shadow of a cat which the passing lamp of the chowkidar's cycle had projected on the wall. Also, he could have dreamt the whole thing. Everyone knew the difficulty with which he had been stopped from attacking the milkman, who he had seen in his dream adulterating the milk.

Tired and distracted, and rubbing his head where the shoe had implanted a bump, Mirzban returned home to find Bano Tamanna and Mushtri up, and, in a spirit of reconciliation and amity which women find naturally in times of crisis and excitement, passionately discussing whether or not there actually was a thief – their opinion being that there *was* one, and that he had slipped away due to the men's carelessness. Mirzban did not hear what they asked him and went inside his room to get some sleep. Salar's snores, which had flowed over the whole commotion undiminished, were sounding louder than ever.

In his late sixties Salar again became obsessed with the idea of getting married. In the beginning Bano Tamanna laughed at it and saw in this activity Salar's dotage antics. But when there was an uncommon spate of mail from anxious parents and widows and spinsters of all description, everyone woke up to reality. Salar was serious and obviously there was a market for him. Realising this he became fastidious.

He severely criticised the widows who had little to offer in riches or looks and asked for the earth, and was equally critical of parents who did not trust a gentleman's word and demanded to see proof of age and property documents. Salar regularly mentioned himself as 'a respectable gentleman in his mid-fifties,' however, he not only kept updating his daughter's age, but actually revelled in the approaching old age of his daughter and never lost an occasion to mention it to her, whereas he himself was now convinced, after two decades of matrimonial-correspondence lies, that he was indeed that which he described himself as. So in twenty years Bano Tamanna's age caught up with Salar's alleged mid-fifties, and always caused bewilderment among spinsters and widows.

On the weekend the newspaper's classified pages were full of matrimonial ads and in the morning Salar moved the chair to the front door to lie in wait for the newspaper. Then he dragged his chair to the kitchen and while Bano Tamanna was making tea for him, he marked with a red pencil the ads which needed an urgent reply from the prospective suitors, and therefore had to be sent with the afternoon mail; the ads which could wait till the next batch of mail was sent, were marked in blue. Salar's letterheads were laced with flowery patterns and white messenger-pigeons flew on the borders, carrying envelopes sealed with hearts in their beaks.

Of late he had become secretive about his correspondence, and wary of people's ridicule for his marital adventures. Bano Tamanna did not know how many houses Salar visited as a suitor and what transpired on these excursions, on which only Muneemji accompanied him. But she always dreaded the day when Salar would embarrass the family by turning up as a suitor at one of her acquaintances' houses, and tried in vain to find a plausible reply to pacify tempers in such an eventuality. It was this concern which Salar had more than once interpreted, as he sat marking the matrimonial ads in the newspaper's supplement, as the look of ridicule. Unable to think clearly he convinced himself that the inheritance of his property being foremost in Bano Tamanna's thoughts towards him, she would naturally be averse to anything that would make him live longer: his marriage for instance. But hadn't he outlived his wife and many children who came after

Bano Tamanna – all of whom had died in their infancy? 'And God willing,' he resolved, 'I will outlive them all – Bano Tamanna and her husband and their daughters. Whom would the joke be on, then?'

Close to where the pigeons were feeding in the courtyard, a beetle crept out clinging to the sides of Salar's slippers, seeking, probably, to hide its considerable mass. A group of black ants who were in the neighbourhood, intercepted the wobbling mite and within minutes, with one ant pulling at each limb, were dragging it to their lair. But there was some lapse on the ants' part and the beetle scuttled away, bulldozing all hazards and provocateurs in its way. As it escaped, the one ant which had got a good grip on its feet was dragged with it for some distance, until, realising the futility of its essays it gave up and came trotting back to its accomplices. It turned out that they were in luck, as they soon came upon a beetle which had fallen on its back from the kitchen wall, and was helplessly wriggling its limbs for a grip, saving the ants a considerable amount of struggle. And in no time the prostrated beetle was sliding on its back down the ants' nest to be quartered.

Salar was sitting on a *moondha* in the courtyard, wearing a *sherwani* and smoking the hookah looking at the pigeons feeding on bird-seed, through the cataract in his eyes. He shifted the hookah mouthpiece to his other hand to turn when he heard Muneemji slowly climbing down the staircase, coughing. 'I am going out to get a tonga. Are you ...?' Muneemji asked Salar from away and Salar interjected without waiting for him to finish, 'Yes! Yes! Indeed I am ready!' Muneemji went out through the gate and Salar kept drawing on the hookah with the mouthpiece clenched tight in his hand. The distinction between an invitation to the girl's house and actual marriage had become blurred in Salar's mind. As he saw the unspoken opposition to his marriage arising from Bano's desire to save her inheritance from division and hence her wish to see him dead, every response to his reply to the matrimonials renewed and reinforced the hanging threat of his marriage over Bano's wishes, as he interpreted them. This gave him a sense of power over her designs and against his own fears of death. For him, to obtain the former was as much an event for rejoicing as the reality of the latter, and therefore he celebrated the one with the vigour of the other.

He heard Muneemji calling him out into the alley in a loud voice. The tonga had arrived. Salar got up from the *moondha* with great alacrity, unusual for someone of his age and condition, and straightening his back walked with a remarkably brisk pace to the gate.

Muneemji had asked the tonga-wala to back into the alley. When he saw Salar, the tonga-wala put out the crate in which he carried the horse's fodder for Salar to step on.

'Put this bloody thing away, crazy man! Do you think I am a cripple?' Salar shouted.

Grumbling to himself the tonga-wala put the crate away. After great difficulty Salar managed to grab the iron bars under the canopy of the tonga cart, and with Muneemji pulling him up from inside and the tonga-wala pushing him from the back for support, he managed to get inside, but it took a while before he could turn to sit and all that effort made him sweat and pant. After they were settled in the tonga the tonga-wala jerked the reins, and the tonga creaked as the horse began to trot in the direction of the Pukka Qila. Salar was still breathing with difficulty and coughing at intervals.

Several times on the way, Salar took off his cap to scratch his bristly head and put it back on. But when he could no longer contain himself he asked, 'What do you say, Muneemji?' Muneemji had noticed Salar's agitation but as it was nothing new to him, he replied in a slightly indifferent manner, 'What is there to say? If they are willing we can have the *nikah* read on the spot. I had asked Ladlay and he told me that Imam Jubba would be a good person to see in this regard.'

'Did you see Imam Jubba then? What did he have to say?' Salar asked eagerly.

'No, I didn't see him. But there is no hurry. He is always available,' Muneemji replied.

'Huh! But what is your impression? How does it auger for me? As they say, even a dead elephant is worth a lakh and a quarter!' Salar smirked smugly.

'Dead be your enemies, Salar Sahib! *Masha'allah* you are young. Are you forgetting Ibrahim Sahib who was circumcised at the age of one hundred and his pious wife who bore the fruit of his loins soon afterwards? You must not undermine yourself! What *is* seventy years!?'

'Don't say seventy, Muneemji! Fifty! A full fifty years!' Salar reminded him in an anxious voice.

'It's all the same. Seventy or fifty. My father took his third wife when he was seventy-five.' Muneemji continued in his indifferent drone.

At the entrance to the alley where the house was situated, a boy was standing guard. A branch torn from a nearby bush was tucked like a sword inside his knickers, which had a large gold-leaf buckle sewn on it. Salar gestured to Muneemji to ask him the address. The moment the boy heard Muneemji ask the address, he turned his back and, running away at great speed and shouting, 'They have arrived! They have arrived!' disappeared inside a small house in the middle of the lane.

'There …! Muneemji! What was I telling you!' Salar said in a hoarse voice overcome with emotion.

'This is but to be expected. You are no riffraff, God knows,' Muneemji replied, imagining how the thing might turn out after the family had been introduced to Salar in person.

As Salar was getting down from the tonga with Muneemji holding him from inside and the tonga-wala propping him from the road, the head of the family came out from the house to receive the guests. When he did not see anyone on the road except Salar and Muneemji, he approached them looking visibly alarmed.

'Assalam-o-Aleikum! Are you looking for the Madaars' house?'

'Yes! Are you Madaar Sahib?' Muneemji asked him. He had got down from the tonga now and was paying the tonga-wala. Salar was in no state to speak a word as he was coughing terribly from the strain of getting down from the tonga and his face had become dark as he almost choked.

'Yes! And your good name?' Madaar asked with a degree of perplexity looking now at Muneemji and now at Salar.

Salar was recovering by degrees and Muneemji turned towards him to see if he would like to answer. Salar raised his hand as he wished to speak and Muneemji kept quiet. 'Salar Jang, and this here ...' Salar took another breath, 'this here is my adjutant ... Muneemji! It is my great pleasure to meet you ... Madaar Sahib!'

In his mind Madaar Sahib was ready to receive a gentleman of fifty and since they always lied about their age in the matrimonial ads, he was willing to overlook a few years. But he had still not come up with a strategy in his mind to cope with the reality of Salar. The only thing he could think of was to invite Salar into the house for now, and then somehow get rid of him. As he turned to go into the house without showing the way to Salar and Muneemji first, Muneemji said in a loud voice, 'This way Salar Sahib!' and both followed Madaar into the house.

The women of the house were peeping through the curtains and Salar could not see their faces because he had just stepped in from the sun into the dark room. He could only hear the women's bursts of muffled laughter and that too inaudibly, as his hearing was slightly impaired. He attributed that to general merriment and rejoicing at the favourable impression he had made on the ladies, and smiled smugly while groping for the sofa where Muneemji was asking him to take a seat.

There were plastic flowers in the vase on the centre table which had been dusted that day. The room was speck free. It was kept closed and opened only for guests, which explained why it was stuffy. The foam seats of the sofa were hard from lack of use, and uncomfortable. A calendar decorated the wall with some framed pieces of verses from the Qur'an. Muneemji saw that Madaar was getting more irritated by the minute and he saw Salar blinking his eyes and smiling through his dentures, unable to clearly see Madaar's face in the slightly dark room. The curtain on the door connecting the drawing room to the rest of the house was slightly parted, and without being able to make out any definite form, Muneemji saw it fill up with light and shadows constantly. Someone inside the house, probably the girl herself could not control her laughter and the noise floated into the room. Madaar went inside and when he came back he seemed even more stolid. Obviously, he did not find it amusing.

Inside the drawing room Muneemji was trying to untie the knot of Madaar's uncomfortable silence without any success. Madaar was deep in thought. He had corresponded with Salar in the guise of the girl's aunt, and after reading his particulars, he had thought that a man in Salar's circumstances was not such a bad match for the girl, who was getting on in years.

Salar cleared his throat of the phlegm rising from the effort of breathing. Steeped in the shyness of the prospective bridegroom, Salar was otherwise quiet, as he usually was on such occasions, until Muneemji finished with the preliminaries of the introduction. Twice Muneemji saw a woman's head peep inside the room through the slit in the curtains and disappear. Then the boy in the knickers who had heralded their arrival walked into the room without any apparent purpose. The branch had been removed from his knickers.

When Muneemji saw himself failing in his efforts to manufacture a conversation into which Salar could be naturally slipped, he leaned sideways towards Salar and quietly whispered, 'Salar Sahib!!' in his ears. It was a hint that now Salar was on his own, and could only rely on Muneemji's assistance once he had made a breakthrough on his own.

Salar cleared his throat and without looking at Madaar asked, 'How, if I may ask, are you related to the lady in question?'

'I am her brother-in-law,' Madaar was forced to reply but he kept his eyes lowered and did not look at Salar while replying.

Muneemji had known for some time the futility of the charade but he kept waiting patiently. He felt like having a cup of tea and decided that at least should not be denied them, no matter how disastrous the outcome. He became more hopeful after the boy was called in and soon returned with a tray carrying two glasses of water and a jug, and was called back inside.

'Very nice. I'd be obliged if you could give my respects to the lady's aunt with whom I corresponded. And please forgive my asking whether she is going to come in or if she observes purdah?' Salar was asking Madaar.

'No, she observes purdah and besides she is not well today. But she asked me to give you her respects,' Madaar replied, all the while becoming angrier and angrier with himself for letting the conversation proceed and prolong and not turning the party away.

Salar for a moment forgot that he had rheumatism and tried to cross his legs but failed in his attempt, and the shooting pain made him gasp. 'Does the lady in question, here I mean the young lady ... does she observe purdah too?'

Salar asked next, now looking at Madaar with his face still contorted from the pain in his leg.

'Yes, she does!' Madaar's reply was abrupt and set to a higher pitch.

A woman's giggle from behind the curtains was immediately muffled. An uncomfortable silence proceeded during which Muneemji felt his chances of having a cup of tea jeopardised. All the more so since the boy now returned empty-handed with the branch tucked in again and looked him straight in the eyes.

'Is there anything I could tell you about myself?' Salar made a desperate attempt to break the ice but was immediately thwarted by an icy 'no' from Madaar.

'The lady's aunt had written that the girl ...' Salar was not to be daunted.

'What she had written doesn't matter now. We have already approved of a match. I am sorry. I could not inform you in time,' Madaar found himself saying and immediately felt a great relief at finally having said something to desist Salar from lingering.

'But would you consider ...' Salar began, but was immediately cut short by Madaar who was drawing confidence from his recent success. 'I am sorry. But as I said, it is not possible. The match has been finalised.'

Salar leaned towards Muneemji and the latter got up. Madaar did not ask him where he was going. Both Salar and Madaar kept sitting in the room. The boy was sitting in a corner beating the rug with his stick. The tapping made the men's silence even heavier. Madaar shouted at him to sit still and the boy ran out of the room. There was now complete quiet in the room. Probably the women too had moved away from the curtains. Salar decided to get up and go outside into the alley to wait for the tonga but he realised that one of his legs had gone to sleep. Fortunately for him, Muneemji soon returned with the tonga and helped him out of the sofa. It was the same tonga-wala. He had not gone away and was resting after tying the horse under a tree, where Muneemji found him.

'It was a pleasure meeting you. Salam-walekum!' Salar said as he turned his back on Madaar and stepped towards the door. He did not hear Madaar's mumble since the boy who had torn into the room when he heard the tonga in the alley, had again rushed inside shouting, 'They are leaving! The hoary old men are ...' They did not hear any more since the door was slammed shut behind them by Madaar.

Salar had returned in a sore mood and ate a little only after Bano Tamanna insisted that he must have something for dinner. Later, Muneemji pulled his chair close to his bed, and in a barely audible voice, and his bald head slowly shaking with malicious joy, caricatured the poor creature and the family members who had refused Salar her hand. Muneemji's evil-minded lampoons cheered up Salar, who grinned in agreement and the two of them stayed up late that night.

Mornings always brought some new tribulation. People woke up to find something or the other laid to ruin, a new problem in the offing, or the portents of one to come. But nothing had made Tabaq Sahib more restless than those mud tunnels which originated from the walls and crevices in the floor of his brick-paved courtyard and terminated in the bedsteads.

'Can you imagine, *janab*,' he asked Basmati and Bhai Qamoosi one evening, 'having the termites in the frames of the very charpais where my family and I sleep? Anyway, I had the mud tunnels destroyed immediately,' he continued, 'but the termites had already tunnelled inside and since there was no knowing in what numbers, we have been sleeping on the floor since.'

'You did the right thing!' Basmati replied, 'They multiply overnight. They'll eat up the whole charpai, jute-string and all, you'll see. My wife came up with a remarkable idea. She asked me to get small aluminium bowls, and filling them with oil, steeped the charpai legs in them. That way, the termites and the ants which stalk them were kept away.'

'Why didn't you tell Tabaq Sahib about it earlier? See how glum he looks,' Bhai Qamoosi said in mock anger. But Tabaq Sahib had already picked up the thread. Realising that Begum Basmati's was indeed an ingenious scheme he protested, 'Is this what you call friendship, Basmati? Your friends tossing and turning on the floor and you happily spread on your bed like an ox? Answer me!'

'Hear me out!' Annoyed by Tabaq Sahib's innuendoes Basmati raised his hand. 'You have this bad habit of picking words off my tongue. You haven't even heard what happened and you've already started your crying and complaining. Huh!'

A relieved look appeared on Tabaq Sahib's face when he heard that something eventually went wrong with Begum Basmati's scheme and he mollified his friend, 'Look at this butterfly! Hardly have you touched him than his colours begin to come off! Come on now! Can't you take a joke?'

'Now listen quietly and don't interrupt,' Basmati continued, flattered by Tabaq Sahib's extravagance of comparing him with a butterfly. 'So I was saying that, Sahib!' he began in a tone calculated to build intrigue, 'I took all those precautions but still I saw the termites creeping out of my charpai leg when I got up one morning.'

'Oho!' Tabaq Sahib exclaimed more in joyous anticipation than in sympathy.

'And the ants!' Basmati said, 'They proved as stubborn as the termites, and soon the aluminium bowls were awash with a thousand dead ants, as their rank and file surged forward to hunt out the termites.'

'Such hardy ants too!' Tabaq Sahib commented with satisfaction. 'What happened next?'

'What do you expect?' Basmati replied, '*Hundreds* of ants swept over the bridges made by their comrades' carcasses floating over the oil, to climb onto the charpais while we slept!'

'That must have upset …?' Tabaq Sahib asked eagerly, his eyes shining.

'Upset!?' Basmati exclaimed loudly and Bhai Qamoosi started. 'Upset is not the word for it!' he continued gloomily, and a content smile slowly appeared on Tabaq Sahib's face. 'Everyone woke up in the middle of the night. There was no electricity and such a rumpus with the ants biting, my wife screaming and the children crying that I can't tell you.'

'So now, you too …' Tabaq Sahib began, but Basmati anticipated him and finished off the sentence, 'Yes! We too are sleeping on the floor now!'

'*Allah*!' an assuaged Tabaq exclaimed and closed his eyes as he took a sip from the steaming cup.

Basmati made the mistake of asking for Imam Jubba's advice the next day, who instead of suggesting some remedy, came up with an original allegory. 'Since Man is made of Earth,' he said, 'and since the termites also dwell in Earth, the time has come for sinners to repent, since it is plain as day that the termites will only stop once they have reached their flesh and bones, and all that has passed was just preparation. To burrow into the sinners' bodies is the quest which has sent them scrambling out of their earthen nests, and that is how the wrath of God will be satisfied, and the outbreak end!'

None of these phantasmic visions came to pass, but they further depressed the already beleaguered friends, especially Tabaq Sahib, who was getting trouble from all quarters.

'God's wrath!' Tabaq Sahib remarked one evening, 'Now that rascal of a contractor has stopped work on the room we are building on the roof for our elder son. With only three months remaining until the marriage! There are no wooden planks to be rented for plastering the walls; that's the contractor's excuse! And what do you know, this morning one of the daily labourers, who worked for him, turned up at my door. And what was he selling? Some termicide! When I asked him what this was all about, he told me that construction work had stopped all over Purana Shehr and daily labourers like him were being hired by the pesticide manufacturers to go door-to-door with their products.'

'They wouldn't let a chance like this pass without making money out of it!' Basmati replied. 'There is no fear of God left in people's hearts!'

New products were introduced every other week, and despite his denunciation, almost every second day Basmati bought 'the newest and the most potent termicide' from these salesmen, all of which had failed to contain the pestilent ranks of the insects. Tabaq Sahib and Basmati both envied Bhai Qamoosi who, unlike the two of them, was still a bachelor and lived on rent. Recently Bhai Qamoosi had moved out into a better place. Because of the damage done by termites, the rents in and around Topee Mohalla had gone down. Also some people had moved to other, less affected areas in Purana Shehr, where they had relatives. As a consequence, Bhai Qamoosi had found a two bedroom apartment for the same rent that he had been paying for a ramshackle room, and he had wisely signed a five-year lease.

Later that week, some children were poisoned by the DDT meant for the termites but luckily it was discovered in time: their stomachs were pumped immediately, and tragedy was averted. But it gave Pesh Imam Jubba of the Central Mosque a chance to declare from his *minbar* that harming something sent by God would not do. Sitting in the back rows Basmati and Tabaq Sahib looked at each other and nodded gravely. Imam Jubba ordered an immediate end to the killing of the termites which had no will of their own and only acted upon the Divine Will. He gave the example of Job who picked up the maggots which fell from his rotting flesh and put them back in his wounds, because they were like guests sent from God.

Later, when Tabaq Sahib told their friend what Imam Jubba had mentioned, Bhai Qamoosi just said 'Huh!' and surprised his friends by mentioning that he would come along for the next Friday sermon. Basmati and Tabaq Sahib were intrigued because Bhai Qamoosi never showed up for prayers except on Eid day. They thought that he was probably joking and did not think much of it.

But Bhai Qamoosi duly turned up that Friday. In his next sermon Imam Jubba furiously denounced those as insect worshippers, who, after hearing his previous sermon, had started feeding the termites, by placing their half-eaten furniture near their nests. 'Such people,' the Pesh Imam bellowed from his *minbar*, 'are those who make insects partners with God, and who will find no refuge in the benevolence and mercy of the Almighty for their turpitude.'

When he heard that Bhai Qamoosi got up. 'Brothers!' he said despite Basmati and Tabaq Sahib's efforts to pull him down by his hands and lapels of his shirt, 'While we are looking at all the possible causes for the termite plague, I suggest we also consider that the termites might have descended as a consequence of the debaucheries of our leadership, and the clergy's perversion, about whom nobody says a word!'

No greater uproar would have been produced if somebody had set off a bomb. A great outcry began in the front row where Imam Jubba's minions were seated. Bhai Qamoosi could see people slowly nodding their heads in the middle and back rows. A murmur had also started but it died as soon as Imam Jubba got up from his *minbar*. He cast a fiery look at the assembly and began to recite the scripture under his breath. There was a deathly silence in the mosque which had subdued even Bhai Qamoosi, when Imam Jubba suddenly bellowed, spit flying out of his mouth, 'It is for God to decide who is the sinner among us!' People quickly nodded their heads and touched their ear lobes. 'And a people deserves the leaders appointed to them, and if ... only if ... they searched within their own dark hearts first,' here Jubba's fiery glance rested on Bhai Qamoosi for just a second, 'they would stop pointing fingers at others!' Basmati and Tabaq Sahib had shifted a little away from Bhai Qamoosi as people were now looking accusingly at him. 'As to the clergy,' Imam Jubba said patronisingly, 'those, who are quick to point out the hair of iniquity in another's eye are mostly blind to the shaft of sin ... in their own!'

Jubba again recited the scripture loudly and after this sombre presentation, began his sermon. Bhai Qamoosi sat quietly for the rest of the prayers. He had made those remarks just to irk Jubba but the latter had had the upper hand. But his feat of taking on Imam Jubba made Bhai Qamoosi popular with some people who were getting tired of Imam Jubba's antics and his harangue about punishment and redemption through termites.

When they met at Chhalawa Hotel the next day, Bhai Qamoosi looked sheepishly at his friends, who also avoided eye contact. Tea was ordered, and the counter-boy put two pastries and a cup of tea with a generous portion of cream floating on top, in front of Bhai Qamoosi. Surprised, when he tried to tell the boy that he had not ordered all that, he was told that it was on the house.

Ladlay was standing motionless in the middle of his bedroom, musing over something with the hint of a smile on his face. After glancing at his watch he stole to the balcony which opened onto the street, and making sure that his shadow was not falling on the curtain, crouched, and from that position, well below eye-level, applied his eyes to the slit between the curtain and the frame of the balcony, so that a casual glance at his window from the street would not betray his post. Right across was Mushtri's window, whose drapes were parted enough to give some idea of the room's depth but although nothing was in plain view, the restless lurking of a woman's form could be descried from its shadow on the curtain. The smile which had faded in the labours of his tactical positioning reappeared on Ladlay's face, and he moved away from the curtain to his gramophone, after another glance at the street.

In a few minutes a familiar tune, the male version of Mushtri's favourite song, emanated from Ladlay's balcony. Immediately afterwards, Ladlay himself casually appeared on his balcony, dressed in a muslin kurta without a vest which revealed his paunch and the many bulges of his anatomy.

The preening of his corpulent form in the small space of his balcony was most admirable. Moreover, it was not a performance to an empty house. The window opposite had darkened when Ladlay surfaced, and the shadow as well as the form of a woman filled up the curtains, the further proof of whose existence manifested itself in the appearance of a hand which clutched the folds of the drapes. The duration of the song was a few minutes and one could see Ladlay displayed to his best advantage during that short time. His cigarette was held majestically between the last two fingers of his hand closed in a fist, and it was most gratifying to see him draw on and puff out the smoke carelessly with a backward throw of his head, and from time to time flick off the ashes with a snap of his fingers. His eyes, seemingly admiring the traffic of the passers-by and the occasional tonga, darted frequently to the balcony opposite him, causing his bold simper to be restored, which he modestly composed, either by pressing the hard bristles of his whiskers, or by circumnavigating his lips with the tips of his thumb and forefinger.

The moment the song ended, the form concealed behind the opposite curtain withdrew, taking with it its shadow. But Ladlay stayed to finish his cigarette and listen to the beginning of the song which followed. Then looking around indifferently at the sight of the emptying street, and with a parting glance at the empty balcony, just as the braying of the washerman's donkey filled up the alley around sunset, he too retired, as naturally as he had materialised, and the gramophone stopped playing.

Muneemji's bald head did not appear from behind the pigeon-coops until some time later. Rising slowly and looking about to see that nobody was watching him, he walked to the edge of the roof and craned his neck forward to look down. All he could see was the canopy over Mushtri's window. Then he raised his head and looked across at Ladlay's balcony. And for the next few moments it appeared that Muneemji was unable to decide which prospect interested him more, as his eyes kept looking back and forth, while his facial muscles struggled with a smirk which ultimately gained the upper hand, and rent his toothless face into a mischievous grimace.

Salar had been up till quite late the previous night, writing something. But the next morning he was out of his bed early as usual. During the night Bano Tamanna had come to see if Salar needed anything. But she could not make up her mind whether Salar was asleep or awake because due to paralysis Salar had lost control of his facial muscles and slept with his eyes open. She had called him softly once or twice and then went away. Salar was awake but he did not reply.

When he heard Bano calling him to the breakfast table he reached for the glass sitting on the side table, where his dentures lay soaking in a mixture of baking soda and water. Salar had been deprived of his original set in his thirties at the hands of a wily tooth-maker who had told him that the constant clattering of teeth while trotting on horse-back loosened them from their roots, and caused much pain in old age. Convinced, Salar sat down at the roadside and in a single hour was relieved of his teeth. On his wish, barely conveyed with a bloodied mouth to the man, the tooth-maker set the false dentures using Salar's extracted teeth.

Putting the supple and wet dentures in his mouth Salar chewed them into place with great purpose until the gums had found their hold and then called Muneemji to ask if Ladlay had been over yet. He was not there but while they were still talking his knock was heard on the door.

When Salar had asked Ladlay to procure for him a piece of vellum and a calligrapher, he was a little taken aback. And only after much circumspection did Salar reveal through Muneemji that he had composed an ode for Noor-e Firdousi which had to be sent to the subject of its verbiage post-haste. Ladlay thought it over in his mind and humbly proposed that vellum was now out of fashion, and that all such presentations were now made on special paper like the one he could see near Salar's bedside. As to the calligraphers, almost all of them worked for religious presses and were so vain that they considered it an unforgivable transgression to draw up anything that was not directly or indirectly the word of God. However, he added, Salar must not lose hope since the letter-writers who sat outside the post office were as good calligraphers as any and would do an equally fine job.

The troop of letter-writers littered the pavement outside the premises of the General Post Office. Purana Shehr was a city of an opiate mood, probably on account of the heat which made everyone sluggish. The one trait which bound the whole city was idleness. And it was due to this property, and not some discipline, that everything, from one's grocer to one's place in the mosque, was fixed. People and their ways were so set, that just walking on a different side of the pavement betrayed one's destination to the observers. For example, anyone taking the Pukka Qila road in the early hours was undoubtedly heading to the vegetable market, where the farmers brought the produce from the hinterland. Anyone seen out of the house after lunch must be off to Mahtab Cinema. And around noon, a young man loitering near the GPO where the letter-writers sat under their umbrellas, was waiting for the heat to clear the rush, so that he could pour his heart out to old Baba Navees, the most seasoned of all letter-writers, who would then edit and compose his passion.

Letterheads, envelopes, aerograms, postcards, and postage stamps lay spread before the letter-writers in polythene showcases. Three pots of home-made ink in shades of black, blue and red stood on the ready to quench the thirst of as many fountain pens hanging heavy in their shirt pockets. A bottle of weak gum was at hand to seal the mouths of envelopes. Their ears, which could grip any number of pens, pencils and other cylindrical and oblong stationery behind them, were a source of endless fascination for boys passing on the street, who attempted in vain to parallel this feat at home and in school. When called upon, their rough hands could weigh and tell to a fraction the postage required, nationally and internationally, for a letter or a parcel's weight. Under one roof they provided letter-writing and letter-reading aids. The letter-reading service, requisitioned in isolation was charged for, and was complimentary with an attendant letter-writing assignment. In that case it was rendered after the fifty-paisa charge for writing the letter had been deposited with the proprietor.

In the science of postures, the letter-writers had their own trade mark. In its shape, it was modelled on the squat, but the body weight was distributed between the heels, pulled together and tucked under the hips, with the back leaning against a wall. It was also a posture which signified general apathy. Seated on the low wooden stools in proximity with these scribes, a man felt by himself, and was encouraged to modulate his thoughts and shape them into lucid rhetoric. Their open-air shops had the air of a wayside dock where everyone willingly unburdened themselves. A long time ago the letter-writers had lost all interest in the affairs of men. They had heard the same story repeated so many times that if they had any interest left in their patrons, they could have recited it back to them. So there was good reason for confidence in them, since nothing was farther from their thoughts than the letter just penned, and their indifference was not a cultivated commodity, but one that had naturally evolved. Sitting at their wayside posts, a pen tucked behind each ear, the letter-writers penned entreaties, sought forgiveness, visited admonitions, pledged love, swore allegiance, promised vengeance, solicited small loans, quoted the different prophets of advice, and sent threats across human civilisation on behalf of their patrons for the consideration of fifty paisas. When idle, their gaze scanned the pedestrian traffic on the road, innocent of any attempt at the unsolicited peddling of services. Each one of them had an established clientele whose patronage had remained loyal for years.

Sheikh Salah, although a little hard of hearing, had at his command a treasure trove of famous quotations, and as a consequence was popular with the parents of delinquent progeny, revenge seekers and remonstrating souls alike. The bald Mumtaz Sahib could string words together just so and create such pathos by his expressions as would force the stingiest of fathers to loosen his purse-strings. And so on. Old Baba Navees was employed by young men of the servant class while communicating in confidence with their counterparts. The letters were tabulated in the patent love-letter format, modelled on the 'Letters to Wives' in a bizarre compendium of all pre-, post- and extra-marital worsts and their remedies, the *Bahishti Kangan*. It fell to Baba Navees's lot to pen Salar's ode to the Nightingale of the Battlefield, in his immaculate hand.

The paper was torn from the pad by Baba Navees and handed out to Salar to read, who was breathing heavily. Salar carefully read it, admiring the script, and after carefully folding it inserted in the envelope addressed to Firdousi. After he had checked twice to see that the envelope was properly sealed, he dropped it in the letter-box and pushing his arm into the letter-box and then carefully thumping it to make sure that the envelope was secure, Salar walked away beating the ground with his stick, his other hand on Muneemji's shoulder for support, as Ladlay moved briskly ahead to get a tonga.

An Ode to the Nightingale of Acaldema

When the crow of war appeared cawing in the skies,
And on motherland's unsullied virtue the evil eye cast,
Ere heavens sent a thousand armed seraphs to defend her throne,
The locks of fury spread out on her fair countenance, the Nightingale,
Rose in the spellbound heavens and mangled
the abject avis with the talons of her ire.
In her scorn his grave, and last perch the bird found.

Mark Thee! Ye who bestows speech to stones,
Thy slave finds himself bereft of Thy bounty,
When he aspires to declare his chaste ardour,
For a creature of Thy very Light, fair Noor,
The Nightingale of the Acaldema.

The heavens now rival me in singing her adulation,
And array their might against my blissful affliction.
Heretofore for rebuking clay one was denounced,
Shall I now be chastised for ratifying Thy light,
And my lot be cast with the Fiend?

On the Eighth day was my passion created,
As a sacrifice to her eternal eyes.
For nowhere is beauty engendered,
But its sacrifice is sooner contrived.

SALAR JANG'S PASSION

When the Heavenly mirror slipped from the hands of Time,
And the love which fired the orb became frigid,
In my passion it was again rekindled,
And in Noor's eternal eyes the world again lived.

Do not deny Thy slave the glory to utter,
One word, NOOR, be it his last. For the agony of his passion,
Can be redressed by a glance of her eyes alone,
And a word, though of reproach, from the Nightingale's sweet lips.

With my life blood nurtured, the tree of my desire,
Sinks roots deeper and deeper into my heart. In its branches
Roost your concurrence, and set down your honeyed carols,
Ere the jealous breath of autumn,
And the treacherous axe of rivalry work their evil, O Nightingale!
– from the humble pen of her Lowly Servant and Vassal, Salar Jang

After Mirza Poya had assumed it unsolicited and unannounced, it was discovered that the office of the film critic of Purana Shehr, lying idle unbeknownst to all, had been ably employed. In the mornings Mirza slogged at the school canteen; but in the evenings he rose from his ashes to hold court at the Chhalawa Hotel.

The hotel was separated from the street by an open drain, a moat infested by vermin which one had to jump over in the formative years of the Chhalawa Hotel. This condition was later remedied by placing a wooden board across the drain. Close to the entrance of the Chhalawa Hotel sat a bench, doubtfully balanced on the periphery of the open drain. A person occupying this seat commanded a fair view of the Mahtab Cinema. This was Mirza's customary post where he sat magnificently perched for the greater part of the evening, and if it was occupied by somebody else when Mirza came in, it was hurriedly vacated for him, and he took it over as a matter of right.

Mirza's grandfather was the author of *Umrao Khanam*, arguably the first Urdu novel which had been translated into a successful film since. By that token of ancestral claim, Mirza Poya, declaring *Umrao Khanam* the paragon of national cinema, was wont to present a critique of every film in its shadow.

In his youth when Mirza had inherited some money, he attempted to gain entrance into the film industry successively through doors reserved for the protagonist, second lead, villain, songwriter, music composer, dance master, scriptwriter and in his last, desperate, bankrupting attempt, the producer. For all those offices Mirza was as qualified as any other man, but luck never favoured him. Mirza had sold his father's house and put all the money in the film. The young Noor-e Firdousi was cast as a heroine in his film which never made it to the box office because half way through the production a fire gutted the upcountry studio along with all the footage stored there. Mirza was not insured against any such calamity, and never recuperated from the loss. It was said that the owner of the studio had orchestrated the fire to declare bankruptcy and escape paying the taxes he had accumulated, but nothing was ever proved.

Devastated as he was, Mirza was not to be daunted in his love for the big screen. Since Chhalawa Hotel was also the habitat of the legal gentlemen, it was incumbent upon the discourse to sometimes flow towards the many legal aspects of the villain's prosecution, who, in Mirza's view, was never adequately represented. That being the thrust, the proficiency of Mirza in legal matters was often called into question by Qabeel Bhutera B.A. LL.B., a renowned prosecution attorney. Mirza always picked up the challenge and minutely went through every single detail of the case from the opening shot to the credit list, leaving Qabeel Bhutera in quite an ingenious statutory muddle. When Ladlay thought of introducing him to Salar, Mirza Poya was up to his ears in legal quagmire, and his sentiments for the sacrosanct *Umrao Khanam* had taken a new turn.

Some disgruntled issue of a deceased *maulvi* who had penned a bestseller on the horrors of the grave had invoked the nebulous copyright laws of the land in order to sue the publishers who had ventured a reprint of the said book without the prior permission of the legatee, after the death of the author. When this case became known Mirza was goaded by his cronies to consider moving court against the director of *Umrao Khanam*. Looking at the facts of the case, which were heavily balanced in Mirza's favour, it was natural for him to give in to temptation. Mirza's grandfather had not been dead fifty years, after which time a book became public property: therefore, the copyright of the book, if any existed, rested with the legatees; and neither the publishers, who had reprinted the book several times, nor the director, who had made a lot of money from the production, had cared to approach Mirza – the sole representative of his deceased father's material claims, for his permission to print or produce *Umrao Khanam*.

Mirza was too decent to put the literary persons in the publishing house through the hardships of the law courts. But where the director was concerned, Mirza was reminded of his triumphant insolence towards him during and after the prodigious failure of his film career. One of his old acquaintances from Chhalawa Hotel had persuaded him to seek legal help, and was eagerly waiting for Mirza to mortgage his apartment, so that the case could proceed.

Mirza had kept in touch with Noor-e Firdousi. That is, every Eid he sent a greeting card to Firdousi without fail. It was never acknowledged, but being the only person in Purana Shehr to have some pretext to continue this annual ritual was enough to make Mirza an authority on all rumours pertaining to Firdousi. Ladlay knew him from Chhalawa Hotel and to him Mirza was the means to gaining more influence with Salar.

For once, even the cunning Ladlay could not see Muneemji's impish smile hidden from him by the latter's stoop; and his double-edged greetings, when he came over the next time with Mirza Poya. Ladlay was right in his assessment. Mirza Poya was the very person to keep Salar's mind occupied with Firdousi. Mirza Poya became a frequent visitor to the house and tried without any great success to quench Salar's insatiable thirst for Firdousi's particulars. When Ladlay dropped in to report the progress on the case to Salar, he would also turn the conversation towards Firdousi but Salar never seemed to have enough of her, and would delve deeper and deeper into the tiniest details which nobody seemed to remember and would often improvise at his persistence.

Mushtri was usually in audience in the veranda whenever Ladlay was by and they exchanged greetings and looks. Muneemji closely followed these encounters and interpreted their commerce of pregnant looks and salutations in the only way it occurred to him that they be construed. But tempting as it was for an old man like himself, so given to gossip, he kept silent, without conveying a word of it to Salar or anybody else. Nor did it escape him that sometimes on weekends when he was out on some errand for Salar, Bano Tamanna was at the bazaar, and Mirzban was holed up in his room and for all practical purposes dead to the world around him, Mushtri would make a cup of tea for Ladlay after Salar had dozed off, and they would have lengthy talks in soft tones. On one occasion he almost caught Mushtri clearing the cups and disappearing into her room, and Ladlay sliding into Salar's room and beginning to rummage through files, as Muneemji walked in one day through the front door which was mistakenly left open.

Trudging slowly and balancing the heavy wicker basket full of vegetables on her head, the shrivelled phantom of Bilotti appeared every morning in the precincts of Topee Mohalla with a cluster of cats in her wake. Including glaucoma and cataract, Bilotti's eyes had suffered manifold ocular ravages, and it was rumoured that her vision had departed behind the round, foggy spectacles secured behind her hair with a string which sat on her cheek bones, and that she only went about with sheer intuition. After being witness to a century and some decades, she was growing a new set of teeth, and her hair was turning black again; as were her whiskers and goatee, although her eye-lashes had fallen and flakes of dead skin fell from her face whenever she rubbed it with her hands.

She had been selling vegetables door-to-door in Purana Shehr for the better part of eighty years. In the small hours of the morning when farmers brought their produce to the marketplace in their mule carts, she was there to haggle with them. After her day's purchase was done she repaired first to Topee Mohalla, carrying the load of vegetables in a hamper on her head. Sometimes a tonga-wala who would be going in that direction without a fare would give her a ride. And around ten o'clock, when housewives would be preparing for lunch after having sent the children to school and dusting the rooms, Bilotti knocked on the doors. She made a meagre profit but the paisa went a long way in those inexpensive times, and Bilotti had no household to claim expenses. She had no possessions either, except for two pairs of amber and silver anklets, her wooden comb, a prayer mat, a change of clothes and her vegetable basket. If they could be counted as equity, the eight small silver earrings which she wore in as many piercings in her ears, could also be taken into account. She kept her money in her waist-band and slid it back and forth by the action of the cummerbund.

Bilotti's appellation had begun in Topee Mohalla. From the beginning the cats had shown a partiality towards her.

They would sit around her when she supplicated on her prayer mat and without being bidden, even the most feral one would come growling to rub its shaggy head against her legs. Bilotti encouraged them by bringing them pieces of sinew and other cheap viands from the butcher. The cats waited for her at the periphery of the neighbourhood and upon catching the whiff of flesh, their tails raised, their backs arched and making happy caterwauls, they tracked her on her route as she plied her trade. When Bilotti beat her well-trodden course knocking at the houses, like an octogenarian ant bent under her burden, some of them sat behind her on their haunches with meditating or sleepy aspects, while some others rubbed their fur against the doors. Sometimes a cat would pursue her on the walls of the houses, halting now and then with Bilotti, and from that vantage point kept an eye on her. Some marchers, like the infamous tomcat, Kotwal, knowing their bearings well, went ahead but kept looking over their shoulders, seeking general navigational endorsement from her direction. The cats who followed her now were probably the twenty-fifth descendants of the felines who followed her in the earlier days. There was not much difference in the circumstances of either except that Bilotti's once stately gait had now been reduced to a feeble swagger and that while the earlier cats had followed her at a brisk pace, they now trailed behind her leisurely.

In this fashion Bilotti went about her daily business goading the cats onwards, swearing at them and invoking the most odious curses upon them. This was another aspect in which the lot of this brood was significantly at variance with its predecessors. Either the cats, who had burgeoned manifold, were becoming a nuisance or, perhaps Bilotti was losing her patience with them. But what in the beginning were sweet nothings, in a few decades' time – as sometimes happens with the best of conjugal associations – developed into a most demonic spiel. The cats were not fed until after her rounds when the hamper was covered with a damp cloth and put away. Then they received their rations along with miscellaneous deserved and undeserved oaths, and turning their backs to each other ate their meal in a hum of guttural notes.

Before she relinquishes their charge, a mother cat carries her kittens to seven houses, so that their smell does not accumulate and attract murderous and fiercely territorial tomcats. Mother Fate either lost count or did not wish to abandon her geriatric kitten, for after changing scores of houses Bilotti was still on the move in her hundred-and-twenty-fifth year. She never had a roof over her head that she could call her own and wandered from house to house. Of late she had become a little querulous and was easily agitated. But all the same, no one dared to cross her without the risk of Bilotti summoning a potent curse for his benefit. When she walked inside a house and sat down there with her basket, it was generally understood that Bilotti had come there to stay and accordingly preparations were made for her accommodation.

One day, a week after Salar's arrival, Bano Tamanna heard Bilotti talking to her cats in the courtyard. She looked out from the kitchen where she was tempering new china mugs in boiling water and found Bilotti sitting in a corner, a little distance away from Salar, who had gone to sleep with the hookah mouthpiece in his hands and his eyes open. Close to his feet a flock of wagtails were bobbing their tails up and down feeding on the bird seed left by the pigeons. Bano Tamanna could well imagine the turbulence with Bilotti's cats and Salar's pigeons and Muneemji's irritability, but there was nothing to be done now. Everyone had to move over to make room. The needful was done and Bilotti was accommodated in the veranda.

When he saw Bilotti's cats taking position near the pigeons' coop, Muneemji did not lose any time nor mince any words in conveying his fears to Bano Tamanna, who passed them on to Bilotti, who said there was no reason to worry. One afternoon, during their feeding time, when all the cats were assembled around her, Bilotti began telling the restless cats the legend about the pigeons who were called Syeds because they embodied the souls of the Prophet's progeny. She told them how anyone bringing any harm to the Syeds was neither spared in this world nor in the next from the wrath of God. To what degree the cats understood the legend of the Syed pigeons was unclear, but although there was an all around smacking of lips accompanied by ominous protestations, the cats seemed to heed her warning and stayed away from Salar's pigeons. That is, all cats except Kotwal.

While their owner reclined casually under the full moon somewhere on a wall, a pair of mismatched blue and green eyes surveyed the world from tufts of dirty, white fur, regarding it with scornful disdain. In this manner Kotwal, the protagonist of many myths and legends and Bilotti's favoured cat, was known to give audience. Kotwal had been around for years and the stories of his birth had become warped with time. His pedigree was believed to be of a hybrid nature, indebted to the lust of a barn owl for a blind cat. And he had been named after the superintendent of police because of his habit of watchful observation. At least two generations of children had grown up dreaming of their perilous adventures with the mighty Kotwal, and no child in Topee Mohalla encountered darkness without feeling a set of blue and green eyes trained on him, watching his every move from walls, windows, ventilators and doorways. The grim truism that Kotwal sometimes made a meal of his own kittens did nothing to lighten the nocturnal burden of these juvenile souls. Kotwal's name was a sedative prescribed to restrain some of the more restive children in their throes of mischief. During the Friday prayers when Pesh Imam Jubba talked about the Fiend, they were naturally reminded of a certain tom whom they sincerely believed to be the gentleman in question. The womenfolk were also responsible for this apotheosis. They *knew* for a fact that Kotwal was an obstinate djinn whom Solomon transformed into a cat, and whose evil had been on the prowl since. In the light of this theology, such stories that Kotwal could drink milk from mugs like a human, holding it in his front paws and tilting the vessel to drain its contents, surprised no one.

While lesser cats were regularly caught, put in sacks and removed to the meat market, Kotwal never saw the inside of a sack. It was widely believed that whoever harmed a single tuft of Kotwal's fur would not only come to a grisly end himself but also commit seven future generations to the guardianship of evil.

In his youth Kotwal had a brush with Bilotti before he became the favourite. Bilotti had three favourites, all females who lived with her permanently, and had been christened in some colloquial tongue. They had a singularly protected childhood and would have followed the destiny of their spinster mistress if Kotwal had not taken it upon himself to lure them out one stormy winter night and strip them of their virtue. Kotwal had watched their passing into maidenhood with an uncommon interest and had indicated his favour by the habitual spraying of Bilotti's hamper every time he was around.

Bilotti was greatly scandalised when she noticed the heavy tread of her cats. But there was no time for lamentations and she soon got herself busy, preparing to harvest the crop of their sins. And abundant it was that season, filling up the three wicker baskets she had bought for their beds. However, Bilotti had made one resolve during the course of all her labours: Kotwal must somehow pay for her trouble. And towards this end, an opportunity soon presented itself.

When the tempting whiff of twenty-odd juicy kittens

sleeping and dreaming in their cosy cots reached Kotwal's nostrils he threw all caution to the wind and descended in Basmati's courtyard where Bilotti was staying in those days. It was a wintry night, not much unlike the one some months ago when three weak-willed cats had been tempted by a lecherous tom.

As he crept stealthily forward towards the slumbering kittens, Kotwal ignored the shadow behind the veranda door. He froze when he heard the whirr, as he was smelling the kittens, but it was a bad time to freeze because Bilotti had just lashed her hand-fan across his back. Her love for her kittens had proved stronger than Bilotti's superstitions about Kotwal's spiritual attributes. She had espied the devil's shadow prowling on the wall from her bed where she was resting after saying her prayers. The infuriated Kotwal was marked twice more with the fan before he could climb the wall and be gone. But no matter how furiously the fires of vengeance blazed in Kotwal's breast, he was, above all, worldly, and knew when the wind was against him. So Bilotti's kittens passed into adulthood under her vigil, and except for the occasional fatality at the hand of the many illnesses cultivated by nature, remained safe from Kotwal's gluttonous misappropriation. But while Bilotti kept the kittens safe from Kotwal, she became more and more attached to him, to the extent that she even encouraged him to come and sit next to her when the kittens were not around. And not long after that Kotwal cut off the three cats completely from Bilotti's supply of affection.

Other cats lived in mortal terror of Kotwal. There was the calico Reshmeen, who, but for her longhaired tail, was divested of all Persian virtue in the course of her mongrel lineage. Once she was part of Kotwal's harem but Kotwal poisoned this relationship twice by eating her kittens and wounding her badly in her efforts to protect her litter. After those incidents when Kotwal tried to mount her, she flew into such a rage that he thought it best to leave her out of his retinue. Bilotti had a soft spot for Reshmeen but did not show much affection to her in Kotwal's presence, for fear of igniting his murderous envy.

Kotwal manifested a special interest in Salar Jang who encouraged and reciprocated that sentiment. Whenever he arrived, Kotwal appeared on the walls of the house and sat there for hours on end watching him bug-eyed with his neck craning forward. That was the only time when his expression changed from its usual contempt to one manifesting an element of savage enchantment. But the moment Muneemji appeared on the scene, Kotwal, his demeanour restored, slowly retreated behind the ledges. He had an altogether different relationship with Muneemji, based on lines of mutual distrust and animosity. On more than one occasion, Kotwal had poached on Salar's prize pigeons as Muneemji slumbered nearby. Muneemji had sworn to flay the burglar but Salar was too egoistic and high-minded to hold such minor acts of vandalism against someone whom he regarded as his courtier.

Ladlay was under increasing pressure from Salar that they pay a visit to the printing presses and get them interested in his collection of poetry. The idea had been at the back of his mind for sometime now and he had discussed with Mirza Poya the various suitable titles that he may use in dedicating the book to Firdousi. He had already had lengthy discussions with Ladlay on the quality of the paper and the typeface to be used in the printing, and during their tonga journey to the largest printing press in Purana Shehr which Mirzban had recommended to his father-in-law, he shared his ideas and Mirza Poya's recommendations, who was highly supportive of such a course of action. But near the press their tonga found its way blocked by several noisy workers who were unrolling huge rolls of newsprint that had been damaged by the termites and the leakage of rainwater from the roof into the storage shed. That press also printed Purana Shehr's local newspaper. In the printing shops the termites had recently laid waste to whole consignments of newsprint, and as a result the newspaper came out in costly limited editions, and was mostly read in the marketplace. Only the day before, Bano Tamanna was obliged to join the chorus of hostile housewives who had encircled the newspaper-man when he informed them of a five-paisa raise in the newspaper price due to the loss of a huge consignment of newsprint, and were demanding to know whose fault it was to have left the paper unguarded.

Muneemji paid off the tonga-wala and they walked to the press. Inside the shed the clamour was even greater than outside. The press was running and a sharp odour of ammonia and ink pigments invaded their nostrils, as they proceeded to the manager's room where a short and restive man could be seen busily tying up a bundle of papers. The way to the door was lined with stacks of invitations to weddings, *valima*, and *aqiqa* ceremonies. The short man, who turned out to be the manager himself, carelessly pointed at the chairs, asking them to sit down and beckoned someone outside to take the bundle away.

'Tell me,' he asked Ladlay who seemed to be the only relevant personality in the company, 'how can I be of help to you?' after he had settled in his chair. Salar had brought out the manuscript from the leather case and he put it on the table in front of the manager, as a boy came in and took away the bundle of papers which the manager had tied up. Salar held the letter from his mentor in his hands.

'This here!' Salar said and pushed the loose pages of the manuscript towards the manager after Ladlay had nodded to him.

The manager did not look at the manuscript. Instead, he took out a cigarette and knocking it once against the table leaned back in his creaking swivel chair to light it. Then swinging forward and extinguishing the burning matchstick by shaking his hand lethargically, and blinking from the smoke that had gone into his eyes, he said, as a mirthful smile parted his lips, '*This here*, is fine! Now tell me,' he looked first at Salar and then at Ladlay, 'What do you want?'

'Salar Jang Sahib would like to have this book of poems which he has composed during the course of his life, published by your esteemed press,' Ladlay decided to intercede.

'More poetry! Why not! Why not!' the manager seemed amused by the idea as he dragged an already brimful ashtray close. Salar looked at the manager in a patronising way. 'That is not all!' he said, feeling encouraged and extending the patron's recommendation letter towards the manager like a trump card, 'See this!'

'What is *that*?' the manager asked looking at no one in particular. He did not take the letter from Salar's hand and sat blowing smoke through his nostrils, leaning back in his chair.

'I was addressing you. Are you listening, *janab*?' Salar asked in an irked tone.

'I think you should take a look at the letter,' Ladlay pleaded, leaning forward with his elbows on the table. 'It is a letter from Dilband Golkandvi Sahib recommending Salar Sahib's body of work.'

'A letter from Dilband Golkandvi! Indeed! I must take a look at what Golkandvi has to say!' the manager leaned forward and pulled the letter from Salar's hand. Then leaning sideways, he flapped the letter carelessly to open its folds. Salar started at the manager's careless handling of the letter and wanted to protest but Ladlay pulled the sleeve of his *sherwani* to restrain him from saying anything. The press manager was reading the paper in mocking quick glances with his lips pursed and his eyebrows raised, in what is the printing world's substitute for a smile of plain ridicule.

'I have read it!' the manager pushed the letter forward to Salar. Ladlay took it and putting it back in its envelope passed it on to Salar.

'So what do you think?' Salar asked haughtily, stuffing the letter into the pocket of his *sherwani* and looking intently to see what impression Dilband Golkandvi's laudatory epistle had made on the press manager. Dilband Golkandvi was a high-flying kite, and was included in the high school curriculum. Such impressive credentials obviously warranted a humble rejoinder from the press manager. But the manager was looking stolidly at him. Then blowing one huge puff of smoke on one side he said, 'We could talk about these secondary issues later. Why don't you come to the point! Huh?'

'I am always one for coming to the point,' Salar replied with renewed enthusiasm, convinced that the letter had done its job.

'The point is,' the manager took one last drag on the cigarette and extinguished it in the ashtray, 'That we print books, that's our job …'

Salar looked triumphantly at Ladlay who made a congratulatory but apprehensive face. 'Now you are talking!' Salar rejoined.

'As I was saying,' the manager continued impassively, 'We are in the business of printing. But let me make it clear in advance that we will not take responsibility for its circulation.'

'What a thing to say!' Salar replied and turning towards Ladlay remonstrated, 'Don't you think the book would sell by itself?'

'Of course I do not know much about the publishing business but I think once the book is published circulation should not be a problem. There is Dilband Sahib's letter and then the dedication. I can see the book selling like anything,' Ladlay maintained a zealous but guarded tone as he knew that the manager had not quite finished with his agenda.

'Very well then!' the press manager pushed his chair back to get up. 'If you are agreed on that then I should give you the estimate!'

'What estimate?' Ladlay asked the manager looking anxiously at Salar.

'Yes, what estimate? For the circulation?' Salar asked in a perplexed tone.

'The estimate for the printing. Also, if you want to have it printed while the termites are around, you must buy your own paper and bring it to the press on the appointed day. And if you want us to buy paper for you, we will not be responsible in case the termites damage it while it is stored in our shed.' Saying that much the manager looked askance at Salar and Ladlay to make sure that they understood all the stipulations.

'But I do not understand,' Salar asked. 'Didn't you just say that you are willing to publish the book?'

'Indeed I said that we will print the book. But you can't have it so good that without spending a single paisa you have the book, what's your name ... Salar Sahib!' the manager said. 'Do not expect us to finance the printing. This is not a publishing house. I have a business to run here! And a publishing house too, if one were to open tomorrow,' he continued in his vein, 'would be printing wedding invitations to keep itself from going bankrupt.'

'But Dilband Golkandvi's letter ...!' Salar protested.

'These letters have no value. Every poet comes here brandishing one. Who knows if this letter is authentic. I can also produce a letter and tell you that it has been written by Dilband,' the manager said as he beckoned to the boy sitting outside. 'Who is to know?'

'Are you out of your mind? You mean ... you think that

Dilband Golkandvi's letter … is fake? How dare you?' Salar's voice rose, his face began to twitch, and he began to cough as he replied after recovering from the import of the manager's blasphemy.

But the manager was not listening. He was quietly telling the boy to send a small kettle of tea into his room. The boy looked at Salar's party inquiringly and asked how many cups. 'Didn't you hear what I just said? Ask your father to have the wax removed from your ears!' the manager gesticulated with his hands as if he intended to remove the wax himself from the boy's ears.

'Manager Sahib, you must not talk like that. Salar Sahib is a very respectable man,' Ladlay pleaded with the press manager after the frightened boy had cleared out of the room.

'Respectable! Fine! Why not! But even if I accept that the letter is genuine, who is to tell if it was really written on the manuscript's merit or it was just one of the many letters which are written by senior poets to make someone happy at a particular time. You know what I mean!' he looked at Ladlay and grimaced.

'Surely this man is mad! What bloody nonsense he talks. Such unbridled irreverence towards Dilband Sahib! You must take me away from here Ladlay Sahib before my anger gets the better of me,' Salar was now shouting and one of the workers looked in to see if the manager needed a hand to set the matter right. 'It is not Gulmoha … or the man would have … been stuffed with … hay for his presuming so!' Salar shouted between choking fits.

'Don't mistake my words,' the manager shouted from behind, tapping out another cigarette from the packet, as Ladlay gripped Salar's arm firmly and led him away. 'Letter or no letter we will print the book if you pick up the tab. I don't want to fight. I have a business to run here.' But when he saw the party clearing his room without a hope of return, he shouted, 'Fine! Don't come back. I am happy enough printing wedding invitations. Who the hell needs a book of bloody poetry!!?' Then, grumbling, he took a long sip from the cup of tea which the boy had brought in and lit his cigarette.

Basmati was complaining of gas to Tabaq Sahib when Bhai Qamoosi directed his friends' attention to the newspaper column he had been reading.

'Put it away, Bhai Qamoosi!' Basmati said. 'Enough of this newspaper nonsense! It's all bunkum! They will write the first thing that comes into their minds, just to fill up the pages. What I am interested in right now is … brrrr!! … a cure for my gas.'

'What is it about?' Tabaq Sahib asked.

Bhai Qamoosi referred to renowned entomologist Dr Adbari's article, 'The History of the Termites' that was being serialised in daily *Qandeel*.

'Here he mentions …' Bhai Qamoosi started but Tabaq Sahib cut him short. 'Not like this! If you want to read it, read it from the beginning.'

'As you wish,' Bhai Qamoosi replied and began reading out loud, while Basmati reclined in his seat and stared at the ceiling.

'The recent outbreak of termites in the south-east of the country, although severe in its dimensions is not a historical oddity. In this series of essays we will study the recorded history of these blind insects, who have been around for over a hundred million years, and comment on the impact of their pestilence on human society from biblical times to the present.'

Bhai Qamoosi looked around and finding his audience attentive, continued:

'The celebrated British entomologist P. E. Howse writes that recorded history of South America was lost to contemporary society since the termites devoured the majority of texts more than a century old. Howse notes, "A variety of the species, *Reticulitermes lucifugus*, was apparently introduced in the region of La Rochelle in ships' timbers. The insect went for a long time undetected, but in 1797 it was found that they had ruined stores of stacked oak for making warships, and in 1820 Napoleon's ship, *Le Genois*, had to be broken up because of the damage done by termites …"'

'Hold it there!' Tabaq Sahib interjected. 'Did you hear that, Basmati!'

'Hear what?' Basmati started.

'The termites eating up a whole ship!' Tabaq Sahib's voice was quivering with emotion.

'It was not a whole ship …' Bhai Qamoosi tried to explain but Tabaq Sahib did not allow him to proceed. 'It's all the same!' he said, and again asked Basmati, 'Doesn't it remind you of anything?'

'What should it remind me of?' Basmati asked nonchalantly.

'Now don't be so simple!' Tabaq Sahib replied irritatingly, 'When it's as plain as day!'

'Whaaa…attt?' Basmati was still yawning, when Tabaq Sahib suddenly yelled, 'Noah's Ark!' startling people at neighbouring tables who turned to stare.

'What of Noah's Ark?' Basmati sat up and looked around to see if people were still watching them. They were, but quickly looked away when Basmati returned their gaze.

'No matter what anybody says, I am willing to bet that these termites were aboard!' Tabaq Sahib replied. 'That's why they haven't found a single trace of the Ark on Mount Ararat, even though the pharaoh's body has been found.'

'If we believe you, Tabaq Sahib!' Bhai Qamoosi spoke, 'Where was the wisdom in carrying such a destructive passenger on board, which could potentially imperil the lives of others, considering that nobody, including Noah himself, knew how long the ship was to remain at sea?'

'All I can say is that these are Godly matters and we cannot poke our sinful noses into it! Noah was acting under God's directions! That's that! Have you forgotten that the termite also acted as a minister of God, when He sent it to fell the mighty Solomon, who, when death suddenly came knocking on his door, propped himself so dextrously against an oaken staff on his throne, that he kept sitting there for many days without the djinns as much as suspecting that he was dead?' Tabaq Sahib asked. 'Who was it that put an end to his almost boundless rule, which extended from the four corners of God's good Earth to the six heavens – the Seventh Heaven being forbidden by holy writ to his slave djinns – by hollowing the staff? The same termite! Who else?'

'*Acchha*?!' Basmati said.

'No longer able to sustain the prophetic weight, the wood snapped, and Solomon lay at the feet of his old trustworthy friend and minister Barkhia along with the debris of his staff! But Solomon had saved the day,' Tabaq Sahib continued, 'and the termites felled him when the pretence was no longer necessary. By this last act of wisdom not only did the great king pave the way for Barkhia to organise a smooth transition of power, but also had the last laugh at the djinns, by cheating them of their freedom even after his death.'

'Why was it necessary?' Basmati showed interest in Tabaq Sahib's story for the first time.

'It was highly probable,' Tabaq Sahib replied patronisingly, 'given the mischievous and rebellious nature of the djinns, who were bound to his vassalage for the course of his natural life, that they would have desecrated Solomon's body and pillaged and plundered his kingdom, were his death prematurely known!' Tabaq Sahib finished his discourse and looked with satisfaction at Basmati whose face wore an incredulous look. Only Bhai Qamoosi looked impassive.

'I say it is an allegory for posthumous yearning for power

and the Democratic Will!' Bhai Qamoosi propounded, unable to contain himself.

'Don't say another word Bhai Qamoosi! Our friendship aside, your insinuation, in view of such prophetic sagacity – invariably guided by Providence – is highly provoking and endlessly deplorable,' Basmati interjected, shaking his head menacingly.

'I was only suggesting …' Bhai Qamoosi backed down.

'Not a word more now!' Basmati growled and Tabaq Sahib diverted the argument by asking Bhai Qamoosi to read on, who immediately began:

'Man himself is also a predator of termites … Smeathman considered roasted termites to be superior in taste to shrimps …'

'What nonsense!' Basmati interposed and Tabaq Sahib nodded his head, but did not say anything more than a derisive 'Huh!'

Bhai Qamoosi read on:

'However, Koening in 1779 reported that an excess of the insects is damaging to the health and that one may succumb to a surfeit.'

'What was I telling you?' Basmati asked Bhai Qamoosi who kept on reading without answering.

'Howse writes that in view of the termite queen's impressive fecundity (up to 36,000 eggs a day), it is scarcely surprising to find that queens are highly prized aphrodisiacs in many countries of the tropics. They are said to be used by Hindus for restoring the lost powers of the elders, but in certain regions of the Congo they are eaten only by the women; if they are eaten by men, this is believed to result in a loss of generative powers.'

Now Basmati looked at Tabaq Sahib and smiling meaningfully, asked, 'What do you say to that Tabaq Sahib?'

'All rubbish!' Tabaq Sahib said.

But Basmati managed to convince Tabaq Sahib to ask Imam Jubba to expound on the aphrodisiacal properties of the termites and tell the assembly about the religious aspect of the issue.

Imam Jubba consulted his adjutants for a few minutes to check whether Tabaq Sahib had been planted by the opposite sect to ask this question. After the Bhai Qamoosi episode, Imam Jubba had become careful. But when his adjutants confirmed that the man was known to them, Jubba cleared his throat and replied, 'To discuss the aphrodisiac merits of termites is beyond the scope of my sermons, although I had been thinking about these issues myself. Also, it is not righteous to exploit to one's advantage a scourge sent by God to punish us. It would be tantamount to imagining prophet Jonah robbing the fish of her ambergris and selling it for profit when he was released from its belly, or prophet Job making a living from narrating the story of his misfortunes in public places.

'However, since the Hindus use the termites to cure impotency among *their* geriatric ranks, we would warn our senior brothers not to indulge in such infidel practices. The Hindus have a penchant for the queer. Many of them subscribe to the healing properties of the cow's urinal discharge, an animal they not only consider holy but also a fountain of filial and maternal passions *nauz'obillah*, and many of them have developed a taste for it without the least signs of amelioration in their heathenish lot. On the other hand, it is known to all that many tribes had converted to Islam during the Muslim conquest of Africa, and therefore if the said brother Muslim tribes in the Congo have arrived at the conclusion that the termite queen instead of curing, *causes* impotency among men, we must follow their example and take heed. However, if a housewife comes upon a termite queen, she can safely eat it, provided that she has her husband's prior approval, for consent in such matters is only conducive to marital bliss. Also, she must not do it with a view to her own carnal satiation, but for the pleasure of her lord.'

It is highly likely that the sudden interest in digging up underground nests to search for the termite queen was motivated by Dr Adbari's mention of their aphrodisiacal properties. Notwithstanding Jubba's diatribe against the Hindus, the hunt for the termite queen went on. The fact that the whole land on which the neighbourhood of Topee Mohalla was raised had become an extended subterranean nest for the termites, did not in the least daunt the spirit of the search parties. Comprising the neighbourhood elders, among whom Tabaq Sahib figured prominently, they thronged the dimly-lit corners of the streets and alleys in the evenings, and lingered around small groups of commissioned workers who even from a distance could be recognised as Lumboo's *lashkar*, the eleven-strong army of the sweeper's progeny, who were notorious for sticking nettles on the clothes of passers-by in the alleys. Its pincers did not come off easily once they had gripped a fabric, and if somebody sat down on them the nettles penetrated the skin, causing much discomfort. In a week's time the *lashkar* had done more damage to the houses than the termites had until then, by burrowing under the plinths. How many queens were dug out during these excavations and what if any were the effects of their consumption was questionable, but as a strategy for containing the termite menace it seemed to work, since many termites and reproductives perished inside their vaults as the nest wall crashed under the blows, and a lot of soldier and reproductive termites were mistakenly eaten for the queen.

Muneemji, who sometimes went out for a walk around the neighbourhood in the evenings, ran into one such group once and told Salar of their exploits upon his return.

'Muneemji, what do you say to bringing me a few of these

queen termites?' Salar asked him softly and anxiously after looking around to see that nobody was listening.

'What can I say?!' Muneemji replied.

'Now look at it this way,' Salar began to explain zealously, 'What can go wrong if I eat a few termites? So many times we eat insects which fall in our food accidentally. So I do not see what harm a few extra termites would do. You can put them inside a sliced banana: that way I won't even taste them. And if you ask me, in my heart of hearts I believe that there is some truth in what people say. What's on the people's tongues is God's own decree. And besides, aphrodisiacs are also good for the mind. They make it sharp and alert.'

Muneemji opened his mouth to say something but Salar silenced him. 'Enough! Keep a sharp lookout, and even if you have to buy some, get me at least one or two of the queens.'

But Muneemji returned home empty-handed every time, either on purpose or perhaps because there were no queen termites to be found, and after grumbling a few times, Salar forgot all about it.

Salar had no patience for the publishers' antics. He wanted a printed copy of his book in his hands immediately, with the dedication written to Noor-e Firdousi. And Ladlay managed to convince him that he should put up some money for the printing himself. 'Who knows – maybe Firdousi will even choose a ghazal from the book, Salar Sahib, when she finds out that the dedication is in her name. I don't know of anybody who has dedicated a book to her. The way to a woman's heart is through her heart only!' he told Salar. And the more the notary went on, the more impatient Salar became, and the greater grew his desire to have Firdousi know that a book had been dedicated to her. For some days now Ladlay had been telling Salar that he would bring him good news soon, when one afternoon he arrived beaming mysteriously.

Immediately he demanded that Salar congratulate him and order sweetmeats. 'Now then, we must know: what is the auspicious occasion?' Salar asked eagerly. 'Has a publisher been found?' he inquired with bated breath.

'It was no ordinary job, Salar Sahib!', Ladlay replied wiping the sweat from his swarthy face on his sleeve, 'I have spoken with someone in the press, who moonlights during office hours, but when he heard that it was a book of poetry, he backed out. He said that the poets kept tinkering with the rhymes and kept asking for new proofs which made it impossible for the job to be done clandestinely. But I told him, 'Listen you fool! This is no ordinary book of poetry. Dilband Golkandvi has written the preface for it, and the stature of the poet is such that every written word is like a word engraved in stone. There is no occasion for such worries.' What do you think? Did I or didn't I give him the true picture here?'

'I must say that I cannot object to anything said as yet,' Salar replied in a haughty voice but in a tone which clearly betrayed how flattered he was. 'But tell me, what did he say?' Salar was becoming more impatient by the moment.

'What did he have to say? He agreed!' Ladlay slapped his thigh with the flat of his hand.

'Really?' Salar began scratching his scalp with uncontrollable delight.

'Yes! But since he has to do the job in a clandestine way he said that he will not meet us again so that nobody suspects him of any wrong-doing. He also knows a distributor who will do the distribution for us. The deal is cheap. Only four thousand rupees for the printing and distribution. But he must have the answer by this evening.'

'Four thousand!' Salar's voice was deeply thoughtful. 'I will have to ask Muneemji to arrange it.'

No sooner were the words out of Salar's mouth than Ladlay reached for and caught Salar's wrist. Without letting go, he pulled his chair closer to Salar's bed and said in a barely audible but agitated whisper, 'Enough, Salar Sahib! I do not think you must involve anyone besides yourself in this.' Then looking here and there in a conspiratorial manner he continued, 'As God is my witness, I have nothing against Muneemji, but he is very close to Begum Yunani. And God forbid, if in a moment of weakness he breathes a word about it to her, one thing will lead to another. And God only knows where it will all end and what shall not be compromised. I suggest you acquire this money directly through your personal account. That way, no one will know.'

Salar was thinking about Ladlay's allusion to Muneemji's soft spot for Bano Tamanna. Ladlay was right, Salar realised. Muneemji was quite protective of her. If he found out that Salar was spending so much money to send a book to Firdousi, he might try to persuade him otherwise. Suddenly it occurred to Salar that Muneemji might even be spying on him for Bano Tamanna. Now that he thinks I am old and might die any day, he has to fend for himself. So he goes wagging his tail to Bano. Ha! How clearly I see it all! How plain are his dastardly schemes! Salar was deep in these thoughts when Ladlay broke the silence.

'And if you are thinking about another printer, let me tell you this. If you go to a printer in the market, he will not charge a paisa less than eight thousand,' he was saying. 'I suggest that you go ahead in God's name. Money is the grime of hand. Eid is just two months away and from next week he will be busy printing wedding invitations and will not have time. Who knows when this opportunity will come again!'

In a month's time Ladlay brought Salar five copies of his book of poetry which he said were all that was left since the distributor had picked up the first bunch the day it was bound and he kept coming for more, so great, he said, was the demand. Salar was beside himself with joy. 'What remains now,' he told Ladlay, 'is to make a due presentation.' The book was packed in two envelopes to ensure a safe delivery, and with the note of dedication underlined, sent to Firdousi's address the same evening by registered post.

Despite his stoop, Muneemji's longitudinal vision was remarkable. A pigeon never broke away from the centrifugal force of his toothless but shrill whistle, when on its daily exercise flight. While to everyone he seemed to be looking at the ground, he knew of every movement of the pigeons in the skies even when they were camouflaged against the silvery sky by the sun's rays which illuminated their undersides as they tilted to make a turn. And that day he had picked up Unnab Khan's cockerel long before his mad fluttering and flapping over their heads surprised the pigeons in their innocent circuitous flight over Mirzban's roof.

The rooster made a semicircle over Mirzban's roof and flapping its wings dropped a little distance away from Muneemji, who looked at him in surprise. Ladlay was taking Salar to a cock-fight that afternoon and he had mentioned that the neighbourhood cock was to be matched. So what was it doing here just a few hours before the fight, Muneemji wondered? It was quite extraordinary for a rooster his size and weight to fly. Raised on an invigorating regimen of buffalo mince, multitudinous grains, dry fruit and electuaries, its stimulus had made the bird spirited, and probably occasioned this demented flight. During a vicious fight early in his career he had broken his left spur and wore its silver substitute during fights. He had survived more weekend battles, and won more bets than any living bird in the small community of the Topee Mohalla cock-fighters. Although he had received a fair share of scars in his profession, and his heavy breast had slowly been divested of feathers from the pillage of hundreds of claws and spurs, the two-hands-high bird sauntered about with the sashaying pride of a seasoned general, and even Kotwal, greatly tempted by his juicy neck and sumptuous drumsticks, kept away knowing of the danger inherent in his deadly beak and spurs, which had blinded a desperate feline in one eye and slashed open the sides of many others. Unnab's life was devoted to his bird. In a corner of his chowkidar father's ramshackle quarters in Topee Mohalla was a coop where Unnab kept his pet. Almost one third of the winnings were spent on his food. The rest Unnab translated into opium balls, which soon dissolved in cups of tea, to cope with the hope of new wins and dread of new failures.

Muneemji heard the water pipes rattling: somebody was climbing up the wall using the pipeline. He moved behind the pigeon coop and from there saw Unnab's crimson, pimpled face slowly appear over the ledge under his thick mop of hair. He was not expecting anyone on the roof and his head was turned away to see if anyone was watching him from the alley. He kept hanging there, looking about with his small watchful eyes. When satisfied, he propelled himself over the ledge and crept onto the roof. Standing still and surveying Unnab with vigilant eyes, the rooster turned its head majestically as he moved forward, making clucking sounds. Unnab picked up the bird and stroked its back. Then he moved forward to look over Mirzban's courtyard. A short while ago Muneemji had seen Mushtri bring out her chair into the courtyard to read the newspaper. He came out from behind the pigeon coop and shouted, 'You scoundrel dog! What do you think you are doing here, you rascal?' Unnab immediately turned and the look of fright upon finding Muneemji standing right behind him made his face even darker.

'Nothing!' Unnab answered hurriedly. 'I just came here to get my cockerel.'

'Why not from the front door – why do you have to climb onto the roof like a thief?' Muneemji confronted him.

'I didn't want to disturb Yunani Sahib's family. I thought they would be sleeping!' Unnab pleaded.

'And why were you hanging around after you had found your rooster? Tell me!' Muneemji came forward.

'Oh ... I saw ... I saw a kite fall on one of these roofs some time ago and I was ... I was looking to see if I could find its skein hanging somewhere!' Unnab's eyes shifted like a cornered animal's as he haltingly answered Muneemji.

'Get lost! If I ever see you peeping or snooping here I will take out your eyes! Get going!' Muneemji waved his arms menacingly. Then suddenly he shouted, 'Watch your step, wretch!' Unnab was moving backwards and Muneemji was afraid that he might fall down from the ledge. Unnab dropped the bird in the alley and climbed down from the pipes. Then he made a salaam to Muneemji and, carrying his rooster under his arm, walked hastily away.

'Who was on the roof, Muneemji?' Mushtri asked Muneemji as he came down.

'Some neighbourhood rascal who had come to retrieve his cockerel from the roof,' Muneemji replied.

'Someone from the neighbourhood, you said?' Mushtri asked.

'Yes, yes, that rascal, what's his name ...' Muneemji looked at Mushtri from the corner of his eyes.

'Unnab?' Mushtri hinted.

'Yes, I guess it was him!' Muneemji replied looking away from Mushtri.

'How wrong it is to climb on people's roofs. I have told Mirzban Bhai several times to have the walls plastered with cleft glass. Hope you gave him a good shouting,' Mushtri went back to the newspaper with a smile of triumph which did not escape Muneemji.

He went to look for Salar. He found him fully dressed, having ignored Bano Tamanna's objections that he should not be seen in the low company of cock-fighters and gamblers.

Muneemji was quiet and when Salar shouted Bano Tamanna down, he did not intervene between the two. He kept sitting in a corner silently smoking Salar's hookah.

Ladlay was full of particulars about the two combatants of the day and briefed Salar about them on the way to the cockpit. Salar, who used to be an avid cock-fighter in his day, kept interjecting with quips about the valour of the birds of his day, and memories of historical fights he had witnessed. Muneemji quietly clung to the tonga frame. It rattled badly on the unpaved road every time the wheels went over the stones scattered by the masons for pulverising later in the day.

The day before the fight, tucked in the crook of Unnab's arm, the cockerel had visited the *qalandars* of the Pukka Qila and returned sporting a new charm around its drumstick which Unnab was now showing around. It was widely believed that the potency of a charm was as much a factor in a fighter-cock's victory as were its agility and finesse. Unnab made many respectful salaams to Muneemji when he saw him, and brought his cockerel over in his arms for Muneemji and Salar to pat its head. Salar bounced the rooster's head with great pleasure but Muneemji quickly withdrew his hand after lightly brushing it. Ladlay looked on with surprise and after Unnab went back he turned to Muneemji. But Muneemji was looking at the cocks. They were some of the many animals born for the promotion of gambling. The roosters too, had the shifty, sidelong, glimmering, trademark glance of compulsive gamblers – the same look which could be seen on almost every face gathered there to make bets.

Unnab held the bird's head in the cup of his hands to blow hot breath on his face, and tug at the charm. The other cock was given similar ministrations at his owner's hands. Then the two birds were thrown together in a circle formed by the veteran betters and onlookers. At the sight of each other's proximity they immediately puffed up their neck feathers, but kept prancing about in this attitude without committing themselves to an all out combat. However, their restive masters forced the fight upon them by goading them into such dangerous convergence with each other that neither was left with a choice but to engage his foe in a decisive battle. Soon a great flurry of blood and down ensued. It floated in the combat zone and splattered the grassy pit as the cocks locked their necks, and their beaks and spurs explored each other's tough flesh for a bloody hold. For a long time no other sound was heard but the fluttering and flapping of wings and the clash of claws and beaks.

The fight lasted a full three rounds. Unnab's cockerel was dominant from the start, hardly touching the ground before he was airborne again, his wings flapping and his claws groping the air for his adversary's flesh. When both the birds were gored, their owners, ready with cold water, sprayed it on the wounds from their mouths. The heads were also sprayed and the wounds were rubbed with salt. By the end of the second round the results were more or less obvious and a withdrawal at that stage would have ensured the losing bird's survival. But his owner, either pressed for or simply blinded by the prize money, did not hold his charge back, counting on his bird finding the jugular of Unnab's cockerel at the last minute, but this miracle did not happen.

On the way back Salar enthused about the thrill of the recently witnessed event, and fell back to reminiscing about the courts of his day and dying traditions like cock-fighting, of which the new generations were raised in blind ignorance. Finding an opportune moment, Ladlay steered the conversation towards Firdousi, and spoke at length on her passion for singing – especially mentioning Firdousi's concert tours which were held every few months. Ladlay hastened to add that she only consented to a concert appearance when convinced that the first and foremost consideration before her sponsor was to promote and propagate the classical singing tradition. That that was Firdousi's only condition, and that where she was concerned, art was akin to religion, before which every other consideration must be shunned, Ladlay emphasised a great deal.

After Ladlay's harangue was over there was an uncomfortable silence during which Salar shifted in his seat thoughtfully. 'For argument's sake, how much would it cost to hold a concert?' he asked holding to his temple the index finger pointing upwards. Muneemji observed that Ladlay seemed engrossed in some complicated calculation, but it was soon resolved, and Ladlay quoted the sum, 'Twenty-five thousand rupees!' Then, hastily, but in a voice pregnant with conviction, he added, 'It may sound like a big capital investment but profits from such ventures are multiplied many times over, always!'

Salar quietly scratched his chin before inquiring about the case, 'And what is the progress at court?' The words were hardly out of Salar's mouth when Ladlay began to enumerate the many problems he was facing. One was that of physical presence, he pointed out. Salar might have to visit his property personally to get notarised copies of the agreement from the defendant's lawyer. The lawyer was not responding to Ladlay's communications, making excuses that he had not received them, although they were sent by registered post and Ladlay had receipts to prove that they had reached the lawyer's office. Probably the lawyer was doing it to get even with Salar who had filed the case in a faraway city and taken away his business, making it necessary for the case to be transferred to a Purana Shehr lawyer. 'It is quite obvious that he is in cahoots with the defence lawyer and between them they are playing games with you. But if you go in person,' Ladlay said, and affecting indifference in his tone added, 'or if someone were sent to represent you, armed with a general power of attorney, the lawyer's bluff would be called, and he would be obliged to surrender the documents, whose procurement would expedite the proceedings.' Muneemji was listening to the conversation with more alertness than he had shown previously. And when Ladlay mentioned the general power of attorney, he leaned back from the front seat where he was seated and almost sprained his back in an effort to arch it backwards to hear the conversation better. Ladlay did not notice Muneemji's movement and kept talking to Salar.

Salar did not like the idea of the general power of attorney being transferred to anyone, but he was expecting Firdousi's reply to his letter any day now. His mail had been opened and destroyed on several other occasions by Bano, and Salar had kept quiet. But now it would be foolish in the extreme to leave Firdousi's reply in Bano Tamanna's hands, Salar thought. There was no knowing what fuss she might kick up if she finds Firdousi's letter. God only knows she might even write something inappropriate in reply to her. His presence in the house was necessary, Salar decided. He asked Ladlay if there were any other options, but Ladlay insisted that the best thing would be for Salar to go himself and finish the business with the lawyer. He even offered to accompany him. Salar said he would consider the matter.

Although he had been unsuccessful in his search for the termite queen, Tabaq Sahib had become involved in the campaign against the termites, and was instrumental in drafting a petition with Bhai Qamoosi's help, getting it signed by the residents of Topee Mohalla, and sending it to the MP from Purana Shehr. The MP tabled a motion in the lower house of the Parliament that the situation facing his city be discussed in the Assembly and relief measures taken immediately. The speaker promised that in due course the matter would be taken care of. The Purana Shehr MP joined hands with a few independents from upcountry, who made a promise in the cafeteria to stand on every point of order and plead his case. In the next session one of the upcountry MPs got up on a point of order and told the House that as yet it was only legal documents that had been appropriated by the insect, but soon it would be the country's constitution. He asked the Leader of the House to specify the measures he had taken to prevent such a contingency. The Prime Minister was taken completely unawares. While he was thinking of a reply, the group of the upcountry MPs shouted that the PM should instruct the old *hafiz*, whose recitation from the Qur'an inaugurated the assembly proceedings, to memorise the constitution. Other spirited voices joined the chorus, and the motion was carried despite the old *hafiz*'s many protestations.

Like everything else discussed in the Assembly, the termite scourge also began to take the shape of a farce, played at the expense of Purana Shehr. When the Purana Shehr MP realised his mistake of initiating a dialogue with the upcountry MPs, it was already too late. The next day, another fat MP from that group got up on his chair and started to undress. But before the man-at-arms could grab him, the man had undressed to a robe made of the national flag. He displayed it proudly, smiling and bowing his head to the applause and whistles of his comrades. When the bemused speaker questioned his conduct, the flag-wrapped MP made a short patriotic speech to the effect that he had taken this precaution to safeguard the national herald in the event of the spread of the termites, and expressed his intention of coming dressed in it until the termite epidemic had subsided.

Upon that the Opposition benches, who had an old score to settle with the fat MP, raised the objection that the speaker must set up an independent commission to determine whether wearing the national flag was not a desecration of the national emblem. The speaker found himself qualified to dismiss the point of order by remarking that the flag was not desecrated as long as it was worn *over* the undergarments.

At that the Opposition benches again asked how they were to know whether or not the respectable MP had undergarments on. The MP in question removed all doubts by quickly disrobing once more to display his silken underwear. But by then the speaker had already hinted to the man-at-arms who dragged him out half-naked and barefoot, amid cries of 'Shame! Shame!' The whole incident was purged from the assembly proceedings to the great dismay of the group of independent MPs.

All these sordid details were reported in daily *Qandeel* and Tabaq Sahib condemned the irresponsible ways of the legislators. In his denunciation of the MPs he remarked that if he were the MP, the ills of Purana Shehr, and especially Topee Mohalla, would have been over long ago. It was one of those careless remarks which have a way of taking on a life of their own. Everyone present at Chhalawa Hotel agreed that indeed Tabaq Sahib would make an exemplary legislator, and Basmati proposed that Tabaq Sahib run as an independent for a seat in the forthcoming local body polls from the Topee Mohalla constituency.

Qudratullah was in a dilemma. One would have credited a once wedded man like Qudratullah to act more boldly, or, at least, to think more courageously, than he had done until now. But Qudratullah's deceased wife had been a matron of stern moral attributes, and though her flesh had been defiled on the nuptial bed, she had risen from that ignominy with her ethereal assets intact. Consequently, her mark had remained indelible on Qudratullah, even in the wake of her demise. Indeed, his attraction to Mushtri Khanam was not without a dash of masochism which congress with women such as his late spouse inculcate in weak-willed men like Qudratullah. Incapacitated by these encounters to ever have a healthy relationship with women, they become self-destructive, develop miscellaneous liver and kidney disorders, and seek out relationships in the visitations of whose torments they pay homage to their long dead and buried conjugal associations.

So Qudratullah was at a point when the entire official scope of his daily audience with Mushtri Khanam had been exhausted. Ever of a reconciling nature, he had become comfortable with that adjustment to such a reckless degree as to imagine that *that* was the intended end of the whole exercise. And the longer it continued the more difficult it became to give another turn to this arrangement without rocking the boat and imperilling one of the two parties to be thrown overboard. However, in the small hours of the night, the devil rode Qudratullah so hard and fast that it robbed all sleep from his inflamed eyes, and under its evil influence his raving mind made maniacal resolves, only to be sapped of all their strength by the morning sun, which saw him repair to the bank on his scooter, his usual meek and law-abiding self.

At home, in his mind, Qudratullah conducted witty conversations with Mushtri, embellished with elaborate arguments and quips. But the moment he saw her, rather as he got closer to the bank, the arguments evaporated, the quips melted away, his face became grim and he felt more and more determined to call it quits. And the moment he stepped out of the bank he was smitten by the pangs of remorse with redoubled force. Not prepared for this stalemate Mushtri Khanam became even more stern and aloof while she received dictation, and for the first time in her life, started coming late to work.

But, for her own sake, that was the one thing which she should not have done. When she arrived late on the third consecutive day, the clerks who were until now jubilant over her back-breaking labour, sat up as a body to take notice of this unusual development. It meant two things. First of all, that she had not received a warning for coming late on previous occasions. Obviously that encouraged her to repeat it. But why she didn't get a warning from Qudratullah was something which needed explaining, and occupied the minds of the clerks for the rest of their office hours. However, being the practical people that they were, they decided that the first step in such a situation would be to follow in Mushtri's footsteps; to forget whatever notions of punctuality they still laboured under, and in the meanwhile to keep working at the puzzle. That was their parting resolution on the eve of the come-late, go-slow weeks which lay ahead of the Desh Bank; the latter idea being an added garnish of rebellion, proposed off the cuff by the cashier, and carried by the unanimous approval of the whole assembly.

They would have saved themselves much anxiety if they had been more willing to take Qudratullah seriously. But they were still hesitant. From his office and over Mushtri Khanam's shoulder Qudratullah could see the clerks leaning across their tables and gesticulating mysteriously to each other with furtive glances at his room. The Pathan gunman was also in much circulation, looking quite puzzled. In this state of mind he inadvertently brought Mushtri Khanam's tea into Qudratullah's office when he brought the manager's cup. Mushtri Khanam, not asking him to take it to her table where she usually had it, and Qudratullah in no moral position to repudiate him, the gunman had returned to the clerks full of new insight, and feeling very superior.

Another trait had become known of the termites: that they constantly developed new predilections and that their taste changed overnight, as if their armies were being guided by some divine oracle, which reached the whole of their multitude simultaneously. In the beginning they applied themselves to the eating of woody tissue. But slowly their tastes began to diversify and they devoted an increasing number of hours to foraging. If during one week they wiped the city out of all woollen objects and material, the next week they rifled the city of all its spices. This kept everyone constantly guessing, and always the least suspected of objects or materials became their target, rendering all precautions futile. By now they had veined into the whole corporal body of the city, and its every natural and unnatural pore was filled with termites. The insects lived not as entities in themselves, but as one organism. A world where neither individual nor individual loss signified anything. The organism had to survive at all cost, and to that end the termites devoted themselves as a body.

At some point the termites viewed tea leaves as an item of food, and Qudratullah woke up one fine morning to find them in the glass jar in which the tea leaves were kept, wriggling and writhing in a black paste. When he ran out of the house in panic to the Buddah *kiryana* merchant's shop to secure a bag or two of tea before it was too late, there was already a mob assembled outside the shop. Those were people who had made similar discoveries earlier in the day.

Chhalawa was in the forefront and holding his ground; he winked and grimaced at everyone knowingly, as the newcomers tried to elbow their way to the front. There were no paper bags in the markets, and people took rice and sugar in their handkerchiefs and dupattas. Chhalawa had turned up with the bottoms of his pyjamas tied up with rubber bands, and when his turn came he loosened his cummerbund and asked Buddah to fill up his pyjamas with tea. Greatly scandalised, Buddah shouted at him to have some shame, but Chhalawa insisted, winking and nodding amid general mirth and jocosity, until Buddah was obliged to fill up his pyjamas with a half of one of the two sacks of open tea he had managed to secure in his cellar from the termites, and which he was blatantly selling at four times the controlled rate. Once Chhalawa had tottered away from the scene with his pyjamas full, the remaining tea was greedily snatched away by people in the front who still had not bought their full allowance of tea in their ration cards, and Buddah quickly pulled down his shutters on the rest, crushing many fingers and arms in the process. Foiled early in the morning, Qudratullah listlessly dragged his feet home. Inside the shop Buddah continued his vigil, to see what commodity the termites attacked next, in order to quickly take it off the shelves, and peddle it in the black market.

If on one hand caffeine destroyed the termites' natural sleep cycle, for whom night and day became one unending work shift, on the other the disappearance of tea had a dispiriting effect on people. Without tea, its addicts became listless and sat on street corners holding their aching heads in their hands. Some reeled and staggered on the roads, creating traffic hazards. It was a rare shop which carried coffee, and the far-sighted people had already hoarded it up in their homes. Without exactly knowing the properties of green tea, people brewed teapots' full, and before its stimulative properties could be ascertained, it was fully consumed. There was a great rush at the Chhalawa Hotel for the first week while its tea rations lasted. But when every tea leaf had been drawn from several times and when it floated on the surface without discolouring the water in the least, Chhalawa reluctantly struck tea out of the menu and roamed the streets out of sheer habit, with his head shaved. People looked away when they saw Chhalawa's face. It reminded them of the forgotten, delectable taste of that heavenly decoction, that was lost to them, perhaps forever. From sucklings to hoary old men, everyone had become languid. Some took out their frustrations in the street, the rest stayed indoors and made trouble. Family life was the first casualty. Husbands swore at their wives across the breakfast tables for keeping the tea leaves in plain view of the termites, broke crockery, and thrashed their children. With heavier objects of cutlery the wives targeted the heads of their better halves, and repaired to their mothers' houses with their progeny. In the office everyone was in a foul mood and snapped at each other.

Since the disappearance of that breakfast staple, an hour past morning tea-time, the signals originating from Qudratullah's cranium warned him to prepare for an imminent headache. He went to office with his head spinning, his eyes watering and a sour taste in his mouth. Of late, the staff of that nationalised bank had shown more than usual belligerency with customers and had surpassed themselves in slothfulness. The customers too, were disposed to riot. Qudratullah had to make a great effort to restrain the fury he felt welling up inside himself by clutching on tightly to his armrest when customers and staff charged into his office shouting. On such occasions the gunman always stood alert with legs apart outside the bank, with the requisite fierce attitude of his duty, away from the trouble.

Complaints piled up. The work was standing still. The whole office seemed to be falling apart, with the exception of Mushtri Khanam's department. It was apparent that Mushtri Khanam's reserves of tea were intact, and her steaming cup was brimful and syrupy. Qudratullah had recurring dreams of Mushtri Khanam making tea for him, a clear departure from his past dreams.

On the extreme west of Purana Shehr stood the celebrated madhouse of Guru Bunder. The absent-minded meandering of the long road which issued forth from the railway station and pottered past the police station, Topee Mohalla, the Sessions Court and the zoo, came to a stop at the approach to this dwelling. Apart from the more excitable citizens of Purana Shehr, who were kept there on the pretext of public safety, many adjoining towns too, whose municipal funds could not afford the luxury of a bedlam, had contributed their gods, prophets and other chief executives of heavenly and earthly domains, to its population over the years.

Although Guru Bunder was built in good faith, its construction was contracted out to some mason who had no previous experience of building strongholds. As a result, the iron bars in the windows, instead of being secured in concrete, had wooden frames. As is usual, when the defect was pointed out nobody was prepared to go through the time-consuming paperwork to remedy it. Also, in a madhouse there was no very great danger of someone escaping, since the thought would not occur as plainly to its inmates as it would to a felon in a jail. Therefore, the matter was laid to rest and there was no further action on it.

In due course the termites appeared in Guru Bunder, but their presence was not noted until one of the inmates, hanging by the iron bars of his windows felt it come loose in his hands. He dislodged the other bars too, and with the characteristic cunning of the deranged, dodged the wardens and under cover of darkness, disappeared into the labyrinths of Purana Shehr.

He had been gone one full night when his escape was noticed. The city was already facing problems, and there were strict orders against spreading sensational news. However, the police were alerted and the superintendent personally assured the hospital administration that he would produce results within twenty-four hours. But the police captured any and all demented-looking characters from the city and stuffed them in a cell. An identification parade was arranged, but the needed item was not there. The police were adamant that they had done the needful. This led to an argument and a row between the representatives of the madhouse and the police, and after this showdown, the superintendent let it be understood that the search for the escapee was no longer a priority.

Cobwebs heavy with dust were draped over books and hung from the ceiling and the angles of the walls in Mirzban's room. The smell of dust and mouldy yellow paper presided over the room jointly with the burning smell of the lampshade's enamel. In a moment of forgetfulness, taking the upper window for another shelf, Mirzban had stuffed his books there, and plugged the only possibility of getting any fresh air. He attributed the mud tunnels running wall to wall behind his books to seepage from the rain, and credited the malignancy of some silverfish for the holes in his books. The shelves in Mirzban's room were chockfull of books, dictionaries, almanacs, magazines. Loose papers belonging to numerous articles, and miscellaneous detritus mixed with the documents of lease, utility bills, his daughters' old school reports, medical prescriptions, X-ray reports, and grocery lists. Mirzban had long ago given up the futile annual labour of sorting them out, and now they were evenly strewn all over. Somewhere in this maze, in the vicinity of the table, a chair was stranded. In this chaos even the pleasure of rocking the chair on its hind legs was not without peril. Once, the chair had disturbed a particularly heavy stack of encyclopaedias behind him, causing them to fall over his head. In the opposite corner of the room, across from the sofa lay a bed. After years of use its netting had slackened and taken the shape of a hammock. But the heap of books piled underneath had risen since, raising the netting proportionately, and giving the bed a hump. With his back arched on the hump, and his limbs dangling on the slopes of the mattress, Mirzban lay there on hot afternoons waiting for the heat to subside so he could go out into the kitchen to make himself a cup of tea. Bano Tamanna had bought enough tea from the black market at an opportune time and the house was therefore well supplied.

In the hot and humid afternoons he could neither rest nor concentrate because of the constant commotion on the roof. Every few minutes the children kept running after lost kites and climbing the turrets. When Salar was visiting, Muneemji's shouts were added to the racket. The children disturbed the pigeons in their cages while running around on the roof, and hearing their flutter Muneemji would come out of the shed brandishing his cane, and cursing and shouting, run after the children on his rickety legs.

During the summer, kites eclipsed the sky. With the investment of a few coins anyone could be accommodated in the boundless skies – which became patched with colourful kites – and find seasonal renown with his skill. A kite in the sky was fair game for anyone to challenge and claim once it was lost in a fight. Shops were thronged day and night and the dimly lit street corners witnessed a great amount of wheeling-dealing in kites, *manjha* and skeins. Those who could not buy expensive *manjha*, manufactured it at home by mixing the yolk of a duck's egg with cement powder and rubbing and drying it onto the length of a skein-spool. Like every sport, kite-flying too had its big and small wheels who had distinguished themselves variously in the discipline of robbing breakaway kites, and in the mid-air dogfights with other kite-fliers. There were some masters who could secure a breakaway kite by entwining their line with the line of the floater, and some other experts who could determine who was at the other end, just by watching a kite's treacherous flight pattern.

Mirzban lay prostrated on his bed, still thinking of the possibility of Eternity emerging out of two phases of Time merging, and listening to the clink-clank of the ceiling fan which skimmed the congested air of the room. The clatter was produced by its ungreased armature which suddenly clanked in the middle of relatively quiet revolutions, and disturbed Mirzban in his thoughts. Of late he had experienced a soft drumming in his head whenever he tried to concentrate on his thoughts. Taking it for the symptoms of overwork, or the result of his recent anxiety, he ignored it. He heard it again now, but disregarding it, persevered in his meditations.

The human measure of Time was taken from the vantage point of the Present. The Time past, and the Time to come. The Present seemed to remain stationary. Even though it drifted forward into the Future, the one who conceived it, moved with it too, and did not perceive its movement; much like beings on Earth who could not conceive of the planet's hurtling motion since they themselves moved with it.

But to evolve into Eternity, this crude phenomenon must have seen extensive refinements, developed new dimensions and co-ordinates, Mirzban speculated, nibbling his brittle nails, and peeling the dry skin off his chapped lips, in succession: recently acquired habits which Bano Tamanna had noticed with mild apprehension. By comparing the crude Time of the mortals and the structure of Eternity, points can be identified where modifications have been made in the latter. To begin with, Mirzban's inflamed imagination surmised, it was difficult, if not impossible, for a finite mortal to imagine an infinite, immortal being. However, the finite Time was a small prototype of Eternity. Both had Past, Present and Future. But while the former's traits with the exception of the Present, were close-ended, he hypothesised, the latter's were open-ended, and stretched to infinity on both sides.

The Present of Time remained in a forward flux, stopped at the definite boundaries of its destined Future, and was annihilated; but the Present of Eternity – even though it moved with the Present of the Time – remained fixed: since a motion in either direction, between two poles of infinity, will always begin and end at the centre, the Present. Likewise, an eternal being could travel to any point in the finite Time of the Cosmos, Past or Future, and remain in the Present!

The state of his emotions being too much to feel any elation at cracking the profound mystery of Time and Eternity,

Mirzban went into a daze by the outcome of his fantastic thesis. The sheer pathos of his feelings overwhelmed him. A sob was stifled in his throat. Tears of gratitude coursed down his sunken cheeks. The very idea that God had found him worthy of His Trust!

Mirzban felt the drumming in his head grow stronger until he realised that it was the noise of running feet on the roof. His ventilator opened on the other side of Muneemji's shack. But sometimes Muneemji made it to his side, sprinting after the kite-chasers. Taking it for one such occasion, he ignored it. But he did not hear Muneemji's curses, nor did the noise die out. Also, there seemed to be more than one person on the roof now. A shadow had darted past his ventilator when suddenly a blood-curdling scream rose from Mushtri's room, or so it seemed to Mirzban, and he froze. The next scream broke the spell and sent him running to Mushtri's room.

That afternoon Bano Tamanna had not gone to bed. For two days she had noticed with apprehension her granddaughters scratch their heads. She was now combing their hair for lice with a fine-tooth comb. The girls resented this ordeal and Bano had to resort to the story of the girl who never combed or washed her hair, and one day the lice which grew in her hair dragged her in her sleep to a pond and drowned her. She had just finished the story when Mushtri screamed and when she rushed to her room, the girls followed.

Mushtri was standing in the centre of her bed, screaming and pointing her finger in a corner of the room where a cat was crouching. The ventilator was open and a host of anxious faces blocked the sunlight, as they peered into the semi-darkness of the room, pointing at Mushtri and the cat. When Mirzban came rushing into the room, the cat bolted from the corner where it was crouching, and scampered into the veranda. From the ventilator voices rose as the cat escaped and hearing them Mirzban recognised Lumboo's *lashkar*, although he could not see their faces with the sun at their back.

In the afternoons, when their parents were sleeping and could not remonstrate with them for playing with the guttersnipes, neighbourhood children joined Lumboo's *lashkar* in killing lizards and geckos on the wall after paralysing them with small catechu balls stuck on top of broomsticks. When the Mohalla grounds became verdant with the first showers, Lumboo's *lashkar* displayed their catch of beetles, stuck to the tips of broomsticks, and with glowing faces the children listened to their high-pitched screeches as they were roasted alive in bonfires.

The cat which had dropped into Mushtri's room apparently belonged to Bilotti because it wore a charm around its neck which had come loose in its struggle through the ventilator. Lumboo's *lashkar* had seen it roaming and given chase, for sheer fun. Finding itself cornered, the cat hid inside the ventilator's shed and scraped at the netting which had become brittle with rust. The noise woke up Mushtri and she was just beginning to wonder about its source when suddenly the room was bathed in sunlight as the ventilator was pushed in, and the cat dropped growling from the roof. The ventilator swung shut, but presently opened again and was crowded with the faces of Lumboo's *lashkar*. Petrified, Mushtri somehow managed to scream.

The children ignored the threats of Mirzban and Bano Tamanna, but finally dispersed when they heard the rustle of Muneemji's pyjamas as he came stealthily upon them and grabbed hold of one by his ear. Bilotti had also got up and upon finding out that a cat was being persecuted, shouted curses at Lumboo's *lashkar* from the veranda where the cat was hiding behind her wicker basket. The children generally avoided Bilotti, who was not above pelting them with cobblestones when she saw them running after cats, and they scampered, with Muneemji following them, to the periphery of Qasr-e Yunani's roof.

Bilotti took the cat away, tearfully remonstrating with her. Bano Tamanna took the girls back into her room and having finished combing their hair, plaited it tight and put them to bed. Mirzban was so shaken by this bedlam that all feelings of light-headedness and vertiginous ecstasy disappeared, and no matter how hard he tried to link his mind again to the source of its rapture, the mocking faces of Lumboo's children kept appearing in front of him. He went straight to his medicine cabinet, and tapping a tranquilliser directly from the bottle into his mouth, swallowed it with a glass of water and threw himself into bed.

Slowly Mirzban overcame the unpleasantness occasioned by the commotion and getting up, retired to his desk. There he sat making notes of his thoughts the whole evening, after which he had his dinner and wrote feverishly till the nocturnal songs of the cicadas faded out, and daylight broke upon the eastern sky with the sparrows' chatter.

Mirzban was to be surprised by the termites a few days later. Opening his notebook where he had made some notes that night, he found it delicately perforated where the writing had been. It was still legible, albeit only in stencil, and the paper was untouched except where marked by the ball-point pen. Over the next few days however, this singular marvel of termitic art was badly impaired by some plebeian band of termites, which drilled the notebook at random, destroying both the paper and stencil.

For ages the *Divan* of Hafiz of Shiraz has variously satisfied lovers in the matter of their desire's requital through the prophetic hints hidden in its verses. The seeker of fortune performs ablution; puts on perfume, preferably oil-based, although there is no compulsion in this regard either by the poet or anybody else; and on the night of the full moon, with closed eyes opens the *Divan* at random and puts his index finger on the page. The couplet thus marked by the finger is supposed to contain the augury. Unfortunately, the lucidity of the poet is such that very little room is left for democratic interpretations of his verses. Failing to discover any propitious bidding in the *Divan* during two successive sessions, Salar's mind became clouded, and he grew sceptical. But Ladlay succoured him in time from the depths of his despondency, by taking him to visit Haji Tota Faal Wala.

A visitor to the Sessions Court premises in Purana Shehr, if not out-of-sorts for some reason, had several opportunities of becoming liberally educated at little expense to his time. For example, he could find out that the single largest buyer of pomade creams and jasmine hair-oil in Purana Shehr was its lawyer community; he could also find out that during the manufacture of an affidavit the impact of a manual typewriter's key penetrated six alternate layers of foolscap and carbon papers to leave a greatly diminished but legible imprint on the seventh; and that the lot of mankind was irrevocably distributed among twenty prophecies of Haji Tota Faal Wala, and that the last mentioned fact, having been amply demonstrated to the utmost satisfaction of Haji's vast clientele had become proof to all human revision and reproach.

Haji Tota Faal Wala's clairvoyancy flowered in the court premises, not far away from where Ladlay's office was parked. This encroachment comprised a mat, furnished by the seat of the proprietor, the said twenty packages of portents, and, on a perch, a hoary parrot of exceedingly grimy plumage. This evil-looking bird seemed the custodian of some ancient sorcerer's soul, who anxiously waited for someone to wring its neck and release him from his misery. But no succour came to the forgotten sorcerer's rescue, and the decrepit old parrot remained undisturbed in its slow and silent callisthenics on the bars of its roost.

The court premises were a strategic location for Haji's trade. Nowhere else was despair found in greater numbers, running on two feet, than in court. The terror which the efficient law of the land and the competent honour of the judges instilled in the people was greatly in need of some wizardry relief. Under those circumstances, the secular augury of a bird, who ostensibly had no interest in the affairs of man, sounded the only voice of reason and was their only solace at the day's end. This was also advertised on the placard which Haji kept by his seat: *The parrot is the medium between man and his fate, and, for the consideration of dole for his rations, would furnish the curious with a ready statement of their heavenly credit.* As for Haji, he sat there in social service, as an orderly to the hermetic bird.

All manner of cases and petitioners, as many as went to the honourable judges, were presented before Haji and his parrot. Everyone wished to know their odds. Men in leg-irons, men in handcuffs, patricidal children, infanticide parents, indisposed possessors, disgruntled heirs, derelict mothers, battered women, petty felons, major thieves, young and old loafers, insolvent businessmen, all found their respective lot in Haji's twenty envelopes. As to the astuteness of these prophecies, let it be said that after the parrot's verdict, men convinced of their guilt went to court with less confidence than they came out with, and vice versa. Generally, the odds aligned themselves in favour of Haji's shop and its subscription never saw the down side. Keeping in mind this state of affairs, the superintendent of police had appreciated the rent, as he saw Haji's trade flourishing, and exacted this toll monthly from the ration money of the presaging bird, of whose labours he was a gratis subscriber.

Salar arrived in the court premises in the retinue of Ladlay and Muneemji. As they passed the ranks of lawyers Ladlay made salutations all round. Chhalawa appeared from a corner in his usual rodent-like manner, and stopped when he saw

Ladlay. The notary ignored him and moved on. Although it took him some time to recognise Chhalawa with his shaved head, Muneemji had noticed the queer waiter and Ladlay's avoidance of him. Haji had got up from his bolster where he was reclining to receive Ladlay and company when he saw them heading his way.

As Haji settled down to conduct his business, Ladlay squatted near him, Muneemji leaned forward on his stick and Chhalawa hurriedly procured a chair for Salar, since he could neither stand nor squat. Chhalawa had followed them to Haji's place and Muneemji saw that Ladlay was looking irritated but acted as if he had not noticed Chhalawa's presence. Just then Chhalawa stepped forward and tugged at Ladlay's sleeve. Ladlay looked up innocently and when he saw Chhalawa he beamed cordially at him. But Chhalawa's face remained solemnly anxious as he rubbed forefinger with thumb and asked Ladlay for his arrears. The latter tried to get up with the intention of taking Chhalawa aside, but Chhalawa held him down and again rubbed forefinger with thumb. Cursing him in his heart for his impudence, Ladlay decided to pay up and not create a scene in front of Salar, who had turned to see what was happening.

After this business was settled to Ladlay's detriment and Chhalawa's satisfaction and the latter had toddled away, Haji lowered the parrot's roost onto the ground. Reciting the scriptures he entreated the parrot to address the anguish gnawing at his client's heart, and stroked his tail feathers. This was a signal for the bird to begin his swaggering journey to the deck of envelopes, and like a butcher, jangling his knives together in anticipation of the murder, the bird sharpened his beak on the wood of the roost and issued forth. For a moment he stopped to look at the men, to anticipate from their eager look their just deserts, and to draw on the basis of these observations. After a decade in this line of work, the parrot had become as well-versed with the twenty prophecies as with the nature of man. And when the parrot's eyes met Salar's, Ladlay ejaculated a lusty *Masha'allah!* as Salar's lips parted in a spontaneous smile around his dentures.

In some instances it so happened that the anguish gnawing at the person's heart was greatly compounded because of that avian whim. But an equal number of times it was also diminished by the same agency. The latter proved to be the rule in Salar's case, on whose spirits the prophecy of the bird acted as a potent restorative. But Muneemji was aware of the subtle exchange of meaningful glances taking place between Ladlay and Haji when parting company, and his resolution was beginning to harden.

Although the state of the Yunanis' penurious circumstances amply justified it, Bano Tamanna never bought second-hand warm clothes from the passing carts on the road. To conduct this commerce she went all the way to the Lunda Bazaar in the Kutcha Qila, a good five miles away from home. Buying second-hand clothes in Purana Shehr, from carts on the roadside, in open view of neighbours and acquaintances, was to compromise oneself to public censure and to be labelled a low niggard by society. But buying clothes from Lunda Bazaar kept one safe from public reproof to a great extent. It was the proverbial bath in which everyone was naked, and a woman could not publicly reprove another for being seen there, without compromising herself. Although autumn was still a distant prospect, the bales had arrived and it was decided to open the Bazaar earlier, to reduce the threat of termites damaging the goods in the storage.

A person seen in Lunda Bazaar was either a trader or buyer of second-hand clothes, or else a bandicoot rat, who lived and multiplied in great numbers under the carts where the sun never shone, and the garbage was never cleared during the four months of late autumn and early winter when turbaned, square-jawed Pathans plied their seasonal Lunda business. The air in Lunda Bazaar was congested with lint from the bales and the narrow passages had become further cramped with the crowding-over of carts laden with second-hand clothes on both sides of the alleys. Standing on the merchandise on their carts barefoot, sporting their wares on their shoulder for advertisement, the Pathans hawked their goods, as Bano Tamanna's hands reached out for jackets and cardigans piled up on the carts, and other women pulled out white shirts from other stacks for school uniforms. Knitted self-coloured cardigans were immediately snatched up because they could be unravelled and woven into new shapes and sizes. The children were trying on colourful pom-poms and mittens. But their interest in buying a sweater or cardigan was short-lived and soon gave way to a sense of gloomy trepidation. It was never safe for children to be seen wearing Lunda clothes. Like love, musk and homicide, Lunda clothes too, were exposed in due time, sometimes by the foreign manufacturer's label mistakenly left on, at other times by the side of the lapels the buttons were sewn on – it happened when a boy wore a girl's shirt by mistake. These iniquities were duly noted and their perpetrators regularly chastised by their peers during the recess and after school, throughout the winter term, and their mothers spent a lot of time stitching the torn collars, and darning the sweaters in places where the wool had been violently pulled.

Bano Tamanna soon finished her shopping, and laden with bags full of her family's winter wardrobe and smelling strongly of grime and mothballs, returned home by her usual circuitous route. Without exchanging a glance with anyone, she made her way between speeding donkey carts, stopping once at the chaat shop to have a spicy snack, and rejoicing secretly at having caught so many of her acquaintances in the shameless act of buying Lunda clothes! She opened up her handbag and once more admiringly fingered the garments she had bought. Her clothes were also in constant need of darning, and she usually made new clothes in light colours so that they could be dyed into darker shades later on, and save the expense of a new suit. Most of these suits were retired as pillowcases or tea-cosy covers. She had bought a cardigan for Muneemji. Due to his back problem he preferred them as they were easy to put on. But when she offered it to him and received the customary compliments and blessings, she saw tears in Muneemji's eyes. Bano Tamanna was greatly alarmed and distressed to find him in that state because she had heard of Muneemji crying only once, at her mother's death, who treated him like her own brother and to whom he was as attached. She beseeched him in her mother's name to tell her what was bothering him.

Muneemji's voice became hoarse as he began telling Bano Tamanna about Ladlay's treachery, but he also became animated as he felt the burden of his forebodings lift off his mind. He recounted every small detail which he had been witness to since it had entered Salar's head to communicate to Noor-e Firdousi for the purpose of matrimony; how he saw Salar playing into the hands of Ladlay, and how Bano Tamanna ran the risk of losing every last penny of her inheritance to that scoundrel of a notary, unless something was done urgently to stop him from obtaining a power of attorney for Salar's estate. Bano Tamanna was at first incredulous at what Muneemji told her, but she became convinced as he explained in detail and began connecting small incidents that had intrigued her in the recent past. Words came out fast from Muneemji's mouth, although not without a tinge of guilt at telling on the employer he was devoted to, but he became more confident as he became convinced of the legitimacy of this step by hearing his own arguments. He loved Bano Tamanna and Salar too much to see one destroyed by some caprice of the other, to which that other was blind, and influenced by the evil agency of somebody else.

Bano Tamanna knew that Muneemji would not deny her his help, considering that that was the reason why he had made the disclosure in the first place, and she realised why he felt so hesitant betraying his master, yet his resolve surprised even her. She also understood why Muneemji had asked her to keep the whole business secret until they had received legal advice. She turned to look at Mirzban bringing out his load of books into the courtyard, and sorrowfully realised the futility of asking him to help out in the affair. Mirzban had shown no interest in filing an application for the allotment of the house in Topee Mohalla either, and it was mostly through Bano Tamanna's efforts that the challan form had been filed with a late fee. She thought that in his absent-mindedness Mirzban might even make matters worse by blurting out something in front of Salar or Ladlay. In that difficult hour she could only rely on Muneemji's help, who, besides having a thorough understanding of Salar's estate, was almost as knowledgeable as a lawyer in legal matters.

Ignorant of his wife's anguished solicitudes, Mirzban kept bringing out new loads of books from his room, frantically slapping them together to free them of any clinging insects, and leaving them exposed to the scorching sun which, as if presiding on the day of judgement, seemed to stand a lance-and-a-quarter high. In the shimmering rays and through the haze of hot air which rose from the courtyard and scorched the nostrils, even nearby objects appeared to waver, as in the desert. When the termites stumbled out in panic from the books onto the burning floor to escape the suffocating heat, they were attacked by the ants while their smell made forays into the bindings to hunt for hidden food. In the strong wind the pages of the old books came loose and soared all over the courtyard, some of them carrying, like small flying carpets, the ants still engaged in combat with the half-dead termites. Mirzban had discovered the destruction of the books too late. The termites had spread to his room when, after Salar's arrival, his daughter's old rocking-horse had been temporarily removed there and which, unbeknown to him, harboured a whole army of termites in its hollow gut.

Muneemji kept an unusually sharp lookout during the evenings for Ladlay and Mushtri's balcony courtship and was usually rewarded for his exertions. But while he did not breathe a word of it to Salar for obvious reasons, he avoided mentioning it to Bano Tamanna out of delicacy. While it was neither wise nor necessary to report anything regarding Ladlay to Salar, Muneemji kept himself from broaching the subject with Bano Tamanna who might be offended at Muneemji's prying into affairs concerning her sister-in-law. For the time being it was enough to warn Bano Tamanna that she must keep his intelligence of Salar's intentions secret from Mushtri. And Bano, too, did not think twice about why Muneemji had emphasised that she must not have the slightest inkling. Indeed, Bano Tamanna thought, there was no telling what new ruckus that woman might kick up, if she knew about it, thus complicating the situation further.

Then one day something new developed. Ladlay had not appeared on his balcony that evening. Earlier in the evening, when Muneemji came down from the terrace to get the pigeons' water bowls which he had washed and scrubbed of the accumulated moss layers, he saw Mushtri's room shut and the light off. It was around the time when the lovers usually enacted their pantomime. Singing softly Muneemji collected the clay bowls and returned to the terrace to continue his vigil, grimacing to himself and singing under his breath:

The eyes of the faithful Laila are watchful for her Majnun!
Expectation rends the heart as does dread,
Both foraging on hope like pestilent worms! Bitch!

The night was humid and quiet and after waiting for some time Muneemji got tired of hiding in his cramped position. The alley was deserted and there was no sign of Ladlay yet. He watered the pigeons, changed their feed and was planning to go down again to ask Salar if he needed anything when he heard Ladlay's door open. Muneemji immediately slithered away to his post behind the pigeons' coop. The light in Ladlay's room came on and was switched off after a while. Muneemji thought it odd that Ladlay would go to bed so early, without his ritualistic song and audience in the balcony. While Muneemji was absorbed in these thoughts, Ladlay's head appeared in the balcony, furtively looking around. At the end of the alley one could hear footsteps going away. Apart from that nothing stirred. Muneemji could not see well because moonlight was in his face, and since the light in Ladlay's room was out, he could barely make out the notary's silhouette. Therefore he could not ascertain why the notary was swinging his arm. Leaning forward in his balcony Ladlay seemed to be flailing his arm. It made another motion and froze, and Muneemji heard something like a stone strike the front wall of Qasr-e Yunani. A few moments later, Muneemji saw Ladlay's arm move again, and again he heard the same sound.

'What's …? Oho …!' Shading his eyes from the moonlight to see better, it suddenly dawned on Muneemji, 'I'd be damned if that son of a whore is not trying to throw an anchor into Mushtri's window!'

Ladlay was successful on his third try. There was a faint sound of stone hitting the metal bar of Mushtri's window. Within seconds Ladlay pulled and disappeared inside his window, gathering the thread after him.

'Love burgeons in secret, and the lovers send missives wrapped in anchors,' Muneemji said to himself. 'How wonderful! If her brother comes to know of this whoring business, that good man will die of shame. And at her age too!' he reprovingly snickered. Satisfied that there would be no more commerce between Ladlay and Mushtri that day, Muneemji went to bed. What could possibly be wrapped in the anchor, Muneemji did not give much thought, convinced that it must be a love-letter that was exchanged that night. And therefore he was soon occupied with other thoughts.

When Muneemji thought over his decision to betray Salar he lacked the courage to take that step. But he had given his word to Bano Tamanna and so he thought of an alternate course of action. He would find Bano Tamanna a lawyer and also accompany her to the court for this purpose. But actively siding with Bano Tamanna against Salar was no longer a consideration. If Salar asked him why he went to court with Bano Tamanna, the excuse that she requested him to accompany her would silence Salar. And even if he did blast him he would take it with good grace knowing that he was doing a service to Bano. He decided to speak to Mirza Poya the next day to see if he could recommend a lawyer. Despite his reservations about Ladlay and his associates, Muneemji felt that he could trust Mirza Poya, whom he found congenial and truthful from the start, if a little soft in the head. Wrapped up in these worries Muneemji went to sleep.

Muneemji found Mirza Poya at his post at Chhalawa Hotel, munching an arrowroot biscuit, sipping a bowl of hot milk with his small finger cocked, and with his other hand nursing his leg. He was looking diagonally across the street at Mahtab Cinema, where the billboards were changing stations. A set of men was at work lowering the old hoardings from the cinema walls with the help of a corroding chain and a pulley. Using the same implements, the freshly-painted billboards of the new release were hoisted and fastened on hoops. Mahtab Cinema's change of facade every alternate Thursday evening was an immutable routine and for Mirza Poya its contemplation was as necessary and as much part of the cinema as the film itself. In his free time Mirza was usually in attendance at Master Puchranga's workshop, the creator of these larger than life canvasses, watching that great artist paint his masterpieces.

The portraits were made on the principle of an improvised collage featuring characters in various attitudes of vulgar ecstasy and grotesque anguish without any connection to each other. So while a locomotive mindlessly steamed its way across the landscape, a matron of considerable girth danced in front of it. Two sinister-looking men, one of whom was the hero, grappled each other over her head in the skies, while a lawyer made his oratorical flourishes inside a gigantic handcuff. The plot of these drawings was so confused that often the light of day and the shade of night fell on the same face. All these objects were the standard components of the films, and Master Puchranga's art was their gist.

Mirza greeted Muneemji warmly and called for another bowl of hot milk. While they were waiting for it, Chhalawa walked in and headed straight for the radio. Muneemji saw him turn the volume up and as the old radio started blaring out a film song and an impossible amount of static, he began shuffling from side to side on his mud-plastered feet with his hands raised above his head. Mirza Poya arranged his Rampuri toupee askew, and saying, 'Wah Chhalawa! Wah!' at intervals, started to drum the table, as his arm moved with the beat of the music, and his neck gyrated like a camel's.

Finally the song ended; the counter-boy who had gone inside the kitchen to shout at the cook for not putting enough water in the gravy came out to turn the volume down and Chhalawa went out carrying a tray of food over his shoulder and jingling the change in his waistcoat pocket with his free hand. A waiter put a bowl of milk in front of Muneemji with a layer of cream and pistachio shavings floating on the surface. Thus settled comfortably, Mirza inquired about Muneemji's errand. Muneemji did not give him any details; he just told him that he needed the services of a civil lawyer and asked Mirza to keep it confidential since it had something to do with some family affair. Mirza assured Muneemji of his strictest confidence, gave him the name of a certain Advocate Parwana, and asked Muneemji to give him his reference for a reduction in the fee. Muneemji thanked Mirza but said that he would rather not give any references because of the delicacy of the matter. Mirza good-naturedly assented to the necessity of that precaution even as Muneemji was explaining.

There was utter chaos in the legal system as several important documents had been destroyed by the termites. Moreover, hundreds of false claims were being filed in the civil courts. Women who had had divorce settlements, complained that their husbands stopped making payments when they realised that the record of the settlement was destroyed. After it was known that municipal records were damaged, scores of people came forward to lay claim to their neighbour's property. To save the roof over their heads, people were forced to file counter-claims. And there was no end to those who filed claims of being mentioned in wills destroyed by the termites. The notaries public, oath commissioners, lawyers, false witnesses, magistrates, and sundry other legal inventions had a field day. The chambers of the judges became auction houses where the lawyers bid, and speculated on their clients' behalf, in the newly emerging market of false real estate and land claims.

In the local income tax office only an old list survived, and the commissioner issued claims against people long dead to remit the overdue taxes or face imprisonment. In a few cases warrants were actually issued for the arrest of the dead since their death certificates could not be produced. When the municipality issued temporary slips for birth certificates to make ration cards, a lot of people, Basmati and Tabaq Sahib included, took advantage of the confusion and managed to get two or more documents made, and later applied for as many ration cards, causing the food shortage to became even more severe. The dimensions of the catastrophe were phenomenal.

In partnership with two other lawyers, Advocate Parwana plied his business from an office measuring ten feet by twelve, adjacent to Chhalawa Hotel. Although it looked more respectable, the fact was that their practice was far less rewarding than the lawyers' and notaries' like Ladlay who were right in the middle of the legal market. But like all legal businesses, those days even Advocate Parwana's humble office was full of petitioners and Muneemji found the din maddening.

It was lunch time when Muneemji's turn came and the other two lawyers, having finished with their clients, stepped out. The old ventilator in the wall which connected Parwana's establishment back-to-back with Chhalawa's was covered with hardboard, but although the hardboard was secured with nails, they had been removed from a corner, so that it could be lifted slightly. Parwana ordered lunch for himself through that conveyance and immediately Chhalawa arrived with the tray and reverently put the things on the table. Muneemji noticed that Parwana promptly paid Chhalawa and witnessing that gave him some measure of confidence in Parwana's integrity.

Speaking on behalf of Bano Tamanna, Muneemji tried to explain the situation simply: after briefly recounting the nature of Salar's inclinations and eccentricities, he mentioned that an opportunist had hooked himself to the old man when he realised that he could be steered by his emotions, and Bano Tamanna feared that if Salar was not stopped from proceeding with his present predilections, she might lose all her inheritance to a scoundrel. At that early point Muneemji thought it prudent not to mention Ladlay's name, lest he turn out to be one of Parwana's friends.

Throughout, Parwana sat listening to Muneemji with a degree of conscientiousness which, although engendering Muneemji's confidence in Parwana's assistance, also irritated him a little since he did not seem interested in any more than what Muneemji had to tell him. Finally, when Muneemji had come to the end of his story, he loosened his tie and unbuttoned his collar, revealing the streaks on the inside edge where hair-oil and grime had left marks. 'There are several possible angles of the case,' Parwana said, sliding forward in the chair and throwing his head back on the head-rest. 'The daughter can reasonably ask for an injunction from the Court to keep Jang Sahib from transferring his power of attorney to someone who is not a legal heir. But it is difficult to prove malafide intent unless someone has actually taken measures to inculpate himself, and in most cases the Court gives the benefit of the doubt to the person against whom the injunction is being requested. So, she could try that option but I cannot say how far she could go with that unless she had some tangible proof of wrongdoing against the person in question.'

'And the other option?' Muneemji asked.

'The other option, and I regret to say this,' Parwana made an apologetic face, 'is to wait until Jang Sahib has wrapped up his business in this world.' Here he paused and looked intently at Muneemji for some adverse reaction to his line of reasoning, and finding his face bereft of any expression, continued, 'Then the court could be moved to settle the claims on Jang Sahib's estate.'

'Provided it has not been sold off by the culprit in question and the money and the perpetrator have not disappeared!' Muneemji interjected.

'Yes! Yes! But if the person is known, he could be summoned to appear before the court,' Parwana said, and looked at the ceiling absent-mindedly.

'Is there no other option?' Muneemji inquired, visibly more dissatisfied with the last option than the first one.

Parwana started talking while still looking at the ceiling, 'In law there are quite as many options as there are cases. The thing is to find the option which best suits the circumstances of one's client, and then weigh the chances of success with that option and compare them to chances of success with the other options which may not suit your client to the same degree.' He leaned forward, looked at Muneemji, and continued, 'My job is to inform you of the options available. In Civil cases sometimes the success of a lawyer's preferred option is undermined by a client's interests. A client may be moved to choose an option which suits his considerations better, but which may weaken his case. All of this I understand, mind you!'

'So there is still some other option?' Muneemji inquired.

'Yes, there is!' Parwana threw a quick glance at Muneemji and continued. 'We can seek an injunction against Jang Sahib settling his estate or any proceeds from his estate on someone who is not a natural heir citing the feebleness of his mind as the reason. It will have to be proved that Jang Sahib is of unsound mind, and if that is ascertained to a reasonable degree, you'd have your injunction.'

Muneemji returned home fortified with this knowledge and glad of the fact that the course was now set to put everything in order. He had told Parwana that the opportunist in question was Ladlay and Parwana's incredulous look had made Muneemji anxious for a moment. But there was no reason to worry. As luck would have it, he could not have run into a better person than Parwana where Ladlay was concerned. In their line of duty Parwana and Ladlay had crossed paths several times, mostly to the detriment of the former. But it had less to do with Parwana's forensic ability and more to do with Ladlay's deep understanding of a corrupt legal system. Although Parwana was aware of the practice of courting the judges with money and provisions in the shape of heads of cattle and sacks of seasonal crop, he never advised it to his clients, and consequently reaped the harvest of this negligence.

So Parwana was delighted when Bano Tamanna signed the document authorising him to be her counsel. That was his chance to get even with Ladlay. The course of action Parwana advised Bano Tamanna to take was to appeal to the court that Salar's mental faculties were impaired, that any powers he may confer on a person without his daughter's consent, who was his only heir, must be considered null and void, and that any person who might stand to gain from his actions must be asked to clarify his position to the court. Parwana was convinced that Ladlay's licence to practise law might easily be revoked if it was reasonably proved that he had tried to take advantage of Salar's deranged faculties by influencing him to his personal advantage.

In the beginning the termites were the obvious target of hatred. There was an unseen camaraderie in the neighbours' ranks against the common enemy. People also became more generous. There were stories of great self-denial and sacrifices. Young brides were not beaten up or taunted if their dowry trunks were found infested with termites, or if something, mentioned in the dowry list provided by their parents, was found missing in the trunk. With tears in his eyes when Unnab carried his cockerel to Buddah *kiryana* merchant, he did not have the heart to accept it, or to turn away Unnab empty-handed. So Unnab returned home with his cockerel in the crook of one arm, and a load of rations in the other.

Despite Mirzban and Basmati's strained relations, their

wives shared each other's housework, jointly looked after the children, and did grocery shopping for each other. In the courtyard, Basmati and Tabaq Sahib prepared toxic mixtures of pesticides and insecticides, and wrapping old clothes over their hands to protect them from contact with the noxious compounds, poured them down suspected termite nests. But several gallons of insecticides later, when the insects appeared undaunted, there was widespread panic. All concerted effort broke down, and everyone did the first rash thing which occurred to his mind as a possible remedy.

In his frustration, Tabaq Sahib set fire to the wooden fixtures and furniture which he found badly infested with termites, thinking that doing so could destroy the insects, and put an end to the menace in his house. The fire not only gutted the furniture and fixtures, but also caught Tabaq Sahib's pyjamas. Fortunately, Basmati was there, and immediately threw the mattress over him, and Tabaq Sahib was lucky to get off with only his hair and clothes singed. But instead of being thankful, he admonished Basmati for jumping on him after he had thrown the mattress on him, and fracturing his small finger with his weight.

One night someone set fire to the old tree in the neighbourhood garden. Everyone supposed Tabaq Sahib had done it, although there were no witnesses. Ever since his close call, Tabaq Sahib had overcome his fear and become an authority on fires. He had also put together a small gang of neighbourhood boys who were all too willing to do his bidding and already this band of amateur incendiaries had been responsible for two conflagrations in the neighbourhood. These were houses where Tabaq Sahib had managed to convince the families that the best cure for termites was to set fire to the fixtures. But luckily the termite-infested wood burnt rapidly, and these fast-dying fires did not spread from house to adjoining house, and no extensive damage to life or property was reported.

Tabaq Sahib suspected the trees of harbouring termites. There were grounds for this suspicion. Sap had began to accumulate under their bark, and soon after it cracked and split, the termites covered the exposed trunk with a layer of chewed plant matter mixed with soil. Underground tunnels made by the termites ran from tree to tree, conveying the residents from one tree to the innards of another. They entered the tree from its roots, drilling up, then outwards, and had reached the cambium, making ring-like furrows in the trunk.

One evening Mirzban found Tabaq Sahib at his doorstep. At first he did not recognise him. Tabaq Sahib was wearing a toupee to cover his singed hair. Behind him were three or four boys from the neighbourhood among whom Mirzban could recognise Unnab. They were all carrying torches and smelling strongly of kerosene oil.

'Please ask the ladies to take purdah!' Tabaq Sahib asked Mirzban, 'We would like to use your back entrance to get to the trees in your backyard.'

'What for?' Mirzban asked perplexed.

'Tell him!' Tabaq Sahib turned towards the boys.

'Those trees in your backyard are sending termites all over the neighbourhood. We have come to burn them!' Unnab answered.

'But I don't want them burnt!' Mirzban replied. 'Besides, I have elderly guests in my house and the smoke will fill up the whole house. And what if the house catches fire?'

'There is no need to worry!' Tabaq Sahib spoke. 'We will be here until they are fully burnt. Relax!'

'But I don't want them burnt,' Mirzban again protested.

Tabaq Sahib caught Mirzban by the hand and pulled him close, whispering into his ears, 'Yunani Sahib! You see these boys standing behind? They have seen the termites hiding inside the tree with their own eyes. Now or later, these trees have to be burnt down. It's better if they are set fire to under some supervision. If tomorrow somebody sets fire to them in the middle of the night, and your house burns down, don't blame me!'

'What do you mean?' Mirzban was getting angry at Tabaq Sahib's condescending manner. 'Are you threatening me?'

'We won't take no for an answer,' Tabaq Sahib adopted a harsh tone now. 'The whole neighbourhood is suffering and we cannot allow you to breed termites in your backyard while they destroy our houses. We are simply asking you to let us pass through your house. We can come from the other side too and then you would not be able to stop us. Don't fight! It does not look nice for a good man like you to be defending the termites. Go inside and tell the women to take purdah and open the back door so that we can pass through. We have to go to two other places tonight.'

Mirzban realised that any argument with Tabaq would be pointless. As Tabaq Sahib had mentioned, he could come from the back alley. Although the trees were in Mirzban's backyard, they stood on municipal land and Mirzban had no legal right to stop Tabaq Sahib from proceeding with his plans. And there would be more danger if Tabaq set fire to them at night as he had implied. Mirzban quietly opened the back door, and the gang of incendiaries filed past. Tabaq Sahib put his arm around Mirzban's shoulder and said to him confidently, 'Rest assured! You will see what short work we'll make of it! Hardly an hour and the trees will be reduced to ashes!' Mirzban was chagrined to see Basmati also join Tabaq Sahib. Mirzban realised that he must have been hiding behind Unnab so that he could not see him.

The banyan and yew trees in Mirzban's backyard burnt slowly, and Tabaq Sahib and his gang quietly disappeared after a few minutes. The trees were torched early in the evening but they lighted the sky well into the night. Their avian tenants angrily circled their burning nests in the skies above and the chameleons jumped from branch to branch to escape the burning heat. Qasr-e Yunani filled up with smoke and Salar had such a terrible fit of coughing that Bano Tamanna began to wonder whether or not she would have enough money to arrange for his burial. Tabaq Sahib had come and gone while she was out visiting the neighbours. After shouting at Mirzban for letting Tabaq Sahib set fire to the trees, she again donned her burqa and went looking for the culprit to give him a piece of her mind. Tabaq Sahib must have been expecting her because Bano found a padlock on the front door. Foiled, she walked over to the Basmatis' house, to protest Basmati's behaviour with his wife. But Basmati was not home either, and Begum Basmati had nothing to offer Bano but sympathy for the damage done, and embarrassment at her husband's disgraceful behaviour.

In the morning the trees were still smouldering, and the soot in the air blackened everyone's face. Half the owls dozing in the shade of the ledges and the parapets were devoured in their sleep by the cats.

Neem trees, untouched by the termites on account of their bitter sap, were the only species of flora left standing in the city, and soon hundreds of birds moved into them to nest. But their peace was short-lived. When people found out that layers of neem leaves placed in the kitchen under food boxes greatly reduced the chances of termite raids, the trees were shorn clean of their foliage. And soon enough the people would have felled the trees for furniture if the carpenters had been slow to point out that neem wood was not pliable. Most of the shrubbery which was not destroyed by the fire was consumed by marauding animals. Months later, when some of the dead trees which had escaped being burnt were felled, their trunks were found full of sand-like matter.

In some houses the wooden fixtures were completely ruined, while in others they had yet to attract the termites' attention. When Tabaq Sahib's youngest daughter saw the furniture in the house of one of her friends intact, whereas in her own house it had been totally destroyed, partly due to the termites but mainly as a consequence of her father's counter-measures, she was driven by jealousy to stick a piece of termite-infested wood under the cushions when she went to visit her the next time. That piece of wood was found and the culprit was brought to light. People became suspicious of Tabaq Sahib's visits, and he complained to his friends of a lack of common courtesy in the neighbourhood. But Basmati did not reply. After she had learned about Tabaq Sahib's daughter, Begum Basmati had refused to let her husband bring Tabaq Sahib over. Other people had also become wary of Tabaq Sahib, thinking that probably he was trying to burn down their houses on the pretext of the termites, after he had almost gutted his own. The innocent also suffered. Even goodwill visits by old, friendly neighbours in whose houses the termites had been established, were not above suspicion, and generally not welcomed. The neighbourhood became more isolated, and the warmth and affability of societal demeanour, so necessary to keep the morale high, were hard to come across.

The termites were everywhere, from between the folds of clothes in trunks to their embroidered details. When Bano Tamanna lifted up the sewing machine over the wooden base to change the bobbin she found them hollowing the wooden base, and nibbling at the thread wound around the little reel. Her granddaughters had discovered them in the refrigerator and in the bowls of the ladles. Lumboo had complained that not a single twig of his broom was left, threatening that he would not collect the garbage with a spade, and asked to be paid for a new broom.

For the termites the whole of Purana Shehr was a giant dining table on which the homesteads, like so many dishes, were arrayed high and low and to which they helped themselves night and day. The only place where there were no termites was the Past and that too was fast filling up with the memory of their devastation.

Along with the lawsuit, a percentage of the property's municipal worth was to be submitted to the court, and after a little circumspection Bano Tamanna decided to sell off her remaining six gold bangles that had once belonged to her mother. It was all the jewellery left with her after her daughters' weddings, although she knew they had had their eyes on them when their dowries were being decided. Her daughters realised that Bano would not part with them and except in jest they no longer bothered her about them.

At the entrance to the shop, Bano Tamanna saw a middle-aged woman looking inside the show window. She was leaning with her nose pressed flat against the glass, regarding the displayed jewellery with a delight which Bano Tamanna understood. Despite the impossibility of her ever acquiring that piece of jewellery, a fact that could be surmised from her appearance, the woman's face beamed with the same pleasure that she might have exhibited admiring her favourite child. Bano had the six bangles inside her purse. Something about the woman reminded her of her own married life and her savings and scrapings through which she had managed to complete one gold set. It was quite light and was ultimately divided between her two daughters. Bano's arms closed around her purse, and for a moment she felt the temptation to go back. But justifying her decision by the comforting thought that she could always buy them back if her property was saved, but if it was lost, they would have to be sold sooner or later, she entered the shop.

The jeweller never tired of passing on his merchandise for inspection and trial, knowing that after holding it in their hands and trying it on, it became difficult for women to deny themselves its acquisition much longer. After passing a set to the customer he had moved away when he heard Bano Tamanna enter the shop and thought that she had come to have her bangles polished again. But even as he was greeting Bano with his full-toothed smile, his eyes were watching the movement of the other customer's hands with the competence of an astute vulture. He was always glad to service Bano since he kept bangles in aqua-regia a bit too long, and always managed to dissolve some of the gold. When Bano Tamanna produced the bangles and asked him for an estimate, he was even more pleased. Buying gold, whether from thieves or housewives, was a commerce done entirely to his advantage.

He told Bano Tamanna that she must forget about the market price of the bangles. When selling, the weight of the putty used to fill up the holes and joints for structural strength was also counted with gold, and in the price the greater composite was always the value of the handiwork. Neither of these factors were considered while buying gold by weight.

'These bangles,' he carefully followed the well-rehearsed routine, 'were crafted in a design which, unfortunately, is no longer fashionable, and therefore does not have a ready market. However, I could keep them for you on consignment, if you so desire, and if and when a customer comes along, who might be interested, I will sell it for you for a thirty per cent commission. Believe me madam, thirty per cent is very legitimate,' the jeweller hurriedly put in when he saw Bano look incredulously at him. 'Business is not too good these days and it's difficult even to pay the rent sometimes. Let me tell you this too. You must be patient. Prepare yourself to wait for a few months before a customer can be found who will pay the right price. On the other hand, a customer could be found the very next day.'

That there were no guarantees the jeweller had made amply clear, and finding Bano Tamanna deep in troubled thought, he then proceeded towards the natural culmination of his discourse. 'You are an old and valued customer and I feel myself morally bound to help you out. Therefore, if you would not find it presumptuous, I would like to offer you the price of the gold in the bangles. You should understand that I stand to gain nothing from such a deal since I would have to bear the price of melting them myself.'

Bano Tamanna returned home with a roll of carefully folded notes in her handbag; a little remorseful at eventually parting with the bangles, but overall satisfied with what she considered a successful wrangling session with the jeweller over the selling price. While coming out of the shop she had noticed the woman still looking at the shop window with her nose pressed to the glass. But now she quickly passed by her.

Ever since he had stumbled upon the key to the unravelling of Eternity, Mirzban had felt a vague unease growing inside him. But he plodded under that burden with dignity and not without a sense of responsibility. As he became gradually emboldened by his status as privy to the Almighty's Sacred Confidence, he also found the courage to pick up the thread of his hypothesis where it had been dropped. And a few days after that riotous afternoon when his reflections had been rudely disturbed by Mushtri's scream, the starry sky found him defining the genesis of Eternity again. But this once, inconsistent though it was to the pursuit of metaphysical postulation, Mirzban decided to keep an eye out for any stray projectiles in the heavens. The clouds had parted, though the air was as damp and humid as before. A cloud shaped like a question mark sailing past in the sky that had partially covered the moon, suggested the needed analogy to Mirzban. Two spheres of Time, one with a fixed Present and infinite Past, the other with a fixed Present and infinite Future, hurtling in the boundless space, had somehow collided, like two giant clouds, he began.

At that very moment, a shadow moved stealthily in the veranda and the rustling of its clothes were muffled by Salar's loud snores that were filling the quiet of the night as usual. It moved on tiptoe and came to a stop at Mirzban's room. From the veranda Mirzban could be seen lying on a charpai in the courtyard but it was difficult to guess from that far whether he was sleeping or awake.

'The resulting impact neutralised the fixed polarities of the Present, allowing the two spheres of Time to be merged, into Eternity. And with a simultaneous backward and forward pull of Time, it remained stagnant, and became Eternal Time. Like the egg and the sperm, which had a linear life until they merged and took on a new existence, the two phases of Time when they merged took on a new existence, which was Eternity. And like all timely dimensions, Good and Evil too, lost their polarities and became plain thoughts and acts,' Mirzban thought.

The shadow slipped inside Mirzban's room and headed for the cupboard where Bano kept her valuables. The doors of the cupboard creaked slightly and the rustling of paper was heard in the lower shelf. Soon after that somebody struck a match and covered it in cupped hands so that the flame produced a controlled light. Mushtri Khanam, her face glowing over the flickering flame, was looking intently at some papers spread in front of her on the floor.

It seemed simpler and simpler to Mirzban, the more he thought. Like joining a series of negative and positive integers with the immovable and neutral zero representing the Present of Eternity. It also occurred to him that perhaps the fear of mathematics in children was nothing but a subconscious fear of numbers which represented Eternity.

With great caution Mushtri closed the cupboard and got out of Mirzban's room. After making sure that Mirzban was lying still, she was threading her way past the veranda towards her room when she stepped on one of Bilotti's cats on the floor. The cat had just turned over his side and was lying stretched to his utmost capacity.

But what was that auspicious moment when this sacred collision occurred? Mirzban wondered. It was at that point that the moon, which had gradually been falling down the south-western wall of Qasr-e Yunani, was eclipsed by a dark shadow, like a dun storm cloud and the painful growl of a cat was heard from the veranda. Mirzban turned his head and sat up. Mushtri had reached her room safely, with just a scratch on her ankle. Except for Salar's snores, everything was quiet in the veranda now.

Mirzban looked up. What he could not see clearly from where he was lying in the bed, and which had seemed to him a cloud at first, was the silhouette of two felines against the moon. On the wall, Kotwal and a fat little cat were humping.

The courtrooms included the twenty-odd rooms of the Sessions Court building which were distributed between three floors. It was an old building with the roofs supported on wooden beams. The sweeper, entrusted with the duty of keeping the place dust free, hardly had time to cart the dust out from the courtrooms in the morning before the judges gave audience, so he found it more convenient to sweep all the dust under the hollow wooden platforms where the magistrates sat. Thus a mound of waste gradually rose under them, permeating the courtrooms with a rich stench not unlike the one around receptacles of waste.

Personal appearance had been the first casualty of the successive power breakdowns and the depressing mist. People often arrived at work with their hair standing up on one side of the head. Clothes were not ironed because there was no power. In most cases they were not washed either as water too was in short supply. Faces shone with oiliness. This state of affairs was also visible in the courtroom and an ever greater number of inelegant faces were in attendance.

Parwana sat through the first trial with a glowering face and answered Bano Tamanna's muffled but agitated queries about the procedures brusquely. After consultation with Muneemji, Bano Tamanna had finally decided to request an injunction from the court citing Salar's unsound mind as the reason for the order. Muneemji had also accompanied her to the court. The magistrate was to conduct the hearing of a case, and as Parwana wished to avoid one of his angry clients, he proposed that they wait for the magistrate in the courtroom and then follow him to his chambers once the hearing was over.

The case of Zubaida Pewandi vs Sarmast Pewandi was being heard. The plaintiff's husband had been missing from the house for some time when somebody saw him in another quarter of Purana Shehr, living in what seemed to be conspicuous circumstances. When inquiries were made by the wife's relatives it was found that he had recently remarried and had set up house with his second wife. After the initial weeping and wailing was over, and after the relatives' entreaties to divorce the second wife were turned down by the man and their innuendoes fell on deaf ears, and it became abundantly clear that he had no intention of returning to his first wife, they incited her to move the court against him. She had nothing further to lose from following such a course. According to the family laws it was incumbent upon the husband to seek written consent from his first wife if he wished to take another woman in matrimony, or else face prosecution. The first wife's relatives thought that just the threat of the lawsuit would be enough to bring the man to his senses, but contrary to their expectations the man had challenged them to go ahead.

The defendant, Sarmast Pewandi, was called to the witness-stand by the prosecution lawyer, Qabeel Bhutera. The oath was taken and the frown on Parwana's face became more apparent.

'Mr Sarmast, is it true that you are now living in matrimony with a lady half your age?'

'Objection, Your Honour! The age of the lady has no significance in the matter,' the defence lawyer interjected.

'Sustained!' the judge barked, annoyed at having to mediate at the very first question, and also visibly surprised at the unawareness of both prosecution and defence lawyers, of the judge's inalienable right to be allowed to warm up to the case without assisting the discourse during the first few dozen questions.

'Mr Sarmast, is it true that you are now living in matrimony with a lady other than your first wife?' Bhutera rephrased the question, forced to realise the error of his ways. He well knew how disastrous a lawyer's trespassing on a judge's rights could be. The defence was also more cautious.

'Yes. I am now living with my second wife,' Sarmast replied in a calm voice.

'Would you explain the circumstances under which you left Zubaida Bibi, your first wife?'

'Gladly. I told her that I felt the need to take another wife since she was barren.'

There was a stir in a corner of the courtroom where Zubaida Bibi was sitting with her sister. The words 'scheming liar' and 'cheat' were heard.

'Order!' the judge listlessly banged the gavel, looking with explicit disdain at the assembly.

'So you told your wife that you intended to marry someone else,' Bhutera continued.

'Yes!'

'What was her reaction?'

'She saw my point and gladly gave me her consent when I asked for her permission.' Sarmast replied. There was some rumpus again. 'Order! Order!' Again, the judge's anger was directed more at his having to call the house to order than at the cause of the commotion itself. The lawyer walked over to his client and asked the woman to be quiet. The questioning resumed but the whispering in the plaintiff's quarters did not stop. Bano Tamanna noted that Sarmast avoided looking in the direction of his first wife and her relatives. When she looked at Parwana from the corner of her eye she found him contemplating the rafters on the ceiling but the frown on his face was undiminished.

'You say that she gave you her consent, willingly?' Qabeel Bhutera put new purpose in his voice which did not seem to bother Sarmast in the least.

'That's right!' he answered in the same complacent tone.

'What did you do next?' Bhutera continued.

'What do you mean what did I do next? We went to the court the next day and she signed the paper.'

Sobs were heard from the corner where the first wife was sitting. But Bhutera seemed to be expecting this answer and the need he felt to move to the next question was greater than the need to placate his client. The defence lawyer was not slow to take notice. He realised that Bhutera had something up his sleeve. Sarmast quickly looked at his first wife and turned his head away. Bhutera looked at the judge.

'Proceed!' the judge said.

'Do you have the document with you now?' Bhutera asked without changing his expression in the least.

'No.'

'Where is it now?'

'We had termites in the house but I didn't know about it. I had kept it with my other documents. They were all destroyed.'

'Huh!?' the judge looked at Bhutera as if to ask where they should go from there.

'Were there any witnesses to the signing of the permission form?' Bhutera continued his questioning without looking at the judge.

'Yes! One was my brother who was visiting from upcountry. He is not here today but the other person is present.'

Unnab Khan got up from a corner of the room to take his place in the witness stand. Bano Tamanna knew Unnab and was a little surprised. Muneemji also looked at Bano Tamanna. He had also recognised Unnab. Parwana just muttered inaudibly when he heard the cock-fighter take oath and became silent.

'Unnab Khan, were you a witness to the signing of the document in which my client, Zubaida Bibi, allowed her husband to marry again because she was barren?'

'Yes! As God is my witness, I was there and the document was signed in front of me. It was typed on stamp-paper and later I put my signature as witness,' Unnab replied.

'Unnab Khan! Can you read English?' Bhutera suddenly asked.

'No! But the notary translated the document for all those present,' Unnab replied promptly. The defence had obviously prepared him for that question.

'Thank you, Unnab Sahib! That will be all for now,' Bhutera said and walked away importantly to his client and stood looking in the air for a few seconds while Sarmast was called to the stand again. Then Bhutera turned with the flourish of a cat tired of playing with the mouse, in full realisation of his hour of triumph.

'So the paper was eaten up by the termites?' he asked Sarmast with great deliberation.

'Yes. I have told you,' Sarmast was subtly displaying signs of irritation at his lawyer's advice, who looked at him with a mixture of admiration and approbation. Bhutera's line of questioning was unusual, and therefore worrisome. But his lawyer had not told Sarmast that, so as not to play into Bhutera's hands by unnerving him unnecessarily. If Bhutera was bluffing, he could not go too far, he thought.

'But you remember having it typed and signed in these premises?'

'Yes!'

The judge moved restlessly in his chair. It irritated Bhutera but he continued after throwing a quick glance at the platform, although he decided to come to the point quicker than he had planned, and felt as deeply grieved as someone who had been denied indulgence in his rightful glory. 'So you remember it very well?' he asked in a rather pensive voice.

'Yes!'

'Obviously it was done on a stamp-paper and a carbon copy was also made?'

'Of course. I know that much law. But as I said, everything was destroyed, including the carbon copy. But if you asked me now who witnessed the termites eating them, I wouldn't know what to say!' Sarmast replied and looked around.

There was an explosion of laughter from the assembled audience. The judge also seemed pleased with the wisecrack. The defence lawyer drummed his desk with his fingers and smiled in approval. The defendant was becoming confident and cheeky by equal degrees, realising that perhaps Bhutera didn't really have anything further to ask, and no direction to proceed in. But Bhutera stood there without the least change in his expression.

The defence lawyer got up. 'Your Honour, please ask my learned friend to come to the point,' he felt encouraged by the beating Bhutera had taken, to press him to conclude the questioning.

'Mr Bhutera, I must say …' the judge interposed.

'Yes My Lord, I will come to the point right away! What I would like to ask the defendant is to produce the register in which the sale of the stamp-paper was recorded. He must have bought it from one of the notaries in the courtyard, and they will have a proof of the sale!'

Parwana showed interest in the proceedings for the first time by un-crossing his legs and sitting up in his chair. Bano Tamanna was also excited about this new turn of events. If the man was unable to produce the record, they might see some instant action.

The judge looked genuinely grieved at this unforeseen piece of cleverness on Bhutera's part. It meant another hearing possibly. Under ordinary circumstances the judge would have looked forward to as many hearings as possible, as he was in no way unmindful of the import of his office and the prestige which his seat behind the sculpted pair of scales bestowed on his person. But under the extraordinary circumstances prevailing in the city, the pressure of the court appearances had begun to take their toll on him, and he wished to bring the termite-related cases to an end as soon as possible, so that his life might again resume its normal dignified course. However, despite all these considerations he controlled his emotions and pressed Sarmast, who was taking an inordinately long time answering, for a reply.

'That can be arranged!' a visibly ruffled Sarmast finally answered when his lawyer winked at him with a nod. Nobody including Bhutera and the Honourable Justice noticed this fine piece of artfulness.

'The register may be produced in the court,' the judge said.

'Your Honour, my client needs time to produce the register,' the defence lawyer now got up. The judge turned to the defendant in the witness box who was looking at his lawyer.

'What would be a reasonable amount of time?' the judge stifled his yawn with difficulty and his eyes watered with the effort.

'A week from now, Your Honour,' the lawyer said.

'Granted,' the judge said, overruling Bhutera's contention that the man could be escorted out to bring in the register. The judge might have been in a hurry to close the case, but he did not wish to set the bad precedent of acting immediately.

That kind of thing had far-reaching consequences. Therefore the hearing was adjourned until the next week.

Bhutera returned to Zubaida Bibi to try and console her. Her husband passed in front of her with his friend without once looking at her. Unnab had slipped out of the room quietly. Chairs scraped, feet shuffled. Some people left the courtroom, and another group took their place.

Bano Tamanna was seriously concerned about the judge falling asleep by the time he was finished with the hearing. But she did not get a chance to share her fears with Parwana who was shaking his head vaguely, disregarding her anxious looks, as the proceedings began for the next case. Muneemji was leaning forward on his cane and Bano Tamanna could not figure out whether he was awake or fast asleep. The judge drank a large glass of water and looked around helplessly, as another party moved forward and settled itself on the front benches.

The municipal inspectors had evacuated some old houses in which the termites had damaged the wooden rafters which supported the roof. There was good reason for this precaution as falling bricks had already injured children in one house. However, the evacuees were not provided any alternate accommodation and after a brief stay in the municipal grounds, they were asked to find themselves a shelter until their houses were repaired and certified fit for occupation by the municipality. The fitness certificates were available in the municipal inspector's office, provided one was willing to cough up a few hundred rupees – still considerably cheaper than the cost of repairs. A family of seven found it a good bargain, and four of them were killed when the roof collapsed over their heads in the rain the following week.

The people evacuated from their homes had by now formed an association. They realised that asking for the suspension of the municipal inspector was not going to benefit them, because the family had actually brought it on themselves, so they decided to sue the municipality itself, for issuing a fitness certificate to a house which was uninhabitable, thereby causing loss of life. The members of the association thought that through legal pressure they might be able to force the municipality to find them alternate accommodation sooner, or, at least have the municipality foot the bill for the repair of some fifteen houses whose residents had been forced out by its edict. The lawyer had built the case on some obscure provisions of the property taxation laws and its strength lay in exploiting public sentiment to force a sympathetic ruling rather than having any legal standpoint.

The lawyer representing the association called the administrator of the municipality to the witness stand. The administrator was a short, stocky fellow who seemed to know the witness box well from previous court attendances in the line of duty. He immediately leaned one elbow on the railing, as if from long habit, and knowledge of how to make oneself comfortable in the stand. The defence lawyer asked him to describe the rationale behind the municipality's action to have families evicted from their houses.

'It is like this,' the administrator started, 'You either leave the people to their fate, or you take steps to keep them from danger. We did the latter and therefore I find myself in the witness stand today.' He looked around with the air of a martyr, and the confidence of a man who knows that no matter how disastrous the results of his presentation, it was the municipality after all, which had to take the brunt. 'The houses from which people were evacuated were in bad shape. The roofs could have caved in any day!' Then looking up at the ceiling of the courtroom and pointing at the rafters which ran from side to side, he added, 'You see those beams here today. But do not be deceived by their appearance. It is quite possible that tomorrow they may come *arrar-dham!* down on you all when the court is in session.' At this unexpected piece of information there was a brief silence which was broken by a murmur. It immediately heightened as the whole assembly began gesticulating and pointing at the ceiling. A few chairs were pushed back as some people got up in excitement to look more closely at the rafters.

The judge called the assembly to order and slowly raised his heavy head to look up at the ceiling. Others followed his gaze. The rafters seemed quite strong but then, what did the municipality administrator just say! 'They look strong, but in reality they may have already become hollow.' One loud noise, one little movement and the whole ceiling will be upon me, the judge's face seemed to be saying. He slowly produced a handkerchief from under his robe and wiped the perspiration from his face. Everyone, including the lawyer of the prosecution, was visibly shaken by the remarks of the administrator standing nonchalantly in his corner, looking more comfortable than ever.

'What do you mean by this remark, Mr Administrator?' the judge managed to ask.

'Your Honour, I am just stating the facts. Our inspectors had done a city-wide survey of the old buildings, and the beams were found infested with the termites in six out of every ten houses. The extent of the damage was different in different cases and therefore we did not evacuate each and every house. Only houses with extensive damage to the rafters were evacuated. We did not force people out unnecessarily where basic repair was deemed sufficient to check further decay. However, one cannot predict the intensity of rain, and the damage it might cause if it continues. Such things only God Himself knows!'

'And you say that the roofs of the court are not safe either?' the judge asked. He had taken the questioning upon himself now and ignored the attempts by the prosecution to interrupt with a question.

'I don't really mean that, Your Honour. They may or they

may not be. Somebody has to inspect them to determine the true picture.' The administrator thought it best not to commit himself on that score, and that was his mistake.

'What do you mean by that?' the judge bellowed, then looked up in terror and suddenly lowered his voice realising the possibility of the roof caving in. 'Didn't you just say that the municipality inspectors had done a city-wide survey? Are you going to tell me now that this survey was confined to the residential sector only?'

'Ea ... it was confined to the residential sector, Your Honour, as far as I know, though ... at the last hour we also decided to include the public schools at the recommendation of the Mayor.' The administrator was now standing erect and was no longer happy with the way the proceedings were moving. For the first time his face betrayed an expression of unease. The prosecution lawyer was in a fix himself but did not find it proper to ask any questions, as the judge was battering the defendant's representative himself.

'How can the good Mayor make an exception in the case of the schools and ignore the safety of other public buildings? I must remind you that all lives are sacred in the eyes of the state, whether they be under the roof of a school or a courtroom!'

'Er ...' the administrator opened his mouth to say something but the judge did not give him a chance.

'I cannot continue to hold court here knowing the danger to which I am exposing the lives of all these people assembled here. I must put this matter before the District Judge. And until such time that he arrives at a decision or makes arrangements with the municipality, and the safety of life has been guaranteed for all, I adjourn this court,' the judge declared to the surprise of everyone and banged his gavel.

The whole thing happened so unexpectedly that everyone was astounded, and only realised the full significance of the judge's remarks when he had risen from his seat and, in what was a clear departure from routine, without waiting to check whether any of those present had risen or not, gathering the folds of his robe around him, disappeared into his chambers, walking at a rather brisk pace.

Bano Tamanna ignored Muneemji's outburst as he began to abuse the judge and the legal system, and asked Parwana to exit the room with her to discuss what they must do next. But Parwana advised her to remain seated. The corridors outside would be noisier. Bano restrained herself with difficulty while the people walked slowly out of the room, and the moment the courtroom became relatively empty, she assailed Parwana with questions regarding the fate of her case. But Parwana could not offer any help, since the matter now rested with the District Judge, as the judge had mentioned. To obtain a hearing date was not possible either. The loss of her gold bangles figured prominently in the dark thoughts which this turn of events engendered in Bano's mind. In the light falling from the tall stained-glass windows in which some panes were broken, Parwana's coat shone in places where it was layered with grime. As he got up after sorting the papers in his file, to Bano Tamanna he looked like one of the fixtures in the courtroom: a very part of the run-down room and crumbling mechanism which was chiefly responsible for her ruin. This prospect appeared clearly before Bano's eyes for the first time.

The District Judge arrived at the obvious solution. The court would remain in recess until the municipality had provided it with a fitness certificate for the premises, and a letter of guarantee against damage to human life. The legal process was halted and everything came to a standstill by this decision. But while some people suffered as a result, a lot of problems were averted, which would have resulted if the cases had been allowed to accumulate at their present speed.

For the past few hours Salar had been discussing the disappearance of his documents with Ladlay. The notary maintained a pregnant silence while Salar was speaking and shook his head to show his dismay at the incident. When Salar was finished Ladlay looked around suspiciously to see if anyone was listening, and said, 'It sometimes happens that heirs to an estate do not see the wisdom of an investment and are sometimes led to commit rash acts. Now I am not naming any names under this roof, but I understand human weaknesses, especially in women, and so should you, Salar Sahib. Nobody can put a stop to people's tongues. They circulate all kinds of gossip, and since Bano Tamanna is a woman after all, she can be swayed by what she hears other people say of Madame Noor. Now I am hypothetically speaking here, but she may think you are giving her rightful share to someone who is unworthy; she may also be moved by self-interest which is understandable.'

'And what about my interests? Am I not entitled to seek my comfort in this world?' Salar asked in a hurt voice.

'Oh, I am sure she would not see that you are only making an investment in your own future,' Ladlay replied.

'Enough!' Salar almost shrieked and broke into a wheezing cough. Ladlay had already stopped and he saw Salar's face become black with anger as he began to speak again even before he could fully recover, 'I would not ... hear my daughter make plans for me. What plans ... what plans could she have for me, I ask? Huh? I am sure her days are ... spent ... waiting for me to die. And that son of a whore ... Muneemji, he must also think I am a candle about to be snuffed out. No wonder that dog ... is wagging his tail now at Bano to secure ... his future supply of bones. Rascal ... I am going to surprise all of them!' Salar shook his head in derision, and began to cough again.

Ladlay had to prepare Salar's mind for the coming days. He realised that the old man's rage was on the rise and he must say whatever he had planned to say at that very moment, as he might not get a better chance. 'Since you have mentioned it, I will take the liberty to suggest that you become more careful. I mean … how should I say it without running the risk of being thought presumptuous …?' Ladlay uncrossed his leg, sorrowfully put the cup of tea on the side table and pulled his chair closer to Salar's bed. Salar was looking at him thoughtfully. 'I must say I am in a difficult position. Here I am enjoying the hospitality of this house, and …' Ladlay shook his head grievously. He seemed to be undergoing some inner conflict. Salar was eagerly watching him. The conflict in Ladlay's mind must have reached a successful resolution for he made a resolute face to brace himself for what he had to convey to Salar. 'I must remain true to my duty,' he said. 'As your lawyer I must advise you to be careful under the present circumstances. In everything, including food. The world is full of surprises,' Ladlay said and quickly searching Salar's face for his reaction noticed a shadow pass over it. He decided that he had taken the risk and he must now complete it. He continued, 'But I must advise you to act quickly. If the tenants in your building get to know that the documents are missing, irrespective of whether the termites destroyed them or whether someone put them out of your reach …' and Ladlay again darted a look at Salar's face, and finding him pensive, continued, 'there is no knowing what mischief they and their lawyer might think of. Besides, they will also get the idea that there is someone with a vested interest who is not inclined to sell the building, and they may obtain a stay order until they find out for themselves who that someone is, involving you in an endless legal battle.'

'So what is to be done, now that the documents are gone?' Salar inquired in an irritated voice, after, what seemed to Ladlay, a rather long pause.

'My advice would be to proceed with your initial plan about

the power of attorney. No one knows that the documents are not with you. And nobody will ever know. In the meanwhile, I will go to the upcountry municipality and get the details about your property. Since I will have the power of attorney, I will have a new registry made in your name. Nobody knows me in the city there and it will be more easily arranged than, for example, if you or Muneemji, who are known there, had to go. Once that is done, I will immediately arrange for a real-estate agent to sell off the property. I don't think it would take more than a couple of weeks, since it is prime property and you have already had offers for it. In my absence you could maintain contact with Madame Firdousi so that she would be ready to make time for the concert when everything is ready.'

'Where will she stay in Purana Shehr?' Salar suddenly asked.

'That should not be a problem. We could rent a house overlooking the river for the duration of her concert. I am sure Madame Noor would like it. That way she could be close to her patron and benefactor,' Ladlay said in flattering overtones.

'Muneemji! Muneemji!' Salar called out. 'I must ask him to start searching for a house.' Just then Muneemji was listening to Bano describe again where she had put the documents in the cupboard and where only some fragments of termite-eaten paper were visible now. Muneemji quietly walked away from Bano, after looking at her in a manner which seemed strangely secretive to her.

Salar was evidently pleased with those encomiums of Ladlay's and underwent a complete change of mood. He kept snickering uncontrollably but would not hear anything about him being a benefactor of Firdousi. He vehemently contradicted Ladlay. 'No, No! *Nauz'obillah*! It is not our place to give a boon to Firdousi. We could rent the house near the river though ... and then how long would she stay?' he asked expectantly.

Ladlay immediately replied, 'Nobody can tell! Madame is very gracious and we could always request her to extend her stay. Maybe, if the first concert is successful, she might like you to accompany her to her house in the Capital. You could stay there quite comfortably too. Also it would be best to keep away from here as people who do not have an understanding of things might jeopardise matters by inopportune remarks. You know what I mean ...' Ladlay looked at Salar again who was nodding his head gravely. Muneemji entered the room at this point and Ladlay became cautious. 'But we must look ahead for now,' he said. 'I see so many things happening within a matter of weeks.' With a satisfied smirk on his face Salar began scratching his head and Muneemji looked on apprehensively as Ladlay took his leave and got up.

Fatalistic by belief, and prone to a supine approval of divine counsels, the people were convinced by Imam Jubba that their own sins had helped bring the termite plague on their heads. And there was no shortage of phenomena to which the bursting forth of heavenly rage could be attributed. As God's policeman, Imam Jubba had rounded up the usual suspects: the decay of youth's morals, the avarice of the merchants, the worshippers of the graves, even the evil of the pets; pious and devoted pets are known to sense a disaster before it visits their masters' heads, and are supposed to take it on their person and die, thus sparing the households any inconvenience. But the animals were hale and hearty, and, if anything, multiplying in even greater numbers than before.

When a grave was dug in the Purana Shehr graveyard, the diggers unearthed a termitarium, which threatened to fill up the grave with the insects. Imam Jubba's advice was sought, and according to his directions a second grave was dug. And again, the spades hit a nest. Imam Jubba, under whose supervision the second grave was dug, made many grave and ominous motions with his head, to the terror of the deceased's family. Then fulminating incoherently, he ordered a third grave to be explored. But the termites had taken over the burial grounds, and despite the lamentations and protests of the aggrieved family, the Imam had the body interred there, remarking that the deceased was a great sinner indeed, and the termites filled his grave each time to show God's judgement on Earth, for others to take example from.

But although he remained as vociferous as before in the condemnation of the sins of his constituency, even Imam Jubba had been taken unawares by the termites. There were standard prayers for ending drought; prayers seeking clemency for the dead in the hereafter; for deliverance from the evil of Satan and his minions and pinions on earth; for warding off wild beasts; for taming reprobate children and headstrong horses; for the bite of the mad dog; for the recovery of stolen goods, and so on; but there were no prayers anywhere in the vade mecum of heavenly petitions which addressed the evil of the termites. But Imam Jubba was not to be daunted. When he saw how the ground lay, he began to blare out with even greater fervour that there was hope yet, but with one stipulation: that the city be first purged of all sins. He forbade anyone to visit cinema-houses, or indulge in playing cards, or visiting the quarters of the *qalandars* from where nobody ever returned sober. He encouraged people to visit the house of God regularly, do ablutions each time they broke wind or defecated, and shower whenever they had sinful dreams or slept with their wives.

Although the termites continued their work regardless of the exercise of these immaculate measures, in the populace they inculcated a sense of chastity and a feeling of moral rectitude, bringing some comfort to the pious in their suffering.

The barefoot *kathputli* walas made their annual forays into Purana Shehr every spring. A turbaned man, wearing garlands of chrysanthemums around his neck, carried the whole marionette theatre in two tin canisters balanced across a pole on his shoulders.

In the old city the fierce handlebar moustaches of the *kathputli* walas raised some apprehensions among children, but their aspects, like the guise of an animal which allows it to conform better to its habitat, were more in keeping with their quarters in the grim desolation of the desert, than with their shy and obliging natures. Their beautiful women stalked down the street by their sides, surveying everything and everyone with their dark, proud eyes, and giggling, perhaps at the sombreness of the city folk, with the corners of their *ghagras* clenched between their teeth. The men played the clapper-drum, and with shrill voices the women announced the arrival of Patay Khan and company at the head of an unforgettable tamasha.

Patay Khan was the prophet of drama. This versatile marionette played anything thrown his way, from the unbelievable inventory of historic roles in the *kathputli* walas' dramatic stock, during the spring of their urban wanderings. The *kathputli* walas' was a wonderful history, no less fantastic than the one taught in schools. But it was far more entertaining, and while history did not fit the interpretations of the school textbook boards, one still wished she was as ingenious in her fiction as the *kathputli* walas were in theirs.

Mirzban had not constructed any rooms in the courtyard, unlike his neighbours, and as usual, when they arrived in Topee Mohalla, the *putli* walas set up their show in Qasr-e Yunani. Bano Tamanna enjoyed the *putli* tamasha herself and with her granddaughters in her train, she bustled about helping the *putli* walas set up in the courtyard, now bringing out the bamboos from the mosquito netting for their tent, and now searching the laundry basket for old sheets for curtains. The news of Patay Khan's arrival spread in resounding waves across the neighbourhood, and sent droves of children trotting over to Mirzban's house.

The marionettes were arrayed on one side of the stage and a man and a woman took their strings out of public sight once the money had been collected. The marionettes were dressed in bright pleated skirts and tinsel-decorated jackets with their arms bent at the elbow. While the lady marionettes walked with the swinging gait of the *kathputli* walas' women, the marionette men got their stilted swagger from that of the clan's blades. In moments of anxiety, not only did their human voices change to the shrill notes of birds but their suspended movements also became so fluid that it seemed they had taken wings. One man squatted on one side of the stage with an organ and clapper-drum to prompt the performance with his narration and orchestra. After everything was settled and Bano Tamanna had taken a privileged seat right next to the stage with her granddaughters, he declared the show open by turning the clock back a few centuries to a period of uncommon commotion in Moghul history.

At that point in time, Emperor Akbar the Great was seething with rage. His only son and the heir to the Moghul throne, Prince Saleem, later known to history as Emperor Jehangir, had become so ensnared by the charm and beauty of Anarkali, one of the Prince's courtiers, that he forgot the court's decorum. That invoked Akbar's wrath, who had the dangerous Anarkali bricked-up alive into a palace wall, while the fat and capricious prince looked on.

By their clever improvisations the *kathputli* walas had greatly improved upon this appalling history. A last minute rescue had been engineered for Anarkali by the gallant Patay Khan, a character unknown to history, who replaces the irredeemable Prince Saleem as heir to the Moghul empire.

According to this version, as Anarkali was whisked away from the clutches of death, in a great din of whistles and bird song, the fury of the Emperor turned upon himself, resulting in self-murder. Patay Khan, putting one foot casually on the throne, declared the empire a republic and called for free and fair elections within ninety days, thus rounding off the Moghul dynasty far more romantically, on the gay and cheerful notes of the clapper-drum.

After the main actors had been lying still on the floor for a few moments, their strings were pulled up. The children clapped, the *putli* walas encouraged them, and another set of marionettes descended jerkily from the roof.

The next story was dedicated to the Father of the Nation. In this matchless play, Patay Khan, the redoubtable Father of the Nation, shows great exasperation with Queen Victoria, played by a grim and ungainly marionette with a tin crown over her head, who, after listening to his petitions, continually refuses to grant him a homeland for his naked and hungry people. The valiant Patay Khan asks her one last time to make up her mind, and finding her irresolute, after a count of three, pounces upon her with his sword drawn. The fat queen, surprisingly agile for her advanced age, gives Patay Khan a good fight. But his swordsmanship soon prostrates the fat slug, and he leaves the palace amidst songs and whistles as usual, vociferating 'Long Live Patay Khan!' and 'Long Live Patay Khan's Buffalo!' (which last mentioned creature never once made an appearance during the summary negotiations, nor indeed afterwards), marching to the familiar beat of the clapper-drum.

The show was hardly over and the *putli* walas were still dismantling the bamboos when Bano Tamanna heard someone shouting in the alley. She was in the kitchen, making tea for the *putli* walas. The neighbourhood boys had again got into a fight over something and their parents were trading accusations, she thought. But she was intrigued when she recognised the heavy, baritone voice of Imam Jubba asking for Mirzban. Muneemji was already at the door and he told Imam Jubba that Mirzban was not home. Bano went to the door, covering her head, to find out what the Imam wanted. Muneemji made way for her, whispering that Jubba seemed angry at the *putli* walas. Their women had already heard the Imam and two of them also peeped from behind Bano Tamanna to see what the shouting was about.

'*Bibi*! Don't you know that these people spread infidel practices and idol-worship in the city? How could a pious family like yours give them a place to enact their depravity?' Imam Jubba asked Bano Tamanna after she had identified herself. He was looking hard at the ground but his stern voice made it clear who was in charge. There were two other short and stocky men by his side whom Bano did not remember seeing before. They too were looking intently at the ground and stroking their beards.

'We always let them come and stay in our courtyard. Children enjoy that ...' Bano tried to answer, not knowing how to tackle this unexpected attack on the *putli* walas. But Imam Jubba cut her short.

'*Allah'o'Akbar*! Children enjoy it! See ...!! See ...!!' Imam Jubba looked at his two accomplices who shook their heads in disapproval of Bano's remarks. 'Children enjoy it!' Imam Jubba took a special delight in repeating Bano's phrase. 'Enjoy it indeed *bibi*! And what comes of this enjoyment? A termite plague, no less! Doesn't that say something to you about the whole game? The entire city has been caught up in the punishment. Now's the time to stop this deviltry, this satanic workshop!' he declared.

When they heard this the two *putli* walas' women rushed inside to ask their group to hurry and pack up. One of their men came over to Muneemji's side who was lighting a cigarette to ask if anything was wrong. Muneemji mumbled something and went inside without answering him satisfactorily.

'But nobody has complained,' Bano protested. She was afraid of Imam Jubba but she was also feeling a little angry that an innocent thing like the *putli* tamasha was being blown out of proportion by Jubba.

'Everyone is complaining! Everything is being destroyed by the termites. The doors are complaining, the windows are complaining. Look at the idols these heathens carry around. None of them have been destroyed by the termites! Why, I ask? Aren't they made of wood? What has kept them from being destroyed but the fact that they are the devil's progeny themselves?'

Bano had no answer for that and she wanted to end this dialogue with Imam Jubba which was made more intimidating by the presence of his two toadies. 'They are already leaving!' she said.

'Very well! We shall wait at the end of the alley until they leave. We want to make sure they do not take their sinful business to another house in Purana Shehr. Come!' Imam Jubba said and walked away with his two flunkies following him, their hands tied respectfully behind their backs.

The *putli* walas had listened to the whole dialogue with dread. They looked alarmed and left immediately. Bano Tamanna put her head out in the alley to see what was happening. The *putli* walas' women had covered their heads, drawn their dirty dupattas around their bodices, and were huddling together. The men were walking meekly, like prisoners, with their heads hanging in dread, in front of Jubba and his two acolytes. When Bano went into the kitchen and saw the tin tray she remembered that she had forgotten the tea she had made for the *putli* walas, and realising that most of it would now be wasted made her even angrier.

Qudratullah could well see his grip on life and career slipping from his hands. But he could not bring himself to state his case to Mushtri Khanam who had now become, as it appeared to him, openly hostile.

One evening there was a pleasant breeze, and having nothing better to do, Qudratullah decided to take a walk with the intention of passing under Mushtri Khanam's apartment, and if convenient, scanning the balcony for any sign of her. What that would achieve, Qudratullah was not quite sure. But its promise of bringing him in close quarters with the object of his desire being a sufficient reason, Qudratullah set out with a palpitating heart, carrying a grocery basket to disarm suspicion.

The guilt of his intentions, and the parallel fear of being caught in the act raged like a storm in Qudratullah's head, raising a whirlwind of apprehensions, and paralysing the flow of sane thoughts. His cold fingers felt cramped around the handles of the basket and his feet dragged heavily. At one point Qudratullah thought he saw the cashier pass by on his bicycle. It was too late for Qudratullah to duck inside a shop. A debate about whether it was the cashier or somebody else, took away Qudratullah's thoughts from ruminations of Mushtri Khanam. He tried to imagine what the cashier might have thought of his heading in the direction of Mushtri's house. But did the cashier know where Mushtri Khanam lived? He might have followed her tonga on his bicycle after work. Qudratullah had thought of it himself before remembering that he could get her address from her personal file. But the cashier did not have access to her personal file, unlike Qudratullah: so in all probability he did follow her and was now in possession of her complete address. But if the cashier had had any suspicions or had seen Qudratullah, he would have stopped to greet him, to embarrass him. Or, knowing him, he might have hung around to see where he was going, or tagged along to hold him back. But he did not stop. So probably the man he had seen on the bicycle was not the cashier!

Here a new thought displayed its fangs to Qudratullah. Could it be … could it be that the cashier himself was proceeding in the same direction? Qudratullah remembered that he lived in the Pukka Qila. Qudratullah had been to his house to condole with him on his father's death. And why was the cashier in such a hurry? He looked so confident, pedalling swiftly and zigzagging his cycle through the crowd. Why were his spirits so high? Mushtri Khanam had been uncommonly strict and curt with Qudratullah of late. The cashier was young, and earned enough to support a family. Together Mushtri Khanam and the cashier could be quite prosperous. And Qudratullah was reminded that it was the cashier who had made eyes at Mushtri Khanam in the beginning, and indeed, he was the one who had initiated the custom of wearing ties and polishing shoes. And even though Mushtri Khanam had not encouraged him in the beginning – something that was not lost on Qudratullah – she might have relented. Things do not always remain the same. Women were fickle-minded. They liked courage, something which he had yet to display. Qudratullah cursed himself loudly and stamped his foot. A woman walking beside him with her two children pulled them nearer her, considering Qudratullah a dangerous lunatic.

But even if it had been the cashier, he could be going anywhere in the whole wide world. Qudratullah returned to the point where a second set of fears had been triggered. And as to the first one, why should he be frightened of the cashier, he thought, and laughed at his ridiculous fears. He had forgotten that he was carrying the basket. Why on earth would the cashier imagine that Qudratullah was going to Mushtri Khanam's house? Going in the north direction certainly did not mean that one was going all the way to the North Pole! But Qudratullah had never taken this route on a week day, and he always bought his groceries on the weekend, like everybody else. What if the cashier passed that way every day on some errand? In that case Qudratullah's itinerary would appear conspicuous to him, and that would certainly raise doubts in his small head. Ah! He should have been more careful. But there was no use crying over spilt milk now. And then there was that consolation: at least the cashier was not going *there*!

The bazaar got its characterising sound-effects from the creaking and rolling donkey carts, cries of vendors of spices and dried fruits, and the notes of the flute, which kept trilling with short intervals of silence, mixed in with the chatter and arguments of the shoppers and shopkeepers. The balloon salesman overrode all these sounds with the constant rubbing and screeching of balloons and the noise of the many rattles he rattled at the sight of approaching children. The pungent odour from the balloon seller's hydrogen cylinder pervaded his surroundings and gave Qudratullah a slight headache as he stood there for a couple of minutes to let a train of donkey-carts pass by.

It was that time in the evening when the buffaloes returned from the pond where they had been driven early in the morning. Qudratullah's timing was bad and before he could discern the cause of the excitement in the street and the reason for the running and shouting, the first batch of brazenly stampeding buffaloes was upon him. With an insufficient guard of two keepers and an overwhelming crowd of street children who excited them by twisting their tails and showering cobblestones on them from both sides of the road, the buffaloes made their way through the labyrinthine alleys out of habit and instinct, as best they could. The terror in their eyes as they flooded into the alleys and grazed past the carts and pedestrians, was the same with which Qudratullah made his way between their charging columns, with his palm-leaf basket as a shield. But the stampede was soon over because once the narrow alley filled up, it did not allow much room for forward movement. And when the dust raised by the buffaloes was settling down on food carts, Qudratullah found he had reached Mushtri Khanam's neighbourhood, where beggars were rolling about.

The rich and the poor had suffered equally at the hands of the termites, and the gourd begging bowls of the beggars were not spared either. In the beginning when they went around with these corroded bowls, charitable citizens were greatly moved by the symbolism, and the mendicants had a field day. But such good luck did not last and soon there was nothing left of the gourds, and the beggars went rattling their coins in tin cans.

The alley had become narrower here. From the second storey of a house, debris was falling from a damaged window frame that was being hammered out to be replaced. A little further down this alley and past the beggar's den, the Memons had their gun-shops. The bearded Memons in their gold-embroidered toupees and caftans were breaking shot guns and cocking rifles to check them. The walnut and rosewood stocks of the guns locked in the showcases had been ravaged, and the cartridges ruined by holes drilled into their thick paper casing through which the gunpowder and the pellets had trickled out. The Memons had closed down their shops temporarily to shift their merchandise to a safer place, and guns wrapped in their green tarpaulin and leather cases were being loaded into a tonga which had partially blocked the pedestrian traffic.

Qudratullah took a detour, passed from the main road into the alleys which led to his destination, and into a new terror. What if Mushtri Khanam were to come upon him all of a sudden?

'Thhisshhhh!' Qudratullah almost jumped at the sound of glass crashing. A new company was selling imitation French unbreakable glasses. But these were eminently breakable, and only in the shop, where the salesman had mastered the precise angle of dropping them, did they bounce up unscathed. Occasionally an excited shopper tried it when the salesman was not looking, and the shop rang with the sound of the unhappy result.

But he had the basket in his hand, Qudratullah again reminded himself after he had recovered from the initial shock of the crashing sound. And Bholoo sweetmeats wala was in the next lane, where he was going to buy rusgullay! And why was he buying rusgullay? He was expecting some guests! What guests? His late wife's parents! No, that would not do. His brother! Yes, that's more like it. His brother had a sweet tooth, too. Qudratullah started swinging the basket with his stiff hand, as if it were moving naturally with his gait. He decided to buy the sweets first. A full basket would be better moral protection against Mushtri Khanam's taking him by surprise. The weight of the basket would also satisfy his guilty conscience at taking a shorter route through her alley. And how could he know that Mushtri Khanam lived there? Manager Qudratullah was not in the habit of poking his nose into people's personal files or following their tongas.

As that comfortable thought occurred to Qudratullah, his right shoe started to bite him just above the heel. The lane was not too crowded, and few people were seated on the benches when Qudratullah got there. Close by, a small crowd of people were discussing the termites, and the half-naked Bholoo was in his usual stupor, the result of a heavy intake of carbohydrates.

In Topee Mohalla children were told the story that, late in the night, after everyone had gone to bed, the djinns came out to buy the leftover sweets and cleared the sweetmeat shops. They could be recognised from their feet which had heels in front and toes pointing backwards, and the children never passed the sweetmeat shops late in the evening without checking the feet of those shopping there. This myth was perhaps intended as an explanation for Bholoo being always busy in the mornings making gulab jamuns and barfees. But the fact was that the djinn who cleared Bholoo's sweetmeat shop in the evenings was Bholoo himself. In the mornings as well, Bholoo's mouth was always full and his shop under constant threat of being cleared any moment, were it not for the industry of his emaciated apprentice who kept the cauldron bubbling, and constantly replenished what Bholoo's rapacious hands had subtracted. Between this simple arithmetic of the proprietor and his apprentice, the small shop flourished and extended to encroach on the pavement, where wooden benches were placed for the customers.

Qudratullah took off his shoe. While he was rubbing his sore foot standing there on one leg and passing his eyes over the array of delicacies displayed behind Bholoo's corpulent and ruminating form, he was startled by someone calling him by name.

With a million misgivings immediately paralysing his thinking, and with his heart in his mouth, Qudratullah looked back, expecting to find the cashier. Instead he found a fat, dark man sitting on the bench eating carrot halwa and smiling at him, in what appeared to the bank manager to be a knowing manner. Qudratullah forgot all about his basket ruse and even though he could not readily connect the short fat man with either Mushtri or the cashier, the thought of being discovered instantly took hold of him. When the man shook Qudratullah's cold hand and introduced himself as a notary public, Qudratullah recognised him as one of his account holders who had been in and out of the bank a few times, like hundreds of others. He tried again, but he could not establish a connection between him and Mushtri Khanam. He thought it most dishonourable of the notary not to charge him with his guilt, and for holding back the blow, protracting his misery.

Qudratullah asked himself if it were possible that he was

one of Mushtri's relatives, her brother even? But he did not look like her at all. But then again, a lot of siblings didn't have the remotest resemblance to each other. Take his own brother for instance. Nobody could say that they were related. Here was Qudratullah, restrained and respectably paunched, and there was his brother, as athletic as a goonda and always ridiculously buoyant. Even their features had adapted themselves to their respective dispositions, and whereas Qudratullah's forehead had given way to the sober folds of the frown, and his deferential face had become assiduously clouded, his brother had developed lines around his mouth on account of his constant guffawing, and an impertinent flash in his eyes.

But Ladlay soon dispelled Qudratullah's fears when he told him that it was regarding business that he sought Qudratullah's advice. Qudratullah's relief at hearing him talk of business, and not of his latent guilt was so immense that he at once became most fraternal to his new acquaintance. Indeed, such was his gratitude that when the notary asked if Qudratullah could spare a half hour from his valuable time (the confidential nature of his business being such that he did not wish to discuss it in a public place like the bank, although he had tried to approach him more than once with that intention), Qudratullah readily consented, remembering that in the last month's board meeting the chief executive had urged all the branch managers to go out and get business from private parties. Also, after struggling with so many internal and external hazards on his way to Mushtri Khanam's house, Qudratullah had imagined his task mostly accomplished. And retreat in difficulties being Qudratullah's second nature, although he had successively overcome the desire to turn back, after his encounter with the cashier and the charge of the mad buffaloes, this opportunity to do some bank business finally inveigled him to retire from his expedition.

But before Qudratullah could safely move away, Bholoo suddenly woke up from his stupor and demanded to know what Qudratullah wanted. The word 'rusgullay' was hardly out of his mouth when Bholoo started weighing them in a big two kilo box despite Qudratullah's protests – who was still labouring under the self-delusion of his brother's visit – that he only wanted half a kilo. But Bholoo had a way of silencing these protests by publicly offering advice on the amount of sweetmeats a good host ought to serve his guests. On such occasions Bholoo was also very generous with credit.

Cursing Bholoo for his slyness, while dragging his load and wondering how long it would take him to finish it, Qudratullah was led to Ladlay's apartment by that gentleman through dark and serpentine alleyways.

The notary's house was on the second floor and the familiar rodent stench came gushing out to greet them when the door was opened. It was now getting dark and a solitary low-wattage bulb hanging pendulum-like over their heads was put on. Opposite the curtained balcony an old gramophone sat next to the water-pitcher. A few popular digests were strewn on the centre table surrounded by two *moondhas*. Ladlay made a small ceremony of removing the newspapers from the *moondhas* and after dusting them, seated Qudratullah there with his back to the balcony. He hurried into the kitchen and appeared with two quarter plates, a couple of aluminium spoons, identical to the ones served in Chhalawa Hotel, and the promise that tea was on its way. Qudratullah cheered up when he heard about tea. He tried to remember how long it had been since he had last had tea and to his surprise, could not. Meanwhile, Ladlay had disappeared and emerged after a while from the kitchen, dejected and apologising, with an empty bowl in his hands. A cat had broken in and licked clean the whole bowl of kheer. When Qudratullah assured him that he would have nothing but tea, Ladlay seemed in two minds as to whether or not to remove the two quarter plates he had put on the table for dessert. Qudratullah got him out of this difficulty by putting the box of rusgullay on the table despite the host's initial objections. Tea was not long in coming, and thus amiably sitting across the table over tea and rusgullay, the two men talked business.

It appeared that Ladlay had recently been appointed executor of a not inconsiderable estate, comprising a commercial building. The necessary paperwork was complete and the power of attorney signed. But Ladlay's honour far above pestering tenants monthly for rent, he had decided to take a mortgage against this property, which being the executor he was empowered to do, and to invest the money into his legal practice. Real-estate prices were at an all time low and it did not make sense to sell it just then. Moreover, there was no time limit set for the estate's liquidation as the owners trusted his judgement. Once his business became prosperous (there was no reason to doubt it, Ladlay being healthy and industrious, and these two qualities the foremost considerations for success), he would pay back the mortgage. By that time the real-estate prices would also have stabilised, as predicted, and he could liquidate it in more fairness to his clients, and hand it over to people better suited to the occupation of collecting rent. Until such time, the bank was to appoint an administrator to look after the estate, and the power of attorney being invested in Ladlay, nothing could be simpler than his appending the signature of approval to anyone's name entrusted by the bank for this purpose.

Qudratullah mustered enough fortitude and self-control not to rub his hands gleefully in front of Ladlay. Here was the very opportunity a bank manager prays for during the term of his office: prime estate in lieu of a highly hazardous mortgage. From his experience Qudratullah knew that only those law businesses prospered on a higher scale where some former attorney-general or an ex-judge of the superior courts was bribed to lend his name to the board. Qudratullah could imagine what a rag enterprise Ladlay's business was likely to turn out, and its dismal chances of survival. The property was as good as in the bank's pocket. But not a soul must know how it had landed into his lap, he reflected sombrely. In the next board meeting he would narrate his success to the chief executive in the briefing hour, with emphasis on the hours he had put in pursuing his quarry after work. It was likely to leave a favourable impression, and would help Qudratullah in the interview when he appeared in the Desh Bank's Assistant Vice-President examination in the next couple of months.

The notary had struck Qudratullah as balmy. He compared him to the clerks in his branch and thought that any one of them coming into property all of a sudden would act equally foolish. They would probably open a general store or a bakery and be out of business in no time. Qudratullah groped his way home in those dark and mysterious alleys that eventful evening, not without a little regret for the loss of about one kilo of the juicy rusgullay, partaken of mostly by Ladlay during the discourse; but all in all a happy man, considering it an investment in career growth. An appointment was made between Qudratullah and Ladlay for the following week, to work out the finer details.

But Ladlay's conduct during his visit was most unaccountable. Ladlay had made him very uncomfortable by looking over Qudratullah's shoulder every now and then, as if there were someone behind him. Several times Qudratullah felt a draught on the back of his neck, making him uneasy in the thought that someone was indeed behind him with a drawn weapon, ready for murder. There were stories in the newspapers of people who had been lured into dark and dingy houses, where they had been discovered slain.

Then Ladlay had put on the record-player quite loud. To muffle his cries while he was attacked perhaps? Out of politeness Qudratullah did not turn back to see what engrossed Ladlay's attention. But when Ladlay went to the pitcher to get himself a glass of water, Qudratullah had quickly glanced behind. Except for the balcony curtain moving with the wind, he could discern nothing. The wind coming in from the balcony had parted the curtain and grazed Qudratullah's neck. So why was Ladlay staring at the curtain? And although they could not hear each other in the din, Qudratullah considered it rude to ask him to turn down the volume. His safe exit from Ladlay's house had dispelled his apprehensions, however, and he attributed these quirks to Ladlay's eccentricity.

Engrossed as he was in these thoughts, the moment Qudratullah saw his bed, his mind was assailed by thoughts of Mushtri Khanam. That night he dreamt of being run over by a herd of buffaloes, and against the skyline he saw the cashier pedalling away, with Mushtri Khanam perched on the carrier, and her hand around his waist for support.

The next day in his office Qudratullah thought he saw the cashier glance at him from the corner of his eye, seemingly busy counting, his fingers moving like centipede legs on the wad of currency notes. He was also convinced that he saw the cashier exchange a wink with the gunman, and the gunman nod his big round head. Mushtri Khanam was her usual crabby self. All these observations made Qudratullah uneasy.

Firdousi's letter arrived a few weeks after Salar's visit to the letter-writers. The postman slowly cycled into the alley, dismounted at the door and rang his bicycle bell to deliver the letter into Salar's hands, who had moved his chair even closer to the door these days to intercept the mail. The rain had smeared the ink on the envelope, and Salar Jang's name was barely legible. It seemed that things had been looking up for Salar ever since the auspicious portent of the parrot.

Firdousi had acknowledged Salar's sonnet, and asked for an introduction.

As Salar's hand shook because of palsy, but moreover since the pen of the scribes had proved so auspicious, he rushed off to Baba Navees again, taking only Muneemji with him to send the following reply to Noor's receipt of his ode:

A Memorandum for the Notice of,
The Light of the Heavens,
The Source of All Rapture in the Universe of the Unknown
God,
The Eyes from which Nothing is Ever Hidden but is Manifest,
The Eye Lashes in which the Villainous Might of the Foe was
Strangled and Annihilated,
The Eye Brows which Decide more Fates than the Heavenly
Tree on Shabe-Bara'at,
To Whom all Offerings Big or Small are at One Level, I
Submit,
Lest Found Guilty of Transgressing my Lowly Station,
The Least of all Offerings,
My Fervent Salutations and Earnest Accolades!

Nothing could be farthest from my humble aspirations than to vie for your heavenly favours, dream of a seat where your comely feet had trodden, and drink a goblet of unsurpassed glory from the illuminated spring of your blessed aspect! Then how shall one who fomented the seed of perpetual sorrow in my existence read this parchment on which her handiwork is inscribed? As an innuendo most unmerited? As an overture where none was solicited? As Heaven is my witness, this missive which finds a cradle in your perfumed hands was created by the same justice which ordained the Earth and the Heavens, and by the same hand which shot me through the heart with the arrow of your love.

And who may this abject hound be who brazenly pollutes the ears of Heavens with his miserable bayings, and impertinently mingles his mournful strains with the angels' chorus? One Salar Jang who is no stranger to the slurs and abomination of Fortune, and well known to the wrath of Time. He who has brazenly and most disrespectfully ordained the blessed favour of dedicating a book of rhymes to one who has indeed neither desire nor need of such shoddy tokens of courtship. And he who, persisting in his unbridled presumptuousness, offers herewith that shoddy tome for the perusal of the object of his fervent but chaste attentions. He who was deposed from the seat of his good fortune and thrown to the dogs of ruination and plague; whose domicile once sheltered the elephants of the royal hunt; whose appellation was once the last word in rhyme and known to the four bearings of the compass; whose eyes commanded the fairest view in men and beasts, on both land and air; whose pigeons were the pride of the morning skies, and the hooves of whose noble horse sparked fire and illuminated the night skies when it trod Gulmoha's earth with his master in the saddle, eager to redress inequity or wrong.

Those halcyon days are now best lived in memory. The ravages of two score years and ten have left their mark on the world of your slave. But the eyes of the mind now see sharper, and the drive for life has been reinforced. A weather-beaten vessel is all the more trustworthy for the sails have become familiar with the treacherous high wind and the frame is no stranger to the blows and saline fangs of the hostile waves. To be regarded highly in the society of men are desired riches indeed – the celebrated Mirza Poya and the worthy Kaskas Brothers – those epitomes, respectively, of intellect and valour, shall be reference enough. However, the goods and chattels (to which this ignoble creature may attach his name, and confer on the one who strikes the match of affable companionship in his dark isolation) are considerable still.

If I had matched the futility of my nugatory requests with your infinite charm, my optimism would have diminished in the inverse proportion of the difference, and indeed my deaths would have been many and endless. But I matched the candour and fidelity of my passion with your infinite rectitude in affairs of the soul, and thus my confidence was heightened in direct proportion, and my restive fancy settled.

On foot or walking on my head, I am prepared to traverse the distance that separates us, so that my tongue and my eyes can submit their own memorandums. I shall leave it to be settled by a prompt of your eyebrows when it shall be bridged best, for although fires rage within me, and devastate me with every moment which passes away from your presence, yet the salve of your fond recollection brings succour to that conflagration, rejuvenates the scorched ground, and makes it verdant once more. Amid this resurrection and death I continue my existence and find myself suspended between the choices of instant self-murder and everlasting bliss.

Of late, Mars and Venus have joined forces. The winds are propitious. The spoor of the jasmine all around could be traced to the lover's dreams. A candle has been lit. A hope has been engendered. The senses have made ablutions in anticipation of a welcome augur. I seal this letter along with my fate and prostrate my person to the charity of your indulgence, and refuse to raise my head until your just heart declares a truce between my longing and its requital.

Grovelling, He Begs of You to Grant him Leave,
The Servant of your Menial Servants,
The Sacrifice of your Enemies,
What Feral Heart was Tamed by the Gentle Spring of Your
Fancy,
The Abject Moth which Eagerly Circles the Omniscient Light
of Your Beauty,
The Lowliest of the Lowly,
Salar Jang.

Noor replied once again, and, what was more, asked for a photograph. Firdousi's letter was brief and to the point, as Salar postulated must be expected of a woman of her distinction. He was in a state of great excitement, and so were Ladlay and Mirza Poya. Although the latter had never received a single word of acknowledgement from Firdousi, for all the Eid cards he had sent her, he was thrilled by the idea that it must be a reference to *him*, after all, which had prompted Firdousi to condescend to reply to Salar's memorial. But what was really stirring his excitement was the hope that if he could gain Firdousi's confidence through Salar's match, there would be no impediments to his glorious return to filmdom.

The auspicious moment called for a celebration, and Salar considered that laddoos, which Ladlay had run to fetch, were not enough to do justice to the propitiousness of the occasion. He invited Ladlay and Poya over to lunch the coming weekend.

While Salar was giving instructions to Bano Tamanna about the forthcoming feast, she remembered the sorry state of the copper pots and asked Muneemji if he could find an annealer to have them polished.

'Eh? Annealer!? What for an annealer?' Muneemji retorted sullenly. 'I say make that rascal Ladlay sit in the corner of the alley and do the job! What else is he good for?' But he helped Tamanna collect all the pots and pile them up outside the kitchen after dinner, and when Ladlay came in the next morning, Muneemji sent him to look for the annealer, while Bano Tamanna emptied the cauldrons of cockroach eggs. Ladlay was not happy being sent away on an errand by Muneemji, but the latter said that Salar had specially mentioned that the dishes should be cleaned up that very day, and Ladlay decided to go. It was not easy to find the annealer because he was on the move, and the whole morning passed without any sign of Ladlay. He had taken his cycle from home and only appeared late in the afternoon, pedalling hard and perspiring profusely. In his tow came the annealing man with his sack of coals, bellows, a mallet, and a boy.

A small fire was made on the ground, and the annealer began heating and hammering all the copper pots and pans one after the other, while the boy, who, from a lack of enthusiasm in his work seemed to be his son, operated the bellows and fed the fire. As Muneemji passed on the pots and pans to the annealer, he kept admonishing the boy for not operating the bellows more energetically. He, therefore, did not see Ladlay slip into Salar's room and only saw him as he was leaving, with a file tied with a ribbon onto the bicycle's carrier.

For special occasions, Bano Tamanna ground the spices herself. But these days she also ground them because the ones sold in the market were almost always adulterated. And the termites had made their state more dubious. It is unclear what attracted the termites to the spices. Perhaps it was the sweet smell of the cinnamon wood, or maybe they were attracted by the saw dust which came mixed with the coriander powder. It could even be the familiar earthen smell of red bricks finely mortared and mixed with chilli powder. Irrespective of the cause, the termites had been seen in the spice container, although not in such great numbers as in other places, but they had wet the ground spices, leaving behind small powdery balls unfit to cook food with.

The grating slab had become slick with use, and the next day Muneemji sent Ladlay out again to get hold of the slab grater, who went around the houses with his chisel-hammer on his shoulder, offering to revive the slab's grinding teeth. Again Ladlay found him with some difficulty and sat outside while the man took the slab and the pestle out of the house into the street, and with his chisel-hammer chipped away at the smooth-surfaced slab and pestle, making small abrasive marks, which the grinding had planed.

His eyes were shut because of the flying chips, but his hammer never faltered against his other hand, laid on the slab to keep it from shaking. Ladlay was also obliged to keep his eyes shut but the shower of chips on his face made him quite uncomfortable and he cursed Muneemji, who had sent him out on the pretext that Salar was sleeping and could not be disturbed. He knew it was a lie because he had clearly heard Salar asking for the tobacco of his hookah to be changed, as he was knocking on the front door. It had led Ladlay to question the extent of Muneemji's knowledge of his affairs. He had witnessed a gradual change in Muneemji's demeanour from the day he had first met him, and it had become openly manifest since. So much so that Ladlay had begun to suspect that in one of his manic outbursts Salar might have blurted out his plan to sell off the property.

Once the chipping was done, the man sent Ladlay twice to bring bowls of water, once to clear the surface of the dust and debris, and again to cleanse the pestle, and the grating slab went back into commission. Ladlay had noticed Muneemji blocking the entrance to the veranda beyond which was Salar's room. He did not insist upon seeing Salar and realised that he must act fast if he did not wish to be caught in the fall-out from the scandal.

Being a delicacy, fish was also added to the menu. Bilotti and the fishmonger were both on their beats in the same neighbourhood, and therefore only the older and weaker cats lagged behind with Bilotti. The young and impressionable cats, on whose olfactory sense the fetid stench of the fish had an enchanting effect, all followed the fishmonger, mewing loudly. They tried to walk between his feet as he was putting his basket down on the steps of the Qasr-e Yunani, with the obvious intention of tripping him over and plundering his goods. He almost stumbled over one of the cats, but regained his balance and kicked another out of his way.

'By God, the fish is fresh! Early this morning I dragged in this catch. See for yourself,' the fishmonger said when he noticed Muneemji poking around the hamper with his bony fingers, tossing and turning the contents of the basket. 'It is not my business to cheat and defraud. You could keep searching the basket till evening and you wouldn't find a single stale fish,' the little man was saying. Most of the fish looked old to Muneemji. Their scales had dried and were recently showered with water. Muneemji shook his head in disapproval.

'What's wrong now? What's wrong!?' the man asked with irritation. He had a short beard and upturned whiskers kept starched by his oily fingers. Thatches of his hairy chest tore out of the neck of his waistcoat and came up to his chin. An oily amulet was roped around his neck in a leather casing, and another oily talisman adorned his arm above his right elbow.

'What's wrong? Can't you see what's wrong? Look at this!' Muneemji held a particularly pulpy fish close to the fishmonger's nose, 'This fish smells like my shoe! When did you catch this, eh? The last time you took a bath in the river?' He picked up another fish and lifted its gills. They were dark and he threw it back into the hamper.

'What do you mean by spoiling my whole basket like that?' the fishmonger shouted as Muneemji kept picking up the fish and throwing them back inside the basket with dissatisfaction. 'You don't have the face that has eaten a fish in its life. Get off! I am not selling you anything,' the fishmonger jerked his hamper and made a move to get up.

'Don't move! Keep still!' Muneemji threatened, without putting the fish back or removing his eyes from the hamper. 'If you moved an inch it will be the last time you are seen in this neighbourhood. If I caught you I will break your legs myself! What do you mean, you rascal, selling rotten fish and then shouting at me, eh?'

'When did I say I was not selling?' the fishmonger now changed his tone to one of helpless protest. 'You said you did not want to buy. I don't want to spoil the first sale in the morning. I want to make *bohni*. Do bismillah!'

Muneemji had picked out two fresh fish from the mixed lot of fresh and rotting produce, and he handed them to the fishmonger to weigh. The little man threw the fish in the pan and began to weigh it.

'Hold it there! What do you think you are you doing?' Muneemji shouted as he noticed the man trying to load the scales. 'Weigh it again, you scoundrel. Do you think I am blind?'

'I didn't do anything. By God I didn't do anything!' the fishmonger almost gouged out his small eyes by poking them fiercely with his fingers while swearing to his honesty. But Muneemji was indifferent to this loud public spectacle of his honour. After he was satisfied that the fish had been weighed correctly he took it and disappeared inside the house without paying. Inside he handed the fish to Bano Tamanna and lighted a cigarette. He smoked half the cigarette, oblivious to the oaths and the denunciations of the fishmonger in the alley and his repeated knockings on the door which progressively grew louder. Then he calmly got up, went out, shouted at the fishmonger for making a racket, paid him and went out roaming. The fishmonger was now grumbling quietly and the cats who were meek witnesses to the sale, without mewing once, were eating the heads and the entrails of the Palla which the fishmonger threw in the alley. For days the alley reeked of what the cats had left uneaten until trampling feet carried it away in all directions.

The humid weather which persisted was the single most beneficial circumstance for the proliferation of the termites. With the severe humidity, all evaporation had stopped, and the air above the ground became as moist as the vapour inside the termitariums. In fact, the air inside the nests became drier in comparison to the atmosphere outside. The extreme humidity outside proofed the termites' vital humours from dehydrating through their flimsy cuticles, relieving them of the need to make tunnels to reach a spot or to descend to the water-table to bring up moist particles for humidifying the nest. And while the humid weather lasted, they were seen crawling all over in plain sight.

The smell of cinnamon and First Grade Rooster Brand *kewra* pervaded the kitchen air. Bano Tamanna was eagerly peddling small onion rings in the oil with her ladle. The newly annealed shining silvery utensils had increased her delight in cooking. The only thing she was afraid of was termites falling into the cooking pots from the wooden railings with which the electrical wiring was clipped onto the kitchen ceiling. It ran right over the stoves. As in the rest of the house, the railing had come loose as the wooden pegs securing it had been eaten away. The termites had etched the exposed copper wires with their sprays, after finishing off the wax-cloth wrapping and the rubber casing, and the deposit on the wires had increased to an extent that the adjoining wires sometimes made contact, causing short circuits, and electrocuting the termites by the thousand.

Mirzban had to stay late at the school to finish marking exam papers and therefore he had excused himself from the lunch. Having the field to himself Salar narrated the story of when, upon his birth, he was taken for his grandfather's inspection, and the old man upon opening the cloth in which he was wrapped, and struck by the portentous testicles of the infant, had made some ominous prophesies. The story was regularly interrupted as Bano Tamanna brought out one dish after another from the kitchen. The knocking of the dishes and the rattle of the cutlery on the table had brought out the blind soldiers. From the labyrinths of its infested wood, they appeared through the many needle eye entrances on the table's surface, marching between the plates, and feeling the straw mats suspiciously which lay in their way, with their mandibles.

Salar was now quite animated and narrated the incident when the Nawab of Gulmoha, hearing rumours of his voracity, had invited Salar for dinner. Salar had a good lunch and in the evening rode his phaeton to the Nawab's palace. That night the Nawab's oven had to be rekindled again because Salar, after devouring the fifty greasy naans and some eighty fowls roasted for the dinner, showed no signs of slowing down. He ate twelve more naans after that with the curry which he had overlooked, and licked clean fifteen clay bowls of rice pudding. Throughout the spectacle, the Nawab sat quiescent, passing the different dishes to Salar, and after he was served, tasted some from each himself. Only once did he betray any signs of displeasure when the flow of the naans from the kitchen broke down. After Salar was finished, he shared the hookah with the Nawab, gossiped about the amorous predilections of his court poets, and left after paying his respects. The next day the Nawab sent him a sword and a *khilaat* with the offer to make him the commander of the palace guards. This offer Salar politely declined but kept the sword and the *khilaat*. The Nawab never forgot Salar and until his death a four-horse coach daily delivered delicacies from his kitchen to Salar's house.

Due to his precarious digestion, however, Salar could not partake of even a morsel of the greasy cow-trotters and shahi tukras. Muneemji being similarly indisposed, and Poya being a small eater, it fell to Ladlay to do justice to the dishes, for himself as well as for the rest of the party. And on that account he amply distinguished himself, from stalking dishes with his eyes to and from the kitchen, to demolishing them one by one with remarkable ambidexterity. Salar was in a jubilant mood, Bano Tamanna was well-satisfied with the cooking. For a while even Muneemji seemed to have been delivered of his dark apprehensions as he joined in the general merriment.

Finding their exits covered by the mats the soldier termites had already started excavating beneath the emptied dishes when they were cleared, and along with the mats they were consigned to the kitchen, still maniacally working their way into the mats.

The power supply from the grid station had been disrupted after the wooden electric poles were felled by the termites, and until the bridge could be opened for the goods train which brought in the timber, there was no hope of it being set right.

From the beginning, the city administration had shown an apathy towards the termite problem. Official bulletins downplayed the gravity of the situation at hand, and at every stage tried to divert public attention from this more immediate and pressing problem to distant issues, for instance by drumming up support for the ruling party's candidates in the forthcoming polls. In his press conferences the commissioner had called for an end to what he termed the sensational coverage of the termite epidemic in the local Press. Also, he had arbitrarily put a hold on the distribution of relief cheques issued by the federal government. He justified this capricious move on the grounds that in the wake of the elections, the public exchequer was hard-pressed to arrange funds and provisions, and it would be a small sacrifice by the citizens to wait for their money until the election results had been announced.

But this was just a ruse. A new law had made fund regulation for electoral expenses mandatory, so that candidates would not spend beyond a certain limit. The commissioner wanted to divert these relief funds to support the election of the local candidates fielded by the party in power, who had promised to replenish the money upon their re-election by transfer of local development funds from the treasury. And in the meanwhile, the commissioner and his cronies in the relief committee were planning to speculate with these funds in timberyards, a business which had recently gone into a slump because of the termite problem. All that gave rise to corruption, since the money had already been sanctioned for the relief fund; the cheques were issued in the names of the individuals, and those willing to grease the palms of the relief committee functionaries were legally free to collect their money. Somehow Tabaq Sahib had got wind of these proceedings and called on the commissioner's office for an appointment, armed with an article meant for publication in daily *Qandeel*, in which the whole procedure for misappropriation of funds had been described in some detail. He was under the impression that under threat of blackmail, he could persuade the commissioner to set aside a couple of thousand rupees for his electoral expenses too, since his wife had forbidden him to touch her savings. Tabaq Sahib really intended to return the money after his election, of which he was confident. What Tabaq Sahib did not know was that it was an open secret and therefore the question of blackmail did not arise. As could be expected, Tabaq Sahib was unsuccessful in his efforts. And after a fortnight, just when he thought that things were looking up, having managed to get an appointment with the assistant commissioner's secretary, Tabaq Sahib was badly injured and confined to bed.

Instead of alleviating the plight of its citizens, the corrupt government functionaries aggravated it at every step with their systematic incompetence. Consequently, with the passage of time the situation became so critical that to hide it any longer was not safe. The home minister had inquired about the city administration's failure to check the situation, and there were reports that an independent inquiry might be ordered into the affairs of Purana Shehr by the federal ombudsman. Unable to decide on a course of action and in order not to appear panic-stricken, the city administration sought recourse in the use of force to quell every dissent. A peaceful procession of Topee Mohalla residents, dispersing after registering their grievances at the commissioner house, was lathi-charged. Tabaq Sahib and Basmati were at the head of the procession. The latter managed to escape when the policemen came charging, but Tabaq Sahib slipped and was roundly thrashed. The District Magistrate had promulgated Section 144 after that incident, prohibiting the assembly of four or more people. Tabaq Sahib did not speak to Basmati for leaving him behind, and only came round after Basmati convinced him that the incident had boosted his popularity, and further strengthened his candidacy as Topee Mohalla's leader.

Thanks to small groups of concerned citizens and businesses, the chaos in the city was settling, although the city administration had grossly failed in its duties. Public servants, finding support in the administration's high-handedness, found all kinds of excuses for their natural indolence; and for unabashed thievery and extortion from those who fell into their clutches the termites provided them with a whole new array of alibis. In the past, a file in the government records which went mysteriously missing whenever needed, could always be retrieved by the clerks for a standard and nominal monetary consideration. But after the termite outbreak, it threatened to become wholly extinct, until exorbitant sums were paid for its resurrection.

The Sessions Court had returned from its long recess. The lawsuits and counter-lawsuits which had clogged the legal system were beginning to clear. The government set up a special judicial commission to study all claims filed during and immediately after the termite epidemic, allowing all false claimants to withdraw their petitions unconditionally, or face severe punishment. Petitions seeking heavy damage compensation from the government for the apathy and the incompetence of the public departments were dismissed as non-admissible under the Force Majeure Act.

Bano Tamanna and Muneemji who had come again to get a hearing date from the magistrate were waiting in the corridor for Parwana when Imam Jubba passed by. Bano Tamanna was still wondering what could possibly have brought Imam Jubba to the court, when she saw Mirza Poya enter. He saw Muneemji and when he found out that they were waiting for Parwana, he invited them inside the courtroom. The hearing of a lawsuit against the misappropriation of the copyright of *The One Thousand and One Terrors of the Grave* was about to start, and Parwana was representing the plaintiff. Mirza Poya explained that he was there to acquaint himself with the salient features of a copyright lawsuit since he was himself considering suing Betaal Baghera for trespassing on *Umrao Khanam*'s copyright.

The publisher of *The One Thousand and One Terrors of the Grave,* someone named Kokabi, had arrived the night before from a business trip, and looked listless and sleepy. The legatee, Maulvi Isfandiar's son, had refused an out of court settlement which Parwana had recommended in the light of the information provided by the defence. The son was adamant that a settlement was not the same as punishment and that nothing short of a jail term for the publisher was going to satisfy him. In that, he could not be dissuaded, and Parwana's explanations fell on deaf ears.

Imam Jubba, who was in the centre of the front row, seemed to be presiding over a cluster of *maulvis* who kept leaning sideways to whisper in each other's ears. As they all looked alike, Bano could not figure out if the two who had called with Jubba the day of the *putli* tamasha were among them. The publisher was called to the stand by the defence.

The publisher confessed to reprinting the book but in a thoroughly edited version. He contended and produced proof that although the original book was titled *One Thousand and One Terrors of the Grave,* in reality it listed only seven hundred and ninety-three. Even the proofreader had lost count somewhere because the items were not numbered, and the book ran through several reprints until Imam Jubba pointed out the discrepancy in a visit to the publisher. Since its author had already become eligible to verify those terrors first-hand, Imam Jubba offered to complete the count and improve on the existing text. The publisher readily agreed but refused to publish it under the same name. Instead, he reprinted it as *Still More Terrors of the Grave*. It was this publication which was in question, the defence lawyer said, but since it was published in an edited form with additions made to it, the question of copyright did not arise.

Next, Imam Jubba was called to the witness stand. He got up stroking his beard, and amidst much handshaking among the *maulvis*, took his oath in a voice loud enough to be heard outside the courtroom.

The questioning began. Parwana knew the helplessness of his situation but he was still trying to extract something to build a case on from cross-questioning. 'Imam Jubba, did you edit and rewrite *One Thousand and One Terrors of the Grave* originally authored by one Mr Isfandiar, at Mr Kokabi's request?' he asked Jubba who seemed to be reciting something under his breath.

'*Alhamd'o'lillah*! I did!' Imam Jubba said and resumed his silent recital.

'Could you tell me what were the changes you made in the revised version?'

'Indeed. And since I am under oath I must also forego my belief in screening others' iniquities. First of all, as you have already been told, the book listed only seven hundred and ninety-three horrors. I don't know what such a grave error could be attributed to, if not to a critical infirmity of belief in the writer himself.'

The *maulvis* in Jubba's camp nodded their agreement and Maulvi Isfandiar's son, tried to get up and say something but was restrained by one of his supporters who held him firmly from the back. The judge turned an annoyed face to them and asked Jubba to continue.

'I don't think that the court is interested in the infirmities of people's beliefs,' Parwana replied. 'Please answer specifically.'

Jubba looked triumphantly around and resumed, 'After I had discovered that error, I decided to read the text more closely, and indeed I was scandalised by the liberties taken by the author. In one place he had mentioned that the guardian dog of Hell had two heads, when all sacred authorities from Adam's times are agreed that the said dog has three heads. It also didn't make sense since two is an even number and no divine entity could have an even configuration. Then there was the question of the length of Hell's Resident Scorpion. Maulvi Isfandiar puts it at seven leagues across and two leagues high (again an even, diabolical number), whereas in actuality that monster is not a hand shorter than fifteen leagues and a full five leagues tall, since, when it snaps its claws (which alone are three leagues long) the sound is heard across a radius of a thousand leagues. Nobody in his right mind could credit or expect a scorpion merely seven leagues long and two high to make such a thunderous noise. Then again, the length of a day in an eternal year was not …'

'Infidel! Infidel!' Maulvi Isfandiar's son had suddenly got up from his seat and was shouting at the top of his voice. 'This man is an infidel and by rights must be stoned to death!'

One of the *maulvis* in Jubba's camp shouted, 'Close his blasphemous mouth! Don't let this mad son-of-a-bitch run away!' and in the flash of an eye was upon Maulvi Isfandiar's son, tearing at his beard with all his might. Suddenly Bano recognised him. Here was one of the two *maulvis*. The plaintiff's supporter, having found a chance, jumped on the *maulvi* who had attacked his friend.

'Order! Order in court!' the judge shouted. The policemen on duty were already buffeting the attacker, Isfandiar's son and his accomplice. In the scuffle, when he tried to get up and move away, Mirza Poya also received a slap across his face. When the *maulvis* had been restrained from further violence, the judge called for a short break after threatening the miscreants with contempt of court. In one corner Kokabi could be seen talking to Jubba, surrounded by the latter's supporters. Parwana took his client to a corner to protest his behaviour but Maulvi Isfandiar's son only waved his hands angrily in reply to his accusations. Both Bano Tamanna and Muneemji decided to leave the courtroom and wait for Parwana to finish his business inside.

Ladlay was coming out from the neighbouring room when he saw Bano Tamanna and Muneemji in the corridor. He immediately stopped in his tracks. What is that woman doing here? he wondered. Does she know? That old depraved Muneemji, is it his doing? Just when he had decided to retrace his steps to see from a distance what the two of them were up to, Mirza Poya came out of the room, rubbing his nose, and saw Ladlay.

'Aha! Our Ladlay is also here!' he said.

Both Bano Tamanna and Muneemji turned around and as their eyes met, Ladlay realised that his game was up.

'Jubba's cronies will jeopardise Kokabi's case. And Isfandiar's son is also bent upon destroying himself. The courtroom had the air of a mosque today,' Mirza Poya was saying.

'How are you, did you get hurt?' Bano Tamanna turned her face away from Ladlay who had come forward to greet them, and asked Mirza Poya.

'Yes, yes, I am fine, it was just a graze,' Mirza lied.

'So what brings you here, Muneemji, Begum Yunani? Is there anything I can do?' Ladlay asked, ignoring Mirza.

'I don't think we need your services, Ladlay Sahib!' Bano Tamanna said in a stern voice. Mirza looked askance at Muneemji but he was staring blankly ahead without looking at anything or saying a word. Mirza remembered what Muneemji had said about the confidentiality of the matter and decided to take Ladlay away but the notary now addressed Bano Tamanna.

'Can I have a word with you, Begum Yunani?' Then he

turned to Muneemji. 'Please ask Begum Yunani to listen to what I have to say. You can also join us,' he said.

'Muneemji! Please tell Ladlay Sahib that we are waiting for someone. Now is not the time to listen to the likes of him,' Bano Tamanna said, unable to control the anger building up inside her. Mirza was feeling embarrassed standing there, and finding Muneemji unresponsive to his questioning looks, he quietly took his leave.

'Begum Yunani!' Ladlay entreated, 'I must beg you to listen to me. We can talk outside, in my office, if you like.'

'Bano, I think we should hear him out,' Muneemji said getting up. 'Let's give him a chance to say what he has to say. Maybe it's something we'd like to hear.'

Bano Tamanna picked up her handbag and the file and reluctantly got up. They followed Ladlay into a room. A lawyer was coming out of the room and from him Ladlay found out that it was vacant. It seemed that the room served as a library or archive. The cupboards were full of old law books and files which were also stacked in the corners on the floor. Some panes were broken and there was layer upon layer of dirt on the books and the bookshelves. The walls were covered with termite tunnels and their network was most extensive behind the cupboards. Ladlay pulled out chairs for Bano Tamanna and Muneemji and they both sat down.

'Without asking your business here, let me clarify whether or not there have been any misunderstandings,' Ladlay began without looking Bano Tamanna or Muneemji in the face. 'Salar Sahib is my client and my legal transactions with him are confidential, but still I would like to assure you that I would not undertake anything which would be detrimental to the interests of a family I feel so attached to. I thought I must say that, at the risk of you considering it too presumptuous of someone of my social standing,' Ladlay said and looked at Bano Tamanna and then at Muneemji to see what effect his words had produced.

Before Muneemji could restrain her, Bano Tamanna burst out, 'We know very well what your plans are, Ladlay Sahib! Do not think that we do not know! And to keep you from executing them we are getting an injunction from the court. People like you should be arrested and put in jail. And a lawyer too! You should be ashamed of yourself! Once we are through, we'll see to it that your licence to practise law is revoked!'

Ladlay seemed unruffled. 'I do not understand what plans you are talking about. All I have done is to follow Salar Sahib's directives. So I do not see why you must get an injunction from the court. And what injunction?' he asked.

Muneemji tried to hold Bano Tamanna from saying anything further, but Ladlay's calm was making her more and more furious and she would not be held back from speaking her mind. 'An injunction that my father is weak of mind and that you were manipulating him. We will prove to the court how you have exploited his weakness to get him to transfer the power of attorney into your name.'

Ladlay sat up in his seat when Bano Tamanna finished talking and without any change in intonation replied, 'Begum Yunani, I would like to repeat what I said earlier, that I feel myself very attached to the family, and I could not ever think of doing anything that could bring any harm to your family. As God is my witness, I would be the first one to relinquish this power of attorney in your favour if only Salar Sahib would give me the slightest hint.'

'As if you would take a hint. Why don't you leave my father alone?' Bano Tamanna interjected angrily.

'Begum Yunani!' Ladlay continued, ignoring her question, 'Salar Sahib knows what I am doing. You surely cannot fault *me* if he does not take you into his confidence. I do not know who is advising you in these matters. Maybe it is Muneemji himself. But I will just say this much: I am a lawyer myself, and I have seen a great many lawsuits where a court injunction was requested in similar circumstances, although in the present case the allegations are totally baseless. But what usually happens in such cases,' he leaned forward in a minatory manner, 'is that the injunction is not easily granted if there is no proof to blight the intentions of the transferee of the power of attorney, and to prove their point, the plaintiff has to go to extremes to prove that the individual against whom the injunction has been sought is insane.'

Bano Tamanna opened her mouth to say something but Ladlay raised his hand, 'Hold on Begum Yunani, I am not finished yet. I hope you realise the full significance of what I am saying. Once you have proved Salar Sahib insane, the case could go either way. You may get your injunction, but at the cost of consigning Salar Sahib to the madhouse of Guru Bunder. Would you like that?'

A shadow passed over Bano Tamanna's face and she found herself unable to say a word.

Ladlay realised his triumph and pressed his advantage. 'Everybody knows what happens at Guru Bunder with the beatings and the starvations and mysterious deaths. No visitors are allowed, and for somebody in the last lap of his life, the final satisfaction of dying with the family close to him is also denied.'

As he spoke, Ladlay kept looking at Bano Tamanna and was delighted to see the results he had striven for manifest themselves so visibly on Bano Tamanna's face. Satisfied with what he saw, Ladlay once more adopted a grovelling tone. 'Begum Yunani, I told you all this not with an intention to frighten you. As I have told you time and again, my intentions are sincere and do not go beyond satisfying Salar Sahib's own commands which I am not under liberty to make known, but which I can say with confidence are in the best interests of the family. What I told you about Guru Bunder is just meant to make you reconsider what you have set out to do, and think again before you get so carried away in your mistaken suspicions, that you compromise the life and safety of your dear father, who loves you more than anything else in the world.'

Bano Tamanna was on the verge of tears when Muneemji took her away after informing Ladlay that they would stay in touch with him. Ladlay had insisted that they let him know if they needed any assistance in court. After Bano Tamanna had verified Ladlay's threat with Parwana and he had confirmed with some reservations what Ladlay had said, she requested Parwana to withdraw the case. But both Muneemji and Parwana prevailed upon her to file a request to postpone the hearing date for the time being and see what happens. They were both hopeful that now Ladlay knew where he stood with regards to them, he might make some mistake which might damn him.

The three friends were gathered on Tabaq's roof, who had invited them over to discuss the strategy for his election campaign. Tabaq Sahib had somewhat recovered from his injuries and could walk now, but his movements were restricted.

That morning Lumboo's *lashkar* had killed one of the crows which nested in the neighbouring garden. The crows had turned out in force and were swooping over the enemies who were still pelting them with sling-shots. There was such a racket that his friends had been unable to benefit from Tabaq Sahib's proposed election strategy. Bhai Qamoosi was reading the newspaper and Basmati, who had lighted a cigarette, was blowing smoke into the air. Tabaq Sahib's wife sent up a few hot compresses and pulling up his pyjamas and applying them on his legs, he asked his son who had brought the bowl, if Lumboo had arrived yet to catch the cat. A tom had recently become interested in Tabaq Sahib's kitchen, and Lumboo, who usually provided the service, was given the task of dumping him in the meat market which offered many diversions for a cat.

Just then they heard Lumboo's lusty shout, 'Oay! Leave these crows! We have to catch your mother!' Lumboo was standing in the alley, in a pair of boots worn without socks, holding with one hand his turban, and gripping a jute-sack tucked under his other arm. Hearing of this new adventure the children followed their father to Tabaq Sahib's house as the crows shadowed them in the air. 'Catching the mother' was Lumboo's expression for apprehending a cat.

Begum Tabaq identified the cat reclining on the wall, and Lumboo began strategically deploying the members of his force at the entrances to different alleys, assigning some to the rooftops and porches. These sentries were given orders to monitor the movements of the cat and to sound the alarm if they saw him taking refuge in a ventilator or a chimney cornice. The cat was now alert and watching the action with alarm. The crows who had followed the children were still hanging over their heads and rending the air with their vengeful cawing.

Lumboo climbed onto the roof, and after respectfully nodding at Tabaq Sahib and his friends, stole towards the cat who had watched all this activity with tense apprehension. Lumboo was flanked by his two sons; his one hand held the notorious jute-sack which was the transit parlour of the cats bound for the meat market, and the other was drawn out to seize him.

When Lumboo came dangerously close, the cat bolted, and surprised by a sentry at the far end of the wall, jumped into the alley. 'There! Catch it!' Tabaq Sahib shouted from his roof. While the cat was struggling, the sentries on top of the roofs proclaimed its whereabouts with shouts and whistles. Lumboo and his sons quickly came down from the roof. Some of the crows who had just alighted rose into the air when they saw a cat so close by. The cat was restless, and it suited Lumboo's purposes well, for the point of the exercise was to tire out the animal with constant stalking, until it lay panting in some dark corner of the alley, unable to go another foot for its life.

Tabaq Sahib, Basmati and Bhai Qamoosi watched as Lumboo stuffed the cat into the sack. With his remaining strength the cat had lacerated Lumboo's arms, and rubbing his arm which carried the bulging and rippling sack, Lumboo walked away in the direction of the meat market.

'There! That's one of my problems taken care of!' Tabaq Sahib said, and turned towards Bhai Qamoosi. 'What became of my article, Bhai?' he asked. After Basmati's assurance that a pesticide dealer was very interested in financing his campaign if only Tabaq Sahib promised to support his company's tender in the municipal board upon his election, Tabaq Sahib had decided to send the article about the relief-fund fraud to daily *Qandeel*. The article had not been printed yet. Instead, Bhai Qamoosi came upon Dr Adbari's second article on the history of termites.

'Put it away!' Tabaq Sahib said. 'I am in no mood to hear any hocus-pocus.'

'But you must listen to this,' Bhai Qamoosi insisted. 'This is a true incident.'

'Come on, Bhai Qamoosi! Let's have it!' Basmati was obviously in a good mood that day. 'What is this true incident?'

Bhai Qamoosi looked up. The crows had become relatively quiet after the dispersion of Lumboo's *lashkar*. He opened the paper to the article and folding the rest of the supplements under it, began:

'In the year of our Lord Seventeen Hundred and Thirteen, the Franciscan friars of the cloister of St Anthony in the province of Piedade no Maranhão, Brazil, were greatly annoyed by termites, which devoured their food, destroyed their furniture, and even threatened to undermine the walls of the monastery. Application was made to the bishop for an act of interdiction and excommunication, and the accused were summoned to appear before an ecclesiastical tribunal to give account of their conduct. The lawyer appointed to defend them urged the usual plea about their being God's creatures and therefore entitled to sustenance, and made a good point in the form of an *argumentum ad monachum* by praising the industry of his clients, the white ants, and declaring them to be in this respect far superior to their prosecutors, the Grey Friars. He also maintained that the termites were not guilty of criminal aggression, but were justified in appropriating the fruits of the fields by the right derived from the priority of possession, inasmuch as they had occupied the land long before the monks came and encroached upon their domain. The trial lasted for some time and called forth remarkable displays of legal learning and forensic eloquence, with numerous citations of sacred and profane authorities on both sides, and ended in a compromise, by the terms of which the plaintiffs were obliged to provide a suitable reservation for the defendants, who were commanded to go thither and to remain henceforth within the prescribed limits. In the chronicles of the cloister it is recorded, under date of Jan. 1713, that no sooner was the order of the prelatic judge promulgated by being read officially before the hills of the termites that they all came out and marched in columns to the place assigned. The monkish annalist regards this prompt obedience as conclusive proof that the Almighty endorsed the decision of the court.'

'Bogus!' Tabaq Sahib said.

'What do you mean?' Basmati asked, 'Don't you believe it?'

'Do *you* believe it?' Tabaq Sahib returned.

'How am I to know?' Basmati's bewilderment was genuine.

'Ask Bhai Qamoosi!' Tabaq Sahib suggested.

'Why don't you ask Bhai Qamoosi!' Basmati asked.

Tabaq Sahib smiled knowingly. 'I know very well what Bhai Qamoosi would say! And therefore, I won't ask!'

Basmati turned towards Bhai Qamoosi. 'Records of animal communication have been around since the time of Solomon,' Bhai Qamoosi said, not looking up from the newspaper. 'My grandfather knew an Englishman who had spent some years learning the language of monkeys and wrote a book on its grammar. What is the wonder in an intelligent man understanding and solving the termite problem?'

'See!' Tabaq Sahib looked at Basmati. 'Now what do you make of that?'

'I for one ...' Basmati was beginning to think of a reply when Bhai Qamoosi interrupted him. 'This time Dr Adbari also provides some strategies to exterminate the insects,' he said. 'Listen to this:'

'It is difficult to provide here a definite method for eradicating the termites. However, a brazier left burning outside the termite nests can prove effective in the following way: Termites are dependent on intestinal protozoa, who parasitise on the termites themselves, to supply them with vital enzymes to digest the woody tissue. Being more vulnerable than their environment, these protozoa die at lower temperatures than the termites. With the even heat of the braziers the nest could be heated enough to kill off the protozoa, while sparing the termites and without driving them deeper into their nests. Once the protozoa are killed, it would only be a matter of time before the termites too, are wiped out. A whole termitarium could also be destroyed by poisoning a few worker termites. Since workers feed other workers and soldiers and the queen, the poison could spread and relieve a household of their menace.'

'Now, Bhai Qamoosi!' Tabaq Sahib started in a taunting tone, 'Why don't you hurry to the bazaar before all the braziers are sold out. One genius got rid of the termites by sending them into the jungle; this man, Adbari, might also prove a genius. And if you don't want to buy one, you could borrow mine. You just have to clean it. Last week my wife had made some shish-kebabs ...'

'Shish-kebabs!' Basmati started before Tabaq could even realise his mistake. '*Shish-kebabs*, Tabaq Sahib?'

'We had some guests ...' Tabaq Sahib's tone was apologetic.

'Now I remember!' Basmati said. 'It was around noon last week, right? I told my wife that I could smell someone grilling shish-kebabs. What a shame Tabaq Sahib! How scandalous that shish-kebabs are grilled behind your friends' backs, and devoured in silence, without so much as a burp. Nobody asked, "How about some shish-kebabs, Basmati, Bhai Qamoosi!" As for me, I have a peptic ulcer and I can't eat spicy food, but Bhai Qamoosi would have liked a skewer or two, perhaps! Right, Bhai Qamoosi?' Basmati turned towards Qamoosi.

'I don't like shish-kebabs!' Bhai Qamoosi replied.

'I am telling you, those guests ...' Tabaq Sahib interjected.

'Now listen to this!' Basmati began, ignoring Tabaq Sahib, 'Why don't you like shish-kebabs, Bhai Qamoosi? But, Tabaq Sahib! I did not expect that of you. Your volunteers too! No, I am seriously disappointed ...!'

'All right, Basmati! You win! Give me the day, and I will make shish-kebabs for you myself. I will also grind the special spices,' Tabaq Sahib offered.

Basmati accepted Tabaq Sahib's surrender with nobility. 'Any day is good for me. My doctor has said that once in a while spicy food is not harmful, as long as I have my glass of milk, and a piece of papaya before going to bed. Ask Bhai Qamoosi when it would suit him!' he suggested.

'I have told you Basmati, I don't like shish-kebabs ...' Bhai Qamoosi interposed.

'Again you have started ...' Basmati turned on Qamoosi angrily.

While his advice on getting rid of the termites by heating their nest was given with every good intent, unfortunately Dr Adbari forgot to warn people about the danger of carbon monoxide poisoning by the brazier. Obviously this method was strictly for outdoor use, but people thought it a good idea to heat the doors and the beams as well as the nests, and they left the coal braziers overnight in badly ventilated rooms. In the first week after his article appeared in the Press, five people were admitted to the hospital with advanced symptoms of carbon monoxide poisoning. But although the people were clearly in the wrong, it did not stop the lawyer for one of the victims from filing a petition against Dr Adbari and the editor and publisher of *Qandeel* for irresponsible reporting.

As an unfortunate consequence of the lawsuit, Dr Adbari's third article never saw the light of day. In that article he had contended that since the termites of Purana Shehr were an unknown variety, and as the city's soil was not their natural habitat, they must have come with Mahmood of Ghazni's carts and carriages, a few centuries ago. In the same paper he had also discoursed on the place of termites in folklore. But more than the false charges levelled against him and the written reprimand which he received from the office of his superior, Dr Adbari was made despondent by the fact that his article was not published. The learned man had been devoutly keeping the cuttings of his articles, and sending copies to his friends all over the country.

The lawsuit against Dr Adbari and the daily *Qandeel* did not stop his word from spreading. It is unclear whether it was some hint in Dr Adbari's learned essay on the history of the termites and their encounter with the Franciscan friars, or a recourse which was imminent, but soon the quarters of the *qalandars* in the Pukka Qila were thronged for charms to drive away the termites. Many charms encrypted with holy words and figures were interred in the termite nests to thwart the evil spirits. All these charms were consumed overnight by the evil they were supposed to ward off, and the school of thought which believed that the termites had come from the Almighty to visit condign chastisement upon the sinners among them, were scandalised when they witnessed that the wrath of this insect was as irreverent with the holy scriptures as with the profane, both of which it devoured with equal relish.

Meanwhile, recipes to destroy termites were being circulated. Some proposed that rubbing bitter almond oil on the furniture would keep the termites at bay. Others thought that nothing was as effective as pouring a cauldron of boiling oil down the termites' nest. Another procedure called for blowing up the nests after stuffing them with gunpowder. But no one method proved feasible. The recurring floods had made the rationing of provisions necessary. The bridge was still not open to the heavy-goods train, and all the private trucks and lorries had been requisitioned by the government for the flood-relief effort. The consequence was that a very thin supply of basic necessities reached Topee Mohalla through privately hired carts. There was hardly enough oil to cook, let alone to waste on the termites. And even in times of peace only the rich could indulge in luxuries like bitter almond oil. As to the gunpowder method, it was speedily abandoned after half a dozen people blew up their limbs along with the termite nests. So the termites burgeoned as before.

The *qalandars* then came up with their own patent recipe for the termites. Most of their cures were animal-based. For instance the cure for flatulence – and a sure fire medicament – was to smoke rabbit droppings in a hookah. They maintained that if the feathers and flesh of a woodpecker were burnt in a house, the termites would as a certainty leave the house and go elsewhere. But first of all a woodpecker had to be procured. The *qalandars* were not into hair-splitting, and would readily sell crow's flesh and kites' feathers in the name of woodpecker's. However, this recipe proved as ineffective as the rest.

Public morale was at its lowest and was soon overcome by apathy. What if there *were* termites? There had been worse things before. The plague for instance. And termites did not harm human beings, contrary to what Imam Jubba had said about sinners. When there was nothing left for them to eat, they would die out or go away. Before long it was reasoned that in fact the termites were working on their own destruction by eating the doors and windows. Once they were consumed, the termites would have no quarters. And they would return to wherever they had come from. Also, such phenomena were not known to last forever. If the termites had gone mad, as some people maintained, or if some disease had broken out among them, which made them behave unnaturally, as some others believed, they could not survive for long. All will be well in the coming days, *insha'allah*! everyone thought.

Despite the restricted access to the bridge to mainland, the food supply was until now intact and those who had expressed fears about its being disrupted had been harshly rebuked and asked to hold their black tongues. Conditions were bad enough as it was and nobody was in a mood to hear what further horrors were to come, or what was imminent as a natural outcome of what had gone before. However, what was around soon turned the corner and stared everyone in the eye. The termites reached the meat market, and although the food supply was not jeopardised as a consequence, life in Topee Mohalla once again took a new turn.

With its mounds of tallow and pungent winds, the meat market resembled the rotting corpse of a leviathan, at whose blubber a thousand sailors were hacking away, without arriving at the inhumed ambergris. There the butchers had raised their wooden thrones, adorned by the scalped heads of cud-chewing beasts, which stared at shoppers with their denuded eyes in raw horror.

Like strings of garlands decorating the nuptial bed, the flayed bovine carcasses embellished a butcher's stall, hanging above his head from steel hooks on a railing. From time to time he raised his knife like a destructive juvenile to pluck those strings and hack them to pieces on his wooden stump with his cleaver, disturbing swarms of bluebottle flies with every thud.

Mixed among the cling-clang of knives, the thud of cleavers, the crunching and crackling of bones, and the squeak of the mince grinder, was the constant growling hum of the cats, fighting over scraps of flesh and bone. Many were born there and several were brought to the meat market with their eyes still ungummed. There were few cats as big and imposing as the citizens of the meat market. But rotund and copious as these cats were, on account of plentiful food, their senses had become dull from lack of employment. Riotous and capricious as the harem of a sterile sultan, they were no match for a shrewd cat like Kotwal who lived entirely on his wits.

Aversion to water came as naturally to the butcher as it did to the cat. Water was a redundant substance in his universe. Even when drinking it, he spat out the first draught, as if to debase it before its consumption. Consequently, a butcher's pride was seriously compromised if his shop was washed with water. The mark of a pedigree butcher was grease. Therefore, grease was everywhere, and ingeniously substituted for many provisions. At closure the shop was laved with a piece of fat, and in the morning it was the inaugural abluent; if the meat was a measure short, a scrap of fat was thrown in for adjustment. If cats or dogs were seen marking the walls, they were chastised by a projectile of fat. In the winters the whiskers of the butcher looked like salt and pepper, wherein the salt was the congealed fat. Even the glib tongue of the butcher, which endeared him to many housewives, who in genteel company would have never allowed certain liberties taken with them, which the butcher was permitted, seemed to have some of the influence of the ubiquitous fat. In the imposing audience of the omnipresent tallow, the butcher, his aspect burnished with grease, sat with a knife clenched between his greasy big toe and the oleaginous second, removing the fat from around the flesh, and making small pieces of meat, a picture of hard work and industry.

But for their tails, the animals had been wholly skinned. The skin on the tail was not flayed to assure the customers that the beef they took home was verily beef, not donkey or horse, and that the mutton was indeed mutton, not dog. This precaution was taken by the respectable butchers after a hurricane of rumours some years back, that a herd of old and decrepit asses and horses had disappeared in the abattoir. Also, there was constant speculation about the one way traffic of pye-dogs inside the slaughter house, through its back door. These scandals had become so familiar with repetition that they had passed into jokes, and when mentioned, never failed to tickle the otherwise sombre butcher.

But the cheaper and busier meat dealers never went beyond the minimum municipal standards of meat safety, whose sum total was a turquoise seal with which every carrion was stamped before it came out of the abattoir. This seal of municipal approval, which could allegedly be bought for ten rupees outside the slaughter house, vaguely defined the meat as fit for human consumption.

It was a custom with visitors to the butcher's shop to touch, slap, thump and probe these carcasses in every possible manner. And to perform this fascinating ritual parents raised their children over their heads, when they could not reach the meat.

Butchery was a trade which still took apprentices, but its discipline was so severe and the character had to be moulded from such an early age that only his natural son could be a successor to the butcher's trade. And thus the presence of the chubby apprentice, an animated transmutation of adipose tissue, sitting by his father's side, plying the mince grinder with a bandaged hand, and pounding the cutlets with the flat of the cleaver, while learning the many tricks of the trade.

The butcher's knife and cleaver had become extensions of his limbs. He flourished them every time he saw a familiar face enter his shop and rubbed them together in a friendly, gleeful welcome. In this gesture the butcher felt his dominance over his client. One of his innocent indulgences was to fantasise about having a quarrel with his tough customers (the type who insist on less fat and bone without shelling out the extra it must cost): he, all armed, and the latter empty-handed. In his mind's eye, the butcher had gone through the whole sequence and the constituent motions many times, and had always emerged victorious, if bloody. That this fantastic match did not end with the kill, but proceeded to flaying and drawing, was a little alarming indeed, but on the face of it there was no harm in an innocuous little fantasy of a good citizen, whose other fancy – when the shop was not too crowded – was to scale his plump and buxom clients in their meat to bone ratio.

Because of power breakdowns, ice had not been supplied to the meat market for three days. Therefore, the evening before the two meatless days, the butchers had salted the leftover meat and hung it on the hooks to dry. When the butchers reached their operation on the third day, they found the cats unusually restless and jumpy.

When the butchers stepped on their stalls, they creaked loudly and sometimes even crumbled under their weight. In one shop, with one blow of his cleaver the butcher's stump broke into shards, scattering the nesting white ants all over the place. The cats snarled, shook their legs with great anxiety and jumped onto the butcher's stall when they saw the termites fall in a spray on the floor. They growled angrily and refused to alight when he brandished his cleaver, and clung on to the meat hanging by the rails when he tried to disperse them with the sweep of his arm. The termites were also found stuck to the meat and when dipping in water and exposing it to light did not help, it had to be thrown to the animals. The real cause for the cats' disruptive behaviour was found out later, when termites were discovered in their claws, biting their way into the flesh.

There was nothing to do but to close down the meat market until the termites had left. Meat could not be sold from the pavements, so the butchers hired donkey carts which had been saved because the cart owners had decided to keep them in motion. There were designated places all over the city where fresh donkeys or mules could be harnessed into the carts. And a cart was not allowed to stop anywhere for more than one hour. There were more animals than carts and therefore it was easily arranged. Also, the cart owners had got all kinds of new businesses because of the termite outbreak, and it was a practical pursuit. They were in constant demand by people shifting their belongings to safer areas, or requiring them to sell something from the carriage as it was no longer safe to store edibles. There was not such a ready supply of horses in the city as there was of donkeys, and therefore in the night the tonga carriages were loaded onto the bigger boats and left floating on the water at a safe distance from the river bank. Some tonga-walas whose carriages had been damaged and who could not afford to feed their horses after the loss of daily wages had let them loose and these horses were roaming free on the streets, helping themselves to whatever pleased their fancy, and destroying whatever the termites had left of people's gardens and hedges.

Early in the morning, butchers carts issued forth from the charnel house loaded with carcasses and blocks of ice. The sky was overcast and, secured between slabs of ice, the meat remained good the whole day. The butcher drove the cart while his apprentice clung to the rear, preventing the meat from falling as the driver, new to the art and caprices of live donkeys, negotiated sharp turns. Over their heads flew the crows and the kites, swooping whenever an opportunity to steal a morsel presented itself. The customers were faithful and their patronage did in no measure diminish under the changed circumstances, even though the price of meat had been raised a little to defray the rent of the carts.

But while these efficient arrangements were made to everyone's satisfaction, very few remembered that the meat market cats would be left without any means of survival until the Market reopened. It was on the third day after the closure of the meat market that the municipal sweepers and the milkman on his bicycle, who were the first people in the streets every morning, saw the alleys of Topee Mohalla teeming with clusters of cats. Of every age and description, their hungry droves were stealing inside houses through open drains, climbing roofs, indulging in skirmishes with the house pets, and bustling all over the place in a state of great excitement. Their loud meows blended with the diminishing dreams of the sleepers and they woke up to find their houses flooded with cats who had been exiled ages ago with Lumboo's help. No matter how hard they rubbed their eyes, the cats did not disappear. With even greater appetites they were returning to the houses which had shut their doors upon them. Some came with families, some alone. Kittens and grand-kittens of old exiles who had breathed their last in the meat market returned to the houses of their ancestors, to make their patrimonial claims.

When Lumboo heard the news, he shut himself in his quarters after securing all the doors and windows, and refused to go out anywhere, convinced that the cats had come for him as a body to seek retribution. He was so fearful of his own convictions that that night, when he saw two particularly large tomcats prowling on his courtyard wall, hunting for lizards and chameleons, he came out with his hands clenched together in repentance, tears streaming down his face, swearing upon his life that he would no longer have anything to do with their tribe. His loud pleas for mercy frightened away the cats as he fell yowling onto his knees on the courtyard floor.

Topee Mohalla was devastated by Lumboo's resolve. There were scores of cats on every roof and their belligerent mood soon took the purpose out of any fatuous resolves of packing them off in sacks to be drowned in the river. They hung around the houses, followed the housewives, and boldly snatched pieces of meat from the pots cooking on the stove. When babies were left unattended, they snatched their banana-shaped milk bottle from them, chewed off the nipple, spilt the milk all over the child, and lapped it up with relish, completely indifferent to the cries of the infant, bawling out his eyes under their sharp claws. When the butcher's cart arrived they scurried out of the house and jumped onto it whenever it stopped, to tear and bite into the carcasses. The apprentice had a hard time keeping them and the scavenging birds at bay.

Bano Tamanna was afraid of the cats' abnormal interest in the rabbits. The rabbits were introduced into the house on Mirzban's initiative to teach his granddaughters the truth and reality of life, which their dolls did not inculcate. On one of their trips to the bazaar with Bano Tamanna the girls had been attracted to a wooden doll-house. Unable to afford the expensive imported model, Bano Tamanna promised to show them how to construct an equally nice doll-house of their own from empty matchboxes. She emptied two carton-loads of matchboxes into a bottle and gave the casings to the girls. And from the next day, after she had explained the basics, the two girls set down to work.

A pair of scissors, a bottle of glue, and sheets of coloured paper were all that was needed. The empty matchboxes were glued together in blocks. Small door knobs were made from pieces of matchsticks, and the matchboxes were cut and flattened to fit in as cupboard shelves and table tops. A row of boxes partitioned the house as walls, and square holes were cut in the middle to make windows and vents. Then the glazed paper was pasted on the surface, painting, carpeting, and tiling the house. A few dolls were clothed and boarded all over the estate. The detachable cardboard roof, neatly fitted in with a chimney, was finally put on once everything inside was completed to the satisfaction of the girls.

Soon enough they fought over the proprietorship of the doll-house, and stopped talking to each other. Bano Tamanna intervened, and to diffuse the crisis proposed a marriage between their dolls. The bridegroom was the elder sister's boxer doll whose punches were operated by two levers on his back. His attire needed a pair of shorts, the toy factory having supplied only a long, loose gown. The bride had been manufactured by Bano Tamanna herself for the younger girl from the cuttings of her old Eid clothes and was stuffed with cotton from an old pillow. Her long plait was made of an old shoelace and the features were sewn on her face by stitches of different length. The boxer appeared on the wedding day attired in a *sherwani* and pyjamas with his mittens on and his arms askew. The elder sister said the wedding prayer. After this auspicious ceremony, the bride and the bridegroom retired inside the doll-house through the roof to celebrate their nuptials, and the matchmakers communicated the next day's programme to each other in the *Fay* dialect, so that the newlyweds might not become privy to their plans. The *Fay* dialect was the secret language of children, in which the *ff* sound randomly punctuated the syllables of speech, and an experienced listener could discern the message by purging the words of the superfluous *ff*s.

Throughout, Mirzban had looked with apprehension at

his granddaughters' minute orchestration of their dolls' lives. The idea that they might grow up to expect the same unconditional obedience from their husbands and in-laws disturbed him. The dolls went along with their fancies without question, and the girls' whims were neither checked nor frustrated. Thinking that a pet might perhaps cure this state of affairs and save his granddaughters from certain disappointment in later life, Mirzban bought them a pair of rabbits from the market. But after their momentary interest in the rabbits was over, the girls ignored them and returned to grooming their dolls.

Left on their own, the rabbits burrowed deep inside Mirzban's old sofa to establish a breeding farm between the alleys of helical springs and straw. From that hole, every two months a new pack of rabbits appeared. They dug up the nursery, stole fruits and vegetables from the baskets, and littered the whole house with their refuse. Once they even stole two mangoes immersed in ice water from a *degchi* left on the floor under the dining table. Under the circumstances Mirzban was forced to consider giving them away. Bano Tamanna would hear nothing of it and objected to it on the grounds that it would leave a bad impression on the girls' minds. Mirzban relented, but every time the rabbits struck he gave Bano Tamanna a disparaging look, and she avoided it by rushing off to the refuge of the kitchen, making way through the sea of rabbit droppings.

Because of the rabbits, Mirzban's house was attracting the growing attention of the cats. In the beginning their watch on the rabbits was of playful alertness, but it slowly grew in intensity. The first step was taken by Kotwal. The delightful keenness with which the meat market cats watched them made him see the rabbits in an entirely new light and one humid night when the clouds were parted and an unfortunate white rabbit shone brightly in the moonlight, Kotwal made his exit through the porch, with the wriggling rabbit suspended from his jaws. Bano's worst fears materialised as that gory act cleared the way for other cats, and within a week there were only eight rabbits left.

The power supply had been partially restored, but because of a heavy load, there were frequent breakdowns. In some places, live wires still lay on the road submerged in rain water, imperilling lives. Children were restricted to their homes. People ventured out in the nights only when necessary and as they groped their way with the help of lanterns and torches in the dark, the blinking and blazing eyes of a thousand cats frightened the wits out of them. Perhaps on account of their size, the cats were now dreaded more than the termites. Stories of how the djinns had transformed themselves into cats, and how potent evil would befall one who harmed them, were doing rounds. It was impossible to get any sleep at night, as the cats growled and the dogs barked at doors and wooden beams which ticked with termites. The madhouse of Guru Bunder also added to this racket.

A certificate of mental health had yet to be issued from this establishment. The treatment was long and laggard, and while a regimen of high-voltage shocks and cold baths made the patients more and more indisposed towards leaving one another's company, it considerably raised the monthly electricity and water bills too, further straining the meagre resources of the establishment. And yet any happy results of this treatment were wanting.

The only sign of progress which the two hundred-odd inmates had shown was in displaying an understanding of the principle of electricity. Whether there was an electrician among them was not known, but what *was* known was that they had recognised as a body that the same energy which brightened their cells and corridors, also powered the electrodes. They made a show of this knowledge in an ungodly uproar every time there was a power failure, leaving the five wardens quite hopelessly employed in addressing them individually with their bamboo staffs. Newcomers to the house who were slow to learn all other codes of conduct, showed no lack of aptitude in picking up this ritual and promptly joined in the outcry. Since most of the power breakdowns occurred during the night, the cries from the madhouse could be heard throughout the length and breadth of the city and disturbed people in their sleep. Mirzban who always slept lightly, would wake up and listen to the noises until they died out close to daybreak.

During the last ten days, two dogs lying on the ground at night were swarmed over by the termites and before their yelping rose the dead, the insects had already blinded them and entered their orifices. The dogs had to be shot and everyone was forced to let their pets sleep with them in their beds at night. This was probably the reason why nobody attempted to drive them away when the cats also jumped into their beds, virtually putting an end to all things conjugal.

While all these changes took place, Kotwal remained the undisputed lord of all cats. The newcomers did not intrude on the affections of Bilotti whose beat remained unchanged. The termites did not bother her, and Bilotti's straw basket with its vegetables, although it remained in its customary place on the ground, was untouched by the termites. The space of Bilotti's cats was not encroached upon either, although the straw baskets they slept in were gone, and at night they were a little uncomfortably perched on the two steel beds Bano Tamanna had bought from the hospital auction to put in the courtyard.

Bilotti's death disturbed the routine in Topee Mohalla further. Bano Tamanna woke up early one morning to the doleful growls of Kotwal who was sitting near Bilotti's head. She had died sometime early in the night because there was already a long line of ants from their nest to Bilotti's bed on the floor. Kotwal's laments soon gathered all the other cats who descended from the walls. That day, many husbands, upon returning from work, found their wives' heads sticking out of the doors to assign them the unpleasant task of going to the Pukka Qila market to buy groceries. As if this was not enough, Bilotti's cats had been in a foul mood that day after being denied their morning meal. They did not even go near the bowl where Bano Tamanna had put some milk and bread for them, and instead were thieving whatever food they could find in the neighbouring houses. Kotwal had struck many times since morning and the losses had amounted to several pounds in choice meats; and from Mirzban's house, in two juicy rabbits who had ventured too close to the casement.

But after that day Kotwal was not seen around for many days. He was believed dead, until one night he roused the slumbering neighbourhood with his hideous vociferation. He had brought in his tow an old debilitated cat, never before seen, who from that day accompanied him everywhere. Kotwal showed utmost devotion to her although she was practically blind and well past her fertile days. Kotwal's neglected harem soon found new lovers in Bilotti's other studs. Other cats avoided this couple for some reason and sometimes, on moonlit nights, when Kotwal guided the matriarchal cat along the walls of the neighbourhood, her feeble swagger reminded people of Bilotti, who once sold vegetables in their neighbourhood.

The Sunday matinée at Mahtab Cinema was usually set apart for the screenings of oldies. And long before Master Puchranga's artwork was hoisted up outside the cinema to display the familiar pose of *Umrao Khanam* with the bells of her *ghungroo* flying all over the place in her last angry dance, Mirza Poya had been circulating within and without Chhalawa Hotel with the news of the great event.

Waves of nostalgia swept the torpid housewives, and early on Sunday morning the smell of sautéed onions rose up from the kitchens in Topee Mohalla. In Qasr-e Yunani, the pestle pounded the turmeric tuber, the garlic bulbs, and ginger roots; and the grating slab pulverised the mince and the condiments, as Bano Tamanna got over her cooking for the day and prepared for the show. She was a regular pilgrim to the Sunday matinées. The big screen was the place where she and her impressionable neighbour, Begum Basmati, took their emotions and tears. While Bano was making the final arrangements, other houses in the neighbourhood were also in a state of great stir. Mothers soothed their young, and sisters sent their younger siblings to the toilet to relieve themselves, so that they would not have to drag them during the interval to washrooms where the many loves of Firdousi were illustrated in fantastic detail.

Bano Tamanna shuffled out of her house and knocked at the Basmatis' door. To her relief she found Begum Basmati ready. They emerged into the main street after traversing the alleys, where they came across others like them, shambling along in burqas and chaddars, leaving behind the redolent trail of imitation colognes and other aromatics. Those who lived close by walked in the sweltering sun, covering the heads of their children with towels; some hired tongas, others rickshaws, and the affluent families putt-putted to the cinema houses on their 50cc Honda and Vespa scooters. It was not an uncommon sight to see four or six children sandwiched between the parents on a two-wheeler, a few more secured in the front basket like baby kangaroos, with the rest dangling by their mother's lapels and, what was most surprising of all, never once falling.

Mirza Poya was standing in queue outside the ticket window, looking furtively at the towering Makrani usher, the best dressed person around Mahtab Cinema. The Makrani's sparkling mirror-studded cap and his golden embroidered sandals were custom-made to his large size. Under his shirt a glittering cummerbund descended from his waist to his ankles as a sign of prosperity and did pendulum duty there. On his wrist he sported a couple of bracelets inscribed with parts of the scripture and wore a gold hoop in his left ear. The rings which adorned his fingers were obtained from the *qalandars* for ministration in his various unholy designs.

The cinema management had decided to screen *Umrao Khanam* for at least a week because of its popular appeal. The first two days were house-full, and the tickets were available in black, being handed out by the Makrani. It was through recourse to this practice that the sparkling Makrani begot his salary as well as that of the ticket vendor. *Umrao Khanam* was an oldie, but always attracted a great number of people, and the seth who owned Mahtab had rightly predicted that selling tickets in black would work.

The Makrani's duties at Mahtab Cinema combined the offices of the usher, sheepdog and doorman in one. On Fridays he herded people into the queue and occasionally disciplined that unruly mob by a combination of abuse, backhand whacks and kicks. There was no male cinema-goer, no matter how meek or distinguished, who had escaped one of the three checks, for in every queue there was bound to be some apostate who attempted to defile its sanctity by shoving and pulling. At such times the queue became the mortar in which the pestle of Makrani's wrath moved indiscriminately. Retaliation was meaningless if not perilous, so his sallies were treated much in the line of the woman's slap, the jester's remark, and the beggar's curse; no one was seemingly discomfited by it.

While waiting in the queue outside the Mahtab, Mirza had frequently suppressed the overpowering urge to pounce upon the Makrani and tear him limb from limb, with bare hands. It was always hot in the afternoons, and with the humidity it was almost maddening to be standing outside the shut window, and to be pushed forward by the surge produced every time someone new joined the queue.

'One push and the bastard would crash against the window,' Mirza Poya suddenly addressed the man standing in the queue in front of him. The stranger looked around to see who was the object of Mirza's anger, and when he saw Mirza muttering curses under his breath with his eyes riveted on the Makrani, he nodded his head and grimaced with the same desperation latent in Mirza's thoughts. The violent urge to knock down the Makrani was totally out of character for Mirza. It was fomented in part by the heat and the rank and humid air inside the cinema house lobby, and in part by the uncommonly turbulent nature of the queue. But Mirza's listener warmed up to his thoughts. 'And why not?' he asked. 'Here we are standing in the heat, that mother-fucking window is closed, and look at these pimplings,' he gestured to Mirza as another man paid the Makrani and returned, counting the tickets, to his family standing in the corner. 'What I want to know is, where are they getting all this dough from?' the man demanded of Mirza.

'Ladies! Give way! Ladies!' the Makrani shouted as Bano Tamanna and Begum Basmati moved forward to the ladies counter at the ticket window. Immediately the Makrani caught someone falling out of the queue because of a strong push from the back, and catching him by the scruff of his neck, the Makrani shoved him back into the queue at random, amidst laughter and abuse from others in the line.

Mirza recognised Bano Tamanna and looked away. He was apprehensive because the man in front of him, having become familiar with him, might pass some unbecoming remark about Bano Tamanna or Begum Basmati, and he was thinking of a way to quickly divert the conversation in such an event, when, to his relief, the ticket window opened and everyone, including the Makrani, the man in front of him and Mirza Poya himself, found each other battling to get to the front.

The Makrani was in his element, now pouncing upon the front row, now jumping to the back, shoving people indiscriminately like someone over-stuffing a bolster with both hands. Mirza was dreading the Makrani's attentions, but fortunately, those behind him were disciplined instead and the surge forward was not quite as strong, by the time Mirza got to the front, as it was before, and he managed to get his ticket without being molested by the Makrani. When Mirza Poya held the ticket close to his eyes to check his seating, he noticed that one third of it was mutilated by the termites.

The interior of the Mahtab Cinema was smelly and damp like a dirty refrigerator's. Although the building was constructed as a cinema-house, its walls crowded with patches of broken plaster, and holes where the bricks had come loose and the swallows had moved in to nest, was vaguely suggestive of an abandoned courtroom. In the darkness, the torch of the Makrani usher marked the seats with a fleeting sweep, and left the people to stomp and stumble in semi-darkness over others already seated to get to their designated seats, while the news bulletin sponsored by a famous pesticide manufacturer blazoned. Slides were shown of the sites the floods had devastated and the relief work in progress. Wearing a helmet over his head, the minister for Public Works was seen jumping over some wooden planks during his visit to the affected areas. Later he was shown handing out relief cheques. After the flag of the fatherland had fluttered at the end of the bulletin, and an abridged version of the national anthem was played, at which everyone stood up, the certificate of the National Censor Board appeared on the screen.

In those days cinema owners were still law-abiding, and although the contents of the censor certificate, like its purpose, were even then extremely vague and illegible, they had not yet started inserting three-minute height-of-delight pornographic *totas* in the films. Nudity was still confined to the Coca-Cola ads in which beautiful, sun-tanned blondes clad in colourful bikinis, fluttering like butterflies, jumped headlong from spring-boards into the Coke bottle, and drowned in the loud effervescence of the carbonated liquid, along with the sighs of men in the audience.

Umrao Khanam was called an epic length drama, but that's where its resemblance to an epic ended. Its theme was a riddle of a most obdurate nature. The infinite unravelling of the same enigma in several other preceding productions hadn't compromised its essence yet. People in general have short memories but the local cinema-goers, it appeared, had the shortest. They hadn't shown the slightest slackening of interest in the story of the anomalous separation of the protagonists by the villain, and their similarly unnatural last minute unison through conjugal oaths.

The people had a taste for the robust where heroines were concerned, and to meet the public demand the film industry had bred a pair of square-jawed and gruff-voiced fillies: literally a match for the finest charger. They were the corporeal ideal of health and crude vigour, and in scenes of intimacy and license their brawny grip had smothered many men. Off the set, the mortal fear they instilled had brought the two male protagonists together in a singularly unproductive relationship. They were themselves sons of retired heroines, who sometimes played mothers or mothers-in-law alongside their sons.

While the film industry was considered well supplied with a pair each of heroes and heroines, it fell short of the mark when it came to villains, having only one article of that denotation. But the evil of this man was immaculately versatile. He appeared in almost every production, was killed in a variety of encounters without fail, and sprang back to menace in the following release like the incorrigible head of the mythical Hydra. As to his screen life it was anything but dull, earning him the title of 'Rape-master'. Being around for a long time he had distinguished himself by the singular honour of defiling the mother, the daughter and the granddaughter of the same natural family on screen. All in all he had a good time and was rumoured to be more popular with the heroines than the two heroes.

The censor board certificate inaugurated the film and it started in a great din of whistles and catcalls. Overwhelmed by a sudden gust of emotion Mirza Poya sprang up to cheer with the crowd but a thundering curse from the projection room plummeted him into his seat, when someone saw him waving his hands in the line of the beam.

The film had run for about an hour when the reel suddenly snapped and the projector light went out. Unobserved from his seat in the circle, Mirza Poya let out a catcall which was immediately answered with greater pathos by the third-class. As if that was a signal, a great pandemonium burst forth from the third-class, soon taken up by the circles. Mostly populated by loafers and street urchins who had purloined enough capital from several familial and unknown sources to lay claim to their admission, the third-class was more brazen in registering their frustration by the cunning use of expletives, but the circles kept their involvement restricted to whistles and catcalls. Listening to this barrage of vulgarity, Bano Tamanna looked at her friend, Begum Basmati, and both broke into embarrassed girlish smiles. The flashlight of the Makrani aimlessly flickered all across the screen in a futile effort to calm the people down. Another minute passed in this activity. Then someone in the projection room signalled to the Makrani. The Makrani shouted, 'Inter-wail!!' The lights came on and the cling-clang of coke bottles and the cries of 'Chips! Cola!' silenced the protesting voices. The clink of bottles also woke the children, who had been lulled to sleep in their mothers' laps. The break had been called before its time because it was taking longer to fix the problem. When the problem was fixed the lights went out and the film resumed.

The villain was causing much weeping and gnashing of teeth all around, but despite that, the restless hands of the mourners found mischief to do. They tossed empty bags of potato chips and bottle tops from their seats in the grand circle, over the heads of the dress circle dwellers, and into the third-class below, separated from the higher galleries like an arena. Their recipients reciprocated this rain of celestial debris with verbal projectiles addressed to the modesty of the grand circle, affording them some respite from the tragic drama on the screen.

The vendor, who always came for his money and bottles, flashing his irritating light after the film had resumed, was pestering the middle rows and diving under people's seats to retrieve his bottles, when black patches appeared on the screen. As someone in the third-class cursed the projector man, the reel broke again. But this time the projector light did not go out, and viewers saw black insects, enlarged a thousand times as in their nightmares, projected onto the screen, creeping leisurely on the lens, wriggling and writhing in their slow, satanic dance. Nobody made a sound, or moved. They sat enraptured by the power of the spectacle in their straw-filled seats in which the termites were already groping. Someone in the projector room cursed and stamped. There was a crash of something heavy falling. The screen turned dark, the house lights came on, frustrating any thoughts of a wild scamper engendered in the conducive darkness. Immediately afterwards, the cinema doors were thrown open and with the sunlight, the Makrani usher materialised, announcing that the show was over. Everyone was told to leave quietly. The house emptied with great expedition because many still owed money to chips and drinks vendors. The vendors were caught behind the crowd and the Makrani, employed in cuffing those persisting for refunds, could not hear their shouts because of the racket in the third-class where a hundred people were elbowing and buffeting each other to exit through the postern at the same time as the swallows, who had been disturbed in their nests by the noise. Bano Tamanna was perhaps the only person who actually stayed back to pay for the drinks. The vendor was in a foul mood because of the absconders and almost snatched the money from her hands.

After the last eventful show of *Umrao Khanam*, and for the first time since the termite outbreak, Mirza Poya felt a genuine hatred for the insects as he noticed them devastate the billboards within a few days. Only the flakes of paint remained. With the wind the paint surface was torn and the passers-by were showered with diverse particles of *Umrao Khanam*'s anatomy, combed out of the hair immediately for fear of termites sticking to them. Springs protruded from the seats in the cinema hall, as the rexene covers and the straw filling disappeared. The projector lens had been broken by the fall. *Umrao Khanam*'s reel was completely ruined, as were several other films lying in the projector room.

One day as Mirza took his usual place on the uncomfortable iron stool in Chhalawa Hotel from where the wooden benches had been removed, and looked across the street, he saw the Makrani hanging a slate outside the Mahtab. Mirza did not even notice that he felt no rancour for the Makrani. The chalking announced the cinema house had closed indefinitely.

Mirzban was not insensitive to the rude manner in which his thoughts had been twice checked just when they were on the verge of connecting the whole riddle of Time and Eternity. Was he treading the proscribed path and exploring the forbidden? In his mind the question had risen more than once.

Had he gone too far in his postulations and hypotheses?

Were they heavenly omens, beckoning him to venture no further in the realm of the Divine?

On both occasions they were so mischievous one could hardly believe they had come about either through holy decree or chaste devices.

Was it then engineered by some profane agency?

All available evidence pointed to that possibility!

Then, was the abominable Fiend officiating himself, or by proxy?

Such were Mirzban's thoughts one evening, as he walked in the direction of the milkman's barn. His granddaughters liked roasted guavas and Bano Tamanna had run out of cow-dung chips for the braziers. The guavas were best roasted in their gentle, even heat. The milkman sold them and the outer walls of his barn were covered with cow-dung chips plastered there to dry in the sun.

'If only Providence would give me a sign that I am on the right path, it would renew my belief that I was not led astray by the Devil,' Mirzban said to himself as he approached a tree on the way. 'Just one sign is all I ask ...!'

The thought had hardly presented itself to Mirzban than he was startled by a rustling in the branches of the tree and a stark-naked man fell in front of him. Because it was dark and he was covered with a profuse growth of whiskers, and tresses which hung down to his shoulders, Mirzban could not see the man's face. He stood there with his heart beating agitatedly and saw the fireflies come out to swarm about the stranger's face.

'Who are you?' Mirzban heard himself asking the man. The thought had occurred to him that probably he was one of the *qalandars*, who sometimes went around without their clothes.

But the naked man remained silent and stretched his arms, as if to embrace Mirzban. Mirzban stepped back. The man did not move. Mirzban found himself in an awkward situation. What would people think if they saw him standing there in front of that man like that? Mirzban was still thinking when the man folded his arms over his chest, and, covering his shoulders with his hands, turned and began walking. Mirzban stood there to see what would happen next. The man took a few steps, then stopped and looked back at Mirzban.

Does he want me to follow him? Mirzban thought. Is it possible that *this* is the sign from God? What should I do? Where will he take me if I were to follow him? Mirzban realised that the man could not go too far. The main street was further down and at that time there would be people around. But what if his presence is really Providential? he considered. Then I shall be held in contempt of a divine augur.

The man took a few steps and again looked back. He obviously wanted Mirzban to follow him, and with a foreboding heart Mirzban let the naked man guide him. He headed straight for the main street and Mirzban followed. The agility of the man amazed Mirzban. He was barefoot and running over stones but his speed never slackened. As he hopped over an open drain, Mirzban felt a pebble get inside his sandals and slip into the gap beneath the right foot's arch. When they were just about to enter the main street and Mirzban was slowing down to see what would happen next, the man suddenly turned and leaped into a dark corner of the alley. At that moment a donkey cart turned the corner at full gallop and if Mirzban had not been alert he would have been thrown under the wheels.

The pebble was moving forward under his instep, and Mirzban shook his foot to get rid of it. But it slipped back under the arch. Mirzban was out of breath. He was also limping as he could not put his full weight onto his right foot, and had to arch it further to keep the stone from getting under the heel. The few times when he tried to shake it out, he was not successful, and he could not wait to unstrap his sandal and get rid of it. The man was moving in the dark alley at great speed and at every step Mirzban feared he might lose him in the darkness. He had come thus far and he was not going to let him slip away now without finding out how this revelation would end.

That it was a sign from God, Mirzban was now convinced, after his miraculous survival of the donkey cart. His head was stormed by images of the possible end to this episode:

Suddenly there would be a blinding flash of light and both he and the naked man would find themselves flying in space without wings: getting closer and closer to a gigantic sphere of light compared to which the sun would be a speck of dirt.

A whirlpool of wind would engulf them and, spinning, they would both be sucked into the presence of absolute darkness; or alternatively, exquisite light.

With great clamour the earth would open in front of them; they would be swallowed into the abysmal depths without a trace, and the earth would become level again.

They would be enveloped by a cloud of incense vapour, ringing with the uproar of djinns reciting *Isme-Azam*, and no sooner would he hear it than his eyes would see the whole world, from its beginning to end, in one complete glance.

'Haaah!', Mirzban shrieked with pain as the sharp end of the pebble got under his heel. And the next moment he ran into a man turning the corner.

When he heard Mirzban's cry behind him the naked man stopped in his tracks for a second. The place where he stopped was lit up, and if Mirzban's cry had not made him look back, with the next couple of steps, he would have reached the cover of darkness where he was headed. But in that brief moment when Mirzban was apologising to the man while staring at the naked man so that he would not disappear, the former managed to follow his gaze and discovered the naked man crouching in the corner. Convinced that he must be the lunatic who had run away from Guru Bunder, and that Mirzban must be chasing him, he immediately raised an alarm, and himself ran after the naked man.

Mirzban stood rooted to the spot, listening to the gradually heightening cries of 'Madman!', 'Get him!', and 'Lunatic!' reverberate in the alley, as he saw both men disappear running into the darkness. As it turned out the naked man was indeed the lunatic who had been at large, and was later caught, but not before he had scandalised a whole family by jumping over their wall into the courtyard where they were sitting for dinner.

Mirzban returned home with a despondent heart and agitated mind.

People were losing their faith in the devices of the *qalandars*, when their fading notoriety was suddenly redeemed through the divine agency of Pir Chamkeela.

On one of his nightly rounds, the zoo-keeper had found the pangolin digging the ground furiously in his cage. A curious man by nature, he put his nose through the bars of its enclosure and found that the animal had dug up a cavity full of termites and was sucking them up with great relish. Apparently many subterranean nests branched out under his cage and the sweet smell of the termites lured the pangolin to expose the tunnels. The zoo-keeper was a man with a fertile imagination, and not one to let an opportunity like this slip him by, early the next day he was in the *qalandars'* quarters.

The city was built around the bases of two geographical slopes. The Pukka Qila stood on the upper step and the lower step had been occupied by the Kutcha Qila and its environs, which included Topee Mohalla. The Kutcha Qila, true to its name, had all but disappeared. There were still some houses and shops under its ramparts, but each rain took its toll when some more mud-plastered bricks from the walls came loose and fell on the heads of unsuspecting passers-by.

Pukka Qila was shrouded in legend and it was held that in its caves was a secret passage which led directly to Mekkah. Another rumour had it that a great lion inhabited that secret passage and he came out every Friday to eat a big bowl of kheer which the *qalandars* especially prepared for him. It was said, the lion solicited mercy for their souls during his audience with God.

The *qalandars* lived around Pukka Qila. At the approach to their neighbourhood was a small platform. Throughout the day a *qalandar* sat there pounding *bhang* in a huge mortar and the jingling of the bells attached to the wooden pestle could be heard from a distance. The *qalandars* wore black robes heavy with dirt and grime; black bracelets; and sported beads strung in ropes under their mouldy beards. They clanged iron tongs in the streets, and sometimes, carrying a black gourd in one hand and a bowl in which incense burned over coals, they went around the city fumigating and purifying the air inside shops and houses for a small fee. In the evenings they retired to their club in Pukka Qila and to their cup of *bhang*. The *qalandars* were assembled there when the zoo-keeper arrived with the pangolin in his sack. The negotiations with the *qalandars* were short, as the zoo-keeper had always brought them good business. The chimpanzee was a case in point.

That chimpanzee was bought off the zoo-keeper by an enterprising *qalandar*, and employed profitably as a delouser in the Pukka Qila market. Although strictly illegal, the practice of buying animals from the zoo was not uncommon. All the zoo-keeper had to do was put a small news item in daily *Qandeel* about an animal's mysterious death and it took care of everything. For this very reason the lions had no young to show for their living in conjugal fashion for over a decade. Sometimes the whole litter of the malnutritioned lioness was stillborn, but in most cases the cubs were either sold to *pehlwans* who kept the cats as their mascots, or to a passing circus.

The chimpanzee sat in the middle of the thoroughfare, wearing a charm for good health and longevity, combing people's hair with his hands for nits and lice, depositing the catch in his ever nibbling mouth, and parting clients' hair with his wet fingers until the *qalandar* pushed them away and made him start afresh on the one next in line: all for the consideration of one rupee. Parents showed this chimpanzee to their children as a sign of God's resourcefulness, whose wrath in olden times had converted sinful tribes into monkeys, in punishment for their transgression of the holy writ; and might do so again.

Late one evening, the singing *qalandars* appeared in Topee Mohalla, ringing their tongs, burning incense, and leading by a rope the garlanded pangolin. They introduced him as Pir Chamkeela, someone dispatched by God from Mekkah through the tunnel to rid the houses of the pious from termites, and provided the following preface for his appearance:

'And Pir Chamkeela was playing with the houris in heaven when an angel came and told him that the pious in Topee Mohalla were praying for him to come and deliver them from the termites. He immediately called for his horse and sword and told the houris that he must go. The houris cried and fell at Pir Chamkeela's feet and rubbing their eyes with Pir Sahib's boots asked, "Pir Sahib! O Pir Sahib! Who will look after us after you have gone?" And Pir Chamkeela replied,

"O Houris! Were I in Heaven to retain a seat,
The termites in Topee Mohalla I must eat!"

'And the head houri held on to Pir Sahib's stirrup and soaked his boot with her hot tears, but God's directive had come. The Great Lion was already sweeping the tunnel with his tail to welcome Pir Chamkeela! Pir Sahib spurred his horse and disappeared into the dust of Hijaz, leaving the head houri crying behind him.'

As the *qalandars* told this story, Pir Chamkeela walked between them, stopping every now and then to smell and scrape the ground. Always alert to the possibilities of a new spectacle, the children were the first to come out of the houses. As the racket of their running and pushing and shouting increased, Pir Chamkeela tried to break his leash and escape. Being unsuccessful in that he curled himself into a ball and lay motionless until the *qalandar* holding his leash jerked it, and dragged him along. Licking his face with his pointed tongue, Pir Chamkeela got up and before long was running at the qalandar's heels. The *qalandars* also shouted at the children to quieten them. The turbulence shifted to the hind quarters of the crowd and, except for the loud chanting of the *qalandars* and the clap of tongs, the procession became relatively quiet.

From the roof Muneemji was looking down at the *qalandars*. Across the alley he could see Begum Basmati peering outside and Ladlay on the balcony. Then Basmati appeared, looked around at the alley and sent his wife inside. He kept standing there himself looking at the *qalandars* and the animal they had brought.

Incidentally, the *qalandars* came to rest at Basmati's door where the ground outside the front wall had been freshly dug by Lumboo's *lashkar*. The clinking stopped, and a *qalandar* chanted something incomprehensible and nodded at Basmati. Not knowing how to react, Basmati nodded back. Pir Chamkeela was smelling the freshly dug ground. It had not been dug deep enough. Probably Lumboo's *lashkar* had dispersed to watch Pir Chamkeela. Muneemji could see their faces in the crowd. A crowd of men had also gathered to see this curious sight. Pir Chamkeela began shovelling the earth with his forepaws. The children tried to climb over each other's shoulders to see the animal better, but for once Pir

Chamkeela kept working. The animal soon dug up a concealed termite nest near the wall, and began decimating it with great dispatch. At this sight there was an uproar. The crowd clapped and bellowed. Again Pir Chamkeela scampered and was violently pulled back. Everyone was tugging the *qalandars* by their sleeves and begging them to have Pir Chamkeela honour their homes with a visit from him. The *qalandars* displayed dissent at such an idea. If the Pir were to visit each house individually, they asked, how would the streets of the city be rid of the menace, an assignment entrusted to the Pir's manifestation. However, the *qalandars* allowed themselves to be prevailed upon by the joint force of appeals, and *nazranas* for the Pir himself. Basmati slipped inside and locked the door the moment it dawned on him what the *qalandar* probably meant by his nod. Ladlay's eyes were now fixed a little higher up and Muneemji realised that Mushtri must be at her window.

At that moment the siren sounded. An air-raid siren had been provided at the mosque by the civil defence administration which was also used to announce the time for starting and breaking fasts. But as this was not the month of fasting, everyone ran indoors to listen to their radios. Muneemji looked up into the sky but saw and heard nothing to suggest an air raid. He could see a blackout happening across the mohalla as the lights went off one by one. The siren was still blaring. Ladlay had withdrawn from the balcony. The *qalandars* were standing in the dark alley looking confused. Then the siren stopped and the lights came on. Slowly people poured out into the alley. It had turned out to be a false alarm. There was no news of an air raid on the radio. In the alley people resumed their solicitations with the *qalandars*.

The siren sounded for three consecutive days when Pir Chamkeela was on his round. Later it turned out that Imam Jubba had sounded it to drive away the *qalandars* from the alleys, and he stopped only after the civil defence authorities found out and restricted its use. The *qalandars* were held in reverence and it was not easy for Imam Jubba to take them on openly as he had the *kathputli* walas. The news about the siren was further confirmed during the next Friday prayers when he took a full half hour denouncing those who sought redress of their miseries in bestial means instead of God, and had therefore inculpated themselves with animal worship.

Pir Chamkeela had proved effective in the courtyards where the floor was not cemented, and although the termites remained undisturbed in the rest of the house, most people were happy to pay and see Pir dig up and consume a few termites in front of their eyes. Houses where Pir either curled up into a ball from fatigue and would not provide service after the *qalandars* had already pocketed the *nazrana*, or where the people complained of termites even after Pir Chamkeela's visitation, the *qalandars* denounced as domiciles of bastards and the impious, thus effectively putting an end to any possible protests.

While carrying Salar's ankle-boots to the cobbler, clamped behind him on the bicycle carrier, Ladlay was troubled by the thought that perhaps Salar had really gone mad. Ladlay cursed himself for getting involved in the affair with Firdousi in the first place. He should have thought of some other way. But now it was too late. He had turned out to be too clever by half and must pay the price. In his ridiculous passion for Noor-e Firdousi, Salar was no longer conducive to hearing about matters of property. At one point he had even frightened Ladlay by mentioning that he may get rid of the tenants' nuisance altogether by transferring all his estate in Noor's name.

From the start forging and posting letters from Firdousi had been a hassle. Although Salar's eyesight was weak, when mailing the first letter Ladlay had taken the extra precaution of smudging the tell-tale post office seal when the counter clerk had turned his back to get him some more stamps from the folder. Although he had been careful, another clerk had seen him touching the letter after it had been stamped, and Ladlay had quickly left the post office. Going out of the main door he had turned back to watch. The clerk was looking at the letter closely. But the letter was delivered and when he heard about it from Salar, Ladlay was greatly relieved.

Then the postal service was disrupted. When Ladlay visited the Post Office to post his second letter from Firdousi to Salar, he saw stacks of mail piled up on the floor and the counters. The strong odour of termicides lying in buckets pervaded the air, and the place looked in complete disarray. Someone told Ladlay that two dozen sacks of mail including state communiqués were stranded in Purana Shehr, awaiting the opening of the railway bridge. That morning a postal clerk had noticed termite tunnels on the walls of the lockers where they had been stored and alerted the postmaster. Fortunately, the damage was limited to only a part of the sack but all other sacks were also torn open and in the ensuing confusion the mail got mixed-up. All of that had to be sorted again, and protected from the termites at the same time. Given the limited resources of a small town's busy post office, it was decided that to save the postal service from collapse, no new mail would be accepted until that already in the pipeline had been cleared.

So Ladlay was obliged to stamp the letter with black ink using one of his own notary seals. Then he smudged it, and paid the postman to deliver it to Salar. The reflection that the measures taken by the post office to choose honest men for the postman's job had failed, afforded him some comfort. During a new recruit's probationary period the postmasters dropped marked currency notes in the letterboxes. The recruits were cautioned that people inadvertently dropped money in the mailboxes when they took out the letters from their pockets. Anyone who failed to redeem these marked bills, obviously could not be trusted with important documents and confidential state mail. But despite these precautions the postmen got corrupted. They held on to telegrams and Eid cards till the very last day, and they were delivered only after a taciturn petition for pocket money had secured their ransom.

It was extremely humid at that early hour of the afternoon and cycling to the cobbler in the heat Ladlay felt like he was wading through screens of steam. In order to generate a solution to the difficulty that presented itself to Ladlay, his mind churned with the same effort as his pedals did. What if the old man had *really* gone berserk? Salar's recent request had set Ladlay's mind thinking. The idea that he stood to gain nothing if Salar totally collapsed was quite clear to Ladlay. However, playing along was also important to get anything out of Salar at this stage, and Ladlay calmed himself down with many self-rebukes for the impatience and frustration he had recently felt.

The notary had convinced Salar that it would be in order to make preliminary arrangements for the concert. If the preparations were to her manager's liking, he would use his influence with Firdousi to get her to agree. Salar was already corresponding with her. All these factors would favour his case. Firdousi was above any material concerns, of course, but it reflected nobly on Salar's part to bequeath a pre-matrimony gift and show his selfless devotion. Salar had written him a cheque and Ladlay insisted that he write it under the head of 'Firdousi's concert arrangement funds' despite Salar's protest that he trusted him fully. Ladlay had already cashed the cheque and transferred the money into another account. Cognisant of Salar's jealous guard of his amorous secrets, Ladlay had utilised his advantage to the full, keeping Salar in the dark about other developments. Recently the Evacuee Trust Property Board had filed a claim on some of the buildings in the area, and Salar's property was included in the list sent to the municipality. If the Evacuee Board's claim was honoured by the court, the owners would be given choice government land as compensation. Then he would have all five fingers in ghee and his head in the *karahi*. Ladlay considered the happy thought and an involuntary chuckle brought relief to his immediate distress.

The ankle-boots were stiff from long disuse, and Ladlay had to wait by the cobbler's side on the wooden box under the peepal tree where two other people were also waiting for their shoes to be polished. They had put on shoes from the many well-worn pairs of sandals lying scattered around. The shoes of one were in a more advanced state of decay than the shoes temporarily available, and the cobbler was obliged to keep an eye on the movement of his feet to frustrate a precipitous flight, while treating his shoes with wax polishes and dandy brushes, spraying them generously with his spit and drying them lightly with a piece of flannel wrapped around his index and middle fingers.

Ladlay dwelt on the new trouble at hand as the odours of polishes and the smell of mouldy leather rose through the cracks of the wooden box under him. The whole matter was so unexpected that Ladlay could not think of a way out. And strangely enough, he himself was to blame.

Ladlay was getting irritated by the long wait when the old Pathan who brought honey dropped by. He had brought the cobbler's monthly supply of bees' wax and therefore another quarter of an hour was wasted in their idle chatter, and in what appeared to Ladlay, pointless laughter. The cobbler wasted some more time in tempering the filaments by threading the cord through yellow balls of wax clenched in his gnarled, blackened hands to check the wax quality, and then got up in the middle of his work to water the small vine he had planted next to his seat, which had found its footing on the peepal's trunk amidst pieces of tanned and untanned leather hanging there, behind Ladlay's back.

Since morning, Salar had been sitting up in bed, smoking the hookah with deep purpose and scratching his chin with a secretive air. When Bano Tamanna opened the scullery to get some more coals for the hookah, Salar asked her to get some for the iron too. He wanted his *sherwani* ironed and Bano had left the coals smouldering in the brazier to do some cleaning in Salar's room before they were ready to be put in the iron. While cleaning the room she discovered the doll-house.

She had kept the doll-house on a shelf, when the girls had tired of it. Left there, the small house had been divested of its miniature inmates and three walls by the termites. When Bano brought it down she found a small nest of termites under its floor. In this diminutive house too, the termites emerged from the foundations, after perforating the glazed green paper of the floor. The doors were eaten with their hinges, the vents with the rooms they were installed in. The chimney and the roof were probably destroyed next as the termites moved up after wrecking the floor and devouring the walls. Some workers were still busy divesting the boxer of his clothes. Of the newly weds only he was left, standing naked, holding his punches in woe, with his cloth bride of not many days consumed whole.

Bano decided to throw it out and replace it with a new one before the girls could discover it in that sorry condition. She stuffed the shreds of the house into a paper bag and put it in the kitchen.

Salar called Bano again to find out if the *sherwani* had been ironed. Bano quickly finished ironing it and left it on Salar's bed. The moths had made fine holes in the *sherwani* and Bano thought about darning them but they were so many that she soon gave up the effort. He would not be able to see them in any case, Bano thought, as she put the needle and thread away and got up. She went to the kitchen to check whether the curd had set in the yoghurt bowl; then she got busy in preparations for the family's evening visit to the photographer's studio.

Bano looked at the paper bag which contained the remains of the doll house and was again thinking with remorse of all the hard work that had gone into its making, when she heard the knife-sharpener in the alley and remembered the kitchen knives. They had become blunt to the degree that even sharpening them against the grating slab did not improve their edge. She went into the kitchen to gather them and was going to ask Muneemji to call the man over when she saw Muneemji standing at the door. He had already called the knife-sharpener over. Muneemji had his back to Bano and she saw him holding a piece of cloth in his hands which looked familiar. When she got close Bano recognised the *khilaat* that Salar had received from the Nawab of Gulmoha. The last time she saw it, the sword had been lying wrapped inside it in the trunk.

The sound Bano heard inside was the noise of the sword being sharpened. The air smelled with the rasping of the siliceous rock and steel. A few times Salar thrust his head out of the veranda to look into the courtyard and give directions to Muneemji, who seemed lost in thought, and when Bano asked him Salar's purpose for having the sword sharpened, he professed ignorance.

Shielding his eyes from the flying sparks as rusty metal met stone, the old Pathan checked the sharpness of the blade from time to time with his callused thumb, and salivated. His antiquated contraption consisted of a flint-stone disk, one foot in diameter, mounted on a wooden axle. It was operated by a single pedal like the foot-operated sewing machines. The stone disk was attached to the axle with a belt, it revolved with the motion of the pedal and sharpened the blade held at an angle to its surface. Bent under the weight of this device of obscure origins and wearing clothes that had shown a steady growth of darned and sewn patches to the extent that it was now difficult to distinguish the original from the graft, the knife-sharpener made his round of Topee Mohalla every fortnight or so.

The sharper the sword became, the more the man salivated. Finally, handing it back to Muneemji, he wiped his mouth on the sleeve of his old jacket, took the knives which Bano Tamanna had left and began working on them directly. Muneemji did not hand the sword back to Salar immediately. He kept regarding the blade, which shone brightly in the sun. The knives were finished soon and Bano collected them when they were ready. Pocketing the money, the old man had hauled up the equipment onto his back and disappeared into the alleys. Muneemji tried to wave the sword in the air but without any success.

After Salar finished his breakfast he went out with Muneemji, leaving Bano Tamanna musing that plans were afoot for another matrimonial overture, perhaps. She did not give away anything to Mushtri when she came asking what all those preparations were for, and why the sword had been taken out. However, Mushtri made Bano uncomfortable by suggesting that she had some notion regarding the proceedings. What Bano could not figure out was why Salar was carrying the sword with him. She was more worried on account of Salar injuring himself with the sharp blade than at the possibility of his injuring someone with it. He could hardly lift it. After Salar had gone out, Bano opened his trunk. The sword was not there. Salar had not taken it with him either. Bano later saw it leaning against his bed, and she kept wondering about it for the rest of the day.

With its frescoes displaying a most inhuman array of faces, advertising the haircutting, shaving and hair-curling services rendered within, the outside of the barber's salon resembled the approach to the freak house in a circus. This impression was further strengthened as one entered the shop, and saw one's figure infinitely reflected in the crooked mirrors fixed opposite each other, along with the spry and mouldy barber's, whose sleazy air no amount of detergent aids could have improved.

Salar's eyes were slowly adjusting to the steamy and dimly-lit room. Waiting for his turn, his nose had already become accustomed to the smell of singed hair from the barber's hot curlers. Somebody was using the public shower. A small boy had entered the shop before him with his father, and since the barber was alone in his shop, Salar had to wait for him to finish with the boy. Muneemji was restless because the boy's father had immediately picked up the newspaper lying on the table and the way he was slowly reading every news item and commenting on it with snorts and nasal asides, it did not seem likely that he would be finished with it any time soon.

Because of his lack of height, the head of the boy was not sticking out over the back of the chair. The barber asked him to get off, produced a wooden plank from under the shelf where the hairsprays stood carafed and nozzled in Pakola bottles, placed it across the arm-rests and asked the boy to mount it. Still not satisfied, the barber raised the chair further by revolving it counter-clockwise with the boy seated on it. Then he produced his notorious cape which had occasioned the Topee Mohalla saying that the barber could just as well have been made the hangman, so tight was the noose of his cape around necks.

The barber pulled the boy against the back of the seat as he struggled to loosen the knot. For an instant his shears twittered in the empty air over the boy's head, then swooped on his mop singing a menacing song to ears which stood idly in their cutting fields. The barber kept sharply steering the boy's head by the lobes of his ears and whenever the boy stirred from the tickling of his scissors behind his ears, he hissed at him to sit still lest the scissors should slip and lop them off. For which reason the children avoided the barber. And knowing this aversion, whenever he stood at the threshold of his shop, sharpening his razor on the strop hanging by the door, the barber always made a scissoring gesture with his fingers at the children playing in the street or passing by.

A while later, the door of the public shower opened and a wet, hairy hand came out to pull the towel from the stand. Then the man inside the shower called the barber over. The boy kept sitting on his pedestal, without moving a hair on his head. The barber went inside the shower and emerged a few minutes later, humming a tune, with a vague, leery expression on his face. The room was again filled with steam from the shower as the door opened and the man came out in his pyjamas, having finished his toilette. Before he could go back to cutting the boy's hair, the barber was once again summoned. Then the man demanded that the barber dust his underarms with powder, something which he had overlooked the first time. Grumbling, the barber picked up the chintz puff which had become flat with mildew, and dusted the man's underarms as the boy in the chair looked on with a mix of intimidation and fascination at their wavy reflections in the mirror. Having done with that, the barber returned. He jerked the boy's head left and right, snipped off an invisible hair, and dusting the nape of his neck with the same chintz puff, loosened and gathered the folds of his cape as the boy slipped off the chair and rushed outside, while his guardian folded the newspaper, paid the barber and walked out of the shop after him. Muneemji immediately grabbed hold of the newspaper, separated the different sections, kept one in his hands and stuck the rest well under his thigh so that anybody coming in after him could not ask him to share the supplements. The man from the shower had put on his shirt and he too went out after paying the barber. The barber lowered the chair and helped Salar into it.

Helpless and half-choking, Salar sat in the chair, as the shadow of the barber's razor glided over his chin, and the clammy hands shaved him under his hooked nose. The steam in the room had subsided a little, and to Salar's eyes his image in the huge wavy mirror in front of him was beginning to clear. Outside, the clouds were parting and sunlight had filtered into the room from the window in the street. The mirror unclouded completely. His murky vision portrayed to Salar's eyes someone in a white shroud covered up to the head. The barber had shaved him once downwards and after splattering his face with another layer of soap for a closer shave, had gone to rub the razor against the strop. Salar felt a shiver of dread grip him. He wished to close his eyes but couldn't, and sat almost hypnotised by the spectre. Another minute and he may have got up in fright, when the sharp voice of the barber brought him out of his stupor.

'Tell me he doesn't look like a bridegroom once I am done with him!' The barber had returned and was addressing Muneemji. Muneemji only answered in a nasal 'Hoonn!' but Salar woke up with the barber's words and the fog of desperation cleared the moment he heard the word 'bridegroom'. His recent dread completely dissolved in the sudden wave of animation he felt. 'What nonsense you talk!' Even this casual reproach was meant to encourage the barber.

'I say, that from a boy of ten until he dies, a man is a bridegroom. Tell me if I am wrong!' the barber retorted, stretching Salar's cheeks with his left thumb and forefinger to shave under the side-burns.

A shadow passed over Salar's face at the mention of death. 'Again the same thing!' he said when the barber had removed the blobs of soap, 'At least don't mix the auspicious with the inauspicious. That is not the proper way to speak.'

'I meant that a man is a man from the age of ten onwards!'

The barber defended himself in a voice seeking his customer's intimate confidence. 'This is what I was telling the other gentleman there. *Masha'allah*, you just have to put on a *patka* and sit astride a horse, and nothing else would be needed to make the *bara'at*.' The barber was removing the last spots of soap from Salar's chin now and wiping the razor on the flat of his palm.

'Are you listening to him Muneemji? Do you hear what he is saying?' Salar asked Muneemji, protesting vivaciously.

'Yes I am listening!' Muneemji did not wish to continue the conversation and gave a vapid answer.

'So what do you say?' Salar would not desist easily.

'He must be right! What else can I say?' Muneemji went back to his reading.

'Haah!' Salar said, half in praise of the haircutter's superior insight and half in denunciation of Muneemji's crabbiness, as the barber began rubbing a rounded piece of alum on his face. The shave and the alum massage done, the barber next brought out the nail trimmer and got down to manicuring Salar's skeletal hands.

Salar's ordeal was almost complete when the tongs sounded close-by and not long afterwards a *qalandar* barged into the shop, gyrating with his incense burner, raising it now over the barber's head, now over Muneemji's, shouting, 'A hundred score and twenty djinns I see inside this shop. Give some sacrifice for the dying, for the dead, whom these evil djinns curse night and day. *Allah! Allah!*' Muneemji had been disturbed in his reading of the newspaper again and he looked irked. 'Ask him to come closer!' Salar told the barber. 'Ask him to do a round over here,' Salar's finger slowly circled over his head.

The *qalandar* did not need any further invitation after that. Salar had barely lowered his head when he was enveloped in incense vapour which became denser and denser as the *qalandar* made revolution after revolution. The barber stood back. Salar began to cough and even then the *qalandar* did not stop. He only stopped after the barber had got rid of him by quickly handing him some change, fearing that Salar might choke in his shop.

When Salar returned from the barber, the *sherwani* was lying pressed on his bed. Salar's joints had become stiff and his elbow hurt him ever since a horse had walled him in and he had broken his arm. Putting on the *sherwani* was such an exertion for Salar that after Muneemji and Mirza Poya had stretched it over his back and forced his arms through the sleeves, he sat for a good half hour panting heavily, and scratching his dandy-brush hair and chin at intervals, with his tongue lolling out. After he could breathe easily, he put on his ankle-boots with difficulty and set his Rampuri toupee, just in time for the tonga, which arrived shortly with Ladlay and Mirza Poya in it. Mirza Poya dragged up the sword wrapped in a pair of old pyjamas. Muneemji's stomach was upset and therefore he had stayed at home. Bano did not see Salar the whole afternoon.

There were times when being a married woman and therefore a decision-maker in her family gave Bano Tamanna certain privileges. Since those occasions were few and far between, she was ever so mindful of them and employed them to her full advantage. The visit to the photographer's studio was one such event. Bano Tamanna was the central figure on those occasions, and from the beginning she had never asked Mushtri to join her in the family photo, leaving it to Mushtri to request her permission to join. As if in acknowledgement of Bano's advantageous position, Mushtri would do what she always did in such instances: shut herself in her room with the excuse of a headache when she received tidings of the programme.

The family went to the photographer's dark and squalid studio once every two years or so. The standard portrait had the parents seated in the two uncomfortable armchairs, the daughters and the sons-in-law standing behind them and the younger ones gathered on the carpet next to their grandparents' feet, pulling out the remaining wool from the depilated carpet. On these occasions the children's photographs were also taken for submission to the school records. If one tallied the children's looks with their official age, inscribed in a corner of the picture, they looked much older. Since it paid to stay longer in government service, Bano Tamanna had cautioned her daughters to keep a comfortable margin of two or three years when registering their children at school. This was by no means extravagant. One of Mirzban's colleagues had recently retired at the ripe old age of seventy-three, after officially turning sixty.

These prints contributed to Bano Tamanna's family album between whose glazed covers their extended families lived. Additions were regularly made to the album upon every new birth, and this pictorial database was revised and reviewed upon weddings and birthdays.

It was the first time that Bano's daughters and sons-in-law were not present for the family photo. She had emptied a whole bottle of perfumed hair-oil in the girls' hair and plaited them tight. Mirzban was sent to get a tonga. It took him a long time to find and slip on his shoes, which had been polished by Bano Tamanna and left next to his table that afternoon.

Mirzban had not slept for two nights in a row. He had bumped into the beds in the courtyard and once tripped over the garbage bin. He would stop from time to time to stare at the firmament, shake his head and continue pacing about with his hands clasped at his back. He seemed normal during the day, although he did not seem to listen to what was said to him, and before dinner Bano had to repeat herself several times before she received a reply from him. Others' nightly sleep had also been disrupted because of frequent power breakdowns and therefore Bano Tamanna did not pay too much attention to Mirzban's nocturnal wanderings around the house and his absent-mindedness, which she attributed to fatigue from insomnia. Also, she realised that Mirzban was no longer young and would be less attentive and alert at times.

The tonga had arrived. Muneemji had fallen asleep from weakness. Since Bano did not wish to wake him up she sent the elder girl to tell Mushtri to lock the front door. Then she left a glass of glucose-sweetened water next to Muneemji's bed and stepped out into the alley. The family secured itself by clinging to different parts of the carriage, and the unhappy, emaciated nag, apparently weighed down by the very plume it was wearing, dragged them with a tired but resolute gait to the hill top where the photographer had his studio.

Throughout the journey, Mirzban sat like a corpse next to the tonga-wala with his eyes fixed on some point far into the distance. And because of him they would have missed the studio turning if Bano Tamanna had not given timely directions to the tonga-wala just as they were about to go past it. The tonga-wala gave Mirzban curious looks as Bano Tamanna paid him and even after he drove away he kept looking back at Mirzban who stood lost in thought in the middle of the road, while Bano and the girls had already moved into the shop.

The photographer was not on his seat at the counter. The studio was inside and the dark room was further down. Bano Tamanna was not pressed for time and she decided to wait until the photographer came out. Their arrival had already been announced by the bell hanging from the front door. She called Mirzban in and they took the chairs lying folded against the wall and sat down across from the showcases.

The shop was a gallery of the nation's pride. The Kaskas brothers could be seen in loincloths, in postures hinting at the machismo of the grapplers, although the formidable maces they carried on their shoulders were hollow. The superintendent of police was spread all over a three-by-two-foot cardboard, standing guard in his black and khaki habit, his kohl-lined eyes open wide in earnestness, and his weight so unevenly distributed as he stood to attention, that it appeared he might fall on his face any minute. There were also Noor-e Firdousi and the President, besieging a table laden with food at one of the many state-sponsored glutting binges. It was a composite picture of the state's power, from its highest to its lowest functionary. Representing the proletariat were a few ruminating gentlemen; some evidently dead, some alive, to make the picture of the commonwealth complete. There obviously was some method in choosing the luminaries to be displayed in that museum but it was never made public by the photographer. Some citizens preferred to have their photographs taken in army and police uniforms, ostensibly for displaying in houses for the behoof of thieves and burglars. But any self-respecting housebreaker knew at a glance the imitation studio rifle which the photographers kept, and the efficacy of displaying such portraits was suspect.

Bano's granddaughters were at first shy and did not stir. But soon the elder sister got up, went up to a showcase and stood looking at the displays. Before long the younger one also joined her. The showcase was wide enough but she wanted to occupy her sister's place. They began to nudge each other with their elbows, at first gently, then a little roughly, as each used her shoulders to displace the other. 'Come back here! Behave yourselves!' Bano called out in vain. Knowing her soft spot for them, the girls ignored her. Bano Tamanna was obliged to get up from her chair and grabbing them, each under one arm, seated them on her lap.

Inside the shop Mirzban's eyes had begun roving. They were moving from framed photograph to photograph, without taking in their contents. The photographs were in the shelves, in the showcases, some of them also hanging from a clipboard. In a few frames the termites had materialised. Finding a foothold on the glass they had made tunnels on the surface and their movement could be observed under the glassy surface. Mirzban's eyes only saw the grey, rectangular shape with the chrome or gilt-plated frame. His heartbeat grew faster as his gaze jumped from shelf to shelf, from showcase to showcase, from wall to wall, and the grey, rectangular forms moved before his eyes in a whirr. These shapes became more fluid as his eyes roved faster, until they began to fly off from the shelves and the showcases, and came together in front of his eyes like one dim, grey curtain bordered with light. Mirzban thought his heart would break out of his rib-cage. The beating of his heart was resonating in the room ...' Thud! Thud! Thud! Thud!'

'It's my heart!' Mirzban cried out in fright, clutching his chest. For a moment Bano Tamanna was confused. She had also heard the sounds but they seemed to be coming from inside the studio. She had also heard someone shouting inside the studio. But right then she was more concerned about Mirzban's condition, whose face had turned deathly pale. He was no longer clutching his heart and seemed to be trying to get a hold of something invisible with his hands outstretched.

Mirzban could see a movement behind the grey curtain with the silvery border. It was a white cloud sailing by. It floated across the curtain and dissolved into thin air, leaving a small wriggling mass in the middle of the grey shroud. The curtain began disintegrating and Mirzban tried to hold it together with his hands. The white mass was still there, at the core of the curtain, and was now taking the definite shape and body of a giant termite. He could hear his heart beat louder than ever.

'What is happening to you? What are these sounds?' Bano Tamanna asked Mirzban.

But Mirzban's ears were deaf to all human voices and his eyes blind to the world. With a smile on his face, he groped his way forward. The curtain in front of his eyes had now darkened, and become bigger and higher so that he could no longer contain it in his hands. Bano Tamanna tried to stop him but before she could put the girls down from her lap, Mirzban had already stepped inside the photographer's studio after parting the curtain which partitioned it from the showroom.

Were the secrets of the universe now unfolding? What was that grey curtain which had suddenly darkened as its silver light disappeared? Mirzban's ears had now stopped ringing. His path was enveloped with clouds. He could see a great sheet of clouds through which a hundred suns were shining brightly. The sky was hanging low, and suspended by a bolt of lightning, a haloed angel in a flowing white robe was floating amidst the clouds. Then he saw a white horse, with a halo over its head as well, drifting among the clouds. A scream of rapture was welling up in Mirzban's throat, and he lost consciousness before hitting the floor.

Bano Tamanna rushed to the studio entrance the moment she heard Mirzban's scream, but as she was approaching it, the door was suddenly shut in her face from inside. That alarmed her further. She began banging on the door. 'Open the door for God's sake! Help! Is anyone there?! Mirzban! Yunani Sahib! Answer me!' The thought immediately occurred to Bano that maybe a thief was robbing the photographer inside the shop and had attacked Mirzban. 'Call someone!' she turned to her granddaughters in confusion, then suddenly realising how young they were shouted, 'Keep still!'

Bano Tamanna heard some clanging sounds inside, and something heavy falling. Then suddenly the door opened and the photographer appeared, dragging an unconscious Mirzban after him by his arms. 'Hah! What happened to him, what happened? Is he OK?' Bano Tamanna shook the photographer by his sleeve. 'Whose cry was it that I had heard inside?'

'Everything is fine, Begum … Yunani!' The photographer had to strain his memory for a second. Shut up in his dark room, he saw the families rarely. These nuclear families made up for him a uniform picture of their natural existence and if he came across one of the individual members, he was at a loss to recognise them. 'Yunani Sahib will come to in a minute. He stepped over an electric wire inside as I was fixing some lights. It is my fault. But don't worry! Here! I think he is asking for something.'

Mirzban was coming to and Bano Tamanna began slapping his cheeks gently. 'Let me get some water,' the photographer said, and disappeared inside the studio closing the door after him. Mirzban was looking around as if in a daze.

'I am very sorry, Yunani Sahib. It was my mistake. You didn't see the wire lying there. I had forgotten to tape it up. I hope you will forgive me,' the photographer had brought water for Mirzban.

'But the angel?' Where is the angel? The suns and the horse flying in the clouds,' Mirzban asked in a faint voice. The photographer turned a concerned face towards Bano Tamanna. 'Begum Yunani, I think you should take him home,' he said. 'He will settle down in a while. Sometimes people hallucinate in a state of shock. Remember to give him a lot of water to drink. That's the best thing to redress effects from an electric shock. Wait a minute. Let me get you a tonga!'

Although Mirzban soon recovered, Bano Tamanna was so worried about him the whole evening that she forgot to ask where Salar had been all that time. Salar and Ladlay arrived late. Muneemji was feeling a little better and Bano had briefly told him about Mirzban's fainting spell. Muneemji was also concerned in the beginning but when he saw Mirzban pacing the courtyard as usual that night, he decided that Mirzban must have recovered. It had been particularly humid that day. The rooms had become very stuffy and Salar had asked that his bed be put in the courtyard. He relented with difficulty to Bano Tamanna and Muneemji taking off the ankle-boots before he went to bed. Muneemji did not get an answer from him about his day's activities. Salar had gone to sleep with his eyes open and insisted on keeping the sword by his side.

Mirzban paced about until he was exhausted, and then he too went to bed. But he kept waking up in his sleep. He had seen it all. No matter what the world would say about it now, he had seen the angel hanging from the skies by the bolt of lightning, and he had seen the shining horse flying among the clouds under the suns. And at long last he was beginning to see how the termite figured in it all!

Like elsewhere in the house, the termites had made their tunnels under Mushtri's bed too. But although she had taken precautions against the termites making holes in the bedpost by soaking the legs in bowls of oil, it did not occur to her to take similar precautions with her wooden-heeled shoes. Over the weekend the termites ate up the wooden heels of both pairs of footwear which she wore to work. Mushtri only discovered them on the morning of the first working day after the weekend, when she looked under the bed. The shoe-shops did not open till late in the day, and besides, she had her high-heels made on order which took at least a fortnight. All her earned and sick leave had been redeemed, but more than that her presence was necessary for an urgent communication which had to be sent that day to the head office from her department, regarding Ladlay's mortgage application. So with a heart heavy with misgivings, Mushtri Khanam repaired to the bank in flat-soled sandals, prepared for surprised and muffled whispers from the clerks.

At the bank the unthinkable had happened. When the clerks returned to work after the weekend, and as was their wont, slammed their chairs hard against the floor to rid them of bed-bugs, which the staff and the clients brought from their bedrooms in equal numbers, the chairs did not bounce back, but lay crumpled on the floor in pieces, sending the termites within groping everywhere for cover. The drawers were full of white ants crawling over irredeemable bank records. And when the bank vault was opened by the head accountant in the presence of the cashier and the gunman, there were only shreds left of the currency notes which had come in a steel trunk from the treasury to be disbursed in salaries to the government employees. Then the gunman's loud curses were heard. The termites had thoroughly bored the stock of his gun and eaten the paper casing of the cartridges where it was hanging on the wall.

At this point Mushtri entered the bank. The reaction to her changed appearance was severe and immediate: the shock and disbelief was profound. The bank was yet to open for the public, and, therefore, Mushtri Khanam claimed the undivided attention of the aghast clerks, in whom the first wave of shock gave way to indignant wantonness. Outrage was writ large upon their countenances. The clerks realised the joke played with their sensibilities. With his neck craned at a critical angle, when the cashier reviewed his hairdo in the cash-window glass, his remorse for the time wasted was as profound as his optimism for the future. Before long a widespread leer decorated every face in the clerks' ranks, as they leaned on each other's shoulders and poured out their bitter confidences. All this while the gunman, dazed by the spectacle, and deprived of his authority to wield a firearm by the termites, sat paralysed on his stool with his mirror-topped snuffbox in hand, staring at Mushtri Khanam with quite indescribable emotions. Qudratullah was in the locker room and had not seen Mushtri Khanam enter.

Mushtri Khanam went to her desk. The drawers had been taken out to empty them of the termites. Some furniture was not damaged and the clerks were beginning to settle down after dusting their work stations. To ward off their hostile gaze, Mushtri Khanam tried to bring into play the potent charm of her sharp looks, but that instrument too, proved ineffectual for the clerks' inflamed spirits. They parried her stare with undisguised grins and bold and loud whispering. Realising that the tables had turned, and that no matter what she did now, her pedestal and all its attendant pomp and glory were forever lost, Mushtri Khanam cursed the termites and Qudratullah's indolence in the same breath. With any other man, Mushtri Khanam thought, she would have been long settled. She sat in her place for a long time, considering and weighing the many options which lay before her. A lot depended on Qudratullah's next move. But it was nowhere in sight. Qudratullah was a hard nut and taciturn. She considered the wisdom of prolonging such an engagement. There were other prospects she had been speculating on, and she could not remain unmindful of them forever.

Qudratullah had gone inside his office after another inspection of the locker room. He had asked for some files and was poring over them. After what had happened, there was nothing to be done but to close down the bank for the day, secure whatever documents were legible or partially damaged, inform the head office, and await further instructions. While these preparations were afoot, the first customers had arrived. Getting wind of the tidings they became alarmed and insisted on closing their accounts and clearing their balance on the spot. Qudratullah tried to reason with a few of them who had barged into his office, but they

were deaf to his entreaties. It was pay day and some ten or
fifteen people were already gathered outside the bank. Upon
hearing the bank manager explain that the bank could not
pay the salaries, they became hostile. The news spread that
Desh Bank had closed down because of a termite attack.
Accompanying this news were rumours that people would
not be paid their salaries for another month.

People's savings were already spent by the end of the
month. On Friday afternoon the shopkeepers had made their
deposits, and that had been sent to the treasury already.
Qudratullah came out to speak to the crowd. He was standing
blocking the portals of the bank, when the Makrani usher of
the Mahtab Cinema, foremost in the crowd of the account-
holders trying to get inside, finding his way blocked by
Qudratullah, butted him. The butcher grappled Qudratullah
as he was reeling, and threw him onto the floor with a
practised manoeuvre. In his struggle to get up, Qudratullah's
dark glasses were trampled on and his collar torn. Someone
inside the bank sounded the alarm, and while the crowd was
breaking the glass windows and indulging in similar railleries
occasioned by mass hysteria, the police party dispatched from
the nearby station reached the scene armed with tear-gas
shells. Section 144 was still in place and when the police
warnings to disperse the mob did not yield results, they fired
a tear-gas shell.

The shell flew over the heads of the crowd and exploded
right under Qudratullah's nose. He ran screaming inside the
bank. At that very moment the gunman, hearing that the
police had arrived, bravely rushed out from under the table,
from where he had watched the proceedings until then, and
felled the first wild-eyed man in tattered clothes he saw
rushing into the bank. Only after the police had dispersed
the crowd did someone realise that it was Qudratullah whom
the stout Pathan had laid low.

Qudratullah was carried to his office. His injuries were not severe but he was visibly shaken. Two policemen locked the bank doors from inside to keep protesters from getting in. The crowd outside had started to disperse and the police in-charge came inside to report. Qudratullah assured him that everything was OK and that they would soon wind up the business. Some closing reports had to be completed and Qudratullah requested everyone, without once looking at the gunman, not to be disturbed by what had happened and to make sure that they finished their work and filled in all the reports before they left.

Mushtri watched the whole spectacle of Qudratullah's humiliation, quite unmoved. And while he recovered his senses, she kept biting her nails, oblivious to his fate. She had made up her mind that now was the time to tackle Qudratullah decisively.

After he had quelled his headache with two aspirins, and wiped the corners of his sore eyes with his handkerchief, Qudratullah had looked around to see why the bank wore an altered air. While looking for aspirins in the drawer of his bureau, he had heard riotous laughter breaking out every few minutes. It could not just be the scuffle outside, Qudratullah comforted himself. The clerks had been simpering smugly before that. And if the clerks had been discussing the scuffle, he would have caught at least one of them looking towards his office from the corner of his eye, since they did not have enough tact or imagination to discuss something without literal references: although Qudratullah realised, and not without bitterness, that the whole episode must have given them immense delight. He was also willing to believe that the Pathan gunman's attack was not an accident. But he had still not figured out the cause for this change. Such buoyancy in the bank was surprising indeed. Was it the prospect of the bank's closure for the next couple of days?

That could hardly be it. If anything the staff would be working harder, duplicating files and sorting and cataloguing papers.

The only explanation Qudratullah could imagine for this change, was through recourse to his worst fears. The cashier had finally won Mushtri Khanam's hand and the engagement had been announced. Qudratullah wondered who would bring the wedding invitation to his office, whether the cashier or Mushtri Khanam herself. It was possible that both might invite him, Mushtri Khanam for the wedding and the cashier for the *valima*. He could already see the gilt-edged card with its fancy golden lettering, announcing the time and the venue of the nuptials.

Qudratullah's nerves had become weak without tea, and unable to continue a struggle with his emotions, he had felt inclined, more than once in the recent days, to surrender his claims on Mushtri Khanam in favour of the cashier. Going without tea for so long now, and after his thrashing at the hands of the Makrani, the butcher, and the gunman, Qudratullah's spirit was completely broken, and it no longer rallied back to support optimistic thoughts. He saw the mirthful cashier and detected in himself traces of what could only be termed fraternal feelings for the man. For Qudratullah, it was a long way to have come, from his native abhorrence of all clerks. But Qudratullah could not lay his finger on the source of this affection. Maybe the deficiency of caffeine had allowed his better self to emerge, or maybe his recent beating had shaken him up and broken all barriers to his heart's access to nobler feelings.

Convoking the testimonials of her abated resplendence, Mushtri Khanam composed herself and the documents she had prepared, and shuffled to Qudratullah's office with a determined heart; to sound her prospects therein, and if found doubtful, to quickly recover her losses, and devise a new strategy for survival under the changed circumstances.

Half way down the hall, Mushtri Khanam was hit by a bray of coarse laughter from the clerks.

They would not break the news to him just yet, Qudratullah thought. He knew that Mushtri Khanam knew that he was a rival, and she would very much wish to keep him suspended by a thread until the last minute, and continue her little game. Such were the caprices of the fair sex. But Qudratullah had seen through the plot! Therefore he would act magnanimously, and readily forgive Mushtri Khanam. To humour her he was even willing to go along with her in her little triumphant parade, as the clown!

But he *must* bring all intimacies with Mushtri Khanam to a firm close immediately, as was only honourable under the circumstances. Her work must also be delegated to somebody else. That would also effectively put an end to the clerks' suspicion of his designs which might have developed in recent days. With this thought Qudratullah felt light and relieved. He resolved to show the world that nothing was farther from his mind than any malice towards the couple. He would be the first one to compliment them after the *nikah* had been read. In his mind's eye, Qudratullah congratulated the cashier under the nuptial canopy and whispered a magnanimous benediction. Some time had been spent in these deliberations, when his ruminations were checked by a loud guffaw. He saw someone waddling round the counter outside his office, and in another instant realised it was Mushtri Khanam. A Mushtri Khanam reduced by a full half foot of her height!

All the possible causes which might have led to the spectacle he saw before him, and the reason for the bank's changed atmosphere since the morning, passed before Qudratullah's eyes as in a dream, making only vague sense. But having once relinquished his claim on Mushtri, Qudratullah could not now stop the retreat which his mind had prepared him for, and he was swept away. If Qudratullah had been in his previous state of mind, the sight of Mushtri Khanam might have floored him. But in his present state it gave him strength. What he saw gave him fortitude, and he reflected on the past events with greater sagacity as he signed the documents given to him by Mushtri Khanam with a firm hand. Mushtri could not believe her ears as Qudratullah told her in clear, unambiguous tones to hand over her present charge to the cashier, and return to her previous responsibilities.

While a small city bank could be conveniently closed for a few days, it was not possible for the shops to shut down. The treasury, on the recommendation of the numismatic commission headed by someone whose family mill supplied paper to the state security printing press, had always minted coins of a denomination lower than the basic currency bill. It was obvious that petty coins could not sustain commerce, but before new currency bills could be distributed from the mainland which could take a day or two, daily business, somehow, had to go on. A meeting of the retailers' union was called post-haste at the local chamber of commerce. It decided that the shops were to remain open in view of the prevailing contingency, and trade using the barter system when a customer could not produce legal tender. Some argued that these were extraordinary measures, others retorted that the prevalent chaos did indeed warrant them, in order to save the people any further hardships. The list of items to be accepted on barter at shops and their corresponding value in terms of grocery items was also quickly charted out and circulated.

This opened a new world. Livestock and poultry had made the list. Already the first pair of chickens were hanging inside make-do mesh baskets outside Buddah's shop: payment for a kilo of molasses. Soon goats and cows were also chained to the shop fronts. The incubator in the market was booked for weeks in advance with a view to growing and selling poultry until the end of the termite epidemic. The goldsmith's shop was also thronged by people securing themselves against financial collapse by buying gold and silver tablets.

Despite the murderous cats, the great dispatch with which the rabbits multiplied promised to keep Mirzban's house well-supplied for the months to come. In the first two days Bano Tamanna bartered five rabbits to buy groceries. Buddah even let her sort out the bigger eggs and the softer bread.

The currency bills arrived on the third day and by the fourth or fifth day the commerce had returned to normal, but exposure to all these extraordinary circumstances greatly altered the city's atmosphere. After a certain hour in the day, the women did not venture out, as the streets became arenas for bacchanal orgies. Cows and goats in heat could be seen running helter-skelter, pursued by the bulls and the billy-goats, their pizzles hanging out, and crowds of provocateurs at their heels. The greedy shopkeepers, covetous of multiplying their profits overnight, were mating their animals publicly.

The bank reopened on the fourth day, and the arrears were cleared. All the credit and loan records of Desh Bank which had not been sent to the head office had been destroyed in the termite attack. The postal service had been restored and when the bank opened, Qudratullah received a reprimand from the head office, censuring him for not taking precautionary measures in view of the epidemic. The insurance firm which covered Desh Bank had sent their surveyors and cataloguers to assess the extent of the damage, estimated to be in the hundreds of thousands. On the allegations of a group of account-holders, the bank also set up a committee to investigate whether someone in the bank had staged this drama to pilfer the money in the vaults.

Bano Tamanna put away the crochet cover she was making

for the water-pitcher and got up. She could hear Muneemji hotly discussing something with Lumboo. Muneemji was shouting at him for not cleaning the washrooms properly due to which the toilet pot was choked and the water closet was filled-up. Lumboo was blaming the municipality sweepers who regularly overlooked clearing the gutters due to which flushes were not draining water as efficiently as they should. There was no water anyway, to regularly wash the toilets with, he told Muneemji.

It was true. Last year Basmati had built a water tank on the roof and bought a motor-operated water pump. The small bribe which he offered the municipality plumber persuaded him to attach the contacts of the motor directly to the main supply instead of the underground water tank where, by rights, they should have been connected. Thus Basmati began to suck up a major part of the neighbourhood's supply of fresh water, although a household of three, which included Ladlay, did not need all that much water. In the mornings and evenings when the fresh water was supplied to Topee Mohalla, Basmati's overhead tank kept overflowing into the drain. The neighbours complained and Basmati made some promises, but things remained unchanged. Then another neighbour bought a motor pump. And then another. Now every second house in Topee Mohalla had a motor pump, and thanks to this arrangement, everyone was again getting roughly the same amount of water they were getting previously in addition to paying a higher electricity bill because of the motor pump. Bano Tamanna had been after Mirzban for some time to buy a water pump too. But there was no money. And to fully utilise a water pump one had to have an overhead water tank which was not cheap to build. And now it seemed almost impossible. The brine had spread from brick to brick and wall to wall. The outer cement plaster was coming off in chunks from the walls where a powdery coating of salt had appeared, causing the distemper to flake. The termites had eaten the straw of the mud-plaster, the mud-filling inside the walls had been washed down, and the structure was crumbling. With the corroding of the walls, clefts formed in the parapets through which rainwater seeped in.

Muneemji came inside grumbling. Lumboo had said that shortage of water was not his problem and had demanded extra money to open the choked water container. Then another problem arose. The sewage drain was common for all the houses in the row, but since the drain was choked only outside Mirzban's house where the gutter sloped a little, the neighbours whose sewage also drained past Qasr-e Yunani, refused to share the cost of cleaning it. In the end Bano paid Lumboo to clean and unclog the whole length of the drain despite Muneemji's objection, who cursed Bano's stingy neighbours loudly.

Mirzban was sitting in the veranda with a bowl of chicken soup in his hands. He had been talking to his granddaughters and Bano Tamanna felt greatly relieved at these signs of returning normality in his condition.

What had happened at the photographer's remained a mystery to Bano Tamanna until Muneemji ran into Mirza Poya at the Chhalawa hotel.

Ladlay was asked to make the arrangements for Salar's portrait which had to be sent to Firdousi. It had suddenly occurred to Salar that the photograph must be an equestrian portrait, with him brandishing a sword. Ladlay's fervent entreaties, that all Firdousi expected was a plain photograph, fell on deaf ears. Salar's mind was made up and he ordered Ladlay accordingly, who followed suit willy-nilly with an ungracious air. The photographer had agreed, but the horse was yet to be found. Salar had already inspected the emaciated tonga horses and rejected them summarily.

Ladlay then took a chance and approached the Imambargah groom who looked after the plump *Duldul* horses, and found him favourably inclined. A saddle and a pair of stirrups were improvised. Ladlay also found a tonga-harness which came fitted with blinkers.

The photographer had made a provision for the horse to stand in the studio by raising his white, reflecting-umbrellas on bamboo poles. He made a podium, and helped Salar climb onto it. Salar was high enough when he stood on it, to roughly measure his height on horseback. Once on the podium, he also found the strength, much to the surprise and wonderment of everyone, not only to hold himself erect, but also to hold the sword with one hand, securely balanced over his shoulders, when the photographer turned on the lights.

The plan was working well. But the insufficient width of the back door through which the horse had to come in now posed a problem. At that point Bano's family entered the shop. The groom tried to rear-in the horse, hoping that walking blind the horse might force his hind-quarters through the door.

But the horse's rump got stuck in the door frame and he took fright. His hind legs were now on the studio's carpeted floor and he was trying to kick. As he struggled, the muscles of his rump contracted and the horse found himself rearing into the studio. In fright the horse kept kicking the air with his head turned to a corner of the room. That was the drumming sound which was heard outside and which Mirzban took for the beating of his heart. Salar was standing frozen, afraid that the horse might bring down the podium with his kicks. Mirza Poya was too close to the horse and did not stir in his chair. The photographer was clinging desperately to his camera to keep it from falling, and kept looking with dread at the lights he had set up on the bamboo pole. The groom soothed down the horse shortly, and he turned from the corner to move towards him.

Mirzban had entered the studio at that point. He stepped in between the horse and the groom, and suddenly screamed and fainted. The horse bolted to another corner, and brought down a pole where the lights had been fixed. The pole came down, and would have crashed over Mirzban lying unconscious on the floor were its fall not broken by the protruding camera lens. The light was also smashed. Salar was not moving, and as his head was turned slightly upwards, with the light in his eyes, he could not see Mirzban. Ladlay asked Mirza Poya not to mention anything about Mirzban to Salar, as it was an accident, and Mirza had seen no point in bringing it up either, after the photographer came back to report that Mirzban had recovered and was on his way home.

Although the photographer had been compensated for his damage, he refused to have any further dealings with Salar who did not seem concerned about his portrait either. He only seemed interested in the horse and kept saying, 'What a noble animal! What a shiny coat! What fetlocks! What spirits!' Mirza Poya told Muneemji that he, too, was charmed by the beautiful horse and while Ladlay and the groom were putting things in order in the photographer's absence, who had gone out to get a tonga for Bano's family, he joined Salar in admiring the horse.

It was then that it occurred to him that the majesty of a horseman would not come out in a photograph. Only a portrait could do it justice, and Master Puchranga, the painter of cinema-hoardings was free those days because of Mahtab Cinema's closure.

To Salar's mind too, it appeared far more glamorous to have a portrait painted than photographed, and he immediately conceded his pleasure. Ladlay was beside himself with rage when he heard of these plans but could not prevail over Salar's determination who also silenced the groom's objections by promising him twice the amount for his pains.

Muneemji had listened to Mirza Poya silently, and now took his leave, shaking his head.

A few days later, a tonga carrying Salar, Ladlay and Mirza Poya rolled into a clearing in the Dyers Colony. At the same time a man leading a plump white horse also arrived. The walls of the Kutcha Qila Dyers Colony were streaked with the colours the Purana Shehr's clothes had been dyed in. A coloured steam rose from the cauldrons where the dyers' family were stirring the clothes boiling in the dye. The head of the family was going from cauldron to cauldron, to check and match every dyed garment. In corners, men twisted the length of the dupatta after starching it to produce the wrinkled effect currently in vogue. Stuck in the quagmire of this hubbub was Puchranga's shack.

Puchranga got up to greet Salar's group. He was short and stout and had a small, rough hand. He was cutting holes for air in a banner, and other banners were lying furled-up in a corner of his shack from the coming *Ashura* parade. Puchranga also did banner calligraphy during the election days, making no bones about ideologies, and fully rendering every party the secular benefit of his skills. But cinema was his old passion. In his younger days Puchranga stuck matchsticks in his eyes to keep them open after two consecutive shows of the same film. He was soon picked by Mirza Poya, in whose person he found a patron and a mentor. Poya visited him often to guide him about the physiognomy of the screen gods and goddesses. The precise angle of the heroine's eyes and the cut of her lips, which had to do with the compassion in her soul; and the expanse of the hero's forehead and the length of his neck, having to do with his noble pedigree, were Mirza's chief areas of interest.

'Hero Sahib! Everything is ready!' Puchranga addressed

Salar. 'All you have to do is to get on this monster, and we will start filming.' Puchranga used his favourite terminology. The horse kept prancing about, making it difficult to saddle it. Mirza Poya had briefed Puchranga, and he was ready with a giant canvas, originally prepared for an action-packed thriller. The alley was relatively deserted due to the heat, except for a few dyer children busy with their work.

Mirza Poya suggested that Salar should be raised on a chair and when the seat of the chair was level with the horse's back, he could swing his legs around, and clutch onto the horse's halter. But Salar being unable to swing his legs because of paralysis, the plan was abandoned. After much debate it was decided that he should lie on his back on the planks of Puchranga's shack, with his legs parted. In that posture he would be picked up by Ladlay from one side and Puchranga and Poya from the other, and with his legs raised in the air carried over their heads on top of the horse from its rear. Once above the horse's back, Salar would be tilted forward and lowered until he was astride the horse. All this while the groom held the horse, covering his eyes with blinkers so that it might not kick. It was not easy, but after a few false starts, it was successfully managed. Salar was in great pain after lying on the hard planks of the shop and then being roughly hoisted. He kept shouting abuses over their heads, and ignored the groom's entreaties to quieten down. Being a consecrated animal, the horse was not used to carrying loads, and it kept rolling up its eyes and cocking its ears in a belligerent manner. The dyer's children had gathered to see the spectacle of Salar being hoisted onto the horse's back, and Puchranga framing Salar from different angles like a film-director, using his two hands. But when everything settled down, and Puchranga got to work, they too retired to their business.

In painting Salar's portrait, Puchranga employed the same

technique he used while painting billboards, except that he did not plot the graph from a photograph.

Salar had quietened down and sat as straight as he could, with his chin up, on the horse, sporting the drawn sword across his breast. Puchranga kept saying from time to time, 'One take is over! First Class! Another take is done! First Class!' Puchranga had already made the outlines of the horse and left some head room for Salar, when he asked the groom to remove the blinkers from the horse's eyes so that he could draw them.

A cauldron of dye was bubbling near Puchranga, and some dupattas were boiling in it. When the blinkers were removed, the view opened to the horse's eye, and the groom saw the dyer's children snap-drying the dupatta too late. A red dupatta flashed, and the air resounded with a crack. The horse reared, displacing Salar in the saddle.

'There! There!' Puchranga shouted in fright. Mirza Poya had frozen in his tracks. Ladlay had rushed forward to help but by that time the horse had already moved.

During his fall, Salar's boot slipped forward. It got stuck in the make-do stirrup when the horse bolted, dragging the terrified groom on one side and the unconscious Salar on the other. Fortunately, the alley into which the horse had run was blocked by two donkey carts on the other side. The horse had not run far when it was controlled by the groom, and Ladlay and Puchranga rushed to disentangle Salar's foot from the stirrup. Mirza Poya was so frightened by the whole scene that he could not move, and stood at Puchranga's shop with his mouth agape. By and by Mirza Poya recovered. Salar was still unconscious and Mirza feared the worst. But Ladlay assured them that he was breathing. There was no time to be lost, a tonga was hailed and Salar was rushed to the hospital post-haste, spread on the back seat, with Mirza holding him from the back for support, and Ladlay catching his head from the front. The groom had not been paid, and after struggling in vain to get something out of Master Puchranga, he returned to the Imambargah cursing everyone, and profaning the ears of the Imam's horse beyond measure, who trotted jauntily at his heels in an attitude clearly expressive of utmost satisfaction.

It was around eleven in the night. Ladlay's balcony was bathed in darkness and Mushtri was snoring. In the background, the cicadas' song could be heard and at regular intervals the croaking of a frog rose prominently from the gutter. Muneemji heard the chowkidar's whistle at a distance, then at close quarters, and the frog stopped croaking. After the chowkidar turned the corner and went past the alley, and the noise of the old bicycle chain died out, the croaking resumed. Two pigeons were sick. Muneemji had put them in a separate cage from the others and kept getting up from time to time to see how the sick birds were doing. He could not sleep anyway, as his mind remained occupied with Ladlay and Salar's affairs. Right then there were too many things on Muneemji's mind. Every now and then he cursed Mirza Poya who had endangered Salar's life through his foolishness, and himself for not pre-empting Salar's next move.

Salar was not too well after his fall from the horse and Bano Tamanna was busy tending to him. He had broken his hip bone and dislocated two joints. His neck was also in a cast. Ever since his injury, Salar hadn't mentioned Firdousi's name once. Either it was the injury which had affected his brain, or the proximity to death, but perhaps for the first time, the reality of his helplessness dawned on Salar, and he disintegrated in the face of it. Muneemji remembered the time many years ago, when Salar, his arm broken, after being walled-in by a horse, had refused to be administered chloroform for the operation. He firmly believed that once unconscious he would never come to. The surgeon refused to operate without a depressant, and Salar refused to budge.

Ultimately an accord was reached between them, and Muneemji summoned Salar's farmhands. They were given strict instructions by the surgeon and six of them held him in place while his bone was joined. During the operation Salar showered his tormentors with the most obscene slurs, threatened everyone with murder, cried to high heaven, and ultimately lost consciousness with exhaustion and pain, just when his servants were about to let him go and run away, frightened by his threats.

Salar was still running a high fever. One evening Salar asked Muneemji to send for Bano, and holding her hand in his, he had asked her to forgive him. But Bano was unable to understand the reason for his tears. Nothing had been heard of Ladlay for a long time. When Bano Tamanna went to the Sessions Court one day to fill up some necessary forms in order to file a complaint to the ombudsman about the Evacuee Trust Property Board's claim on Salar's building, of which she had been informed by mail, she found a new face inside Ladlay's van. The notary had sublet it to him a week ago. Although he had heard that Ladlay was out of town for a couple of days, the man could not tell Bano Tamanna where he had relocated. Begum Basmati had also confirmed the news, and Bano was afraid that Ladlay might have gone upcountry in connection with the property.

There hadn't been any overt communication between the notary and Mushtri of late, and Muneemji assumed that the two must have found some other way to communicate. He had a strong premonition that Mushtri was somehow responsible for the disappearance of Salar's property documents but he had no proof on which to base his allegations. After Bano Tamanna's encounter with Ladlay at the courthouse, Muneemji had told Ladlay that his explanation to Bano Tamanna had removed many misunderstandings and that she had decided not to recourse to legal action. Ladlay knew as well as Muneemji did, what the real motive for this change of heart was, and although he must have inwardly congratulated himself, on the face of it Ladlay had been full of profuse vows of fidelity to Salar and his family, and warmly thanked Muneemji for helping them see the truth. Muneemji had sworn to himself to get even with Ladlay. And now he was always on the alert for the slightest slip from Ladlay or Mushtri which would betray them to Bano Tamanna's gain.

The moon was up. Muneemji lit up a cigarette and went to sit on the porch from where he commanded a good view of the alley, and saw two cats chasing each other on Ladlay's roof. He could hear their muffled growls but after they disappeared behind a parapet, the narrow alley fell quiet again. Muneemji was so occupied with his thoughts that he forgot to draw on the cigarette and the cheap, thickly shredded tobacco went out. He searched his pocket for the matchbox and not finding it there, was going to get up and fetch it from under his pillow when he saw a shadow lurking in the alley. Muneemji stayed still in his position. Because of the heat he had taken off his shirt and was wearing his dark pyjamas otherwise the moonlight would have betrayed him. Two thoughts immediately came to Muneemji's mind: either it was a thief, looking for an opportunity to break into someone's house, or else it was Ladlay, who had come back and was looking for a chance to consort with Mushtri. But didn't Muneemji hear Mushtri's irksome wheezing? Was the bitch awake and making those sounds to fool everyone?

'Hah! What's that?' Muneemji said to himself as the man turned the corner and walked into the alley with hesitant steps and stopped right under Ladlay's balcony. It was evidently not Ladlay; Muneemji could see that much from where he was. The man turned his head towards Mushtri's window. Muneemji had no way of knowing if there was any activity there, but from the consistency of her snores and from the pin drop silence in which the whole house was bathed it did not seem probable. After standing under the window for a while and scratching his head, the man walked away, dragging his feet. And until he turned the corner and disappeared, he kept looking over his shoulder.

It was a most singular occurrence and gave Muneemji food for much rumination. However, after the man had walked away, and waiting long enough to make sure that he wouldn't return, Muneemji came down from the roof, and stopped outside Mushtri's door, listening intently. Nothing was stirring inside and Muneemji went back to bed wondering who the man could have been.

Out of curiosity he kept his watch at the same hour the next day. Tabaq Sahib's son was getting married that day. The house was a few lanes away and earlier in the evening when Muneemji went out to buy some cigarettes he saw young boys armed with staffs climbing the walls to mount a watch for Kotwal. They had surrounded the house on two sides and a few of them had also taken positions on the roofs of the adjacent houses. Kotwal had a strange fixation for nuptial celebrations and he always crashed them, even at great peril to himself. Perched on the roof of the house during the course of the night, he bellowed and wailed like a ghoul. His caterwauls were so doleful and ungodly on those occasions and his wailing so pathetic, that it caused the brides to turn frigid and grooms to lose all procreational intent. He left only around sunrise, in the retinue of his harem whom his wailing had gathered, leaving the walls of the house drenched with his steaming, corrosive piss. Therefore the mention of Kotwal's name by the bridesmaids made chaste virgins blush crimson, and bridegrooms swear absurdities in rage. The clandestine deployment of sentries like the one Muneemji witnessed that evening, to thwart this ritual, had already been foiled on several occasions by the mercurial cat. Muneemji knew all those stories. Some houses away he could also see the silhouette of someone guarding the roof, and therefore he could not help smiling when he saw Kotwal jump onto the roof and make haste in the direction of the groom's house without waiting to sniff the pigeons' coop. The old hammer-head cat trailed behind him at some distance.

The chowkidar had just made his round of the alley, and Muneemji had looked up to see a bat fluttering about when the man from the night before again walked into the alley. After making a round or two under Mushtri's window irresolutely, he stood listening to something. Muneemji also listened but there was no noise other than the soft strains of the wedding song accompanied by a lone *dholki* which he could hear further up in the neighbourhood. The man turned back after a short wait. As he walked away, Muneemji slunk out from the front door. Before going to bed he had oiled the hinges of the door and it did not creak when he opened it.

The man perambulated as if drunk, oblivious even to the occasional sounds which Muneemji inadvertently made as he stumbled upon rocks. Muneemji's only fear was that the man might look back like he did on the first night. But that day the man did not look back once. They passed close to the wedding house where Muneemji stepped on a paper bag, but the sound was muffled by the singing and the man went on as unsuspectingly as before. Now and again he would break into a ditty but Muneemji could not make out the words. Soon they were on the open road. Muneemji was a little more relaxed. If the man saw him now, he would take him for one of the people returning home from the railway station. Then the man again took to the alleys and Muneemji followed him for another ten minutes until he disappeared into a house at the fag end of a dark alleyway. Muneemji watched him from the corner of the street. After he had gone in and Muneemji saw the light come on in one of the windows, he carefully moved into the alley. There was a name plate on the door and Muneemji lit a match under it. 'Qudratullah, 12/B Turap Ghitti,' it read.

What is going on? Is he also one of her consorts? Muneemji pondered. Next, men would be jumping over the walls! He would change his name if that woman did not turn her brother's house into a whorehouse soon! Muneemji considered telling Bano immediately. He wondered if he had made a mistake by not informing her earlier. After all, he was there to guard her interests. But Mushtri was Mirzban's sister and he was after all, a servant. It would not do. At present, apart from Ladlay, nothing much had happened. A man had appeared in the alley for two days and stopped under Mushtri's balcony while she slept. Was it sufficient ground for him to cast doubts about Mushtri's virtue? Obviously not! Trying to think of some strategy to solve this new mystery, Muneemji returned home.

His shirt was sticking to his back from perspiration and he could feel the mosquitoes hitting against his face as he made his way through the swarms which rose from the stagnant puddles. When he looked up Muneemji was surprised. Hundreds of bats were hovering above his head. Muneemji instinctively waved his hands to drive them away and his palms struck one. The bats rose a little further up but kept swooping to prey on the mosquitoes.

On the way home Muneemji's mind again went back to the issue with Ladlay. He was still very much occupied with Bano's problem and considered that although Ladlay had stopped them from obtaining an injunction with craftiness, it also freed them from all restraints. He could now follow any course he chose. As long as they remained out of the court, anything which happened to Ladlay's detriment was to Bano Tamanna's advantage. Muneemji had also thought about using Mirza Poya's testimony against Ladlay, in case he came upon some evidence which could be used against Ladlay in court, without having to obtain the injunction. But even if Mirza could be convinced to be a witness, Muneemji was not sure how he could be utilised effectively by the prosecution. Mirza Poya was not always sixteen annas to a rupee and might ruin the case.

'Aaaoor! Aaaoorr!' Muneemji heard Kotwal crying. He stopped to look up and saw him walking on the ledge of the wall. Tabaq Sahib's house was further down and shortly Muneemji heard loud voices inquiring about the cat. The ledge was lower than the wall and although Muneemji could see him from the alley, Kotwal was hidden from the view of the boys guarding the roof. The sound was reverberating in the narrow alley, making it more difficult to ascertain the source. Muneemji also saw Kotwal's old mistress, ruefully watching Kotwal make his protestations, sitting still on the wall of the adjacent house. Suddenly Kotwal stopped. Muneemji was moving away when he saw Kotwal crouch and move stealthily under a ventilator shade. A head appeared on the horizon and a boy asked Muneemji from the roof, 'Do you see the scoundrel cat here?'

Muneemji could see Kotwal lying still under the ventilator shade, whom the boy on the roof could not see. 'No!' Muneemji answered without hesitation, 'I heard a cat a short while ago!' After the boy had withdrawn and moved away, Muneemji turned his head towards the wall where the old cat was sitting. It had disappeared! He had not seen it move in either direction and it was improbable that it would have jumped on to the other side from so high up. Curious about where the old cat might have disappeared, Muneemji decided to go around the wall which bordered an empty lot where the drains fell into the sewer.

Muneemji walked up the alley. On the way there another voice asked him from the roof if he had seen a cat but this time Muneemji kept walking without replying. After staying quiet for a few minutes, Kotwal began caterwauling again, and his noise rose distinctly above the songs and the drumming of the *dholki*. Muneemji heard Tabaq Sahib shouting and threatening to call the police on the cat. As

Muneemji turned the corner, he heard the muffled sound of something being pounded hard. 'Clog, Clok! Clog, Clok!' Somebody was forcing something, that was sure. But what? It could not be someone forcing a padlock. The noise stopped for a few minutes and then started again. Muneemji was not very far away from Mirzban's house. If he was not quite close to it, it would have been difficult to hear the sound because of the noise of the songs. Was it some burglar trying to break through to steal the dowry? Muneemji was quite close to the source of the noise now. Whoever it was, he was just around the corner. Oblivious to the danger, Muneemji suddenly came upon the man crouching by the drain with a hammer in hand, and caught him by the scruff of his neck.

'Rascal!!' Muneemji shouted.

The man tried to slip away but Muneemji brought his cane down on his head and was about to raise the alarm when the man fell at his feet crying and calling him by his name to take pity and have mercy. Muneemji recognised Lumboo's voice and was greatly scandalised to find him there at that hour of the night. A hammer was lying close-by where some bricks had been removed from the open sewage line.

'Muneemji, I have young children. They will be ruined. We will all be ruined. Forgive me. Have mercy. I swear on my father's grave never again to be seen here! Let me go! I will pray for your life! My children will pray for you for the rest of their lives! Have mercy!'

Irritated, Muneemji gave him one kick. 'Bastard! What were you doing? Trying to break into the house?'

'No Muneemji, By God, no! My father's penance from breaking into a house. I was just digging for earthworms.'

All these adventures in one night had been too much for Muneemji. Without a thought he took off his slipper and hit Lumboo over his head. 'Tell me, you bastard, what were you doing here or I will either give you to the police or murder you myself!' Muneemji raised his voice. 'Then all the earthworms will come out by way of your arse!'

Under constant pounding by Muneemji's slipper and his dire threats, Lumboo confessed that it was he who had single-handedly brought the imposing tackle and horsepower at the disposal of the municipality to nought, and defied the efforts of a whole battery of sweepers to maintain an efficient sewage flow. Profoundly knowledgeable about the waste repositories and rubbish conveyances of the city, Lumboo had sabotaged the open drains of Purana Shehr, which stretched over a mile and connected the row of houses serviced by him. After plugging the drains with plastic bags, Lumboo broke the upper banks of the drain, causing a close-ended shunt to fertilise the neighbouring soil. By the next day the gutter had been completely choked. Also, by this time the well-manured and moist soil irrigated two nights ago attracted scores of earthworms. While Lumboo got commissions to clear the drains and flush the gutters, like he did at Mirzban's house the other day, his *lashkar* was assigned to repair the drains. In the course of these repairs, the earthworms were dug up and later sold on street corners as fish-baits. When Muneemji threatened to bring his slipper into play once more, Lumboo also confessed that he underwent his midnight toil a couple of times every month in different parts of the city and never struck the same place twice.

In the beginning, the municipal forces responsible for city sewage and water supplies had conscientiously attended to the choked gutters and overflowing drains. But as they were inundated with these complaints, their ears became immune to the outcry, and the municipal records too, began to corroborate the theory promoted by Lumboo that the drainage system of the old city had become antiquated and needed a major overhaul.

Muneemji threw down the slipper from his hand and pulled up the sweeper by the scruff of his neck. Regarding

Lumboo contemptuously, as he stood there barefoot and shaking, with his sparse moustache twitching curiously, Muneemji started as something suddenly occurred to him.

Mirzban woke up that morning with the matter in his eyes partially blurring his vision. He had awoken from a dream in which two luminous blue and green whirling spheres were moving towards each other with a thunderous roar. The table lamp was left burning from last night. A whole stack of papers had piled up on his desk. Mirzban removed the papers with a sweep of his arm. When the table surface was cleared the green rexene cover of his writing table reflected the table-lamp's light. It struck Mirzban as being a miniature of the green sphere of his dream. At the same time he also became aware of a termite making its way right under his nose with a grain of wood sticking to its pulpy cuticle. Rubbing his eyes, and leaning forward to see better, Mirzban noticed its slow progress in a tangential line. After pausing for a few seconds to wave its mandibles aimlessly in the air, the termite disappeared into a hole with its burden. Shortly afterwards, another insect head, slightly bigger than the one which had entered it, blocked the entrance from within; but not before Mirzban's thoughts, following the termite into its hole, and in complete oblivion of the ink which had spilled on his papers when he was clearing them, had emerged into the boundless cosmic expanse.

An image did not have to do with just the physical. It extended into the realm of the spiritual and the social. If man was created in God's image then man's world was created in the image of God's world. The issues before a man were the issues before God. The world of man reflected the world of God in all its details. So the termitic act of separating the Constituent Part (grain of wood) from the Whole (table) had broader significance. What he had seen in the photographer's shop was very clearly a termite. The Universal Termite! He had seen it with the spheres of Time. It was separating the part from the whole. It was separating Eternity from the confines of Time by removing the boundaries of the constant Present. In that manner was born the everlasting and infinite Eternity, out of the womb of ephemeral and finite Time!

The next night Muneemji lay in wait for Qudratullah. It was almost half an hour past the usual time and he did not appear. Muneemji was cursing himself for not taking action the previous day when he saw Qudratullah stagger into the alley, singing rather loudly. And after singing some incomprehensible strains of the song under Mushtri's window, he tottered away. Muneemji followed him as before, but this time he was holding his cane firmly by its ferule. They came out onto the main street and Muneemji picked up speed to bridge the gap. The moment they stepped into the alley again, another man stepped in front of Qudratullah, making him stop abruptly, and Muneemji's cane shot forward and its handle hooked Qudratullah's neck. The other man came forward and secured Qudratullah by his collar.

'One sound and we will give you to the police, creep!' Lumboo's whisper sounded in the dark alley.

'He is drunk! Get him inside. Hurry!' Muneemji told his accomplice and Qudratullah, who had lost his voice with the pressure on his windpipe was dragged, helplessly flailing his arms, by both Muneemji and Lumboo into the sweeper's quarters.

'What to do now, Muneemji?' Lumboo asked impatiently in a frightened voice after he had shut the door behind him.

'Son of a whore! What have you been doing outside my house?' Muneemji slapped Qudratullah without answering Lumboo's question. Lumboo's *lashkar* had got up and were watching the proceedings.

'I ... let me go, I was passing there, I don't know who you

are ... let me go ... or ... or ... I will call the police!' Qudratullah stammered.

'Hear this! Now this pimp is going to call the police! Qudratullah! Now isn't that your name, you gutterbug?! Want to ask me anything else?' Muneemji slapped him on his nose.

If Muneemji's slap had not done the job, Qudratullah woke up when he heard Muneemji call his name. And what Muneemji said next made Qudratullah more wakeful than he had ever been in his life.

'For three days you had been passing by, singing songs under Mushtri's window! You think that I am deaf and blind like your mother's cunt?' Muneemji shook Qudratullah by his collar. He took off his slipper and waved it threateningly in Qudratullah's face.

'Don't you dare say a word about my mother!' Qudratullah suddenly became furious, but Lumboo had a firm grip on him. Muneemji slapped Qudratullah with his slipper this time, who needed just that to lose his newly found anger. 'Stand still!' Lumboo shook him, 'If you don't want me to fit a carrot up your arse and bring out my billy-goat!' Realising the hopelessness of his situation in Lumboo's strong grip, Qudratullah broke down sobbing.

'Forgive me! It's all my fault. Miss Mushtri had nothing to do with it. I must take all the blame. It was all my doing. Your daughter is not to be blamed,' Qudratullah was trying to convince himself that somehow he was in the alley at Mushtri's behest and encouragement, and was now valiantly defending her honour in order to induce himself further in this illusion. That Muneemji must be Mushtri's father, he was convinced beyond a shadow of doubt.

Muneemji signalled to Lumboo and he stepped outside in the alley while Muneemji interrogated Qudratullah further.

'And what were you doing at Ladlay's house?' he asked.

The floodgates of Qudratullah's confessions were lifted

and he was willing to answer any question now, whether or not it had any bearing on the issue at hand.

'I went there only once at his invitation. He wanted to discuss a loan against some property.'

'What have you got to do with the property and the loan?'

'He wanted to ask my advice as a banker.'

'What bank?'

'Desh Bank. I am the manager there,' Qudratullah wiped his tears with the sleeves of his shirt as his words reminded him of his respectable status.

Muneemji was not a little surprised to hear that Qudratullah was Desh Bank's manager. He knew that Mushtri worked there. He loosened his grip on Qudratullah's collar a little.

'But what were you doing under his balcony two nights ago?'

'Whose balcony?'

'Ladlay's!'

'I don't know what you mean. Ladlay …? Does Ladlay live there?'

'The balcony across our house, that's Ladlay's.' Muneemji was getting irritated. Now it was Qudratullah's turn to be perplexed. Ladlay had taken him home from the back door after threading his way through the winding alleys of Topee Mohalla, and Qudratullah no longer even remembered where Ladlay lived. 'Does Ladlay live across from your house?' he asked in a thoughtful tone.

'Right across!'

'I was trying to read the name on the door because I was not sure which one was your house, Yunani Sahib. But I didn't see Ladlay's name plate,' Qudratullah grovelled.

'His name plate is not there. That's why. Now what about that property loan? Tell me more about it,' Muneemji had it at the back of his mind all this time.

Qudratullah wondered what Muneemji meant by that question. 'It was some property upcountry which Ladlay had been made in charge of. After initial work, I handed it over to your daughter. From then on she has been dealing with the file. But why are you asking about all that?' he asked.

The papers were in perfect order. All the necessary documentation was appendaged. Although the loan Ladlay was negotiating was considerable, the property was dearer yet, as confirmed by the appraiser. The approval letter from the branch headquarters had come directly from the vice-president, not his assistant, and it lauded Qudratullah's efforts in finding business for the bank even in a time of crisis. Qudratullah was in seventh heaven. Now all this interrogation was making him nervous.

'Did you see the property documents?' Muneemji ignored his question.

'Yes!'

'Do you remember the name the property was in before Ladlay was made in charge?'

'No, I don't remember the name. But he had the general power of attorney and all the property documents, which were all that we needed. But you must tell me what you have to do with all that!'

Muneemji called Lumboo over. He came rushing to clobber Qudratullah, but Muneemji stopped him short.

Although Bhai Qamoosi had come up with some explanations, to the greater part, only speculation could answer why there had been no recent report of major termite damage anywhere. Bhai Qamoosi who had recently shown an active interest in the termites, tried to explain to his friends that when it became hot and dry again, the termites sank into the earth, no longer insulated by the wood which they had hollowed. And here too they faced retreat as the continuous rains had raised the water table, and with that the salt in the rocks underneath had spread into the termites' subterranean nests, making them uninhabitable. It was also possible that, Bhai

Qamoosi explained, from their developing omnivorous habits, some dietary plague broke out among the termites. Or that in a madness which sometimes descends on a species, they attacked and consumed each other. Or maybe the different species of the termites which had been living peacefully until now due to an abundance of food, developed property conflicts, waged wars against each other and were wiped off in great numbers when food became scarce.

But just as Bhai Qamoosi's interest in the termites was building up, his friends' was on the ebb. In the beginning Tabaq Sahib had listened to him with some interest; with an eye to incorporating the theme of the termites into his election slogans, but until his campaign pamphlets went into press, the termites had shown no signs of diminishing, and Basmati had advised him against following such a course. And now that they had been printed, a change of course would have been tantamount to political suicide. Then Tabaq Sahib had got busy with his election preparations and his visits to the Chhalawa Hotel had become infrequent. Basmati, who had failed to persuade Bhai Qamoosi to join Tabaq Sahib's election campaign, had become likewise unavailable. In need of companionship, Bhai Qamoosi had turned to Mirza Poya, and recently even Chhalawa, and discovered in the two of them rapt listeners to his hypotheses.

Ladlay bedaubed his ample cheeks with a shaving brush, a towel stuck in his shirt collar like a bib. His balcony curtain was still drawn but he seemed disinterested in it, since he did not look at it even once. His visit upcountry had been successful, although it had taken longer than he had expected. The municipal registry office was being transferred to another floor within the same building and therefore everything took longer, and Ladlay was given a good run around by the clerks. However, now he had all the necessary documentation. He glanced with satisfaction at the file lying laced up on his table.

The thoughtful delicacy with which he dipped the brush in hot water was worthy of an old master dipping his paintbrush into the paint before embarking on a lifetime project. And his strokes which spread soap across his countenance were equally masterful since they did not violate a single bristle of his newly trimmed whiskers. All this he witnessed with a great deal of satisfaction in a small mirror, which stood on the table as if riveted by his gaze. When the soap had been churned to its utmost lathering capacity, Ladlay picked up the open razor, and raising the tip of his ear with the other hand, applied it to the lower periphery of his sideburn. It acted on him as some sort of cue, like the lifting of the symphony conductor's stave, as the moment the blade touched his skin, Ladlay started humming, and throughout the operation, with practised gasps for air, kept humming like an inexhaustible bee the same ribald song of many evenings before. His hand glided like a surgeon's across his facial expanse, leaving no cuts. At the end of that operation he applied the well-rounded alum bar and indulged himself a little with the sharp, but pleasant and cool aftershave sensation.

Some weeks ago Qudratullah had privately revealed to him the figure he had recommended to the branch headquarters, and being a modest amount for the property being mortgaged, he had told him that there was no reason why it should be devaluated. Ladlay had driven a hard bargain and at one point indicated that he might take his business elsewhere, but he let Qudratullah prevail upon him, and finally the client having relented, the two parties reached an accord.

After his toilette was done, Ladlay carefully put away his shaving kit, picked up the file, threw one parting glance at the room to make sure no item of importance had been left behind, and apparently satisfied on that account, walked out of the door. The tune faded out with his exit.

It was a humid day, and Qudratullah's unventilated office felt like an incubator. The bank's lawyer who had come to vet the papers and make sure everything was in perfect order was there too, perspiring profusely, and arguing heatedly with Qudratullah on some point. In due course Ladlay arrived at the bank with his face beaming, and regally made his way between the rows of clerks and the line of people who were waiting listlessly for the cashier to finish his gossiping with the gunman and tend to their business. The bank lawyer stopped talking when he heard Qudratullah mention Ladlay's name. Mushtri Khanam was crouching over her desk and looked up just once to see whom Qudratullah was greeting, then slunk back into her work, as Ladlay went inside the manager's office.

A marked change had become apparent in Mushtri Khanam's demeanour and work ethics ever since her last meeting with Qudratullah, in which he had asked her to continue with her earlier assignments until she was given a new set of duties. He had also requested her to hand over the charge of certain accounts to the cashier, who was to be promoted to accounts clerk. He had evinced a blind man's surprise at her changed appearance and had spoken to her in changed and business-like tones. If that silly fool was playing hard to get, Mushtri Khanam had thought as she staggered out of his office humiliated beyond measure, he was in for a shock. For someone trained to read resolution in human countenances, that day Mushtri Khanam's face would have been an engrossing study.

Mushtri Khanam had discontinued wearing her high-heels altogether, because it would have looked foolish flaunting her past glory after such humiliation. She came early to work and had all the paperwork ready before Qudratullah arrived. The back-log was fast diminishing and Mushtri Khanam had awoken the head office with her inexhaustible correspondence back and forth. And so it transpired, that what had previously taken a month to accomplish, now took only a fortnight; and what document before went to and fro on the clerks' desks, and went missing sometimes, to be found a month or two later buried under some file, now promptly landed on Mushtri Khanam's table and with the necessary follow-up was sent to the head office by priority mail the same day. At the branch head office, Qudratullah's recent feat had imparted that momentary importance to all correspondence originating from his branch, that everything was readily answered and summarily dispatched with an arbitrary vigour. So before Mushtri Khanam handed over the files to the new accounts clerk, most of them were closed by her industry. And with a couple of days remaining in the fortnight deadline, Ladlay received the approval letter from the Desh Bank headquarters, thanking him for reposing his trust in that remarkable financial institution, and seeking a long and mutually fruitful relationship with the notary.

That day Ladlay did not seem to be in a hurry. He gossiped with the bank lawyer on the termite scourge and other unrelated matters at length, although Qudratullah, who kept looking at his watch, was a bit restless. When some more time passed and nobody even offered him tea, Ladlay decided to get to the point without further delay. But just as he was going to say something, Qudratullah got up from his seat to greet someone. Ladlay was greatly surprised to see Parwana enter the manager's office and decided to wait until he left before he broached Qudratullah. But it seemed that like him, Parwana too, had all the time in the world.

After some more time had passed and Ladlay found Qudratullah avoiding his questioning glances, he uncrossed his legs and sat up. At that point the bank lawyer who had been watching him closely until then cleared his throat and addressed him. 'Mr Ladlay, I do not want to discomfit you with the news but it seems we have a slight problem,' he said looking first at Qudratullah and then at Parwana.

'What kind of problem, something to do with the bank procedures?' Ladlay did not betray his considerable uneasiness.

'No, I am afraid it's not that!' the lawyer replied.

'I am sorry but I don't follow. I received your letter and therefore I came,' Ladlay said, 'Now you tell me there is a problem!'

'Yes Mr Ladlay. But I think Mr Parwana would be able to help us here,' the bank lawyer gestured towards Parwana who had opened his briefcase and was sorting out some papers. When the lawyer mentioned his name, Parwana looked at Ladlay who forced a pained smile.

Parwana did not smile back, which made Ladlay apprehensive. Instead he cleared his throat and still looking at the papers, began. 'My client, Begum Bano Tamanna Yunani, daughter of Mr Salar Jang had asked me to move court to obtain a stay order against any sale, lease, mortgage, letting or sub-letting or any financial or legal transactions regarding a certain property upcountry on which my client has a claim.' Saying that much Parwana looked at Ladlay who was gaping at him and continued, 'The court granted the stay order yesterday, after a competency hearing was held at my client's residence by a commissioner appointed by the court. A copy of the stay order was duly forwarded to Mr Qudratullah, Manager, Desh Bank, yesterday. Mr Qudratullah has assured me that Desh Bank will not involve itself in any of the said transactions and has been very kind in inviting me here since you were coming here today. I thought I should meet you and answer any questions that you might have.'

But Ladlay sat riveted to his chair without saying a word or taking his eyes from Parwana's face, who realised after a while that Ladlay was not looking at him. The whole situation was revealing itself in front of Ladlay's eyes. Bano Tamanna had managed to find out about his bank business. It was immaterial who had blundered: Mushtri or somebody else with the knowledge of this transaction. The only other person was Qudratullah, but why would he do such a stupid thing? It went against his own interests. He was so enthusiastic about it from the beginning! No, it must have something to do with that old demon Muneemji. Now it would not be a problem for Bano Tamanna to prove his malafide intent in court, and he would not be able to secure Salar's help in proving that he was doing something at Salar's behest because then Salar would have to be told that his property documents were neither eaten by the termites nor secreted away by Bano Tamanna: that they were with him all along. His game was up and Ladlay saw it clearly. However, he was still in possession of Salar's fifty thousand rupees, and decided to leave the city before they could get wise to that too.

'No I do not have any questions. Of course if Begum Yunani has any objections, Mr Jang himself, whom I represent by virtue of the general power of attorney he had kindly vested in me, to conduct this business on his behalf, would not like to proceed with the transaction. Since his word is my command, there are no questions or doubts. But I feel grieved that I was not informed by Begum Yunani herself earlier, otherwise things would not have come to such a pass. Probably there was some family tension. But then that's our occupational hazard, you know that kind of thing …' Ladlay managed to make a small speech and looked at the bank lawyer to share his joke, all the time wondering whether Parwana had something else up his sleeve. But Parwana did not seem to have anything more to pounce on him with. The others kept sitting there and Ladlay quietly got up and left.

As he came out of the room he saw Mushtri at her desk, who threw a questioning glance at him. There was the faint hint of a smile on her face. She doesn't know a thing, Ladlay thought. If Bano Tamanna knows that the documents were at the bank, she might also know how they got there. Does

Mushtri know that she is also in trouble? Ladlay felt something tender awake in his heart, despite his recent anger at the possibility of her making a blunder which had compromised him.

Qudratullah was still trying to fit the pieces of this puzzle together. What was Ladlay's part in this scheme? Was there something between him and Mushtri? Was the cashier completely innocent? How many men had Mushtri lined up? What was his role in Mushtri's scheme of things? Did she ... was she still using him? Did she leak any privileged information to Ladlay? What were his chances now ...? The onslaught of these questions had completely befuddled him. Unable to think any longer, he reached inside the drawer for some more aspirin after Parwana and the bank lawyer had left.

Before the termites died out entirely, people had begun claiming credit for their eradication through the efficacy of their methods and agencies. Foremost among such people was Imam Jubba. He was hailed by the prayer group when he boasted of his efforts to fight the termites, and taking advantage of the occasion he quickly distributed among the assembly the one thousand odd *navafil* which he had pledged in the wake of their destruction. As leader of the neighbourhood, Tabaq Sahib got the lion's share. Using even that to his advantage, he recalled his own role in effectively putting an end to the termite problem in many houses through recourse to fire, and reminded people to acknowledge his services by voting for him on the election day. The mayor of the city likewise gave all the credit to the efforts of his municipality. The pesticide companies also ran self-congratulatory ads in different newspapers for effectively curtailing the menace through their individual concoctions. The *qalandars* went around seeking *nazrana* for Pir Chamkeela. Even the police found some ridiculous reason to believe and advertise their efficiency in purging the city of the termites.

Some of these claims were partly legitimate, in the sense that since the termites were already on the ebb, any reasonable remedy only speeded up the process.

Once the dog days were over, the miasma which had enveloped the neighbourhood disappeared and the sun came out shining brilliantly, and it became so hot that one could not sleep in the courtyard at night as hot air wafted up from the heated floor. Bano Tamanna had bought limes for pickling. She sliced them up, rolled the pieces in salt and spread them out to dry on a muslin sheet in the courtyard. The slightest exposure to water could ruin the pickle, and Bano had to watch Mirzban when he sprinkled the floor, water hose in hand, before the mattresses were put on the charpai, to make sure that he did not spray any water on the limes. The charpais' legs were no longer immersed in bowls of oil. It was not that the termites had totally disappeared. But they were slowly disappearing, and all their activity was now confined indoors.

Someone knocked on the door. It was Unnab, collecting money from the neighbourhood houses for the Moharram *haleem* which the neighbourhood boys were cooking in a corner of the alley. Mirzban gave him some money, put away the water hose in the bathroom and returned to his room. He tried to read from the papers lying in front of him on which he had written some nights ago but although he saw the words on the page, the letters did not make a comprehensive pattern and his eyes kept sliding at the contours of the words, unable to read a word. Mirzban pushed the papers away. He felt that the crickets were unusually noisy. When the smell of the burning enamel of the lampshade became too overpowering, and the racket progressively increased, he decided to take some fresh air in the garden and investigate the reason for the crickets' unrest. But except for an odd insect calling out for company from under a flowerpot, all was quiet. Mirzban decided to wait, because sometimes the crickets stopped ticking when they heard approaching footsteps. But there was no audible difference in the level of noise, and Mirzban's mind was returning to the problem that was left unresolved, when he remembered the difference in the ticking of the crickets, and the clicking he had heard in his study, punctuated by a vibrating hiss. Tracing his steps back to his room he found it ringing louder than before with the same characteristic sound.

It was definitely not crickets, Mirzban thought. Then what could it be? The noise was not coming from under his desk or his table, he realised, when he strained his ears to determine its origin. Coming from all corners, it was like the seconds ticking in a wristwatch, only quicker, and at a higher pitch. It stopped for a short while and then commenced again. Sometimes when the ticking became louder, it was augmented by vibrating hisses. It was not the hiss of a cat either. A snake! Yes! Snakes sometimes made such noises, Mirzban remembered and recited *Surah-e Noor* in his heart. Carefully, Mirzban looked under his table, but except for a sleepy rabbit who scurried away behind another pile of books when he saw Mirzban peeking, there was no sign of any snake. Mirzban was checking behind the door when he ascertained the source of the noise as coming from inside the frame of the door. The termites within the walls and door frames and portals were making these sounds. Mirzban was surprised to find them in such great numbers in his room because they had been receding and in some places had vanished completely. As Mirzban's disturbed mind could not return to its thoughts, he switched off the light and sank onto his bed to get some sleep.

As his head hit the pillow Mirzban realised that the noise had stopped the moment he had switched off the light. Curious, he got out of bed to switch on the light again, and sure enough, the moment the bulb was turned on, the noise started all over again. Mirzban switched it off and on a couple of times, and every time the termites corresponded.

That must be it, Mirzban thought. Eternal Past is Darkness and Eternal Future is Light. Life is a mixture of Darkness and Light and the true glory of Eternity is not in its promise of infinite Past, which is Darkness, but in infinite Future, which is Light. One did not worship the Past but the Future of Eternity. The ticking must be the termites praying. That attested not only to their celestial roots but also to an enlightened awareness in their ranks. Claims by people that the termites had disappeared because of prayers or human efforts were foolish. Termites were not *a* factor in the scheme of things. They were *the* scheme of things.

While Mirzban was absorbed in his thoughts, Salar was slipping into delirium. When Bano Tamanna came into the room before going to bed his condition was normal apart from the fever he had been constantly running since the time he got injured. His body temperature suddenly shot up later that night.

Images from his life flitted past. He saw himself as a child the day a horse had run off with him in the saddle and thrown him over, and when the wounds on his legs were being dressed he had heard one of the stable-hands remark at his portentous testicles. He saw himself the night his first wife died, a guilty and unhappy man, and he remembered his uncalled-for slurs and wrongs to Bano Tamanna, who roamed around the house like a spectre and was a constant reminder to him of his unfair and cruel behaviour towards her mother in her last days. He saw himself relinquishing his pigeons to his adversaries a month after Partition. He saw himself presenting his book to Noor-e Firdousi and the singer reciting from it in the concert. In his mind this one fantasy had stuck as truth, and in his last moments he clung on to it. He saw himself lying in his daughter's house, dying an old and broken man, who had come very near to compromising after a foolish whim the estate that he should have bestowed on Bano much earlier to amend his wrongs. When Muneemji told him that nothing was lost and the upcountry property had been saved, Salar saw his error being reversed and his hopes of a comfortable future for Bano were rekindled.

Muneemji sat by Salar's side the whole night. Towards morning he was beginning to nod off when Unnab came knocking on the door to deliver their share of the *haleem*. Muneemji got up to open the door. Before he went out he touched Salar's forehead with his fingers. His temperature had fallen but there was no perspiration. Salar's face, long drawn out in anguish, began slowly to smooth out under Muneemji's eyes.

Salar had already been removed to the bathroom by Imam Jubba and his apprentice for his last ritual bath when the water stopped. Imam Jubba began shouting and his apprentice came out complaining of columns of ants on the bathroom ceiling, some of which had been falling on Salar's body and could not be easily removed. Begum Basmati left her pile of beads and rushed out of the house to arrange for water. Basmati brought over two buckets and only then did Imam Jubba's reproaches end. After Salar was bathed, he was enveloped in the tarpaulin shroud. Muneemji had picked it up earlier in the day from the cobbler's, who had been asked to stitch it at Salar's instructions. He did not wish to be buried in the more expensive cotton cloth customarily used for shrouds, knowing that it was an invitation to cloth thieves to desecrate the grave. Salar had shrunk further and covered in his death shroud looked like a mummified child. For the benison of Salar, mothers had already posted their children to shoo away any flies that might alight on him. It was held that the souls of the dead were as weighed down by insects as the living are by the weight of rocks. A cat was also sitting close to the group of lethargic boys fanning away Salar's posthumous burden, trying to catch the buzzing flies unsuccessfully with his paws. Mixed with camphor vapour which rose from the veranda where Salar's etherised body was kept on ice slabs was the smell of resin varnish and freshly painted wood in the courtyard.

To anyone outside of Qasr-e Yunani it seemed as if a giant woodpecker was trapped inside the house. The racket so reverberated and resonated that it seemed the bird was either sounding out the walls with the intention of knocking them down, or was already at work on one. The white-haired carpenter was driving nails into the planks of an old door he was provided with to construct Salar's bier. Usually the bier was provided by the mosque but only last week a corpse on its way to the graveyard had fallen out from it, when its handles, which had been almost hollowed by the termites, snapped during the funeral procession.

Partly from habit and partly in her confusion Bano Tamanna made the mistake of asking the carpenter if the bier was strong enough, and he mounted it and began illustrating his point by pounding it with all his body weight. Alarmed by the prospect of his demolishing the bier, Bano Tamanna entreated him to step down. Later, when Bano Tamanna objected to his spitting betel-juice all over the courtyard, he pretended not to have heard her and keeping his head down, kept marking the wood with his pencil. When Bano persisted, he began complaining loudly about the cheap old wood provided to him; about the ruin of his matchless tools upon contact with such knotty and jointed material, showing Bano the brittle iron hammer-head whose flesh was regressing in thick metallic curls after years of pounding, or his plane or saw or other implements that were in a similar state of decay. Flashing his gold tooth to its best advantage and without calling the Yunanis stingy, he gave an example from among their neighbours, who had been generous in letting him choose fresh and smooth wood. This silenced Bano Tamanna

who, embarrassed at her family's poverty, took flight at the
carpenter's remonstrations, leaving him to dirty the walls
and the floor of her courtyard with even more license.

It was around noon and Mirzban was sitting with other
men on the *chandni* spread in the veranda, when he looked
suddenly at Bano Tamanna, although she had been crying at
intervals since morning. One of the *pehlwans* said something
consolatory to her at which she had again broken down. The
Kaskas brothers were in Purana Shehr and they had arrived
the moment they heard about Salar's passing away. Everyone
noticed that Mirzban had not spoken a word the whole day,
and there were no traces of grief on his face either. Mushtri
Khanam's eyes, on the other hand, were red. Knowing well
that in the disturbance she might have to skip a meal, she
had quietly slipped into the kitchen and finished off the whole
bowl of spicy *haleem*. Her eyes had been watering since then.
She looked around. Enough people had gathered. In a short
while they would begin to leave. With a heart-rending cry
Mushtri Khanam began to wail, the moment Bano started
crying again, and the women holding Bano Tamanna quickly
left her to console Mushtri.

It was the ninth day of Moharram and a huge crowd was
gathered in the streets to see the dress rehearsal of the *Ashura*
parade. Spectators lined the roads and their columns covered
the pavements. To contain the crowd, a rope was stretched
for furlongs between the members of the spectators and the
parade. Houses whose windows opened onto the street were
packed with heads. The sky was dotted with eagles and kites,
and it was the kind of heat that made people look up to see
when the birds might drop an egg on their heads. The diligent
mourners were at the head of the parade, beating their chests
and wailing in a state of supreme agitation. Then came a less
dynamic column of mourners, similarly engaged, but with
far lesser affectation, bracketed by the two standard-bearers
carrying their bloodstained burden. Neighing gently under

the placid influence of poppy, the *Duldul* horses bedecked with replica swords and shields of the martyrs, plume crowns, and richly caparisoned in satin and silk sheets, trotted behind this group and in front of the *tazias*. Here the clamour was loudest since close to the *Duldul*s' tails marched the tumultuous orchestra of drums and cymbals, supplying the marching beat to horses and men. The *tazias* brought up the rear of these artefacts. The *Shah Tazia* was in the middle, flanked by two smaller ones. The three giant structures sailed on slowly in the sea of humanity which surrounded them on all sides. Salar's funeral procession made its way through the columns of mourners whose cries were echoing from the walls of the buildings enclosing the parade's route.

It was Salar's dying wish that a seven-foot high vault be made in his grave so that when the two angels of reckoning entered his grave, he could make rejoinders to their queries, and plead the circumstances of his position standing up, as was only respectable for a man of his distinction. Perhaps he thought that this precaution would at least give them no excuse to hold disrespect to God's plenipotentiaries against him, in addition to the many minor and major transgressions from the path of the virtuous, which he well knew would be accounted for. The gravedigger had charged extra for burrowing deeper than the standard four feet and the carpenter had added to the bill for providing wooden planks for the door of the vault.

On the last trading day of the week before the public holiday of *Ashura*, business in the Pukka Qila market was brisk. The vegetable stalls were laden with produce. The fruit stalls were similarly brimful. As usual the lanes were crowded, but empty of the usual idlers and loafers who had drifted along the route of the parade, and were loitering there. More than the funeral procession itself, which never fails to attract the pedestrians' attention although it throws a pall over the surroundings, the onlookers were interested in the *pehlwans* who took it upon themselves to be Salar's pallbearers most of the way, and perspiring and reciting the *kalma* and other prayers half lost to their heavy panting, did not slacken their pace until the confines of the graveyard were reached. But they were continuously detracted by the Purana Shehr pigeon fliers, who were watching the skies and who repeatedly tried to distract the covey of Salar's prize pigeons which flew over their heads in the direction of the graveyard, as the procession made its way through the crowded bazaars, chanting from the scripture. Mirzban was the last among the pallbearers who shouldered Salar's bier to his final resting place. He walked at an easy pace, well behind the others.

After he was placed in his grave and the planks laid in place, the vault was sealed with sand, and the mourners retraced their steps, except for the pigeons who had alighted on a nearby tree. After giving some money to the gravedigger to cover it with more sand, and buying bird seed for the pigeons, Muneemji got a tonga and brought Mirzban and Bano Tamanna home.

There they found Tabaq Sahib waiting for them, looking very disturbed. He had to attend a meeting at the district magistrate's office and had just arrived to offer his condolences. It turned out that the message he had sent to ask Mirzban to delay the funeral procession had been delivered too late. Tabaq Sahib was inconsolable at missing the opportunity to be seen publicly allaying the grief of his future constituents, walking at the head of the funeral procession shouldering Salar's bier, loudly chanting the *kalma*.

On Salar's *soyem* the grave was found collapsed and the gravedigger informed the family that the wooden planks had caved in the previous night, and in the morning he had seen some pigeons furiously pecking at termites in the grave. The gravedigger had refused to listen to Muneemji's suggestion that the grave should be unearthed to see how Salar was faring.

Bano Tamanna wanted to go and visit the grave but Muneemji strictly forbade her from doing so.

The *Naskh* engraver was never found, and Salar lay buried an unknown poet, in an unmarked grave. Master Puchranga kept Salar's unfinished portrait furled up with other old cinema canvases of films which kept making regular comebacks. When the next local body elections came, he remembered Salar's portrait. It was taken out, dusted, stretched with nails on the wall and after a few additions, hung prominently from a pole outside Pukka Qila. Salar's contours had been whited out to use the canvas for an election poster. The Horse had been approved as Tabaq Sahib's election symbol.

Mushtri had received Ladlay's letter two nights ago. The contents of the letter had forced her to arrive at a decision. Her relationship with Qudratullah had already been jeopardised. Now it was only a matter of days before Bano Tamanna found out the truth, and then she would make her life miserable too. Moreover, Ladlay, if threatened with arrest for the wrongful possession of Salar's property documents, could easily inculpate her. He had Mushtri's handwritten notes which were exchanged over the balconies. But regarding Ladlay, that was not the only point which forced her to consider seriously the offer he had made in his letter.

Mushtri Khanam had been wooed at all tiers of manly passion. But never as devotedly and unabashedly as by Ladlay. The notary's regular courting from his balcony had driven away Unnab, who was just beginning to haunt the municipality light opposite her window, armed with a pocket-comb. The packet of tea which she found sliding down the anchor one evening from Ladlay's balcony when the whole city was going without tea, was another token of his fidelity. Mushtri had kept the bag secure from the termites until the house ran out of tea. Then she started having her breakfast closed inside her room. To make her tea she would steal in a cup of boiling water, and later drain the tea leaves in the toilet. And now in that letter Ladlay was telling her that Muneemji had not been entirely successful. To his last, Firdousi's concert remained a reality in Salar's mind, and therefore he did not alert Muneemji about the money he had given Ladlay for arranging the event. Mushtri saw that Ladlay had exposed himself by admitting to the possession of Salar's money. He had made himself vulnerable and given her power over him. This realisation pleased her no end.

A masterpiece of ornate verse, heavily embellished with flamboyant imagery, and authored by Salar, the marriage ode of the Yunanis hung from a nail in Mirzban's study for a long time until Bano wrapped it up in the gutta-percha *gharara* from her wedding and put it away in her trunk for safe-keeping from the termites. There was a lot more to this piece of art than just florid verse. Calligraphed on vellum, it was composed in that archaic Lucknow school style which flourished early in the nineteenth century and, due to its uncommonly vexatious character, immediately afterwards became extinct. Only a few specimens of this style were extant, which could be read equally meaningfully back to front and length-wise as well as breadth-wise, without in the least compromising the order of words, or the import of the couplets. In this obsolete form Salar had found the symbolism for the social institution of marriage. To him a successful marriage, to which only Death brought a natural end, was from its commencement to its culmination one whole of Love which could be viewed from any point in its course, without in the slightest measure altering its delineation.

One day when Bano Tamanna opened her trunk she discovered the damage to that figurative parchment of their marital life and the shreds of the gutta-percha *gharara* in which it had been wrapped. This discovery came within a week of her finding a hairline crack in the aquamarine stone of her ring, and she naturally thought of these events as ill omens, and her fancy, already excited by the household chaos and sleepless nights after Mushtri's elopement, saw in it many ominous possibilities. The vacant look in Mirzban's eyes and his nocturnal soliloquies did nothing to give her any hope. Mushtri's dowry trunk was found empty. Later, some cloth sacks were also found missing from her linen closet in which possibly the dowry was carried away. There was a note on her desk addressed to Bano in which Mushtri had poured out all her bitterness against her and accused Bano Tamanna, among other things, of turning away good matches from the door so that she could have her as a servant in the house when Mushtri was past the marriage age and living the life of a spinster at Bano's mercy, in her house. Bano Tamanna did not know what to make of these wild allegations and said as much when she showed the letter to Mirzban. He remained seated in his chair and kept looking at her with glazed eyes as she gave him Mushtri's news with her letter. Bano noticed that there was a lingering expression on his face. It was the petrified look of some mysterious horror which had etched a painful expression on the tablet of his face. That bizarre mien receded during his waking hours, but it reappeared the moment sleep closed his eyes.

Muneemji had to tell Bano what he had witnessed on all those evenings and explained his reasons for keeping it secret from her for so long. She understood and requested him not to mention it to Mirzban. Bano realised that Ladlay had been introduced into the house because of Salar and Mirzban might hold it against her. In those trying times Muneemji's presence was Bano's only support. He had gladly accepted Bano's offer to continue as supervisor of Salar's estate, and stay with her family in Purana Shehr.

Muneemji was wracking his brain to remember what had

happened the night Mushtri ran away. He was tired and had gone to bed early. He had brought his charpai down and now slept in a corner of the courtyard since the pigeons were no longer kept in the cages on the roof. Therefore he had not paid any attention to Kotwal's caterwaul, as he sauntered restively over Mirzban's roof. But a short while later, when he heard a long painful wail and saw Kotwal retreating speedily over the wall, he had wondered what could have caused that flight. He was not aware of a catapult being fired at Kotwal from Ladlay's balcony.

Ladlay had disappeared without a trace. Bano Tamanna contacted Begum Basmati but she had no clue either. Ladlay had just told Basmati that he might be away for a few months and as he could not afford to hold the apartment in his absence, he had decided to let it go. The notice was rather short but as Ladlay had already paid the month's rent in advance Basmati decided not to kick up a fuss. Mirzban's neighbours were given the story that a good match was found for Mushtri and as the boy was leaving the country, only a simple *nikah* ceremony had been arranged and Mushtri was sent off the next day. Begum Basmati took such offence at her exclusion from this secret ceremony that she did not speak to Bano Tamanna for a full week until Bano took her a small jar of the lime pickle she had made. Bano also improvised a letter of resignation from Mushtri and sent it to Desh Bank. As a result of that letter Qudratullah materialised at her doorstep. But Bano Tamanna made short work of his long and lugubrious queries and Qudratullah went away more confounded than ever.

If Time was the germ of Eternity, the Termite was the germ of Nature. And what was Nature but God? But whereas the Creator both created and destroyed, as it could move both forward and backward in Eternity, the creation only destroyed (or consummated), since it could move only forward, its positive movement in Time, as affirmed by the law of entropy. It seemed plausible to Mirzban that after the termites had reached the pinnacle of their destruction, there was nothing to tempt them any more. The challenge which a solid city, standing proudly on its foundations, had posed to the Termite, had been met: the city had been hollowed, eaten from its core.

A lover's insipid listlessness when the object of his passions is met and the desire requited, might just as well mirror a termite's emotion after perfectly laying a city to ruin, as it might God's, after He had reached Perfection. However, the talent of the Creation being restricted to destruction (or consummation) alone, it resurfaces in self-indulgence; whereas the Creator having perfected both creation and destruction, becomes indifferent to both.

Mirzban's mind was on fire. Creation was the office of an imperfect being. The imperfect World was the creation of an imperfect God! Once Perfection was reached, there was no delight left in creation. However, in linear Time, Perfection could not be reached, because there was no perspective, and the Creator and the Creation moved together, making positive movement. But it was simple to define eternal presence in Eternity, as the Creator was free to effect both positive and negative movements. Then no matter to what extreme point He travelled between the two poles of infinite Past and infinite Future whose centre was Present, He would find Himself at that point and at Present *simultaneously*! And if the spheres of Time had not merged yet, the Perfect God and Eternity still existed in linear Time, *with* the imperfect God, until the imperfect God was annihilated by reaching that point in Time when the spheres merged into Eternity.

That defined everything! His head was thrumming, a film came over Mirzban's eyes, and he started. He could feel a bitter taste in his mouth: the cruel paradox that had frightened him in his momentary daze had now become clear and Mirzban could now see it in all its miserable hopelessness. An oppressive pall of irredeemable doom seemed cast over all Nature. Mirzban found himself in the courtyard. The weather had again become hot, humid and gloomy. The air was laden with the smell of dust and incense. The sky was overcast. The excruciating thrumming in Mirzban's head had renewed. Of what use was Eternity if it brought no succour even to the wretched finiteness of life? And in that light, how pointless and absurd was the idea of a Hereafter. Until God was Perfect and Eternal, the World could not become Perfect. And the moment God became Eternal, it would not become Him to undertake to make it perfect. The World, and therefore human life, were meant to remain imperfect!!

Mirzban was feeling slightly lighter in his head and could not feel his feet under him as he walked back and forth. Something was stirring in his loins. He gasped with pain.

A *qalandar* was out in the streets with his incense burner at that late hour. It was going to rain soon and he was making his way to his quarters with great haste. From his bed Muneemji could hear the cling-clang-cling of his tongs coming closer. Just then it began to drizzle. Cursing the rain, as Muneemji was getting off the charpai to roll up his mattress and take it indoors, he saw Mirzban step out of the house, into the alley. A little concerned, Muneemji looked out of the door. Basmati was returning home with Unnab after chalking Tabaq Sahib's election slogans on the neighbourhood walls. Mirzban was walking behind the *qalandar* without covering his head. Muneemji called out to him to ask if he should get him an umbrella; Basmati also tried to get him to attend to what Muneemji was asking, but Mirzban did not look back or answer. What seemed to them oddest of all was that every time the *qalandar* clanged his tongs, Mirzban would leap impetuously like a child and kick up his heels. He kept following the *qalandar* in this manner until they both disappeared from sight at the turn of the alley, into the downpour.

The rain stopped. It had washed away the incense vapour, and the air was clear again.

For a current catalogue and a full listing of Summersdale books, visit our website:

www.summersdale.com